IN THE SHADOW OF THE KINGMAKERS

VAHID IMANI

Stormtop Publishing

P.O. Box 132

Solvang, Ca 93464 U.S.A

stormtopublishing.com

www.stormtopublishing@gmail.com

Editors: Jeanette Morris, CA, Freelance Editor www.jeanette-morris.com

Susan Leon, NY, an independent book editor

Todd Summar, Illinois, The Artful Editor www.artfuleditor.com

Interior book design: Norma Hinkens

Cover design: Germancreative

Author's photo: Laurie Zander Photography

ISBN 978-0-9911103-5-3

ISBN 978-0-9911103-3-9 (hc)

Library of Congress Control Number: 2019900146

Library Subject headings:

1- Historical thriller-Fiction. 2- Post World War I-Fiction. 3- Middle East-Fiction.

4- Petroleum industry history-Fiction.5- International Relations-Fiction.

6- Iran-Fiction. 7- Bahai faith-Fiction. 8- Great Britain-History-Fiction I. Title

To my uncle Djafari
who gave me the spark.

IN THE SHADOW OF THE KINGMAKERS

VAHID IMANI

Stormtop

Publishing

1

PREDICAMENT

Tehran, Iran

Saturday, July 5, 1924

"WHO PAID YOU?" The thud of a powerful punch followed by a low moan accentuated the question.

James Malcolm stood at the doorway of the dim basement hidden beneath the courtyard of an old abandoned house. The flickering light from a kerosene lamp illuminated the bloody, half-naked body of a man, his arms stretched by chains attached to the wall to keep him upright. The pungent smell of blood, sweat, and urine didn't bother Malcolm. He actually liked it. It made him feel part of something important. Besides, the intel could prove to be valuable.

When he entered and stepped onto the dirt floor of the musty room, a pinpoint of orange glowed, then vanished in the dark corner across from him. The reek of cheap tobacco blended with the odors of suffering. Malcolm merged his slight frame into the shadows to observe. He felt at home there. Some of his best work had been born on the dark side.

But this dank hole didn't suit him at all. He'd been assigned to his covert post at the British embassy in Tehran to protect the precious petroleum interests of the United Kingdom. More specifically, to keep the Americans away from Persia's oil fields. However, protecting the UK's interests in Persian oil included keeping a close eye on the Russians, whose underbellies scraped against unsavory places such as the one where he stood. Lenin's death in January had created a power struggle within the Russian leadership. The main challenge had developed between Stalin, the secretary of the Communist Party, and Trotsky, the Commissar for War. Trotsky's views on spreading the Bolshevik's revolutionary ideology throughout the world was particularly worrisome to many countries, including the Great Britain. And the new Soviet Union was ready to pounce on Persia.

"Let's try this again," the interrogator screamed, his face just inches from that of the writhing man. "Who paid you to sabotage the oil refinery in Abadan?"

The person smoking in the corner shouted, "Was he a Russian or a German?"

Malcolm recognized the voice. Ibrahim was already there and doing his job. The interrogator slammed a whip onto the prisoner's bare and bloody back.

The prisoner looked to be in his early forties, no older than Malcolm himself. His torn, once-white shirt hung about his waist, exposing thick, black chest hair that matched his mustache. "Have mercy on me!" he screamed. "I have a family to feed. They *all* are dependent on me. Please stop! I told you many times that I don't know him."

"Did he speak with an accent?" the interrogator probed.

"I don't remember. Please let me go! My children are wondering what happened to their father."

Malcolm recognized the tall, lanky interrogator—a gendarme on Ibrahim's payroll. As no one else was in the room, it was safe for him to make his move. Malcolm ambled over to Ibrahim, pulled the cigarette from his lips, and stepped quickly to the prisoner, pressing the hot end on the man's right nipple.

An excruciating scream filled the room, echoing in the cavernous space. The interrogator gawked at Malcolm in obvious surprise, his bulging eyes and gaping mouth the perfect picture of horror. Malcolm, unconcerned, signaled the interrogator with a quick jerk of his head to repeat the question.

"Did he speak with an accent? What was his name?"

The man cried and screamed uncontrollably as Malcolm pressed harder, bending the cigarette.

The gendarme pulled the victim's hair back with blunt force. "Answer the questions or we'll start to cut your body parts one by one!"

"Yes, yes, he did … my cousin called him *Monsieur* Roossi."

Ibrahim spoke from his corner. "So was he French or a Russian, you idiot! How did he look?"

The prisoner shook his head, flinging drops of sweat onto the floor. "I don't know for sure. My cousin … he is not very bright. He calls any foreigner *Monsieur*. But … the man was big, heavy, and bald. Please. Give me a glass of water. Please."

The interrogator took a large ladle and filled it up with water from a pot on the ground. He poured it on his victim's head. "You will have your water when you tell us exactly what he said."

The man moved his lower lip, franticly trying to catch a few drops in his bleeding mouth. "He … he gave us the explosives. And on a map of the refinery, he showed us exactly where to put it. He said that the … the Britons are robbing our people, and this will slow them down. Water please, you promised!"

The interrogator laughed and threw the ladle onto the floor.

Malcolm dropped the cigarette into the water pot and left the basement in haste, taking the stairs up two at a time. Ibrahim followed him out, his short legs sprinting to catch up with Malcolm's brisker pace.

The darkness of the night had not yet dissipated the summer heat, and Malcolm had a sudden urge for a cold drink.

"That trick with the cigarette worked," Ibrahim said, his words breathy with exertion and admiration.

"It was effective. It produced the result I wanted."

"I don't think I could do it."

Malcolm didn't answer him. What was the point of such a discussion? Either Ibrahim would learn to carry out his duties without remorse, or he would be replaced.

"What do you think? Was it Boris?"

"Yes, Ibrahim, of course. Make certain no one finds out about this interrogation."

"Right, yes. But, German spies have sabotaged our oil production before. What makes you think this man was a Russian?"

"The man's description fits Boris. Russians are displeased with the recent oil deal." Malcolm picked up his pace, hoping Ibrahim would quit his constant chatter.

"The Bolsheviks are becoming ... more aggressive," Ibrahim panted. "This new breed of Russians are not wasting any time."

"You are correct. We must up our game. It's time to activate Project Miracle."

"Do you mean the one with the Baha'is?"

"Yes, precisely. Meet me in the teahouse, *ghahve-khaneh*, in the Ferdosi square tomorrow morning at nine."

"Yes, sir," Ibrahim replied, then abruptly changed his course and disappeared into the darkness of the Tehran night.

Finally alone, Malcolm relaxed his pace. He wasn't going home; he didn't have anyone waiting for him there. Instead, he chose the route to his office in the British embassy.

The serenity of the warm, dimly lit streets was illusory to the chaotic order of the politics of the country. Tehran was a hot bed of spies such as himself, each vying for the chance to loot the newly discovered black gold. The race to convert navy ships from coal-based fuel to oil- based was moving at full speed among the great powers. Britain was at a substantial disadvantage as its vast coal reservoirs would be rendered useless in a modern, oil-based navy. The UK's hold and control of the oil fields in its over thirteen million square miles of territories was vital to her survival.

Malcolm was well aware of this crisis for his homeland. However, he was also a firm believer that the threat of communism, and particularly, the exporting of it under Trotsky's leadership, was equally crucial to England's political and economic stability. And Russia's lust for access to the free waters through the Persian Gulf was as important as their hunger for control of all Persian oil fields.

Based on what he had just learned during the interrogation, he had to adjust his plan. The Russians were moving faster than he had anticipated, so time was of the essence.

Once inside his tidy office, he poured himself a glass of Gordon's Old Tom gin and sat on the high-back, oak swivel chair behind his desk to think. The pace of recent events disturbed him.

It was time to act decisively, but what was the right move?

He shuffled some papers on his desk and found the document he had started reading earlier that day. The author's name drew him like a powerful magnet. He picked up where he had left off and soon became lost inside the pages ...

"Ho there! Malcolm! What is this blessed text that has taken you completely out of our existing world?"

Malcolm startled. His right hand reactively went to his desk drawer where he kept his trusted Colt pistol. British Army Major David Thompson loomed large over his desk. He turned the page face down on his desk with his left hand and slowly moved his right hand away from the drawer.

5

"Hello, Thompson."

"You were quite absorbed in that text. What is it?" Thompson's fit, uniformed body cast a shadow over the document.

"Nothing of importance." Malcolm sat back in his chair. "What has brought you here, Thompson?"

"Nice try, old chap. But no, I won't allow you to change the subject. I'm totally intrigued now. What is that writing?" Thompson moved to snatch the paper.

Annoyed, Malcolm swiftly secured the papers into his desk drawer. "It's a private copy of a piece by a bloke I knew in college."

"And who would that be?"

"Thomas Edward Lawrence."

"Blast me! You mean you know Lawrence of Arabia? He is on his way to becoming a legend. I just finished reading *With Lawrence in Arabia*. A fascinating book."

Malcolm looked down to avoid Thompson's gaze and smiled. "Yes, quite charming, I'm sure."

"Ooh, do I sense a bit of jealousy blossoming here?"

Malcolm took a sip of his drink, angered that he might have shown some vulnerability to Thompson. "No, not at all. What has brought you here so late at night, Thompson? Aren't you stationed in Mashhad now?"

"Yes, but I had a meeting with Colonel Fraser today." He moved away from the desk and looked around the office, as if he were in search of something.

"Mashhad is about nine hundred kilometers northeast of here. It must have been an important meeting!"

"It was. The Russians are becoming more aggressive in the northeast lately. Adding to the mix is the recent Turkmen's rebellion and their quests for independence. This country is rapidly becoming unstable."

Malcolm nodded his head and smiled, "That is exactly how a military man would look at it."

"What are you saying? Is there any other way to look at it?" Thompson asked, helping himself to the liquor on the side table.

Malcolm flashed an all-knowing smile. "Well, there are other angles. For example, a politician may say that the recent disagreements and turmoil in the petroleum contracts is the major root of instability."

Thompson carried his glass of gin back to the desk and sat on a chair in front of Malcolm. "Tell me, how do you know Thomas Lawrence?"

Malcolm swirled his drink, taking pleasure in the tinkling of the ice cubes against the crystal. "Oh, I didn't claim knowing him. We went to the same college, the Jesus College in Oxford University. We were in the same classes for a few subjects. We also went to the same prep school. That's all."

"Is that where you're from then?" Thompson took a big gulp of his drink.

"Yes, I was born and raised in Oxford."

"Look here, Malcolm." Thompson moved to the edge of his chair. "Lawrence doesn't have the monopoly on being the hero of the twentieth century. He was just at the right place at the right time. We can be heroes too!"

The major's disposition entertained Malcolm. Thompson came as near to being a friend of Malcolm as anyone ever had, entering his life a few years before the Great War in Damascus. Malcolm saved Thompson's life, and career, by intercepting a German sting operation intended to seduce and kidnap Thompson, who at the time was stationed in Cairo with knowledge of sensitive information about secret British military outposts. Through the years, he had developed a sort of kinship with Thompson. But Malcolm wasn't quite certain where Thompson was going with his argument. It was 1924 after all. The Great War was over, the Arab revolt was over, and many new countries had already sprung up. He decided to humor him.

"Is that so? Tell me, my friend, exactly how can we become heroes?"

Thompson returned to the liquor table and grabbed the bottle of gin. Bringing it back to the desk, he filled his glass for the second time and topped off Malcolm's before sitting down again and putting his boots up on the desk.

"Yes, by all means, make yourself at home," Malcolm quipped. He would have to re-polish the desktop after Thomson left.

Thompson grinned. "Yes, you can mock me, sir. But, we *are* in Persia, a gem of a land that superpowers throughout history have always coveted. Obviously, as a locale of significant strategic importance and endless resources." He moved to the edge of his chair again. "But, my friend, I believe we are at the right place at the right time to make history too, just like Lawrence, the king-maker of the Arab world—"

Malcolm interrupted, "I'm afraid that's the gin talking now."

"No, sir. Who knows, perhaps you will go into the history books as Malcolm of Persia. Or, I will be known as Thompson of the Near East."

Malcolm laughed. "Oh, my friend, your fantasy is farfetched, I'm afraid. Lawrence loved Arabs and their culture. I despise these Persian bastards. They are cowards, they lie, and they'll do anything for money. The country is broken, divided, and weak. The only good thing about Persia is their oil, and we already have it. All we need to do now is protect our kill from hyenas such as Russia and the U.S."

"I cannot speak of your personal preferences, Malcolm." Thompson leaned back and crossed his legs. "But historically, Persians helped us greatly in the last five hundred years or so, by holding the lines and containing the Ottoman Empire's advances to the east. For what it's worth, as a nation, they have shown bravery and victories when they were united."

Malcolm shook his head and smiled woodenly, wishing to return to his reading.

Thompson continued. "That's the key my friend—united. That is what Lawrence did. He united groups of nomads, and because of that, borders were drawn and new countries were born. That is why we live in an exciting world, brother!" Thompson held his drink with his right hand and shook his clenched left fist. "We are serving the greatest country in the world, Great Britain, and that privilege, my friend, has given us the power and the opportunity to change history!"

Malcolm clapped his hands. "Great speech, Thompson! But I'm still not certain if it's the alcohol talking, or you truly have the fire in you."

"Well, my post is a military one. Basically, I'm there to stop the Russians from getting to the Indian Ocean." Thompson swallowed another sip of his drink. "Just as we successfully pushed the Russians back out of Mashhad not so long ago. But you, my friend, you are in the capital, where politics is the main game. You have Russians, French, Germans, and now the newcomer to Middle East politics, the Americans. You are surrounded by opportunities."

"Let's drink to that, then." Malcolm raised his glass. "To the main game!"

"Here, here!" echoed Thompson, and the two men drained their glasses.

The liquor swept through Malcolm and relaxed him. He put his legs up on his desk opposite to Thompson's. As he crossed his ankles, his pant leg slid up to reveal the old scar along his calf.

"Is that a souvenir from the Great War?" Thompson asked, pointing to Malcolm's leg.

"What, this one?" Malcolm pulled up his pant leg to the knee, revealing the nasty scar that ran from ankle to knee. "No, not a war injury; this one was a gift from my stepfather, something to remember him by. But I do have some other cuts from the war. Would you fancy seeing them?"

"Not really. I'm more intrigued by your stepfather story."

Thompson leaned forward to examine the scar more closely. "What urged him to give you this perfectly symmetrical cut? It must have been deep as well. Such a permanent gift!" Thompson said and laughed at his joke.

Malcolm didn't reply and gazed into his glass. Reflections of light broke through the cuts of the crystal and bounced into his eyes as he rotated it. The effect of the colorful prism was hypnotic. A picture of his fourteen-year-old self, fast asleep under his cozy bed quilt, formed in his mind's eye.

"That night, like any other Friday late night, George, my drunken stepfather, pounded on the front door, screaming and cursing my mother to open it. Next, I heard the hinges squeaking. Heavy footsteps, then the sharp smack of a slap, a scuffle, and then my mother's desperate voice, pleading for George not to beat her."

Malcolm took the bottle of gin and poured some more into his glass. "It was Emma, my little sister's frightened screaming that got me to spring from under my blanket and fly down the staircase to the lounge."

"Did he hurt your sister?" Thomson asked.

Glaring at his glass, Malcolm answered, "My mother's face was covered in blood. She hovered over Emma to protect her from that beast. I couldn't take it anymore. First, I hit him in the face with my forehead, then tackled him to the ground. We rolled around on the floor, kicking and punching each other like street fighters. George was taller and heavier, of course. He hit me quite hard. I was curled into a ball of pain on the ground when he grabbed a bottle of wine from the sideboard, struck it on the edge of the dining table and shattered it." Malcolm took another sip of his drink, "I stood up and went after the old man again. George ducked low, bent his knees, and swung at me with the broken wine bottle, slicing down the length of my bare calf. I dropped to the floor."

He paused for a moment, anger descended, like a dark veil across his soul. "My mother charged at George. He swerved, and she missed him, falling to the floor. On her way down, George swung the broken bottle-neck and cut her arm. The sight of Mum's blood did it to me. Rage consumed my fourteen-year-old wits, and I grabbed a large piece of broken glass and lunged for his neck. The bastard dodged the swipe, but the broken glass in my hand sliced his wrist wide open. Blood spurted with the rhythm of his heartbeat." He paused. "The last image I remember is George gripping his wrist, staring at me in shock. I felt faint and blacked out."

"That's awful, old boy. What happened to him afterwards?" Thompson asked.

"He didn't make it."

Silence took over the room. Malcolm stared into his empty glass. "That was the first time I killed a man," he muttered. Then, as if coming to his senses, he put down his glass, took his feet off the desk, sat up straight, and declared, "Well, you have a long journey back tomorrow, and I have an important meeting in the early morning." He stood and extended his hand to Thompson.

Major Thompson took the hint. After shaking hands, and with a quick nod, Thompson left the office. Malcolm locked the door behind his uninvited guest and went back to his desk. Moments later, he was lost again in his reading. The tales of Lawrence of Arabia fascinated him, not because he found Arabia exotic or felt any particular fondness toward Arabs, but because of Lawrence's wisdom and his intelligent choices on how he played the highly complicated game.

"If I could only be that smart," he muttered.

The clock on the wall chimed midnight when he finally stopped reading. He cleaned his desk, locking his important documents inside it. Leaning back on his chair, he stared at the wall— the only wall in his office where he had hung a picture. An oil of a white rose quite similar to the one which had hung in his mother's bedroom.

Malcolm of Persia! It did have a nice ring to it. Creator of a new political reality in the Middle East. The thought pleased him. His current operation was almost ready to activate. If successful, it could become his ticket into Russia, where he thought he could be the most effective.

"Yes, I'm certain I can change the game here," he said, rapping the wood on his desktop, just above the tales of the kingmaker.

2

GHAHVE-KHANEH

Sunday, July 6, 1924, Tehran

THE RAPID, rhythmic clash of saucers and small tea glasses gave off the impression of busyness as Ali, a lanky teenager, washed the dishes next to several large samovars in the teahouse, *ghahve-khaneh*. His boss, Hassan *agha*, a man in his fifties with a greying beard had told him that the sound added to the overall charm of the place and lured in customers from the street. Either way, Ali was glad he had a job.

In the center of the teahouse, a water fountain splashed in a small pond inlaid with blue tiles, a few nightingales and canaries sang beautiful melodies, the hookah-like *ghalyans* gurgled, and an occasional burst of loud laughter echoed from darkened corners. The aroma of brewed Persian black tea mingling with tobacco smoke from many *ghalyans* put its stamp of authenticity on the place. On the walls, large paintings with vivid hues of red, green, and blue depicted scenes from *Shahnameh*, pre-Islamic Persian mythology, epic poems, and famous religious battles of Shiite imams. The ambiance allowed an escape from Tehran's scorching summer sun.

"Ali, make sure you don't mix the *farangees* glasses with the rest," shouted his boss behind the counter.

"Why, boss?" replied Ali, picking up the pace of his dishwashing. He needed this job and didn't want to disappoint Hassan *agha*.

"Because those foreigners are not Muslim, and so they are unclean, *najess*. Anything the unclean touch, you have to wash seven times, at least one time with dirt so it gets scrubbed well."

Ali turned his head around and scanned the cafe. "Okay, boss, but where are these *farangees* sitting?"

"Over there." The older man jerked his head toward the far corner.

Ali turned his head to the place that Hassan *agha* had gestured. Three men sat on the wooden platform covered with a crimson and blue Persian carpet. The dim and smoky atmosphere in that teahouse often veiled the customers' faces. But none of them looked like foreigners to Ali. They smoked *ghalyan* and their heads were bent toward one another as if deep in conversation. One of the men had a bald head, one was slim with olive skin, and the other had a light complexion and grey hair.

"With apology boss, how do you know they are not Muslim? They sure are dressed like us."

"Ali, listen to me! You are only fourteen years old. I've worn out more clothes than you have. I have heard their tongue before. I am sure they are non-Muslim. Do as I say. I don't want my regular customers to go to hell because we didn't do our religious duty."

Ali studied his boss. The combination of his large Roman nose, his balding head, and the way he jerked his neck when he was very serious about a subject amused Ali. He controlled his urge to chuckle. Obviously, that would be disrespectful. "Of course, boss, I will be careful with the glasses."

"Ali!" yelled one of the so-called *farangee* men in the corner group.

14

Ali put down the dishes, dried his hands on the red dishtowel he kept handy on his shoulder, and rushed to the customer in the corner. He recognized the man who had yelled for him—Ibrahim, a bald Persian who had been in the shop before. Definitely not a foreigner.

"Bring another round of *chaiee*," Ibrahim barked in Farsi. He hovered back, looked around to see if anybody watched them, and quietly spoke in another language to his companions.

Ali thought it sounded like English, but the surrounding noise against their soft speaking manner made it hard for him to correctly recognize the language he had been studying for the past year. He needed to hear more to be sure.

He fetched a tray of hot tea glasses for the three men and slowly, a bit slower than necessary, set the glasses down one by one in front of each customer. His ears targeted the conversation, and he instantly recognized the distinctive accent of the Brits.

"Yes, Colonel, I have learned that the new American vice consul, Major Imbrie, is an astute photographer and quite an adventuresome chap with an amusing background," said the third man, a slender foreigner wearing local clothing.

The English words excited Ali. He sent a silent prayer of thanks to God that his British mentor, Rose, had insisted on teaching him. The thought of her brought a smile to his face.

Ibrahim nodded. "You are quite right, Mr. Malcolm. I saw him and his friend the other day photographing a building in *Ghavom-ol-Saltaneh* square. People had gathered around them to look at his new contraption." Ibrahim put a sugar cube into his mouth, then took the small glass of tea and poured it in its saucer. He blew on the hot tea and sipped it from the saucer. "Ha! But, he better not take any photos of women or religious monuments." Ibrahim smirked and took another sip.

The place was familiar to Ali, but he didn't understand the word "photographing." What was going on in *Ghavom-ol-Saltaneh* square? Ali couldn't follow all of the conversation, but he figured that Mr. Malcolm, the slender man, was British. The fact that he was dressed like any other Persian man in that teahouse settled nicely with him. This foreigner obviously felt close to the Persian traditions and, unlike other foreigners, he wasn't looking down on them. He decided to tell his boss about Mr. Malcolm. Maybe the old man would think better of the *farangees*.

Ali needed an excuse to stay near Ibrahim and the foreigners. He took his red towel from his shoulder and wiped a table near them.

He watched the slender man, Malcolm, circulate his right hand's middle finger on the rim of his tea glass several times, gently gliding his finger down the glass's hourglass shape, as if deep in thought.

The man Ibrahim called Colonel was watching Ibrahim with an expression of disgust. Then he said, "I must confess, I never liked sipping tea from the saucer."

Ibrahim set his saucer down and smiled. "Colonel, relax. This is the traditional way to drink hot tea here. We are not patient people when it comes to drinking hot tea."

The colonel stroked his well-trimmed, dark mustache and glanced at the thinner man to his left. "And it seems *you*, Malcolm, are romancing your tea! Anyway, for what it's worth, you brought up a good point, Ibrahim *agha*. The men in this culture become rather angry if someone takes a photo of their women, don't they?"

"Sir, it is very dangerous." Ibrahim's large, jet black eyes opened wide when he said that. He continued, "Their anger can quickly feed into hysteria, and the end result can become very risky in the worst way. He needs to be very careful. It is dangerous for foreigners to take photos here in this country, especially Americans."

Ali could hardly believe what he was hearing. Very dangerous? Major Imbrie? What are they talking about? What is this "photo" that is very dangerous for this man? Ali wished Rose was there to help him better understand what was going on. She was smart.

And, of course, her English was perfect. He wiped the table next to the three strangers again and looked for another empty one near them to clean.

"Rest easy, Ibrahim, Major Imbrie's dossier is quite colorful." Malcolm took a sip of his tea. "He is rather experienced, I might say. A perfect fit for phase two. His photography projects for *National Geographic* Magazine have provided him a cover well suited for clandestine..."

"Ali, get back here!" shouted Hassan *agha* from behind the counter.

Ali jolted at the shout of his boss and rushed back to Hassan *agha*, disappointed to miss the rest of the conversation. He repeated the word "clandestine" in his mind so he could remember to ask Rose about it. And that other one—a magazine. He didn't recognize it. He couldn't wait to tell Rose about his unexpected lesson.

"Yes, sir?" Ali reported to his boss.

"Take this tray to the customers sitting outside."

"Yes sir, right away." Ali hustled to fulfill his boss's command, reminding himself again that he couldn't afford to lose this job. After his father's sudden death, a year prior, he became the only breadwinner for his family. His mother and his four younger siblings relied on his income. He knew this job was just a stepping stone to something bigger. He longed to travel to different countries and become an even better merchant than his uncle, who ran a caravan of camels.

After delivering the food, he returned to wash more dishes. But his mind whirled to find an excuse to get back to the foreigners in the corner. He remembered what he wanted to tell Hassan *agha*.

"You know boss, one of the *farangees* in the corner is dressed just like one of us," Ali said, dipping his hands into the dish water. "Isn't it comforting that not all the foreigners are stuck up? Some of them actually like our traditions. Look at them, see how easily they smoke *ghalyan,* just the way we do."

Hassan *agha* turned around and squinted his eyes to see what Ali described. "Nah, it's too dark. I can't see what they are wearing. But I don't trust any foreigners." Hassan *agha* turned back to his task. "So, Ali, any new camel adventures?"

"Camel adventures?"

"Yes, didn't you tell me that you often ride camels?"

"Oh, yes boss, but occasionally, not often. When my uncle runs his caravan through Tehran, he asks for my help. I take care of the camels and occasionally he lets me ride them." Ali smiled at his recollection of the experience. "Riding a camel is not as easy as it looks."

"Well, I suppose it's a good thing that God made you taller than the average fourteen-year-old boy. So, you won't get stomped on by the large beasts!" Ali's boss let out a loud laugh at his own joke.

Then his face froze.

The doors to the teahouse burst open and three Cossack soldiers marched in, chests puffed and backs erect, meticulously scanning the customer's faces, one by one. Swords and daggers hung menacingly on the fronts of their belts. Their hats, Russian-style Cossacks' trimmed with Persian lamb's wool, reminded Ali how intimidating his friends had found his father's Cossack aura.

Ali and his boss greeted the soldiers with a half bow and offered them a table. But the soldiers ignored them. After another quicker inspection of the room with their hooded eyes, they approached a local sitting at a table by the water fountain.

The soldier in front grabbed the man's shoulders and lifted him out of his chair. "You miserable weasel, you think you can hide in here?" He flung the man onto his back on the table. A few saucers and tea glasses scattered and hit the ground, breaking into pieces. Men seated near the table jumped away and cleared the area around the soldiers, shouting words of caution.

"I'm going to cut your belly wide open right here," the lead soldier said and drew his dagger. The other two soldiers held the man down.

"No, no not here, please take him outside," begged Hassan *agha*, sweat dripping from his forehead.

"Shut up!" shouted the soldier in a thunderous voice. "This man owes me money and respect!"

The entire shop went silent. Even the canaries stopped their songs. The man struggled to release his neck from the grip of the strong soldier, but his effort only made the soldier squeeze harder.

The lead soldier placed his naked blade against his victim's throat. The man cried and begged for forgiveness and another chance to pay his debt. The Cossacks' notorious brutality prevented anyone from intervening. The patrons watched the horror in silence.

The sense of pride and joy that Ali felt when the Cossacks first walked in the teahouse turned to anger and disgust as he witnessed their violence and vulgar language. A wave of flushing heat swept through his body, flooding his face with warmth. Sweat broke out above his lips. This was not the way his father described Cossacks. They were supposed to be disciplined, honorable, and humble. He had a sudden urge to intervene and took three steps toward the soldiers, all his senses on high alert.

"Ali, step back," whispered Hassan *agha*. "Don't be a fool."

His boss's command broke through Ali's rash behavior. He sent a silent prayer of thanks to God for the protection.

As the sharp blade touched the skin of the victim, one of the other soldiers elbowed the aggressor. He looked up toward the direction his comrade was pointing. In the dim recesses of the teahouse stood two men in two separate locations. At one table, the local champion, Reza *pahlevoon*, stood tall and assertive, his muscular physique intimidating to an average man. The combination of his body mass, his thick, black, horseshoe mustache, and his lowered, tight eyebrows signaled strength and determination.

Ali recognized Reza *pahlevoon* from a few visits he had made to the local sport club, *zoorkhaneh*. Reza *pahlevoon*, similar to other local champions, was revered as a person with physical strength, high morals, and impeccable integrity. Ali envied the champions' code of conduct that had been engraved into their rigorous exercise routine for thousands of years. Their eagerness to stand up and help the feeble was legendary. Ali had heard on the street that Reza *pahlevoon,* like many other *pahlevoons,* never missed an opportunity to help others.

In the other corner stood Ibrahim. His eyes peered directly into those of the lead soldier and his eyebrows were scrunched in a tight knot. Ibrahim didn't seem to notice Reza *pahlevoon.* Instead, he focused on the soldier. When their two eyes locked, Ibrahim shook his head in disapproval. Then with a rapid, sideways gesture of his head, he ordered the soldiers to leave.

Ali shifted his eyes back and forth between Ibrahim and the lead Cossack. Would the soldier obey? Did Ibrahim have that much authority over these menacing soldiers? Ali's heart thudded against his rib cage and his mouth went dry. He swallowed hard. In a few seconds, he might witness the most brutal act of his short lifetime. Mentally, he psyched himself to jump the lead soldier if he pressed the blade. He couldn't just stand by and silently allow such a brutal crime. His father would be so ashamed of him. He hoped, no, prayed that Reza *pahlevoon* would come to his aid once he tackled the soldier.

But the Cossack released his grip.

Ali breathed a loud sigh of relief. And the victim didn't waste a moment. He ran for the door and disappeared into the street. The soldiers hoisted their weapons and, without any words, left the teahouse.

Everyone's eyes followed the soldiers. The moment the doors were shut behind them a loud roar of *"Marhaba,* congratulations!" broke out inside the tea house. Many patrons released their tension with laughter and more shouts of congratulation to Reza *pahlevoon,* who smiled broadly. He acknowledged everyone's admiration with a few nods and returned to his chair and his tea.

Ali smiled, turned back toward the counter, and looked at his boss.

"Ali, what are you waiting for?" Hassan *agha* ordered. "Hustle up! Take a glass of hot tea and a new *ghalyan* for *pahlevoon!*"

As Ali moved rapidly to take care of his boss's instruction he heard, "One more *ghalyan* over here!" It was Ibrahim.

"I got it, boss. I'll take it to them." Ali wanted to use every opportunity to stay close to the foreigners and eavesdrop. He wanted to find out more about Ibrahim. Who was this man that associates with foreigners, speaks English so fluently, and why does he have such power over the Cossacks?

"*Marhaba,* well done, *pahlevoon,*" Ali said. "This is on the house." He placed the tea and *ghalyan* in front of Reza *pahlevoon.* He played along with the illusion. He knew it wasn't the *pahlevoon* who had resolved the situation. He took a *ghalyan* to Ibrahim and his British friends, ears attentive to their conversation in English.

"Are you certain?" Malcolm asked, staring at Ibrahim's eyes.

"Yes, yes, of course. They won't be back. I guarantee," Ibrahim answered, nodding his head briskly.

"Be that as it may, we don't want any incidents while we are in a location like this," snapped the colonel, "Now, back to our earlier conversation, where is this place?"

Ibrahim replied, "It is in *Sheikh Hadi* street. It is called the miracle of *Sheikh Hadi's sagha-khaneh.*"

Ali gasped and looked at Ibrahim, but quickly turned his head back to the table he was wiping. He knew that place! Why were they talking about the holy *sagha-khaneh?* He reminded himself to be more careful. His intuition counseled him to keep his understanding of English a private matter.

The colonel had a confused look on his face. "I am sorry, I am a bit lost here. What is *saga-khaneh,* and what miracle are you talking about?" he asked, butchering the Farsi word.

"Ha," Ibrahim laughed and turned his face toward the colonel. "It is called *sagha-khaneh* not *saga.* The 'gh' sound comes from back of your throat. *Sagha-khaneh*. You can find one in almost every neighborhood."

Malcolm laughed. "Oh, we don't mean to alarm you, really. Just our little cake that we are baking, Colonel Fraser. You know what I mean?"

The colonel sat back, crossed his arms, and glared at Malcolm. "I detect a hint of menace in your voice."

Malcolm looked Fraser in the eyes. "With America's thirst for oil and the Bolsheviks' aggressions, projects like this come in handy. Who knows, *we* may need a miracle soon."

The colonel continued to stare at Malcolm a bit longer. Then in a louder voice asked, "Again, what is a *sagha-khaneh*?" This time he improved his pronunciation of the Farsi word.

"It looks like a shrine," explained Ibrahim with animated arms. "Often it is an indentation in the wall about a meter deep. It is usually built near a natural spring. The water is considered holy and people drink the water, light a candle, pray, and ask their saints or God for a specific request. It is considered the holy place of the neighborhood."

"So, what are the premises of this miracle that you chaps are cooking up?" the colonel asked.

"People believe that saints have blessed this particular *sagha-khaneh*," Ibrahim continued after a puff on the *ghalyan*. "The rumor is that the water of this *sagha-khaneh* blinded a Baha'i man. Then it healed his blindness after he repented and made a contribution to the Shiite saint. People from all over Tehran and even nearby villages travel there to see it," Ibrahim explained.

Colonel Fraser squinted his eyes and gave an inquisitive look to Malcolm. "Rumor, huh?"

Malcolm jumped in. "Anti-Baha'i sentiments are high currently. This attraction will give us a helping hand when we need it."

Ali had completely lost the thread of this conversation. It seemed they spoke in riddles. Malcolm's last statement made no sense at all. Ali couldn't imagine a covert world filled with cold-blooded operators existing right under the skin of his ordinary life. His world was much simpler.

The colonel nodded his head, picked up his delicate Persian tea glass by its narrow waist, and sipped his hot tea. All three men went quiet for a few moments, as if contemplating what had just transpired.

Ali could feel Malcolm's eyes on him as he wiped and re-wiped the table. He glanced at the other men. Ibrahim made eye contact. "That's enough Ali, leave us," he said in Farsi.

"Ye—*baleh, chashm*, of course." Beads of sweat popped across Ali's forehead. He almost replied in English instead of Farsi. He had nearly revealed his secret weapon.

3

DOUBT

Sunday, July 6, 1924

MALCOLM FOLLOWED Ali with his eyes. "Does that boy understand English?" he asked Ibrahim, motioning back with his head to the departing Ali.

"Who? Ali? Nah." Ibrahim laughed. "He's just a camel jockey. No, don't worry."

"It doesn't hurt to be extra careful these days," Malcolm replied, scanning the room for the boy's whereabouts. He had not selected this teahouse because of its charm or quality of its tea, but for its clientele--the Persian working class. Members of the upper classes did not dare enter *ghahve-khaneh* for fear of damaging their reputations. This was a place for donkey drivers, street vendors, porters, or anyone who wanted to pause from their grueling daily work. The perfect place to meet undetected.

The teahouse doors opened, and two men walked in. Malcolm quickly assessed them. One wore a dagger in his sash. But that was normal. They could be just two ordinary guys coming in for tea. Malcolm's eyes shifted to Hassan *agha* as he greeted the new customers, his hands busy sharpening his knives. The blades glinted in the light from the fixture above. From where he was sitting, Malcolm thought he could see four, maybe five knives. Upon his arrival, Malcolm had located the boilers in the shop on the counter adjacent to the east wall, and he made a mental note of how many were operating. Hot steam escaped from the faucets of all four. As an experienced operative, he watched for such things and always planned for contingencies. After all, in his business, the mood of a place could shift in a moment.

Colonel Fraser, oblivious to what just transpired between Malcolm and Ibrahim, broke his contemplation. "I see. This indeed may come in handy soon. The Persian prime minister has recently ordered the military and police not to intervene in any religious demonstrations."

"Are you referring to the fiasco at the Parliament's courtyard? The PM is becoming very careful not to enrage the clergy these days," Ibrahim elaborated.

Malcolm decided that Ibrahim needed some education in local politics. "Well, my friend, it is a bit more complicated than that. Reza Khan, the PM, is a spirited and impatient man. It seems he has no appreciation for the art of politics and—"

"Well, of course not!" the colonel interrupted. "He is a military man. We are all to-the-point and demand results."

Malcolm didn't mind Fraser's interruptions. "Yes, I understand. So, in his rush, the PM prematurely introduced his bid for a republic."

"The Republic of Persia, can you imagine that?" the colonel interrupted again, this time with his trademark sarcasm. "Sorry Malcolm, do continue, I just couldn't help it."

Entertained by the colonel's interjection, Malcolm turned his face toward Ibrahim and continued. "The clergy knew if the bill were to pass in the congress, it would end their influence in politics. They sensed his hidden agenda to separate the church and the state."

"Church!" Ibrahim argued, "We are a Muslim country. We have mosques."

"It's a figure of speech," Malcolm clarified. "By church I mean the religious establishment. Anyway, supporters of the cloth in the Parliament shut down the idea of the republic. His rough handling of the clergy's demonstration in the Parliament's courtyard caused him to be summoned to Qom, the city of religious power. The Muslim leaders forced him to denounce the discussion of the republic. This is jeopardizing his beloved oil bill, which basically is his American Program." Malcolm stopped to sip his tea.

Ibrahim sat up straighter and extended his neck. "American Program! I have never heard of it. What precisely is the American Program?"

Malcolm ignored Ibrahim's question and kept his attention on Colonel Fraser. "Especially after last week's blatant assassination of Eshgi, that famous but outspoken writer and opposition leader. Reza Khan is treading very carefully as the political situation is highly charged."

"Well, he sent a clear message that he won't tolerate any rebellion," the colonel said. "He is a military man, strong and focused. The question is whether his move was a political mistake."

"I don't think so," Malcolm answered. "He doesn't mess about. America may enjoy his decisiveness. This may help him to get his American Program back on the right path."

"And the blessed Americans are digging in and won't quit," Fraser added.

Malcolm nodded, acknowledging the colonel's lack of patience when it came to Americans.

"What is the *American Program*?" Ibrahim repeated. "Is that why the topic of Major Imbrie came up today?"

"Never mind, Ibrahim *agha*," Malcolm jumped in. "Your job is to help your soldier, police, and other friends make some good money when their skills are required." Malcolm delighted in his expertise in changing the subject to what was dear to Ibrahim and away from information that he didn't want to disclose.

"Do you mean oil their mustaches?" Ibrahim took the bait, threw his head back and laughed.

"Yes, precisely." Malcolm moved closer to the table and continued, lowering his voice. "In the meantime, I must inform our friend Major Imbrie of the rare opportunity this miracle *sagha-khaneh* provides for his friends at National Geographic. I am sure he would love to take a few exquisite photos from *sagha-khaneh*. By the way, I have seen his photo essays in the *National Geographic* magazine. He's quite good!" He paused for a moment, then gave a roguish smile. "The trouble is, he made such a splash in Russia that the Russian intelligence apparatus would love a personal interview with him." He sat back and finished his tea.

Ibrahim looked around the teahouse, then leaned in toward Malcolm. "No! I don't think this is a good idea," he said in a quiet voice. "People at *sagha-khaneh* are simple, religious folks. They don't want to see foreigners near their holy sites. They consider these guys *najess*, unclean."

Malcolm knew exactly what Ibrahim was referring to. People may get upset and chase Imbrie, or even rough him up. But Imbrie wasn't new to trouble. Malcolm was confident Imbrie could survive. However, time was of the essence now if the plan was to come together, and Ibrahim's attitude worried him.

"Oh, I am quite certain that Major Imbrie will be polite." Malcolm shifted on his chair, put both his elbows on the table and in a softer voice said, "Rest easy. As I said before, he is well traveled and has experience with simple folks. He has been in Africa, Turkey, Eastern Europe, Russia, and other places ... many of them were conflict zones. So, be that as it may, my friend, Imbrie is a well-rounded individual." He sat back and added sarcastically, "Besides, this will be a rare opportunity for the entire world to get acquainted with Persian art and culture through his lens." Malcolm laughed.

Ibrahim stood up. "Gentlemen! Please. I was not joking, especially with the rumors of Baha'i conspiracy—"

Malcolm cut him off. "Lower your voice, Ibrahim. I am well aware of the situation. I know what I am doing. Imbrie will be our decoy. Americans need to feel the pressure."

Ibrahim shook his head and left in haste.

4

ROSE

Sunday, July 6, 1924

"NATIONAL GEOGRAPHIC ... PHOTO ... CLANDESTINE ... DANGEROUS ... PHOTO ..."

Ali repeated the new English words as he hurried through the residential dusty back alleys of Tehran on his way to his second job as an assistant gardener at the British embassy. This route was a bit longer than the one on the main roads. But those streets were too busy and chaotic for him. Bicyclists, street vendors, noisy motorcycles, motor vehicles, donkeys and horses carrying loads, people or carts weaving in and out—it put him in a bad humor and sapped his energy.

In the alleyways, he experienced the pleasure of inhaling the comforting aromas of Persian food cooking in family kitchens. The smell of sautéed onions dominated the air as its application was used in many Persian soups and sauces, but he could also smell popular foods such as *gormeh-sabzi, gheimeh and lobia-polo.* His belly growled, but he didn't mind.

A few small boys darted back and forth in front of him, rolling wooden bobbins with sticks. Not that long ago, he had also played with his neighborhood friends without a care for the future. But those days were over for Ali.

"Dangerous ... photo ... clandestine ... national," he repeated out loud.

The British embassy was located on the relatively quiet Ferdowsi Avenue. A wide canopy of large sycamore trees provided much needed shade in the heat of summer on that street. The embassy's enormous compound was protected by tall brick walls. Ali reckoned the walls must have been over four meters tall.

Reaching the embassy, he waved to the guards and passed through a set of large wrought-iron gates to enter the compound. Most guards knew him. Only occasionally would a new guard stop him and ask for his ID card. The coat of arms of the Great Britain with the golden lion and unicorn on the gate shone brightly against blue sky. Large assortments of indigenous trees, manicured bushes, and aromatic flowers provided a cool and lush atmosphere much like a botanical garden. Ali loved his job as an assistant gardener there. Not only because of the lower stress level of the job, compared to the teahouse, but also because it had a most wonderful side benefit, his English lessons.

Ali checked in with his boss. "Good morning *agha* Reza, what would you like me to do today?"

Agha Reza was on his knees, hunched over and busy digging and planting a few new shrubs. He looked up. "Oh good. Hello, Ali. Hassan and Jamsheed are cleaning the fountain on the west side today. You go to the east side and prune the bushes there."

Ali retrieved his tools from the tool shed and went to the east side of the compound to begin his pruning job. The work was easy, and he soon was deep in thought, pondering the three men in the teahouse who conversed in English. He repeated the new words in his mind as he worked.

"Psss...psss."

From his kneeling position on the ground, he couldn't tell where this noise was coming from.

"Psss ... psss," came again from his left.

He put down his pruning shears, stood up, and spun around.

There stood Rose—a few meters behind and to the left, holding her cigarette not too far from her mouth. Rose exhaled smoke and said, "Good afternoon, Ali." A smile stretched across her face.

Ali imagined most angels in heaven must look like Rose. She had white, milky skin, a pair of blue eyes and blonde hair, which was neatly tucked under her nurse's cap. That day, as usual, she was wearing her nurse's uniform with its white pinafore apron.

"Rose! What are you doing here?" Ali asked in English, returning her smile with a big one of his own.

"I'm on my break. What's new with you?"

Ali looked down on the ground. He felt a rush of warm blood running up his neck and onto his face. He couldn't help smiling. "I am good."

"I have a few more minutes left of my break, so let's have your English lesson."

"Rose, it is no good now. I am working. Big trouble for me, if *agha* Reza see us."

"I don't think a few minutes break will delay any major gardening project. Don't worry," she insisted. "I'll take full responsibility for it."

Rose sat on a stone bench nearby and tapped the spot next to her a few times, inviting Ali to join her.

He left his tools and sat about a meter apart from her. The gurgling of a small waterfall provided a perfect buffer for their voices as they talked.

She exhaled another puff of cigarette smoke, gazing at the sky as she did so. A few pigeons flew across the sky above them. "I never understood why pigeons sometimes flip in the air!"

Ali looked. "There must be a *kaftarbuz* around here."

"Wait, don't tell me. I know that word. Um … it means a pigeon fancier, a person who keep and trains pigeons, right?" She laughed.

"Yes, do you remember Ahamad *kaftarbuz?*"

"He worked here briefly, didn't he?"

"Yes, he is a *kaftarbuz*. What is it in English?"

"A pigeon fancier."

"Yes, yes, pigeon fancier. If want you, no, hmm…if you want, one day I get you a *chador* to cover yourself, and we go out and visit his house and his many pigeons."

"Perhaps someday we'll do that. Did you know those pigeons are called homing pigeons? They can carry messages. They come in handy during wars and troubles."

The word *troubles* reminded Ali of what happened in *ghahve-khaneh.*

"Rose, you know about Major Imbrie?"

"Major Imbrie? No, I can't say that I do. Who is he?"

"I not know. I hear his name in *ghahve-khaneh* this morning. And, what is *photo?*"

"Photo … hmm. How do you describe photo? Oh, I know, photo in Farsi is *aks.*"

"Ah…" Ali paused and then asked, "What is Nation Geoghrafy?"

"I think you mean *National Geographic*. It is a magazine about places, people, and animals."

"It have *aks?*"

Rose smiled. "Yes, many *akses*. But you should say *photo*. Say, does it have photos?"

"Does it have photos?" Ali repeated.

Rose put her cigarette in her mouth and clapped her hands.

"And what is danger-oos?" Ali said, pleased with her applause of his effort.

"Oh, where did you hear that word? In the teahouse?"

"Yes."

"Dangerous. Well, it means not safe, harmful, bad, very bad. Let's see if I know it in Farsi. I think in Farsi it is *katar.*"

"Do you mean *khatar?*"

"Yes, that. I can't pronounce the *kh* sound correctly."

Ali dropped his head and pondered for a moment. Major Imbrie's taking photos at *sagha-khaneh* will pose danger. But for whom?

"What is clan ... clandes—" A buzz next to his ear interrupted his concentration. He looked up and saw a red ladybug had landed on the front of Rose's white nurses' cap, not far from a small scar on her forehead just below its rim. That scar bothered Ali. Not only did it mar her otherwise perfect face, but how had it gotten there? Had someone harmed her?

"Rose! Stay calm. Let me." Ali's fingers slowly approached Rose's cap and gently picked up the ladybug. He placed it on back of his hand and let it crawl.

"That's a ladybird. Very pretty! What do you call it in Farsi?"

He closely examined the ladybug and let it freely roam around on back of his hand. "Yes, pretty. Sometime beauty is closer than we think. It just need willing head to see. We call it *pinehdooz.*"

They both observed the ladybug for a few moments in silence.

"Rose?"

"Yes?"

"You believe fate?"

"Do I believe in fate? Hmm, fate ... you know, that's funny. A few days ago, I read a poem about fate by one of your countrymen, Hāfez. I think it went like this:

"The place you are right now, God circled on a map for you."

Ali pondered her words. Should he tell her what he heard in the teahouse? "Hafez was wise man. I have one more word. What is clan...destine ... clandestine?"

"Oh, that's a good one. Hmm, clandestine is something secret. Like if something is done in secret. Now you are making me worried. Where did you say you heard these words?"

"In *ghahve-khaneh*, where I work. I feel something dan- dan-ger-ous is about to happen."

"Oh, what is it? Ali, you look a bit pale. Are you all right?"

Ali lifted his shoulders. "I not know. I feel something bad coming. Something big. My *pedar*, father, before he die, tell me, 'Always do right thing, son, no cost'."

"I think you're saying always do the right thing regardless of the cost. But what is bothering you?"

"You know Baha'i?"

"Yes, I know Baha'i. Isn't it a branch of Shiite Islam?"

Ali shrugged his shoulders.

Rose continued, "Well, some of my good friends are Baha'i. They're very nice people." She paused for a moment, and then she added, "I also know Dr. Moody, Dr. Susan Moody. She is a believer of the Baha'i faith and an American physician who founded, or maybe cofounded, the first school for Baha'i girls in Tehran."

Ali shook his head. "Bad news. Baha'i big trouble. Major Imbrie in big trouble."

"I don't understand. Why are Baha'is in trouble? Is Major Imbrie a Baha'i? Is he a troublemaker?"

Ali decided to tell Rose what he heard. He needed to talk to someone, and she seemed the only one that would possibly be able to help him understand the situation better. He showed three of his fingers. "Three man, no, men in *ghahve-khaneh*, talked English. Bad, very bad for Major Imbrie. Photo *sagha-khaneh*," and then he violently shook his head. "No good, photo is no good. Dan... dan-ger-us."

A knot appeared between Rose's eyebrows and her lips formed into a frown. "All right, let's see. You are saying that there were three men in your *ghahve-khaneh* who spoke in English. Yes?" She looked him in the eyes when she asked.

Ali retuned her look and nodded his head. He could see that she was taking him seriously.

"And you heard them saying something about a man named Major Imbrie who is taking photos of a *sagha-khaneh* for *National Geographic* magazine. Right?"

Ali nodded again.

"All right, now here comes the mystery. In what context did you hear the two words *dangerous* and *clandestine*?"

Ali lifted his eyebrows in dismay. "I don't understand context. What is context?"

"In other words, what else did they say? What sentences did they use with those words? Did you hear anything else that can solve this puzzle?"

"Taking photo of women in *sagha-khaneh*. That is no good. It is dangerous. I also heard one of them say it can be very risky in worst way!"

"Are you certain?"

Ali shrugged his shoulders. It was becoming too complex for him. But he recalled Ibrahim was actually excited when he said, "the end result can become very risky in the worst way."

"Ibrahim said it!" Ali exclaimed.

Rose shook her head. "This sounds complicated. I'm not certain that a youngster of your age should be too concerned about what adults say or may do. Perhaps you shouldn't be involved in it."

Ali looked out into the garden, trying to collect his thoughts and come up with the right English words. After a short pause, he said, "I know not. Maybe it my duty to help an innocent foreigner not get hurt. It is right thing to do."

Rose turned her head away from Ali and he followed her gaze. A few butterflies were fluttering their colorful wings and traveling between flowers. Sparrows were fighting over a small piece of bread on the ground. Life seemed to continue peacefully despite the serious conversation.

A moment later, Rose turned back toward Ali. "Let us not worry about it now." She was wearing a smile and playfully tapped Ali's knee. "I'm changing the subject to something more pleasant. A big banquet is coming up here in the embassy. Ask your cousin who works in the kitchen to get you a job for it. It will be a valuable experience for you." Her smile turned into a glowing grin.

Ali enjoyed watching Rose's right cheek crinkle to a dimple when she smiled big. He had never seen that on anyone else.

"A big banquet? What is banquet? A big man like a big general?" Ali asked.

Rose laughed and looked up in the sky. "No silly, a banquet is a party with lots of food and music."

Ali chuckled too, as her laughter energized him. Despite the lingering thoughts of the suspicious plot of the men in *ghahve-khaneh*, Ali joined in Rose's jubilee. "Are you going?" he asked.

"Yes, of course! Lots of people, including diplomats and military men will be there." She found a big rock next to her and put out her cigarette against it. She looked him in the eyes and said, "I have to go now. Take care of yourself and don't worry so much!" She patted his knee again and then turned toward the embassy building behind them, disappearing into the garden.

Ali waited a few moments longer until he was sure Rose was inside the building. A quick survey of his surroundings assured him of privacy. He picked up Rose's cigarette butt and examined it. Taking up smoking had been in his mind lately, but he couldn't afford it. As it was, his earnings were barely enough to support his sizable family.

A faint trace of red at the end of the butt piqued his interest. Gently, he placed it between his lips. A strong temptation to inhale came upon him, but he resisted. Instead, his lips softly covered the red silhouette left by Rose's lips. To feel her lips, he closed his eyes.

5

THE GREAT WAR

Monday, July 7, 1924

THE INSISTENT KNOCK on Malcolm's office door interrupted his concentration on the letter he was composing to his superior, Admiral Sinclair in London, in regard to the latest activities of the Bolsheviks in the region. He put down his fountain pen. "Enter!"

A young British military officer appeared in the doorway. "Sir, your presence is requested."

"By whom?"

"Colonel Fraser, sir."

"All right, I will be there at once. You're dismissed."

On his way the colonel's office, he didn't take the usual direct route. Instead, he passed through several corridors and stopped by a small courtyard. There, he picked a pink camellia. When he reached the reception desk in the large tiled hall of the wing where Colonel William Fraser had his office, he presented the flower to the young woman in her mid-twenties sitting there. "Good morning, Sandra."

A big smile spread across Sandra's freckled face. "Oh, Mr. Malcolm, you are always nice to me!"

"And you always shine like a ray of sunlight in the midst of a cloudy day. Is today a busy day for Sandra?" Malcolm hovered over her desk, eying her with admiration.

"Not particularly." She ran her fingers through her short, sandy-colored hair. "We've just received one visitor, a diplomat, Mr. Adam, from the Foreign Office." She leaned forward on her desk to get closer to Malcolm, and, in a rather seductive voice, asked, "Dinner tonight?"

He smiled, and with the back of his index finger he gently caressed her cheek. "No, not tonight," he whispered. "I'm busy. But soon, dear." Then in his usual tone, "A light day today! Make the best out of it. Cheerio!" He continued on to the colonel's office, pleased with himself for still being able to attract a much younger woman.

Colonel Fraser's secretary was sitting behind his desk, next to the office door, when Malcolm approached. He stood up, "Good morning, sir, please proceed. They are waiting for you," and then he opened the office door for Malcolm.

Unlike Malcolm's office, Colonel Fraser's quarters were spacious and fully furnished with leather armchairs, a plush, leather sofa, a round table for small conferences, and a large oak desk. Military paraphernalia decorated the wainscoted walls. Heavy brocade curtains blocked the sunlight, giving the office a rather gloomy, yet luxurious atmosphere.

"Good morning, Malcolm, come on in," the colonel greeted him. "This is Mr. Adam from the Foreign Office."

The two men shook hands and nodded their respects. Adam, who was tall and heavy about the shoulders, had a pleasant, open face and thin lips. A typical diplomat, Malcolm surmised.

"Mr. Adam has been touring the Middle East region and just arrived from Baghdad yesterday," the colonel explained.

"Is this your first trip to the region?" Malcolm never trusted diplomats, especially rookies.

Adam sat down on a leather chair and crossed his long legs. "This is my first time to Persia, but I have visited the Arabian Peninsula many times." He lit his pipe, took a slow draw, and continued after a deliberate exhale. "However, on my way to Tehran, passing through the Khuzestan region, I arranged for a meeting with Sheikh Khazal."

"Sheikh Khazal?" the colonel repeated, his face twisted with concern.

"Yes, Sheikh has served us well in keeping the oil region of the south trouble free," Adam said, holding his pipe in his left hand, "but apparently, he is not very happy with the British command these days. Nevertheless, despite his dissatisfaction, we had a pleasant meeting. He is a most delightful host."

Colonel Fraser covered his mouth with his fist and coughed. "Well, he has served his purpose. Pardon me." He cleared his throat and continued. "Nowadays, Sheikh, with all his rhetoric about independence, is becoming a nuisance."

Adam shifted in his chair. "Nuisance to whom, Colonel? The Foreign Office finds his request intriguing. If the central government in Tehran doesn't gain control soon, independent Khuzestan may serve our purposes just fine." He shifted his legs and took a draw from his pipe. "Gentlemen, I do not need to remind you of the fundamental importance of the role of the navy to Great Britain's survival and the significant impact of its fuel needs. Since we have started to convert our navy's fuel from coal to oil, countries such as Persia have become strategically important to us. The Anglo-Persian Oil Company must be able to provide our required oil continuously and safely."

Malcolm jumped in. "Not to alarm you, but the trouble is that Americans have already started to dabble in Persian oil. I am certain that you are aware of Mr. Sinclair's proposal with the support of the United States government to the Persians."

Adam impatiently shook his pipe and replied crisply, "The foreign secretary, Mr. MacDonald, has clearly explained our stand to the British charge d' affaires, Mr. Ovey here. He is required to explain to Americans about the complex nature of the oil business in this country and ask them not to support Mr. Sinclair's adventurous dealing in regard to Persia's northern oil fields."

Colonel Fraser got up from his chair and went to the side table where he kept the liquor. He set out three crystal glasses and dropped two ice cubes in each glass, then half-filled them with whisky.

"Setting priorities straight, it is not prudent to discount Reza Khan's tenacity for absolute power yet," Malcolm said, accepting a glass of whisky from Fraser. "He may be the PM now, however, that may not last long. He has demonstrated clarity of vision and purpose. Among other things, he has developed quite a fondness for Mustafa Kemal, our very first president of the new Republic of Turkey. Have you met Mustafa Kemal, Mr. Adam?"

Fraser offered the third glass to Adam and, oblivious to Malcolm's attempt to size up Adam, he said, "Yes, they both were capable military officers. I put my wager on General Ironside's choice. Reza Khan is a no-nonsense man. He can be the answer to a stable Persia. With stability, we can secure the flow of oil from the entire country, south and north. He is highly disciplined and focused."

"In other words, he is predictable," Adam countered.

"And he follows orders," the colonel finished his thought.

Malcolm took a sip of his drink. "We anticipate he will follow the same agenda as Mustafa Kemal and vigorously pursue secularism. Assassinating Mr. Eshghi, a vocal opponent and a famous, well-loved writer, was a clear indication of his razor-sharp focus." He admired Reza Khan for his ruthlessness. And although the cold and brazen killing in the broad daylight had not been proven or officially linked to him, Malcolm had his strong suspicion that Reza Khan had ordered the act, and it was that ruthlessness, which would allow him to do anything. As to the present company, something about Adam made him uncomfortable.

Adam took another draw on his pipe. "Yes, that's jolly good, gentlemen, but wasn't Mr. Eshghi loved and supported by the clergy?" He paused to look at both men. "With over thirty thousand people pouring on the streets for his funeral, one could conclude that Reza Khan has actually further assisted in destabilizing the country." For a moment no one spoke. Then Adam continued, "Gentlemen, a word of advice. The element of religion, used correctly, can be an extremely useful tool. We have been successful in mastering this tool. It has served us well in many continents throughout the ages. We don't want to lose what we have now in this region. We want to stay in control of the religious element."

Fraser shook his head, went behind his desk, and sat on his leather swivel chair. Leaning back, he said, "Our military is spread too thin. We are facing multiple challenges throughout the world. New lines are being drawn. To secure our position in the world, our military forces need to be where they're needed the most. A semi-independent, unified, and strong Persia can help us keep the new Soviet Union's aggression checked without exhausting our own military resources." He seemed to reflect for a moment. "Reza Khan can deliver that for us."

Adam's presence and his demeanor reminded Malcolm why he never developed fondness for the Foreign Office diplomats. He found them to be a group of arrogant bureaucrats with no actual field experience yet were allowed to make policy decisions. Nevertheless, he kept his calm. Gazing at his crystal glass, he said, "Bolshevik agents are actively recruiting and organizing indigenes Communist parties here. Lenin's vision of world revolution is still going strong, regardless of his recent death. Their military has crossed Persian borders multiple times, and they are nervous about American thirst for oil in the north of Persia. My directives are very clear, Mr. Adam."

Adam narrowed his eyes and looked at Malcolm. "And that is?"

"Stop the spread of communism," Malcolm replied and took a quick gulp of his drink.

Adam remained in the same position, stared at Malcolm for a moment in silence, then inhaled and said, "For what it's worth, may I mention that the number one objective for you gentlemen is, and has always been, to protect our oil interests in this region. The *world revolution* concept of Lenin may soon join its creator in hell. Especially if Stalin rises to power and successfully eliminates Trotsky and Kamenev."

Malcolm responded back swiftly, "Hope is a tease, Mr. Adam, designed to prevent us from accepting reality. Regardless of who replaces Lenin, communism will push for expansion. We must not exhaust our will nor divert our attention from stopping it at every corner."

Adam shifted on his chair and moved up to the edge, his eyes staring into Malcolm's. "Gentlemen," he said, "I don't need to remind you that the best defense against godless communism is Islam."

Colonel Fraser glimpsed over at Malcolm, then quickly turned his face toward Adam. "Yes, we know that very well, Mr. Adam. No reminder is required. However, Reza Khan has proven himself a strong and capable ally. Organized religion can spread religious zealotry throughout the world like a cancer. No conventional weapon can combat religious zealotry effectively. Mishandling the politics of religion can backfire."

Adam had looked away as Fraser spoke but turned his gaze again to Malcolm. "We have heard of your adventurous strategy, Mr. Malcolm. Of course, we do not endorse such a dangerous proposal. If pressed, we will adamantly deny any awareness of such an attempt. However, if the plan moves forward with your anticipated results, it will be the most satisfying and perhaps the most significant change in the modern history of the region."

Malcolm nodded and glanced at the colonel.

"However," Adam continued, swirling his whiskey. "I am curious. Why are you targeting this particular American, Major Imbrie?"

"He has been around. This is not his first assignment. I'm fairly positive that he is able to handle himself well in difficult situations," Malcolm snapped.

"No, Mr. Malcolm, my question was more in reference to his infamy with the Russians. Apparently, it was just a few years ago that the poor chap's cover was blown in Russia, which led to his arrest and beating by Cheka. I also heard that the Russians have actually set a large reward for his head. "Bottom line, Mr. Malcolm, we don't want him dead."

Malcolm sighed and emptied his glass. "Noted. We shall be cautious. The Russians are extremely aggressive in this region and their network of operatives is expanding daily."

Colonel Fraser added, "The Americans are actually our ally in helping us contain the Bolshevik's expansion. Russia's thirst for the warm waters of the south is too strong. We can use all the help we can get."

Adam jumped in. "We have reports that Imbrie's assignment is to open up an intelligence office to spy on Russians in the north of Persia. Once in operation, that office can help you in your efforts."

Malcolm shook his head. "I doubt it, and Major Imbrie has a history of blowing his covers. It won't last. He is a loose pawn."

Adam turned toward Malcolm and stared at him for a moment. "Nevertheless, I advise extreme caution. We don't want an international catastrophe on our hands, especially not with America. You can surmise from my words, gentlemen, that we are watching this operation with apprehension. Any mishaps will be detrimental to your career, and that would be the least of your worries. Don't slip up. The stakes are high."

Malcolm nodded. "People who play this game take risks." He set his empty glass on the corner of the table and excused himself from the meeting. He'd had enough of Mr. Adam.

"It was nice meeting you, Mr. Malcolm," said Adam. "And by the way, I heard that you are fluent in German."

"Yes, and four other languages plus three dialects," the colonel jumped in, answering for Malcolm.

Adam continued probing. "I heard that during the Great War you were captured by the Germans. Is it true?"

"Yes," Malcolm answered on his way to the door.

"I read in your personnel file that you were tortured by the Germans during the Great War."

Colonel Fraser frowned. "My understanding was that SIS officers' files are Most Secret and limited subscription."

Adam never took his focus off Malcolm. "SIS still functions under the Foreign Office. I assure you, sir, that I do possess such a clearance."

Malcolm directed a piercing glare at Adam. "Mr. Adam, do you have another question for me?"

"Yes, as a matter of fact, I do." Adam looked up at Malcolm with eyes steady and cold. "Your file indicates that you were captured in September of 1915 and were kept at Magdeburg's *Offizierlager*, the officers' prison camp. Then in July 1916, you escaped, were captured again, and put in the dreaded Ingolstadt reprisal camp. And then in February of 1917, you were moved to Burg bei Magdeburg until you escaped again in the summer of that year."

Apparently, Adam had access to confidential files. Where was he going with his comments? Malcolm's heartbeat sped up, but he knew how to control it. He took a breath to calm himself.

"You have studied my files well, Mr. Adam. However, I fail as yet to detect a question."

Adam sat back in his chair, playfully turning and examining his crystal glass. "The curious thing, Mr. Malcolm, is that I happened to have a dear friend who was in Ingolstadt camp the same time you were there. He remembers you well."

"I'm glad your friend confirmed my whereabouts. Now if you'll excuse me, I'm needed elsewhere." Malcolm turned the door knob.

"But he recalls that you were at Ingolstadt camp only for two weeks. Exactly where were you between August 1916 and February 1917, Mr. Malcolm?"

Malcolm stopped, gave a quick glance at Colonel Fraser, and then looked over his shoulder at Adam. A moment of uncomfortable silence blanketed the room. Malcolm calmly inhaled and exhaled. "Patience, Mr. Adam. If you play your cards right, one day, your clearance level will fetch you the answer."

6

HOME

Tuesday, July 8, 1924

IT WAS AROUND seven and the sun was dipping just beneath the horizon when Ali arrived home. The family lived in a rented room in a large house that accommodated six separate living spaces. Each room opened into an enclosed courtyard that contained a large, oval shaped utility pool in the center, which all the families shared. The house had one kitchen, one toilet, and a basement. Each family had a separate access from the shared courtyard. The owner of the house was a widow who occupied one room and rented out the others. Ali and his family had moved into that house after the death of his father two years prior. Ali had just started seventh grade when his towering, strong father died of pneumonia. His father's unexpected death accelerated his childhood to adulthood in a flash. He had to quit school and work multiple jobs to support the family.

That evening, Ali arrived with his large handkerchief wrapped around four small Persian cucumbers, a cantaloupe, two potatoes, and a tomato that he had selected for his mother at the open-air market. The cucumbers were especially tasty, which he knew because he ate one on the way home.

From the entry courtyard he climbed up five steps to get to their room. On top of the stairs, he stopped in the small patio to remove his shoes and set them next to the others outside the door to their room. Since the room's floor was frequently used for sitting, eating, praying and sleeping, it was important to be kept clean and free of street dirt.

"God bless you, son," said his mother as he handed the parcel of food to her. "You are such a good provider. May God always keep us under your shadow." Premature grey streaked her otherwise dark hair, making her look at least a decade older than her thirty-five years. Ali had also begun to notice a few extra kilos collecting around her waist. But he adored his mother and understood that the stress of losing her husband had taken a great toll.

Ali opened his coat and pulled out a few roses from his side pocket. He was careful to make sure that they weren't damaged. "Mother, will you please put these in a vase?"

"Son, you have such a gentle soul. These are beautiful flowers." Her eyes gleamed at the sight of the well-formed and colorful roses. The twinkle in her eyes wiped away Ali's fatigue from his long and laborious day of work.

"Mother, I don't know why, but roses have such a calming effect on me." Ali caressed a single petal of a pink rose.

"No wonder," said Miriam, his skinny, twelve-year-old sister. "They're pretty, they smell good, and they go well with other flowers mixed in a bouquet." She entered the room from the yard with three-year-old Zohereh in her arms. Miriam had been taking care of her little sister since she was born.

Ali smiled at Miriam and gently patted Zohereh's reddish hair. He would miss Miriam's sharp mind when she married and left to form her own family. Soon suitors would start asking for her hand.

"Yes, my dear, roses have a lot of good qualities. But beware, they also have thorns. Don't let the thorns prick your hard-working hands, my son."

Not the Rose I know, Ali thought, but he didn't dare tell her mother about his Christian tutor.

His mother left the room and went to the common house kitchen in the courtyard. On her way down the stairs, she called the kids who were playing in the yard and asked them to wash up and come up for dinner.

Ali's younger brother, Hassan, entered the room from outside and charged at him with a loud shout. Hassan was a skinny, eleven-year old. Their loud commotion attracted eight-year-old Kazem, Ali's other brother, to join in the wrestling game.

Mother entered the room with a round aluminum tray of food she had prepared in the common kitchen. "Dinner is ready, boys! Miriam, spread the *sofreh* on the floor and place the plates, utensils, and bread on it."

Miriam obeyed immediately and spread the white cloth, *sofreh*, on top of the Persian rug. Hassan and Kazem helped their mother with the tray. "What's for dinner, Mother?" Kazem asked.

"*Ahbgoosht*, lamb stew, dear,"

"Oh, I love *ahbgoosht*," Ali rubbed his hands together in excitement. He was hungry, and nothing felt better to him than coming home after a long hard day of work to a fabulous dinner. He served the dish often to customers in the teahouse, and when he stayed after the lunch rush, he ate the leftovers. But nobody else's *ahbgoosht* was as delicious as his mother's.

"This was your father's favorite, too, God bless his soul."

Everybody went quiet at the mention of their father and took their places around *sofreh*.

Ali took over the pounding of the meat for the stew. Someone strong or with a lot of tenacity would usually take the masher and pound a mix of cooked lamb, tomato, potato, garbanzo beans and white beans. The unspoken rule was that the head of the family should pound the meat. The tender lamb would blend with the other ingredients to create a mash consumed with bread.

Ali noticed the somber atmosphere and decided to change it up. "I remember Father throwing a coin up in the air and shooting a hole through it with his Luger side arm."

Kazem slapped a spoonful of mashed meat on a piece of flatbread, grabbed a handful of fresh greens from a large bowl of basil, mint, green onion, and radishes, and added to the bite. "Was he a soldier or a gendarme?" he asked, his words muffled by the mouthful of food he chewed.

Mother poured soup into a bowl for each person. Miriam grabbed Ali's soup bowl, dropped in a few pieces of bread and stirred it for him. Ali finished and put the bowl of meat mash in the middle of *sofreh*. He looked at everyone with affection, the warmth and love he felt for his family bringing a satisfied smile to his face.

"You were too young to remember," Hassan explained, "He was a soldier, but not just a regular soldier. He was a Cossack!"

Ali anticipated the question Kazem would ask and added, "The Cossack Brigade are the toughest soldiers and extremely loyal to Reza Khan."

"Reza Khan, our neighbor next door?" Kazem pointed to the room next door.

Everyone laughed. "No, you silly! Reza Khan is our country's prime minister. He was a Cossack general before he become the prime minister."

Hassan jumped in, "Wasn't he a soldier first and then he was very brave in battles and then become a general of a Cossack regiment?"

"Yes, exactly!" Ali answered.

The family enjoyed the first few minutes of their meal when a loud knock on the door followed by a thunderous voice of a man jolted the children.

"Salahm-ol-aleikom!"

Ali jumped up and went to the door. His mother and Miriam hustled to retrieve their *chador*. A man's voice meant that they needed to cover their heads and bodies before he entered the room.

At the door stood Seyyed Hussein, a heavy-set young man dressed in the trappings of a mullah—a deep brown robe, a white long shirt over his pants, a green scarf around his neck and a white turban on his head.

"*Salahm-ol-aleikom*, hello, Mullah," Ali greeted him with the door half open to prevent him peeking inside.

"Who is it, son?" Mother called from inside the room. The door had blocked her view of the caller.

"It's Mullah Seyyed Hussein!" Ali kept the door half open.

"Come on in, Mullah, and join us over dinner!" Ali's mother called from inside the room.

Ali opened the door fully and gestured Mullah to come inside.

Mullah took his slippers off and placed them next to the other shoes, then entered the room. Miriam and her mother got up to get an extra plate and bread. Seyyed Hussein, a friend of the family, was as tall as Ali, but since he was heavier and, wearing a robe and turban, he looked much bigger. He held a long strand of prayer beads in his left hand.

"Thank you, you're most kind. I was in the neighborhood and thought to stop by and visit," Seyyed Hussein said followed by a verse from Quran in Arabic about the importance of kindness, and then translated it into Farsi.

"You're most welcome, Seyyed. Please sit and eat with us," Ali's mother repeated her invitation. "Of course, as always, I have prepared enough for guests."

Seyyed Hussein sat on the floor by the white cloth next to Ali. As Miriam set a plate and a bowl in front of him, he stole a quick look at her. "God bless you, sister!"

Miriam blushed and tightened her *chador* around her face. She moved to sit next to her mother on the opposite side of the *sofreh*.

Little Zohreh turned toward her mother. "How come he has so many names and I only have one?"

Everyone laughed. "Zohreh *jon*," Mother explained, "Mullah is not his name. It is his job. Seyyed is his title. All Seyyeds are respected. The Seyyed title is carried only by direct descendants of Imam Hussein, the grandson of our beloved prophet Mohammad."

"Peace be upon him," Seyyed Hussein interrupted. Everyone repeated that phrase in Arabic, the proper way in Islam.

"Do you see his green scarf?" Mother asked Zohreh, and she nodded in reply. "The green scarf is to remind people that he is a Seyyed, and we all need to respect him for it."

After finishing his meal, Seyyed Hussein scooted back, rested against a cushion by the wall, and lit a cigarette.

Ali got up and went in search of an ashtray. He found one and put it in front of Seyyed Hussein. Miriam brought a tray with a pot of hot tea, two slim-waist tea glasses, two china saucers with small flower imprints and a metal sugar cube holder. She set the tray on the floor, placed a set of glasses and saucers in front of the two men and poured hot tea for them.

Seyyed Hussein watched her with fondness in his eyes and said, "Thank you sister, may God give you tenfold in return." He called her sister as a sign of respect.

Miriam didn't look up as it wasn't appropriate. But she nodded her head, thanked him, and went to the other corner of the room next to her little sister.

"Ali, let's take our tea and go to the courtyard by the pool," Seyyed Hussein suggested.

Ali welcomed the idea. His mother and older sister would appreciate not having to cover themselves with a *chador* any longer. The night was warm and the air inside their room was stuffy.

Seyyed Hussein and Ali got up to slip on their shoes. Miriam handed Ali a kerosene lamp as their house did not have electricity yet. Outside in the courtyard, the full moon and a cloudless sky provided ample lighting, however the lamp would be useful if they needed to go to the outhouse. The sweet fragrance of jasmine flowers mixed with the aromas of Persian cooking traveled on a gentle breeze and created a comforting aroma in the evening air. He and Seyyed Hussein sat on the raised edge of the utility pool. Seyyed blew out a large puff of cigarette smoke. Despite the background noise of crickets, frogs, and neighbors' shouting, Seyyed Hussein moved his head closer to Ali before he spoke.

"You have heard of the Baha'is' conspiracy, right?" he whispered.

"No, Seyyed, what conspiracy?" Ali inched away from the mullah. He didn't feel comfortable being that close to him.

"Well, brother, we live in a challenging time. Enemies of Islam are lurking everywhere."

"How so, Seyyed?"

"Baha'is have penetrated government, schools, and hospitals, and they have plans to take over the country! Their blasphemous beliefs are spreading. On the other hand, Russia's new government is run by a bunch of non-believers who are imposing their damned atheist thoughts on our nation's youth. Brits are robbing us by taking our oil and dominating our affairs. Didn't you hear about the fiasco in the Majlis?"

"No! What happened?"

"Where have you been, brother?"

"I've been working three jobs to feed my family since my father passed."

"Family is fine but..." Seyyed Hussein recited another verse from Quran about the duties of Muslims. Then he continued. "Your number one duty is to God. First is God, then your *ummah*, your Muslim brotherhood, and then your family. I'm talking about our battle in the parliament's courtyard. There were over five thousand of us demonstrating, and then it turned to a fight against two regiments of Reza Khan's soldiers. All for the sake of our *ummah* and our country!"

"What? I thought now that Reza Khan is the prime minister, things would improve." Ali was confused, "He was the commander of my father's regiment. My father always talked very highly of him. He said Reza Khan was a brave, bold, and smart man."

"You are young and naïve, Ali. *Sheitan*, Satan, can easily influence the heart and soul of the bravest men." He paused for a deep inhale of his cigarette and continued, "It was just a few months ago that Reza Khan proposed the idea of changing our country to a republic. Do you know how dangerous that is?"

Ali shook his head. "No. I don't even know what *republic* is or means."

"It is satanic! It was Satan who proposed it to Baha'is. Ten or fifteen years ago, their leader predicted that our government will be a republic. Guess what happened to Turkey when it recently became a republic?"

Ali shook his head again. Seyyed's rhetoric was making him feel stupid and childish. What did Seyyed want from him?

Seyyed continued, "The secular regime took over and Muslims lost. They removed the Muslim government and forced people to give up their beloved religion and be condemned to hell! Praise God that our religious leaders, *olama*, took the matter in their hands and denounced the idea of a republic. We are fighting back, Ali!"

Ali sighed. "This is way over my head, Seyyed. What is it that you want from me?"

"Come and join us in the battle against Satan and the Baha'is."

Ali shook his head. "I'm just a kid! All I want is one day, soon hopefully, to go back to school, get my diploma, and find a respectable job. Baha'i people haven't done any wrong to me. I've seen Baha'i people. They seemed very nice. They never looked satanic."

Seyyed dramatically raised his hands toward the sky, looked up, and in his booming voice declared, "God, please forgive him, he's young and naïve. God, please have mercy upon him." He slapped Ali on the back of his head. "Say *astagh-firullah*, you idiot, and ask for God's forgiveness before he devastates you and your family for your blasphemy."

Ali was caught off guard with the slap and fell off the curb onto his hands and knees. While he was down, he looked up toward the heavens and loudly repented, "*Astagh-firullah*, God, please forgive me, I don't know better. I'm still learning. Please forgive me." Somewhat intimidated and partially baffled by Seyyed's action, Ali looked over at him, and in a quiet voice said, "So, you see I repented, but what did I say that was so wrong?"

Seyyed Hussein stood up and bent over and offered a hand to help Ali get up off the ground. "Come to *masjid* and we will educate you. You'll learn how the blasphemous Baha'is denounced our twelfth Imam, our savior and messiah. We will help you to defend Islam and the righteous way of life."

Ali grabbed Seyyed's hand and pulled himself upright. Brushing himself off, he replied, "How did you get this booming voice? I don't know if it was your voice or your slap that threw me off balance!"

Seyyed let out a loud laugh. "Years of practicing and reciting my Islamic rhetoric in the religious theaters, *ta'ziyeh-khaneh*."

"Oh yes." Ali said, "I remember a few years ago my father taking me to *ghahve-khaneh* to watch *ta'ziyeh*. Now I recall seeing you there enacting the tragedy of Imam Hussein's last battle, the battle of Karbala. You were really good. You could arouse the crowd's emotions with that story every time. How does it feel to get a crowd so excited?"

Seyyed's face beamed with Ali's compliment. He nodded his head. "Real good, brother, real good. It's glorious to serve God and be praised by the creatures of God. If you are interested in learning how to become a mullah, I can take you under my tutelage. If you learn it well, and do it right, you will have everything—glory, respect, money, and social status!"

"I appreciate the offer. Let me think about it. By the way,

Seyyed, what do you know of the miracle of Sheikh Hadi's *sagha-khaneh?*"

"That's an example of how miracles work, brother," Seyyed replied. "Sheikh Hadi's *sagha-khaneh* is a sacred place. Our devoted flock has been granted many wishes by our saints. Recently, a Baha'i man disguised himself as a Muslim and drank water from *sagha-khaneh*. He became blind when he praised a Baha'i saint, Abbas Effendi, and refused to make an offering to Imam Mehdi, our beloved twelfth Imam, our savior. His sight came back after he repented and made a generous offering." Seyyed Hussein dropped his cigarette butt on the ground and crushed it with his foot. "Ali, we need your help."

"But what can I do?"

"We need as many young and strong men as we can find to help us cut the hands of the infidels running our government. We must ensure that Islam stays strong in our country. Come and join us Saturday night at Nasser Khosro Avenue."

"What's going on there?"

"We're going to show the American infidels how strong our *ummah* is."

"Americans? What's with them?"

"Satan is turning some Americans to Baha'is. They come to our beloved country, infiltrate our government, and push for changes in favor of Baha'is. An American Baha'i woman named Dr. Moody, who lives in *Nasserieh*, is very active in Baha'ism. She is the founder, or maybe a board member, of a Baha'i girls' school in Tehran. She is turning our innocent daughters and sisters away from Islam. We have given her many warnings, but she doesn't listen. Now it's time to show her our wrath. Bring as many friends as you can."

Ali felt a chill go up his spine when he heard about the Baha'i school for girls. Rose had mentioned that she knew a few people there, including Dr. Moody.

"I don't know, Seyyed. I have to be with my family. I'm the man of the house now. I need to be careful."

"Ali, this is the time that your religion needs you. You have obligations to your religion too. Who is going to help your family in time of need? Who is going to protect you and your family? Your *ummah*, your *masjid*, and your Muslim brothers. Not the government and certainly not Baha'is. Don't turn your back on us."

"No, no, I'm not turning my back on my brothers. Okay, I'll be there."

Seyyed Hussein patted Ali's back. "Good brother, I never doubted you. Now, go and be the man of the house. I'll see you Saturday night. Give your mother my thanks for her hospitality." Seyyed embraced Ali and the two kissed each other's cheeks. Seyyed departed and quickly disappeared into the darkness of the Tehran night.

Ali didn't go back to the room where his family waited. He couldn't. Life was becoming too complicated. He thought about what he heard in the teahouse. He thought about Major Imbrie and the potential danger he was facing. He also thought about Rose.

"Ali! Ali!" His mother's call brought him back to the time at hand. "Are you alone?"

"Yes, Mother, I'm coming in." He picked up the lamp and went upstairs.

Ali was quiet when he entered the room. His younger siblings were playing in a corner on the floor. His mother was going through a large platter full of watermelon seeds. She was picking out the white seeds and removing any excess watermelon left after a day of drying out in the sun. Roasted watermelon seeds were among the favorites of the family.

"That Seyyed Hussein is going places. He's an ambitious, bold and devoted young mullah," she said, while observing Ali's every move.

Ali didn't answer her. He went to a corner of the room and sat on the floor with his back resting on the wall.

"What did he say to you in the yard?"

"Nothing much."

Miriam was stitching a patch on a hole on Kazem's pants. She looked up from her work. "You spent a long time in the yard for saying nothing."

Ali did not reply, as if he didn't hear his sister.

"Ali *jon*, what did he want?" Mother asked again.

"He asked me to go to mosque," Ali mumbled.

Mother smiled. "Well, that's a good thing. I totally agree with him. You should listen to him."

"He also asked me to join a group of people to demonstrate against a Baha'i woman Saturday night."

"Oh my God! You have to go!" Mother exclaimed. "It is your religious duty to defend us and rid our society of infidel Baha'is."

"These are difficult times, Mother. If I get arrested, who will support you?"

"My dear son, do your duty to your God, and God will provide for us. Islam comes first and then family. If, God forbid, you and your Muslim brothers are sent to jail by misguided police, I will send your brother Hassan to work. He's almost twelve—he can handle it." His mother's serious face left no doubt in Ali's mind about her position on the subject. After several minutes of silence, she spoke.

"These days, at every *dars*, or other religious gathering I go to, I hear about the Baha'is threat and how these Baha'is are infiltrating the minds of our youth. Our beloved religious leaders, *mojtahedin*, are warning us to be aware and vigilant about Baha'is penetrating our schools, government, and every aspect of our lives. We need to be stronger and fight back. So, go, my son. Go and be proud that you are defending Islam and your family."

That night, Ali's mind became a battle ground for his opposing thoughts. On one hand, he never had any interaction with any

Baha'i person, so he didn't really know if they were dangers to the society. Furthermore, if some Americans and British people were helping girls to learn English and math, then what was the harm in that? He was learning English from Rose, and he thought that was good. On the other hand, Islam was very important, and as Seyyed said, he had to protect it. He also didn't want to harm anyone. He was taught that in Islam harming even animals was a sin. He also didn't want to disappoint his mother. His restless thoughts and mounting fears kept him awake until nearly dawn.

7

THE BANQUET

Wednesday, July 9, 1924

THE EARLY EVENING arrival of ladies dressed in elaborate evening gowns and gentlemen decked out in formal military or civilian attire signaled the beginning of the gala at the British embassy. Ali arrived an hour prior to the opening to help in the kitchen and set up the hall.

The vast hall with its polished, rich mahogany floor covered with Persian carpets were beyond anything Ali had ever imagined. The tall ceiling was supported by walls decorated with delicate plaster inlays and fancy moldings, some floral and some with geometric patterns. Several long windows ornamented with heavy lace curtains draping down to the floor circled the room. Four enormous oval mirrors were imbedded in the walls, but the most magnificent for him were the two towering paintings. One was of a man and the other of a woman standing in the most majestic attire he had ever seen. The large wooden crown carved on top of each colossal picture frame gave Ali the impression that the paintings were of the British king and queen.

About twenty-five other helpers were moving several large Persian carpets, chairs, and tables around in preparation of the hall for the festivity. Upon his arrival, he had been issued a black suit, a white shirt, a bow tie, and a pair of white gloves to wear. Twenty minutes before the opening, he went back to the kitchen and changed to his uniform.

HE WAS NEATLY ARRANGING Persian chickpea cookies on a serving tray when his cousin gave him the signal to go ahead and serve. Ali froze in awe as he entered the hall where musicians played pleasant, yet unfamiliar music to Ali's ears under large crystal chandeliers lit with electric bulbs. This was his first time seeing that many electric bulbs burning in chandeliers. The mirrors reflecting lights, the large paintings, and countless bouquets of flowers lining the banquet hall added to the regal aura. He had never seen such a superb display of color, light, music and most importantly, people dressed and behaving with such elegance.

"Don't stare at people, Ali, no matter how strange they look. Focus on your work and be polite, as always," his older cousin, Majid, instructed. As headwaiter, Majid exuded professionalism with his dark, clean-cut hair and commanding height.

Ali acknowledged the advice and circled the room with his tray of appetizers. He felt strange in the provided uniform. Nevertheless, he walked tall and never looked the guests in their eyes.

When Rose entered the room, Ali's face broke into a large grin. She wore a red silk dress that stopped right below her knees. It was embellished with trimming of tinsel braid ribbon. Her outfit accentuated her blonde hair that was freely draped over her shoulders with soft curves along the ends.

She looked even more beautiful without her nursing uniform, he thought.

He shot a covert glance at her while serving guests and saw that she was appraising him as well. After a brief smile, she raised her right eyebrow. Ali understood the signal and walked toward Rose and her friends.

His cousin's short instructions had asked him to carry and offer the tray with his right hand. He asked Ali to practice offering the try with his right hand while placing his left hand behind his back. But that was against Ali's upbringing and Persian culture. It was rude to offer a tray with only one hand. So Ali offered the rectangular silver tray to Rose and her friends with two hands, holding each side. The tray had Persian chickpea cookies arranged in a neat and orderly fashion. These delicacies were shaped like small stars, and in the center of each star lay green pistachio crumbles.

"Isn't this exquisite?" Rose whispered, "You look so handsome dressed like this, Ali." She then carefully lifted a star chickpea cookie from Ali's tray with her middle finger and her thumb. Her red nail polish, the same color as her dress, set off her milky white skin. He was close enough that her sweet jasmine fragrance made him dizzy.

Ali blushed. "Thank you."

He turned around and continued circulating through the crowd and offering his tray. A few moments later, what he saw stopped him in his tracks. He felt his hot face go cold. The Englishman from the teahouse stood only a few meters from him. He was the one Ibrahim had called Malcolm. What was he doing there?

Nursing a cocktail, Malcolm was dressed in a tuxedo and buffed-to-a-shine black leather shoes. Quite a drastic change from the Persian peasant look Ali had seen in the teahouse. Ali changed direction and moved out of Malcolm's view. His heart was pounding. He didn't want Malcolm to recognize him.

Ali remembered the conversation between the three men in the teahouse—about a banquet and Major Imbrie. Many foreign dignitaries and men with impressive military uniforms crowded the room. He wondered if he could pick out the American major. Ali watched as Malcolm circulated through the hall, and noticed he spent a good amount of time with a certain tall and rather loud middle-aged military man. The man spoke English, but his accent sounded different than any other Englishman Ali had ever heard. That man could be the American Major Imbrie, he thought.

Ali scanned the room and found Rose near the musicians, engaged in conversation with a few women of her age. Since his tray was empty, he went to the kitchen to pick up a full one. The kitchen was chaotic—waiters rushing back for more finger foods and drinks, head waiters barking orders and cooks busy with making more appetizers. There was no time for any talk or even complaints. Ali picked up another tray, this time, the tray contained *dolmehes*, cooked stuffed grape leaves, a Persian delicacy. Back in the hall, he noticed the crowd had expanded and the hall was nearly full. He went straight to Rose, offered the tray to the group, and with a slight head jerk signaled her to follow him away from the other women. He took only a few steps away and turned his tray to Rose, who had followed him.

"Do you know two men by the corner door?" With his head Ali pointed in Malcolm's direction.

"What?" Rose yelled. "I can't hear you over the music. Speak louder!"

Ali repeated his question a bit louder.

"There are so many people! What men are you pointing to?" Rose asked.

"Corner next to big red curtain and horse," Ali whispered. "A big tall army man and English man."

"Oh, you mean next to the bronze horse statue? Yes, I see those two men. Hmm, no, I don't know them. Why?"

"The man in military uniform, is he English?"

One of Rose's friends had moved near them. She heard Ali's

question and answered, "Oh, I know that uniform. He's an American Marine!"

"American! Thank you." Ali nodded his head and walked away from Rose and her friend. Could the American Marine be Major Imbrie? The same man that they were talking about in the teahouse? The one that they were conspiring to send to the dangerous *sagha-khaneh*?

Ali eased his way near the two men and offered his tray to people passing by. He stayed watchful of Malcolm but avoided making eye contact. He managed to get close enough to eavesdrop on their conversation.

"Mr. Malcolm, it is good to see you!" A well-dressed Persian man in a white jacket and a black bow tie extended his hand to Malcolm. His jet-black hair was swept back and oiled, and his moustache deftly trimmed. The scent he was wearing, a strong, oil-based Persian amber fragrance, was different and much stronger than that of other foreign men in the room.

"Oh, yes, good evening Dr. Akbarie." The two men shook each other's hands. Malcolm then introduced the man he was speaking with to Dr. Akbarie.

It *was* Imbrie!

"An American? We appreciate your government's serious interest in our country," Dr. Akbarie said to Imbrie. "We like Americans. They have always been helpful to us. Do you know Mr. Millspaugh? He is an American gentleman."

"Not personally," Imbrie replied, "but I've heard of him. Isn't he the treasurer of your government?"

"Yes, yes, and a very good one, I might say!" Dr. Akbarie beamed, "Our prime minister, Reza Khan, is listening to his advice more than anyone else these days. Mr. Millspaugh, just like his predecessor, Mr. Shuster, another American, is winning the heart and soul of our government. Mr. Shuster, as the Controller General, brought sanity to the Persian government's treasury twelve years ago. Did you know that?" He leaned toward Imbrie's ear and with a softer voice said, "But Mr. Millspaugh is a bit uptight these days, you know." Dr. Akbarie, elbowed Imbrie and chuckled.

Imbrie stepped back a foot. "No, as a matter of fact, I don't. Why would he be uptight?"

"Well, Mr. Millspaugh is denying our prime minister an expanded military budget."

Malcolm turned his head and scanned the room. Ali noticed and quickly turned his back to Malcolm and his group. He then turned around and positioned himself behind Malcolm. That way, he could see and hear Imbrie, but it was harder for Malcolm to spot Ali.

"Great!" Imbrie replied, "I'm happy that our bean counter came in handy for you folks. But he's just a bean counter. What does he know about military? Cutting costs is in his nature! Like a scorpion, you know?" Imbrie curled his index finger, imitating the tail of a scorpion, and let out a loud laugh.

Dr. Akbarie wrinkled his face in confusion. "Pardon me? I don't understand? Bean? Bean counter?"

"Oh, never mind." Imbrie answered. "What do you think of Mr. Sinclair's proposal for Persia's northern oil fields? I bet the ten-million-dollar loan that is in the package will tickle the right spot." He laughed.

Dr. Akbarie was about to sip on his tea, but he stopped, his eyes bulging and eyebrows raised in delight. "Oh, we love it. The parliament, m*ajlis*, is seriously looking into the American proposal. The more competition, the better it is for us. But I am worried about the meddling of Standard Oil, Mr. Imbrie. Their partnering act with the British APOC is not helping. They are actually working against Mr. Sinclair's proposal." He stepped closer to Imbrie and in a conspiratorial tone asked, "Can't your government control it? Standard Oil is a very dangerous organization, Mr. Imbrie. They have done terrible things in other countries. Are you familiar with their history?"

Imbrie took a step back. "Oh, you surely understand, Doctor, that we are a capitalist country. Our government doesn't meddle, as you say, with corporate affairs."

Dr. Akbarie stood where he was and projected his voice as if he wanted other people to hear him clearly. "Well, we like the American government. Since Mr. Sinclair has the approval and backing of your government, our parliament is more likely to look at his proposal positively, despite the heavy pressure from APOC, the Russians, and even the French. But as I said before, the more competition, the better it is for us." Dr. Akbarie glanced briefly at Malcolm, turned to Imbrie and added, "But, I'm not sure that our friends here, the Brits and Russians, that is, enjoy competition as much as we do."

Ali was impressed with Dr. Akbarie's fluency in English. He wondered if he should become more serious about learning English from Rose and go into politics. Or become a merchant like his uncle. But instead of traveling to India and Arab countries, he would travel to England where Rose was from. If it wasn't for supporting his family, he would have been in school. He enjoyed wearing the fancy clothing and working as a server, but he preferred to be more like Dr. Akbarie, a respected guest at such fancy parties instead of a servant.

Malcolm, who stood nearby, consulted a watch that he drew from his waistcoat pocket. Dr. Akbarie looked at Malcolm again and extended his hand to Imbrie. "I'd better leave before Mr. Malcolm becomes really annoyed with me, but I also want to tell you that we much appreciate Mr. Baskerville's sacrifices for us. He is a true American hero to us."

As Imbrie shook Dr. Akbarie's hand, he tilted his head and said, "I'm afraid I don't know who Baskerville is and what he has done."

"Oh, my God! It was less than fifteen years ago that Mr. Howard Baskerville died for the Iranian revolution! He led the Iranian revolutionaries in Tabriz, northwest of Iran, or as you westerners say, Persia, and—"

"Tabriz?" Imbrie cut him off. "I'm supposed to go there soon."

Dr. Akbarie looked at Imbrie for a brief moment and continued, "Oh yes, he fought alongside our revolutionary leaders against tyranny and dictatorship. You should read about him. Especially if you are going to Tabriz soon."

Imbrie gave a shake to Dr. Akbarie's hand and ended their conversation with, "I will, and I appreciate your country's hospitality. I am glad to be here."

Dr. Akbarie nodded and moved off to speak to another group of men.

Ali continued circulating among people near Imbrie and offering them appetizers, but always maintained his position out of Malcolm's sight. He made every attempt to be polite, courteous, and helpful to the guests, like the other workers there. The money was good and they all wanted to be called back. Ali also enjoyed watching the guests move about in their fancy and elaborate outfits. He was especially amazed at how freely women moved about and conversed with the men.

An attractive brunette woman in a midnight blue gown walked toward the two remaining men. She grabbed Imbrie's right arm, lifted herself on her toes and planted a kiss on his cheek.

Malcolm turned his head toward the woman. "Mrs. Imbrie, I presume?"

"Yes, sir," Imbrie replied.

"I must say that you're a lucky man, Major! Your wife is quite charming." Malcolm bent and kissed her hand. "James Malcolm at your service."

Imbrie's wife chuckled. "Katherine Imbrie. How do you do?"

Imbrie looked at his wife, raised his wine glass to her and said, "Yes sir, she sure is!" Then he turned his face toward Malcolm, started to speak, hesitated, then said, "With Lenin gone, and Trotsky's push for the top job, how do you folks take the Bolshevik's desire to spread? The warm waters of the Persian Gulf are not too far away!"

Katherine didn't let Malcolm answer Imbrie's question. "Warm water, what is that? I'm not trying to be rude or anything, but I have heard this many times. Why are you people so worried about Russians getting to the warm waters?"

Imbrie seemed surprised by his wife's interruption, took his eyes away from Malcolm, and with a little chuckle answered, "Oh honey, by warm water we are talking about warm water ports." He shifted his weight. "A warm water port is a port where the water does not freeze in winter. Because they are available year-round, warm water ports or free water ports give great advantages for trade and military."

Malcolm took a step closer to Imbrie and added, "Geography has been very cruel to Russia in the sense that it has left her virtually landlocked. Even in the north, her access to the world is frozen in winter. Russian leaders in past centuries pursued a fix for this unfortunate problem with a steady and relentless drive to the open sea. Peter the Great, about fifty years before the birth of the United States, in his will advised his subjects to approach as near as possible to Constantinople and India. Whoever governs there will be the true sovereign of the world."

"Hah, that's funny!" Imbrie gave Malcolm a pat on the shoulder. "And the British empire has the control of both."

Malcolm nodded his head gently, smiled, and took a sip of his cocktail.

Ali moved around and took a better look at Imbrie. He stood close to two meters tall with a thick neck and broad shoulders. His chestnut brown eyes and hair, well-chiseled features, and high forehead gave him a rather intimidating presence.

Major Imbrie took a sip of his wine and turned toward Malcolm. "How long have you been stationed in this country?"

"Far too long, sir," Malcolm mused, "but I must admit, this country has its own unique beauty, if you have the eyes to discover it."

"Well, I'm asking because my hobby is photography, and I'm

passionate about my hobby!" Imbrie laughed. "In fact, I just got my new color plate auto-chrome equipment. Now, I can take color photos. I'd love to take it out for a test run. Do you have any recommendations for me? Something unique and colorful, as you say?"

"Hmm, intriguing!" Malcolm paused for a moment, looking down. Then he looked up with excitement and said, "Actually, it's funny you asked that question, Major. For what it's worth, a few days ago, I heard a story about a *sagha-khaneh* in the old part of town. It's called the miracle of Sheikh Hadi's *sagha-khaneh—*"

"Wait, I'm sorry you lost me there," Imbrie interrupted., "What's the first word? *Sagha-khaneh*? And what's the other one?"

"Oh, yes, my apologies, I forgot you are new here. The language is quite the bugger. The place is Sheikh Hadi..."

Ali couldn't grasp all they were saying, but he recognized the name of the place. There it was. Malcolm was telling Imbrie about the miracle. Ali needed to get closer. He inched himself to within a meter of the men. It wasn't working. Between the music and the general hum of people talking, he couldn't hear the conversation clearly.

Someone took the last *dolmeh* from his tray. He returned to the kitchen to refill it.

Not long after, Ali hovered near the two men again, holding a freshly filled tray of finger food.

"I'll be damned," Imbrie said. "That's an interesting story about the miracle. Definitely a glimpse into the culture. Would you join me for a photo shoot? I'll certainly be photographing the miraculous *sagha-khaneh* sometime within the next few days."

Malcolm appeared to think for a few seconds and then snapped his fingers. "Oh bother, I shall be traveling outside of the area three days from now. But if you can wait, I can certainly join you toward the end of next week."

Imbrie shook his head. "I'm sorry, Mr. Malcolm, I can't wait that long. I'll be photographing the Sheikh Hadi's miraculous *sagha-khaneh* sooner than later! Thanks to you, I have a rare opportunity I don't want to miss."

"Okh, okh!" The loud sigh escaped Ali's lips before he could stop it.

Malcolm turned his head toward the sound.

Ali quickly turned away but could feel Malcolm's stare on back of his neck. Ali dropped his head and quietly stepped away from Malcolm and Imbrie.

"Excuse me! Excuse me! *Garcon!*" Malcolm commanded Ali in perfect Farsi, "You! Stop!"

Ali stopped and slowly turned half-way around. After a brief glance at Malcolm, he dropped his head lower and raised his tray up to cover his face, offered the appetizers.

Malcolm examined Ali with an inquisitive look, slowly walking toward him. Again, he spoke in Farsi. "Don't I know you from somewhere?"

"No, sir," Ali replied in Farsi.

Major Imbrie wore a blank expression. Of course, he didn't understand any of that exchange. He smiled, walked toward Ali, and said in English, "Oh, great! I'll have a couple of them." He reached out and picked two items from Ali's tray. "Also, will you take my empty glass, son?"

"Yes sir," Ali answered in English, took the empty glass and walked away briskly. He worried that his response to Imbrie may have worked against him. He didn't want Malcolm to remember that he had waited on him in the teahouse.

"Waiter, wait," Malcolm ordered in English this time. "I'd like some, too."

Ali stopped again and turned back with his head down offered the tray to Malcolm. He felt Malcolm's stare on him, so he didn't look up.

Malcolm in English asked, "Do you speak English?"

Ali felt Malcolm was testing him. He responded in a short Farsi phrase, "A little." He bowed to Malcolm, and keeping his head down, turned and walked away.

Ali searched the hall for Rose. He found her smoking in the opposite corner of the room near the balcony, an exquisite silver and jade cigarette holder between her fingers. He rushed toward her.

"Next few days. That means soon, yes?" he whispered.

Rose smiled at Ali, exhaled smoke away from his face and said, "Yes, it means, not tomorrow but perhaps in three or four days from now. Why are you asking? What is happening in the next few days?"

"Oh no," Ali mumbled and walked away from Rose, lost in his thoughts.

"What is happening?" Rose followed him a few steps and asked again, "Talk to me!" Rose raised her voice as he left, "Ali!"

Malcolm heard a female voice shouting and swiftly turned his head toward the sound. The server who had just left them was disappearing into the kitchen.

"Ali," Malcolm whispered. A common name. But ...

"Excuse me, Mr. Malcolm," Major Imbrie said in an apparent attempt to bring Malcolm's attention back to him. "You know, you really shouldn't think of Sinclair's proposal for northern oil fields as America competing with Britain over the same thing. Think of us as your partners or neighbors who're sharing the same street. There's plenty of oil to go around for everyone. We just want a piece of the action."

Malcolm forced himself back into the conversation with Imbrie. "Yes, yes, of course, but, my friend, Americans are already our partners in the oil business. Standard Oil and APOC are equal partners in the Persian northern oil fields."

"Yes, yes, but ..." Imbrie inhaled and looked down for a moment then he looked at Malcolm. His lips were press together.

"Standard Oil is a private party. Mr. Sinclair, however, has our government support."

"Say, wasn't Mr. Sinclair's name mentioned as one of the people involved with the Teapot Dome scandal?" Malcolm asked automatically. "Correct me if I am wrong, Major, but I believe he is accused of bribing Senator Fall, the interior secretary. Didn't it cause the senator's resignation last year?"

Imbrie shook his head and shifted his weight back and forth a few times. "You know, Mr. Malcolm, my father used to say, 'Robert, believe none of what you hear and only half of what you see.' He was a wise man, God rest his soul. All these accusations you hear about Sinclair are nothing but hogwash. None is proven. These rumors are simply horse manure fueled by his rivals, people who work for outfits like SOCONY, the Standard Oil of New York." He raised his voice. "You know how cutthroat this business is. I vouch for Sinclair, he is an outstanding citizen."

Malcolm noticed that he had hit a nerve with Imbrie and he didn't want to lose him. He needed Imbrie to go to the *sagha-khaneh* and take photos of people there. Without it, his plan would not work. He changed the subject slightly. "It is not us that you need to worry about. It's the ambitious Bolshevik Russia that is eager to expand their oil business into Persia's fields in the north. Not to discount their centuries-old ambition to have access to the warm waters of the Persian Gulf."

"Damned Bolsheviks! We can handle Russia, trust me on that, sir. We'll keep them boxed in."

Satisfied that Imbrie was still on board, Malcolm decided to break off the conversation and check on that boy, Ali. "Major would you please excuse me for a moment?" With a nod of apology to Imbrie, Malcolm followed Ali to the kitchen. It bothered Malcolm that he couldn't pinpoint with clarity where he had seen that boy before. He took pride in his keen ability to recognize faces.

The first person Malcolm encountered in the kitchen was the

head waiter. "Do you have a worker named Ali here?" he asked in Farsi.

"Yes sir, we have two Alis."

"The young boy who came here a few minutes ago, is he Ali? He is around fifteen or sixteen years old."

"Oh, yes. He is my cousin. Is he in trouble?"

"No, no, quite the opposite. He is doing so well that I thought I'd give him a tip, if that is permissible. Where is he?"

"He left, sir. He was sick. He went home."

"Does he work anywhere else?"

"Yes sir, in the garden here in the embassy."

"What I meant was, does he work anywhere else outside the embassy?"

"Yes, he helps our uncle with camels. We call him the camel jockey."

"How about *ghahve-khaneh*? Does he work in a teahouse too?"

"Oh, I don't know, sir. He's a hard worker. His father died, so Ali must work for his family. He'll work anywhere."

"All right, then, give him this money when you see him." Malcolm handed him a few bills.

"Thank you, sir, it will help his family very much. God give you many more in return."

Malcolm turned around to leave. Then had another thought. "Does Ali understand English?"

"Yes, sir. I don't know where he learned it, but his English is better than all the other workers here."

Malcolm made a mental note to talk to Ibrahim about Ali. If it turned out that Ali is the same boy who served them in the teahouse, then he might have heard what they talked about. If that is the case, he must be contained. But for the time being, he returned to the banquet hall in search of Major Imbrie. He had to make sure his lamb would be ready for the slaughter.

8

***

THE AMERICAN EMBASSY

Thursday, July 10, 1924

THE FOLLOWING MORNING, Malcolm decided to pay a visit to Imbrie in the American embassy in Tehran. Since Imbrie had not set a date for his visit to *sagha-khaneh* yet, Malcolm needed to do a bit of prodding in order to find out when to set his plan in motion. As he sat in the lobby awaiting Imbrie, a diminutive woman who looked to be in her early seventies stormed into the lobby and paraded straight to the information desk. She looked distraught and disheveled. Clumps of straggly gray hair protruded from under her wrinkled scarf.

With her right fist, she pounded the information desk and demanded to see the ambassador. "This is the third time! I'll not leave until I talk to Murray."

The clerk sitting behind the desk seemed unperturbed. "Dr. Moody, the ambassador is out of the office. Perhaps we can make an appointment for you."

Dr. Moody shook her head and loudly protested, "No! I will not leave. This is a matter of life and death!"

"Sergeant, man the desk till I return," the man behind the desk instructed the guard. He disappeared into the corridor.

Malcolm had heard of Dr. Moody. He knew she was an American. Her name had come up in some reports—but where?

A few minutes later, Imbrie appeared in the lobby. He went straight to the woman. "Dr. Moody?" He extended his hand to her and continued. "I am Vice Consul Robert Imbrie. How can I be of assistance?"

The woman stood and shook his hand, not seeming at all intimidated by his stature. "I'm Dr. Susan Moody. I'm an American citizen and my life is in danger. I've received death threats."

Imbrie frowned. "Please come with me."

Malcolm raised his hand and waved hello to Imbrie, hoping Imbrie would include him in the discussion with Dr. Moody. He had a strong feeling about her being useful to his plan.

Imbrie did notice him and gave him a quick smile. He turned to the woman and extended his hand to show the way to his office. He took a few steps, stopped, and said, "Forgive me doctor, would you mind if I invite this gentleman from the British embassy to join us?" He pointed to Malcolm. "He is well acquainted with this country."

She shrugged her shoulders. "That's fine with me. Maybe the Brits can bring some sense to you people and teach you folks a thing or two on how to protect the lives of your own countrymen."

Imbrie flinched at Dr. Moody's jab, and invited Malcolm to join them with a quick head gesture. Malcolm sprung out of his chair and followed them into Imbrie's office, just a few meters down the hall.

"Please, have a seat and tell me all about the death threats." Imbrie showed Dr. Moody a chair in front of his desk. "And Mr. Malcolm, make yourself comfortable anywhere."

Malcolm sat on a chair near the door. Dr. Moody began her

story even as she was settling herself. "I'm not new to death threats, you know. In my fifteen years here, I've been threatened many times. But this time, I have credible sources that it is real. They are trying to kill me and my friends. Ever since the trouble in *majlis*, the Parliament—"

Imbrie interrupted her. "Dr. Moody, please slow down. I'm new to this country. I don't know who is after you and why. Can you give me just a brief background about yourself, and then tell me who you think is after you."

Dr. Moody shifted in her chair, "Oh boy, they gave me another rookie. Okay, let's start with me. You got my name, right?"

"Yes, but what are you doing here in Persia?"

"I'm a physician. I have my own private practice and also work in *Sehat* hospital. I cofounded the Tarbiyat school for girls here in Tehran and—"

"Great," Imbrie interrupted again. "It's clear you have made some notable contributions to the Persian society. Who then would want to kill you and why?"

"Well, I'm a proud and active member of the Baha'i faith!"

There it was. Malcolm recalled the context of his intel on Dr. Moody and confirmed his intuition that she could be useful. Shiites, the majority of the population, detested Baha'is and considered them infidels. This might fit perfectly, he thought.

Imbrie shrugged his shoulders and glanced at Malcolm, who was ready with his quick interjection into the conversation.

Malcolm moved to the edge of his chair. "Dr. Moody, please forgive my intrusion. So, you are a follower of Abbas Effendi?"

"Yes!" she answered and turned around with apparent physical discomfort. Looking at Malcolm for the first time since the meeting started, she said, "Why don't you sit closer so I can see you better. You look like a smart man!"

Malcolm moved to a chair near her so she didn't have to turn around to speak to him.

She turned back to Imbrie. "I can see that you haven't been

briefed about the hostilities directed to followers of the Baha'i faith by conservative Muslims in this country."

"No, ma'am. I've just been assigned to this post and have not been fully briefed yet. But to my knowledge, many different religious groups live in this country in relative peace. There are Sunnis, Christians, Jews, Zoroastrians. What makes Baha'is different?"

"You need to ask a Shiite clergy that question, not me. To me, Baha'i is the most peaceful, non-discriminative religion in the world. You should come to one of our weekly meetings. You may be pleasantly surprised!"

Ignoring her invitation, Imbrie turned to Malcolm. "What is your take on this?"

"Well, I concur with Dr. Moody. The climate is intensely charged for Baha'is nowadays. The Jafari Shiite Muslims are the majority in Persia. They see Baha'is as infidel foes."

Imbrie addressed Dr. Moody. "What is the story behind the death threats and why is it credible this time?"

"I've heard rumors through my connections," Dr. Moody cleared her voice and continued, "that conservative Muslim groups have prepared a list of several hundred Baha'is to be killed. I've been told my name as well as my roommate's, Elizabeth Stewart, is on the list. Their plan is to create a riot tonight in front of our residence, drag us onto the street, and kill us. You *must* help us." Her voice held a trace of fear mixed with anger and irritation.

Malcolm noticed Imbrie drumming his fingers on his desk in rapid succession. But he kept his calm demeanor otherwise.

Dr. Moody studied Imbrie for a few moments and then continued pressuring him. "Look, the embassy's indecisiveness in a similar case a few years ago nearly cost two American Baha'i women, Dr. Sarah Clock and Lillian Kappes, their lives. At the time, Kappes was the director of the Tarbiyat Girls' School. The school I founded."

Imbrie shook his head, "I don't recall any briefing about that incident."

"It was before your time." Dr. Moody gestured her hand dismissively and continued. "They were badly beaten and robbed."

Malcolm was aware that Imbrie was an intelligence agent and his title, Vice Consul, was just a cover. He jumped in. "Forgive my intrusion again, madam, but didn't it happen around 1913?"

"That was years ago!" Imbrie exclaimed, throwing Dr. Moody an exasperated look.

"It doesn't matter!" Dr. Moody shouted. "What matters is that the situation is hostile. The current political climate is highly charged. American lives are on the line—the very lives that you're supposed to protect."

"Very well, Dr. Moody. I'll take care of it." Imbrie replied, clearly wanting to end the conversation.

She persisted. "Excuse me if I say that's not good enough. I need to see some action."

"I understand," Imbrie said and turned his head toward Malcolm. "Mr. Malcolm, do you have any suggestions?"

"Yes, I do," Malcolm replied, seizing an opportunity to test the reactions of the local police, who could possibly, and ignorantly, be of use to him. "With respect to the current sensitive political climate, it may be best if you encourage the local authorities to handle the situation. Chances are, they are not even aware of this gathering."

Imbrie nodded his head in agreement and went to his office door, half opened it and shouted, "Johnson, Johnson!"

A man showed up at the door. "Yes, Major."

"Send a messenger to the chief of police and tell him to expect my visit in his office within one hour. I have an urgent matter to discuss with him."

He turned back to Malcolm and said, "Will you accompany me?"

"With pleasure," replied Malcolm. "If I may, I would like to suggest that Dr. Moody also accompany you to the chief's office. That way, the chief of police will hear firsthand about her concerns."

Imbrie turned to Dr. Moody. "Will you accompany us, madam?"

Dr. Moody nodded. "Whatever you boys think will get the result. Let's go." She nearly leaped from her chair and scurried to the door.

A hint of a smile rippled across Malcolm's face. Imbrie's appearance in public with Dr. Moody, a blacklisted American Baha'i, would most certainly strengthen his plot. The meeting with Imbrie, whose cover as a diplomat left much to be desired, turned out much better than he could have hoped. Imbrie's vulnerabilities were many and obvious. This goose was all but cooked.

9

THE FIRST TIME

Saturday, July 12, 1924

BUSINESS HAD BEEN slow at the teahouse. Ali's boss had dismissed him once the lunch rush was over. Ali walked home through the usual narrow dirt alleys, without stopping to watch the kids play. He was preoccupied. He didn't even notice when a kite being flown by some kid on a roof top, crashed in front of his feet. The protest outside Dr. Moody's house was scheduled for late that afternoon. He was lamenting the protest and whether he should participate in it or not.

Inside the courtyard, Ali's noisy brothers played hide-and-seek with their friends and were running around the utility pool. They didn't even notice his arrival. He washed at the utility pool and went inside to his family room to proceed with the afternoon prayers. The musky aroma of Persian tea, which his mother always kept ready, had a soothing effect on him. He saw the thin figure of his sister Miriam by the window cleaning the greens in preparation for dinner. Once in a while she glanced outside to check on the noisy young ones in the courtyard. The normal rhythms of family life in the sanctuary of home calmed his troubled heart.

Ali retrieved his prayer rug from the closet, spread it on the floor in his corner of the room, and faced southwest, toward the Ka'aba in Mecca, and began. At the end of his prayers, he sat on his knees in a meditative posture and silently attempted to connect with God. He was in need of guidance. What was the right move? He asked God to give him a sign and guide him to do the right thing.

His mother, in the opposite corner of the room, hummed an old folk tune as she patched the holes on some pants and socks. When Ali finished his prayer, he raised his head. She looked up from her work. "Ali *jon*, isn't today the day that Mullah Seyyed Hussein asked you to be somewhere for him?"

Mother remembered. Ali didn't answer her and tried to pretend he was still praying.

"Ali, did you hear me?"

Maybe God was speaking through her. He must remain honest.

Ali covered his face with the palms of his hands and slowly slid them down his cheeks, signaling the official end of his praying. As he wrapped his prayer rug to put it away, he answered. "Yes, Mother, it's today. But I'm not sure I want to go. I have a bad feeling about it."

His mother stopped sewing. "My dear, when God calls you, you must respond. It is your religious duty to be there. You're a Muslim. You must protect your faith."

"Mother, it's not God calling. It is Seyyed Hussein. My problem is, I don't have anything against Baha'is."

Ali's mother dropped her sewing, looked up to the heavens and raised her hands as if to pray. "*Astagh-firullah*, God, please forgive my son!" Then she faced Ali again. "When Seyyed Hussein asks for your help to save Islam, you go. No, you rush. Do you hear me? You don't need to second-guess him or ask questions. You rush to his side. Your first duty is to God. No questions, no hesitating, no thinking; you rush! Do you hear me?" A crimson flush rose up her neck and face.

"Mother! Calm down. I will go. I will go right now." Ali strolled over to the door where his shoes lay, trying to waste more time.

Ali's mother followed him with her eyes and did not return to her sewing. "I'm glad Seyyed Hussein saw me in the market this morning. He specifically asked me to remind you of this." She kept up her nagging as Ali put on his shoes. "May God protect you my son. Make me proud."

"Yes, Mother. I'll make you and *Allah* proud. But don't wait up for me."

***

The street by Dr. Moody's house bustled with people rushing, carts pulled by tired horses, donkeys or old men, bicycles, motor-cycles, and the occasional motor car. The shouts of vendors peddling their services, loud bugle horns, children's laughter and noisy motors created a chaotic tapestry of sound. Everything appeared to be another regular day of late afternoon summer in Tehran. Ali didn't see any signs of an out-of-the-ordinary event about to happen. But he had never been involved with such an affair before. Perhaps he was too early. He would wait and see. He was glad his mother had pushed him out of the house. By showing up in the *Nasserieh* location early, he could assess the situation before fully committing himself.

He found a spot on the edge of the *jube* where he could rest his back on the trunk of a maple tree and get out of the direct rays of the sun. The maple tree's leaves provided ample shade. A few spar-rows were fighting over a piece of bread near him. The gurgling water flowing through the *jube* had a peaceful effect on Ali's anxious mind. He sighed and closed his eyes. He prayed again for guidance. He didn't want to hurt people, but he understood that as a faithful subject of God, he had to obey.

The distinctive aroma of barbecued lamb liver tickled his nose and awakened his appetite, bringing him back to the moment. He looked to his left. Ten meters away stood a street vender next to his small grill, meat smoking away on top of it. The vender skillfully cut the liver into long narrow strips, slipped them onto skinny metal skewers, and placed them on the grill. Next, he sprinkled salt and fanned the charcoals. While fanning his grill, he belted out a melodious chant, calling passersby to sample his tasty barbecued liver. The smoke of barbequed lamb liver smelled heavenly to Ali. But he couldn't indulge himself to buy the tasty food. He had to save his money for his family.

He pulled some weeds from the ground and nervously ripped them to small pieces. Things could go wrong, people could get hurt. What if the police arrest him? What would happen to his family then?

Ali closed his eyes again, searching for an image in his mind that could calm his nerves. Rose's smiling face appeared. Her controlled demeanor and her kind blue eyes comforted him. To him, her face, with such an exquisite proportion of features, colors, and forms was an undeniable proof of God as a master sculptor, absolutely the best. He loved his God! A grin erupted on his face and instantly lowered his mounting stress over the protest.

When he opened his eyes, Seyyed Hussein, wearing his black clergy robe and white turban, stood in the distance, greeting and talking to people as if he owned the street. Ali adjusted his position, shrinking behind the maple tree so that Seyyed Hussein wouldn't see him. He noticed a familiar face on the other side of the street. The man crossed the road and approached Seyyed Hussein. Seconds later, the two men embraced each other and placed the customary kisses on each other's cheeks. It was Ibrahim! Ali stood up and changed his position to get a better look, using the trunk of the tree to hide his body. What was Ibrahim doing with Seyyed Hussein?

He stayed focused on them, observing every move. Ibrahim put his arm around Seyyed Hussein's shoulder and guided him into a nearby alley. A street vendor pulling the reins of his donkey carrying saddle bags full of onions blocked Ali's view. Ali moved around the trunk of the tree again to keep them in view. But they had moved too far into the alley and the light in there was dim. He waited for a small caravan of camels to pass and then he crossed the street and followed the two men, staying back to avoid being detected. When they stopped, Ali hid himself in a corner at the head of the alley and watched.

Suddenly, something struck him on his knee. Looking down, a small wood dowel lay at his feet. He picked it up and rubbed his knee to soothe the pain, glancing down the alley to see if Ibrahim and Seyyed were still there.

A young boy ran up to him. "*Agha*, that is my dowel. Give it back to me."

"Why did you hit me?"

"I didn't, my friend did." The kid pointed to a corner of the street, where about four other boys his age were gathered. "But it's not his fault. I swear, we were playing *alak-do-lak*. This dowel accidently was thrown too far, and it hit you. I'm sorry. Can I have the wood back?"

Ali flipped the wood dowel a few times, looked at Ibrahim *agha* and Seyyed Hussein huddled together at the other end of the alley, and then looked at the kid, putting on his most grown-up expression. "I'll give the wood back only if you do something for me first."

The kid shifted his weight from side to side a few times and looked back at his friends waiting on the street corner. "What do you mean?"

Ali knelt down to get close to the kid's ear, pointed at the two men in the alley, and whispered, "You see those two men? I want you to go near them, pretending you are playing, listen to what they say, and come back and tell me exactly what you heard."

"I do all that to only get my own piece of wood back? What else can you offer?"

Baffled by the clever kid's request, Ali said, "Wow, you're pretty shrewd. Okay, I will also give you this." Ali took a small wooden spool from his pocket and showed it to him. "I primed this spool myself. It's ready for games. I was going to give it to my little brother, but it will be yours if you do what I asked you."

The kid reached for the toy, but Ali put it back in his pocket. "Not till you report back to me."

"Okay, here I go," said the kid. He pulled a couple of marbles out of his pocket and rolled them toward the two men.

The marbles rolled near Seyyed Hussein and stopped about a meter away from him and Ibrahim *agha*. The kid ran toward the marbles, picked them up, and threw them against the wall in the alley, pretending to play.

It seemed to Ali that the two men were arguing about something and didn't notice the boy near them. At one point, Ibrahim *agha* turned his head around and scanned the area. He noticed the boy playing nearby, but it didn't seem to bother him. He reached into his pocket, drew out a bundle that looked like cash, and handed it to Seyyed Hussein. Immediately, Seyyed Hussein placed the bundle under his robe and looked around.

Ali yanked back his neck and pressed his back against the wall.

Why would Ibrahim *agha* give money to Seyyed Hussein in a dark alley?

Ali turned back and peeked into the alley again. Seyyed Hussein shooed the kid off. The kid picked up marbles and ran back to Ali.

"What did you hear?"

"The fat man told Mullah that today is a test and the real deal is in a few days. Mullah said that it can get dangerous and asked what to do if the mob gets out of control. Then the fat man answered that he should let it take its own course and not to interfere. He then pulled a lot of money from his pocket and gave it to

Mullah and said the next one will be even more." The kid extended his hand and asked for his payment.

Ali gave him his piece of wood and the spool as he had promised. The kid grabbed the items and ran off to show his friends.

When Ali looked back in the alley, it was empty. He turned around and walked back toward the *jube*, his maple tree, and the fragrance of grilled meat. But before he reached the spot, a hand grabbed him from behind.

"Ali! You made it! I'm so proud of you, brother. Come and join us. We are about to start." Seyyed Hussein put his arm around Ali's shoulder and guided him toward the crowd, where about a hundred people had gathered in the street.

Ali recoiled. He wondered if Sayyed saw him spying.

He slowed his steps. "Perhaps, before we start, we should have some of that tasty barbecued liver."

Seyyed Hussein turned his head to look at the vendor, looked back at Ali, paused for a second, and then after an earsplitting laugh said, "Why not, Ali, why not!" He yanked Ali's neck closer to him and with joy in his tone said, "I'll buy you all the liver you can eat tonight. You deserve it. I'm so glad you showed up!"

"Thank you, Seyyed Hussein, that's very generous of you. But can you afford it?"

"Yes, yes, my brother. Not to worry about money. God will provide. When you work for his cause, you will be showered with many returns and rewards, in this world and the world after. Let's order." Seyyed Hussein kept his arm around Ali's shoulder and they stepped up to the street vendor and ordered their liver.

The vendor arranged four cooked skewers in a large piece of Persian flat bread, *sangak*, and pulled the skewers out.

"Yes! That's exactly how I want my barbecued liver, with the juice soaked on the bread," exclaimed Seyyed Hussein and let out a loud laugh.

Ali smiled and nodded his head in agreement as he took a large bite.

The two talked and ate their dinner like old friends. Seyyed Hussein took the opportunity, with his mouth half full of food, to continue educating Ali about the virtues of fighting infidels. When they finished eating, they walked into the crowd. By then, a much greater number of men had gathered, which made Ali nervous. But Seyyed Hussein was far from nervous. He shook hands, hugged, and kissed many of them. They seemed eager to begin. Seyyed Hussein continued greeting people and moved away from Ali.

Standing alone again, Ali searched the crowd. To his surprise, Ibrahim stood just six meters away, engaged in a conversation with a man on a bicycle. When they finished, Ibrahim handed him some money and patted the bicyclist's back. The man took the money, gave a half-bow to show appreciation, got on his bicycle, and pedaled away.

Why was Ibrahim paying the man with a bicycle? First, he paid Seyyed Hussein then he paid this man. Whom else has he paid? And why?

Moments later, Seyyed Hussein stopped a vendor who was pushing his four-wheeled cart with some apples on it and climbed on top. He stood on top of the street vender's cart and began projecting with his thunderous voice, "People! Infidel Baha'is are robbing us! They are insulting our religion, belittling our beloved saints and poisoning our world!"

The crowd shouted and raised their fists.

An old man standing right next to Ali raised his fist and shouted, "Stop Baha'is!"

"Dirty foreign Baha'i must go," another man shouted, his neck veins bulging with tension.

Ali stood frozen in the midst of the shouting. He had to make his decision. This was it. Was he in or was he out?

Seyyed Hussein continued, his words rising above the shouts of the crowd. "This foreign Baha'i woman who lives across the street is the worst kind of Baha'i. She is infesting our youngsters' minds with her heresy. She's a creature of Satan!" Seyyed Hussein recited those words with a tone as if he was in the religious theater, *tazieh.*

Then the bicyclist Ali saw speaking with Ibrahim *agha* rode his bicycle into the crowd and shouted, "Kill the foreign infidel Baha'i. Kill the woman who is the enemy of Islam and our nation." He pedaled his bicycle through the crowd repeating those sentences over and over.

The crowd became more agitated. Men yelled, raised their fists, and demanded the removal of the woman. Rocks, shoes, potatoes, and eggs flew toward Dr. Moody's house.

Ali had never been in situation like this before. Goose bumps rose on his skin, in spite of the stifling heat. So much hate, so much charged emotion. He couldn't relate to this violent mentality. He didn't know the woman, Dr. Moody, personally. She had never done any nasty thing to him. Why was he there? His mother's words rang in his mind. "It is your religious duty to defend us and rid our society of infidel Baha'is."

His heart pounded in his chest like the hooves of a Cossack's war horse. He didn't want to be a part of this, but he also couldn't get away. What if this was his destiny? What if God wanted him to be there? What if he was supposed to be there, to drag the enemy out of her nest, to slit her throat and let her evil blood stain the ground. Make a clear and a strong message to the enemies of Islam? Another chill ran up his spine. No, impossible to do such a violent act. His stomach clenched and bile rose into his throat.

People joined the crowd from every direction, forming a mob. The chants become shorter and protestors become more animated. "Baha'i go" ... "Baha'i go." Men propelled their fists in the air with vigor and anger.

The man to the right of Ali jumped up with his arms thrust in the air. When he landed, his hip bumped Ali. The man to his left pushed him back and kept shouting. Ali was tossed back and forth by the crowd like swells of a sea, but he remained silent. Someone to his right screamed with such force that Ali turned his face toward him—shocked—and curious about such a vulgar person.

"Death to the infidel!" he sputtered, his spittle spraying over Ali's chin.

Disgusted, Ali wiped away the spit with the back of his hand. "Do you know this woman?" he asked the young man.

"No, I don't need to. Mullah said she is a Baha'i infidel, and that is enough for me." He continued his shouts. "Death! Death to the infidel!"

Someone grabbed Ali by the forearm. "Don't be shy, boy. Raise your fist and shout. Claim and fight for your religion, boy. Do it!" he ordered.

Ali's heartbeat raced and his throat closed in fear. He moved away from the man, pushing through the thickening mob, now totally convinced he could never join this wild menace.

Several men had crowded around Dr. Moody's door, not far from where Ali stood. They pounded on her door with their fists. "Give yourself, up!" they demanded.

They could break her house door and drag her out on the street and slit her throat like a lamb! He didn't want to witness this tragedy.

Ali scoped the best route to exit and made his move, but loud whistles stopped his retreat. He turned toward the sound and saw a column of police, batons drawn, rushing toward the crowd and him!

He tried to move away from the path of approaching police, but the press of the mob stopped him.

Wham! The blunt strike of the policeman's baton fell across his back and arms. Down he went, his face pressed into the dust of the street. People scattered in every direction, some stepping on him as they ran.

He felt a sharp, paralyzing sting in his back and legs. For a moment, an image of the angel of death swirled across his dizzied vision. But the pain of failure and disgrace was far more potent than the physical pain. His father would be appalled if he saw him on the ground, eating dirt and being trampled. He had to propel himself to get up and run.

Suddenly, rough hands lifted him. When he looked up, two policemen with raised batons were about to hit him in the face. He tried to say, *stop*, or *please forgive me*. But no sound came out. Ali covered his face with his arms and closed his eyes.

"I got him. You move on," one of the policemen ordered.

Ali lowered his arms and stared into the officer's face. He couldn't believe his good luck.

"Ali? What are you doing here? Your father did not raise you to be mixed with this kind of crowd. Get the hell out of here before you get arrested!"

He was *Sarkar* Reza, a good friend of his father. *Allah-o-akbar!*

Ali never ran so fast in his entire fourteen years of life.

***

Away from Dr. Moody's neighborhood, only the croaking of frogs and the droning of summer bugs permeated the summer night. At home, the darkened windows alerted Ali that everyone had already gone to bed. The sky was clear, and the moon was shining at its fullest. He sat on the raised edge of the utility pool in the courtyard for a little while and pondered what had just happened. He replayed what he had seen—the images of Seyyed Hussein in the alley with the man from the teahouse, Ibrahim, the money exchange, the bicyclist and Ibrahim again, the wild, angry crowd, and the police.

He praised God for his good fortune, crediting his narrow escape to a lesson his God wanted to teach him, because God is merciful and compassionate.

He turned around, knelt, and splashed the cool, cleansing water of the pool onto his dusty face. He remembered that he must proceed with his night prayers, especially after such a rescue.

He commenced with *vuzoo*, the pre-prayer ceremonial washing. He washed his hands, cupped his right hand and threw water on his face three times, then cupped his right hand again and poured water on his left elbow and washed from the elbow down. He repeated the same for his right hand and then he put three wet fingers on his head and slid them down to his forehead. Next, he put his soaked fingers on his right foot, slid them from toes up to his ankle, and repeated it for his left foot.

Yes, he was ready for prayers now. The washing had calmed his mind.

Stepping softly so as not to disturb his family, he climbed the stairs, removed his shoes, and gently opened the door. Everyone had their beds on the floor and were fast asleep.

Moonlight penetrating through the windows illuminated the room. He knew exactly where to find his prayer rug, which he had inherited from his father. He rolled it open on the floor, again in the corner of the room toward the direction of Mecca. He placed the *mohr*, a round piece of clay brought from Mecca, on the center top of his prayer rug. Using respect and care, he surrounded the *mohr* with *tasbih*, the prayer beads. He caressed the prayer rug gently and closed his eyes, remembering the numerous times he sat on that rug next to his father during prayers.

The small rug had become his island of comfort. When he unrolled it, the fragrance of rose petals secreted from a small, dry-flower sachet. The velvety texture of the prayer rug, the round *mohr*, and the wooden prayer beads evoked many pleasant memories for him. More importantly, he considered that rug his vessel to connect with God, his only true confidant.

He stood, raised his hands to his ears, and started his prayers—the uninterruptable sequences of bows, bends, and drops to the ground to feel the touch of the *mohr* on his forehead.

At the end of his prayers, he sat on his knees with his palms up, resting on his lap. He felt close to his Creator. The quiet room and the dark, serene atmosphere provided a refuge for his turbulent thoughts.

He called on his God and asked if he should join Seyyed Hussein's vigilante group. But he wasn't in favor of the hatred Seyyed Hussein promoted. He paused for a moment, feeling very close to God. He dared to ask if God had created all men equal, and if that was the case, why some hate each other so much.

His most difficult question was concerning the two conflicting views. One argued about protecting Islam by harming or killing non-believers, and the other maintained that Islam was a peaceful religion and much grander than a few feeble non-believers.

He shifted on his knees and asked why would the most loving and forgiving God sanction such violence. Perhaps his mother and Seyyed Hussein were wrong, and violence was not the answer.

At the end of his prayers, he raised his arms toward the sky and confessed to God that he was not afraid to die for Islam and begged for wisdom for making the right decision.

He dropped his arms on his knees and sat quietly for a while, his eyes closed and relaxed. After a few moments of total calmness, he rubbed his face and rolled his prayer rug back up.

Moonbeams illuminated the room just enough so he could safely avoid stepping on his siblings' sleeping bodies as he found his way to his sleeping spot in the corner. He smiled when he saw his bedding already spread for him. In appreciation of his mother's care, he prayed for her.

He lifted the blanket and crashed onto his bed. Soft rays of moonlight traveled through the window over his bedding. When his head rested on the pillow, a small, pure white feather escaped its casing and lightly danced its way onto his face, gently landing on his right cheek. The touch felt like a tender kiss.

He let the feather rest on his cheek for a moment. The sweet fragrance of jasmine flowers from a bush climbing the wall near his window reminded him of the perfume Rose preferred to wear.

He took the feather from his cheek and examined it. The

moonlight accentuated its purity. *Pure white.* He held the quill and gently caressed the feather. It felt so soft. Just like Rose's skin—at least, that's how he imagined it would feel.

He lifted the feather as high as his arm could stretch. Then, he released the feather and watched it gracefully dance down onto his cheek again. He repeated the action several times.

Finally, he kissed the feather ever so softly and placed it on his pillow next to his cheek. He pulled up the blanket and closed his eyes.

The image of Rose appeared, smiling.

All was well. At least for now.

1 0

IN THE GARDEN

Tuesday, July 15, 1924

BEHIND THE TALL walls and iron gates of the British embassy's compound, large sycamore and walnut trees provided much needed shade in the hot afternoons of July. Ali searched for Rose every chance he had while tending the grounds. He searched every outside patio and in every quaint corner of the multiple gardens in the compound. No sign of her anywhere.

He went over his talk with Rose during the banquet to see if he had done anything wrong or had said something to offend her. There were no incidents that he could recollect that would have upset her and caused her to avoid him.

Perhaps she was in trouble because of his talk about Major Imbrie. Or maybe she wasn't used to rich Persian food and became sick. His mind raced through several possible scenarios on why she had abandoned him these past two days. Some of them were pretty awful; he didn't care for those. He couldn't bear the thought of losing Rose.

Images of their first encounter rushed through his mind. It was last fall. He had just started the gardening job at the embassy. His boss asked him to clean the pond in the east garden. The edge of the pond was slippery, and he fell into its chilly water. The water in the pond was not even waist deep, but not knowing how to swim, he got scared and yelled for help.

Rose had been in the east garden on her break when she heard Ali's cry for help. She had rushed to the pond, taken off her shoes and waded across to where Ali lay splashing. First, she helped him to sit up, then assisted him to stand on the slick pond bottom. They both slipped and fell back into the water.

Finally recognizing that the water was shallow, Ali got up by himself and laughed along with Rose.

They sloshed through the water and climbed out of the pond, their clothes soaked through. The chilly autumn breeze had them shivering in seconds.

Ali was only out of the pond for a moment when he felt his boss's thick, earth-stained, hand's slap on his face. He scolded him for his clumsiness. An embassy staffer ran to assist Rose by taking off his jacket and wrapping it around her. Someone else rushed out of the building with a blanket for her.

Ali shivered as he recalled the bitter chill of the air, the sting of his boss's slap, and the embarrassment of working in drenching wet clothes. But more importantly, how it all went away when, for a split second, he dared to look back at Rose and his eyes entangled with hers ...

TOWARD THE END of his shift, Ali was busy cleaning the bed of a rose garden in the east side of the compound, when he came upon a white rose bush. The purity of the white rose had always attracted him. Gently, he touched a petal, so soft and velvety. He was disappointed that his fingertips had become calloused by his hard work, and he could no longer feel the delicate surface as he could just a year ago. But he could remember the sensation. The consistency and purity of the white color amazed him. The cup-like sepal of the flower, supporting all the petals, seemed to him as a receiver of pouring divine influences, and in return, emitting a heavenly sweet fragrance for admirers to enjoy. The white rose, to him, was an example of God's masterwork. He put his nose in the flower and inhaled the spicy-sweet scent. He held his breath as long as he could to take in the heavenly aroma. He slowly exhaled and brought his head back, when he smelled cigarette smoke.

Disappointed with the intrusion, he looked up. Rose stood over him smoking her cigarette.

"You looked very handsome at the banquet!" Rose said with a smile.

"Oh, hello, Rose. You okay?" He answered with a concerned look on his face.

"Yes, of course, why shouldn't I be?"

Ali stood up, scanned the area, and looked busy with his broom. "*Alham-dolelah*, thank God, you are happy!"

"I'm curious, however, as to what urged you to leave the banquet with such an urgency?"

"I not understand," Ali replied.

"Why did you leave in such a rush?" Rose asked again.

"I am sorry, Rose. But I had to run."

"What was the rush?"

"He came after me!"

"Who? Who was after you?"

Ali looked around, moved his face closer to Rose and whispered, "He followed me in the kitchen!"

"Who?" Rose asked in a higher pitch than her usual voice.

Ali put his index finger on his nose, signaling hush, and said, "Ssss!" He scanned the area again and continued, "*Engilisi* man … English man." He noticed Rose's puzzled look. "He saw I speak English, then I run!" He used his right-hand fingers to gesture running.

Ali, you're not making any sense. Why did you run? Who cares if you understand or speak English? Not all English men are evil. Look at it from a positive point of view. You may get better jobs!"

"No, no, my dear. He see me in *ghahve-khaneh*. He talk to another *Engilisi* man and Irani man, Ibrahim *agha*."

"And this is important because?"

Ali's explanation became animated. "I told you! They talk about Major Imbrie, they talk about *sagha-khaneh*. They talk about Major Imbrie take photos of people. Bad; very, very bad. Hmm ... dange-rous!"

"So far, I haven't heard anything very very bad or dangerous," Rose quipped, exhaling her smoke.

"No, no; it very, very bad!" Ali opened his eyes as wide as he could and raised his eyebrows to emphasize his words. "In *sagha-khaneh*, village people come for miracles. No man like. Hmm, don't like, photo their women. They get very very mad."

"Ali. Calm yourself. Maybe the two British gentlemen and the Persian man were planning to help Major Imbrie *not* to get in trouble. Have you thought about that? Not everything has to be dramatic or bad."

Ali paused a bit and pondered what Rose said. Something didn't fit. Particularly after what he saw Ibrahim *agha* do on the day of the riot outside Dr. Moody's house. He had paid the two mob agitators. They caused trouble. Why would anyone want to agitate a mob, especially after the writer Eshghi's massive funeral? They must be after something bigger. Ali shook his head. "They say Baha'i man cursed or poisoned water of *sagha-khaneh* and God blinded him to punish. And, and, mob was going to kill the foreigner Baha'is, Doctor Moody. Is she Engilisi?"

"No, she's American."

Ali dropped his head down and said, "Oh, yes, Seyyed said so." After a moment of pause, Ali shook his head and hit his forehead with his right hand, "Oh American? No, no, not good! This is very, very bad! They will think Major Imbrie is Baha'i. That is very bad, Rose. We need to help him. They will hurt him!"

"I don't get it, Ali! What is the connection between Dr. Moody and Major Imbrie?" Rose raised her voice as she put out her cigarette.

"They two American." Ali's hands were energetically moving around as he tried to explain. "Dr. Moody is Bahi'a and ... and mob want to kill her. So, if people see Major Imbrie insulting Muslims in same *sagha-khaneh*, they see as Bahi'a war. If people become very mad, they will hurt him!"

Rose put her hands on her hips. "Ali, who wants to hurt a nice man like Major Imbrie?"

Right at that moment, forty meters behind Rose, Malcolm strolled toward a building in the embassy. Ali's first reaction was to use Rose's body to block himself from Malcolm's view.

"What's the matter?" Rose exclaimed.

"Ssss, there he is, right there. He walking, that way, there." He bent over forward, half way hiding, and pointed his finger toward Malcolm.

Rose turned around, following Ali's cue, bent over half way and looked toward the direction of Ali's finger.

"What are we looking at?" Rose asked.

"The *Engilisi* man. Right there, walking. He is one who followed me in kitchen. He talk with Ibrahim *agha* in *ghahve-khaneh*. Very bad man. You see? You see him?" Ali inched away to hide himself under the nearby branches of a small fruit tree.

"Well, I see a man, but I can't see him well enough to tell if I know him. And now he's disappeared. I think he went into the building. Shall I go into the building to see who he is?"

Ali stood a few feet from Rose facing the opposite direction, his attention distracted and his thoughts troubled. He vaguely heard Rose's voice, but did not grasp her words. What was Ibrahim *agha*'s business with Seyyed Hussein and the man on the bicycle before the mob attack? Does the English man know?

Ali turned and grabbed Rose's arms and shook her. "Rose, listen! We need to save Major Imbrie. Rose, find him and tell not go to *sagha-khaneh*. Now I must run before the Engilisi man see me, good-bye."

Rose squeezed Ali's muscular arms. "Find who?"

"Major Imbrie," Ali answered and freed himself from Rose's grip.

"But, Ali—I don't know him!"

He ran out of the grounds as fast as he could.

11

THE NIGHTMARE

Thursday, July 17, 1924

MALCOLM SPRANG UP IN BED, drenched in sweat and panting heavily. The same nightmare about his childhood friend, Bobbie, had visited him again. In a foggy, cold dusk in some desolated landscape, Bobbie was pointing at Malcolm with his right hand, but half his left arm was cut, blood was gushing out of it, and his face was torn and bloody from multiple shrapnel wounds. Images of the half-decomposed bodies of his comrades mixed with relentless shelling from enemy artillery.

The worst part was when Bobbie raised himself up from the ground, grabbed Malcolm's leg, and pulled it toward him. It was as if Bobbie was trying to pull him underground.

"James, James, help me! James, what's happening to me? Don't let me die here!"

Bobbie's voice was still echoing in his mind.

Malcolm sat up in bed, inhaled deeply, and swung his legs

toward the floor. He slid out from under the sheet in a single movement. His head hurt.

"The same nightmare?" The groggy voice of the woman next to him asked.

Who is she? It was too dark to see her face clearly. Malcolm couldn't remember her name—only that a warm body seemed inviting at the time. It didn't matter to him. He never loved any woman. Well, except Abigale. But that didn't count. He was only sixteen when he met her. And it didn't go anywhere, regardless. Loving someone made him vulnerable, and he couldn't allow it. He had buried that feeling long ago.

"Yes, go back to sleep," he mumbled. Grabbing his cigarettes and a lighter, he walked toward his balcony. The stench of gun powder and human carnage mixed with heavy smoke and dust from his nightmare was still fresh in his senses.

He opened the French doors and stepped onto the third-floor balcony. The image of his German interrogator's twisted face appeared, so close that he could smell his foul breath. The man let out a hideous laugh and burned Malcolm's bare nipple with his smoldering cigarette. He'd felt an excruciating pain and screamed.

The cool night air hit his face. It felt good. He lit a cigarette and gazed down at the dark silhouette of Tehran.

***

The same day in the late afternoon, Malcolm put on white pants, a white shirt, white shoes and a white cap. He looked forward to some healthy exercise at the British embassy's tennis courts where Imbrie and his wife, at his invitation, were waiting for him.

Large sycamore and acacia trees and lush gardens provided canopies of shade and cool surroundings for the club and the courts. The fragrance of roses and jasmine along with the soothing sound of several water fountains helped visitors there remember a pleasant experience, and a welcome respite to the heat and noise of the Tehran city streets.

The club's staff, decked in head-to-toe white uniforms, were on hand for any needs of the embassy's guests--from preparing and delivering exotic drinks to catching stray tennis balls.

"Here he is. We thought perhaps you forgot our match!" exclaimed Imbrie. They also wore white outfits. Mrs. Imbrie was in a long, pleated skirt and blouse and a soft-brimmed white hat to shield her face from the sun.

"James, do you remember my wife, Katherine?"

"Yes, of course. We met at the banquet." Malcolm bowed and kissed her hand, "Lovely to see you again, Mrs. Imbrie"

"Mr. Malcolm!" she exclaimed with a smile. "What a gentleman! And please, do call me Katherine."

Imbrie scowled and bounced a tennis ball on the ground. "Okay, let's get it going. Where is your partner, James?"

"Partner?"

"Yes, we agreed on a double's match. Did you forget?"

"Oh, I'm sorry," Malcolm said, looking around to see if he could find someone willing to play. A woman sitting in a chair on the adjacent court attracted his attention. He gestured *one moment* with his index finger to Imbrie and ran toward the woman. Once near her, he asked, "Pardon me, madam." The woman turned around. Malcolm continued, "May I ask if you would like to join me in a match against my friends there?" he pointed to Imbrie and his wife.

The woman smiled. "Are you in need of a partner?" She spoke with a British accent and looked in her late thirties.

Malcolm returned her smile. "Yes, indeed. I can always use a partner. James Malcolm, at your service."

The woman extended her right hand to Malcolm. "Jane. Mrs. Jane Berkley." She wore a white headband around her auburn curls, Malcolm noticed her skirt was shorter than Mrs. Imbrie's. He could almost see her knees.

He took her hand and slowly planted a kiss. "Enchanted."

"Great! Game on," Imbrie announced.

"Oh, and the opposing team members are Major Imbrie and his wife, Katherine." Malcolm extended his arm, making the introductions more like an afterthought. He enjoyed the mental aspect of tennis even more than the physical.

"Good afternoon. Americans, I presume?" Mrs. Berkley waved.

Major Imbrie lifted his racket. "Yes, ma'am, full-blooded Yankees."

Mrs. Berkley nodded to Mrs. Imbrie and moved into the tennis court next to Malcolm.

Imbrie served. The two couples played a few sets, the Brits taking the advantage. As the sun beat down on the court, someone suggested a break. The foursome scurried to the benches in the shade of some acacia trees. The wait staff appeared almost immediately with cold drinks.

"Katherine, let me introduce you to the women on the next court," Mrs. Berkley suggested, "that is, if you fellows don't mind." She smiled sweetly at Malcolm.

"By all means, you ladies enjoy yourselves," he replied.

As Mrs. Imbrie and Mrs. Berkley took theirs drinks and joined the women who were gathered a few yards away, Imbrie leaned in toward Malcolm. "I appreciate your help on Dr. Moody's case. Without the timely police intervention, she wouldn't have survived the mob attack. Thank you for your good advice."

"Oh, don't mention it. I'm glad I could help."

"Well, you did. Say, what is with this Bahi'a fixation these people have? Aren't they both Shiite Muslims?"

"Yes. Perhaps it is similar to the sixteenth century situation between Protestants and Catholics. As you know, Catholics didn't take it lightly."

"Well, I think maybe it's more like the Church of England and Catholics."

"Yes, but we don't kill Catholics."

"But you did during Henry the Eighth's era." Imbrie replied, then laughed, a bit too loudly.

Mrs. Berkley, probably noticing Imbrie's loud laugh, turned to look at Malcolm. He raised his glass and smiled at her. She smiled back and returned her attention to the ladies.

"Leave her alone. She's married, you know," Imbrie advised.

"She seems a good player," Malcolm answered, ignoring Imbrie's warning and wondering why he hadn't seen or heard of her before. Quite a looker. It was his nature to pay attention to details and question everything. He contributed his very survival to his skepticism.

Mrs. Imbrie strolled back to join the men, her glass clinking with ice cubes. Without so much as an "excuse me," she inserted herself into their conversation. "Mr. Malcolm—"

Malcolm interrupted her. "James. Please do call me James."

She smiled and continued, "James, someone planted a ludicrous idea of taking photos of some sort of religious site in Robert's head. Would you please explain to my stubborn husband how dangerous it is for him to take photos of that silly religious site? Especially now, after the Dr. Moody incident."

Imbrie roared with laughter. "Honey, it was James himself who suggested it first." He continued his laughing. "But, really, you don't need to worry about me. I've been among much more primitive people than these folks, and I've survived. Honey, I'm like a cat, always landing on my feet."

Malcolm turned to Imbrie. "Actually, Katherine is right. The situation is a bit flammable now. I would take extra precautions."

She turned to her husband and said, "Bob, listen to him. Cancel it for now."

"Nonsense. We'll soon relocate to Tabriz, and I won't have this chance again." Imbrie turned to Malcolm. "Why don't you come with me? I know I've asked this before. But frankly, I don't' remember your answer."

"When are you going?" Malcolm asked.

"Tomorrow morning, when the light is at its best."

"Yes, James," Katherina pleaded. "Please go with him."

"Unfortunately, early tomorrow morning I am bound for Mashhad. I have urgent business there."

Mrs. Imbrie laid a hand on her husband's forearm. "Then, honey, please take someone else with you. Don't go there alone."

"Okay, dear. I'll take someone with me. Don't worry." He kissed his wife and filled his glass from the pitcher left on the wooden table near the benches. His wife smiled triumphantly and left to rejoin the other women.

Imbrie rested his back on the table. "Mashhad, huh?"

Malcolm looked toward the horizon. "Yes."

"Look, you don't have to make up stories if you don't want to go with me tomorrow. I totally understand."

Malcolm was taken off guard by that awkward, yet accurate surmise. "No, no, truly. I'm required to travel there early morning tomorrow. But I'll be looking forward to seeing your photos when I return."

Imbrie turned his head toward Malcolm and looked at him in the eyes. "I know why you are going to Mashhad, James. I got the report, too."

"What report is that?"

"About the Soviets. How they've ramped up their communist insurgency in Mashhad, and that's not sitting well with you Brits. I don't blame you. I hate those bastards, too. They are so eager to spread their diseased communism across the world. The last thing we want is a bunch of no-good Bolsheviks gobbling up Persia and getting access to the Persian Gulf. But your government formally recognized those loonies a few months ago. That makes it much harder for you folks." He patted Malcolm's back. "Hang in there, brother, things will change. We won't let them get to the Persian Gulf."

"Any word on when the U.S. is going to recognize them?" Malcolm asked.

"I hope not for a long time. It's complicated." Imbrie took a sip of his drink. "Did you fight in the Great War?"

"Yes, at Mons."

"Mons in Belgium?"

"Yes."

"That was the first British deployment! Oh boy, that must have been hard to lose your first battle."

"Quite the contrary," retorted Malcolm, "we consider the battle of Mons a victory. We held the German First Army for forty-eight hours. Our first objective was to prevent the French Fifth Army from being outflanked. We accomplished that and killed five thousand Germans within forty-eight hours. We, the BEF, that is, were the most effective force at that time. Our average soldier was able to hit a man-sized target fifteen times a minute at a range of three-hundred yards." Malcolm knew he was bragging, but it always annoyed him when people discounted the BEF's heroic battle of Mons. He'd lost Bobbie there, his best friend. And not just Bobbie. Many other friends and fellow soldiers perished in that battle.

"Yes, but the British Expeditionary Force lost over sixteen hundred men in those forty-eight hours," observed Imbrie. "It must have been hard to see your friend's head blown away. One moment he is talking to you and then, in an instant, he loses half his body. I was there too. I saw all that. As a matter of fact, I was not too far from where you were. I drove ambulances for the French army at the time. I saw it all, brother. I also fought at Verdun and on the Salonika fronts."

Malcolm didn't respond. Instead, he finished his drink. Imbrie's comment evoked his repeated nightmares.

Imbrie put his arm around Malcolm's shoulder. "Did you make it back?"

Malcolm moved away from Imbrie, irritated by the intimate gesture, and put his glass back on the table. "No, the Germans took me."

Heavy silence settled on the pair. Malcolm lit a cigarette and took a deep draw.

"It never quits haunting your soul, you know?" Imbrie said, shaking his head.

Malcolm finished his cigarette in silence, dropped his cigarette butt on the ground and stepped on it. He looked into Imbrie's eyes. "That's only if you have a soul."

Imbrie reacted as Malcolm expected—shocked into a wary silence, searching Malcolm's steely eyes. Perusing for his soul, perhaps. For a moment, he let his inner demons stare Imbrie down. The two men stood face to face. Then both burst into laughter.

The two women returned to where the men stood, Mrs. Berkley wielding her tennis racket. She strutted toward Imbrie and announced, "Well, well. Mr. Malcolm, do you think the American team has given up to British supremacy, or are they willing to give it another go?"

Imbrie jumped in. "Heck yeah. We're beating you in the Olympics this year and we'll beat you here today as well, my dear. We demand a rematch!" He then swatted his wife's behind with the racket. "Honey, let's show these proud Brits some American might."

Mrs. Imbrie startled at the spanking but said nothing and ambled toward the court.

"Just for your information, Major, the British Empire currently rules over a quarter of the earth's population. So, your American might doesn't concern us at all," Mrs. Berkley quipped.

"James, your partner is quite a corker!" Imbrie exclaimed.

Malcolm smiled at Mrs. Berkley and followed it with a wink. Bouncing the tennis ball on the ground a couple of times, he declared, "We start the serve."

Everyone bent their knees slightly in the sport-ready position. Malcolm faced the break point. He toed the line, bounced the ball, and right before he hit it, Imbrie shouted, "Honey, let's show these Brits how their luck just ran out."

Malcolm could not suppress his smile.

12

THE MANIPULATOR

Friday morning, July 18, 1924

MALCOLM DONNED his old man disguise after a quick breakfast of tea and porridge. The baggy black pants, knee-length white shirt, white wig and long gray beard had transformed him into a cranky old Persian peasant. He put a well-used black felt hat on his head, slipped his bare feet into a pair of *givehes*, the traditional Persian shoes made from strong, coarse cotton cloth on top and rubber on the bottom, grabbed a cane, and left his apartment.

As a self-imposed discipline, he slipped into his new character from the moment his disguise was completed. He talked like a peasant, walked like one, and even forced himself to think like they did. It was one of the necessary tools of the trade required to avert any suspicions when under disguise on the streets.

Before he opened his door, he put his ear against the wood and listened for any sound in the hallway or nearby stairwell. Hearing nothing, he cautiously stepped out of his apartment door and went downstairs.

Using his cane, he stepped out on the street and walked with a hunched back for a few minutes to distance himself from his flat. A precautionary measure, in case his flat was under surveillance. It was Friday, the sabbath for Muslims, the day of rest and prayers. Streets were quiet as most businesses and schools were closed. Once he felt assured that he wasn't being followed, he hired a coach to take him to Sheikh Hadi street.

The sky was clear and the sun's rays were heating up the streets of Tehran—just a typical July day in that part of the world. Once he arrived at Sheikh Hadi street, Malcolm found a shady spot under a sycamore tree by the *jube,* across from the miraculous *sagha-khaneh.* He took off his shoes and soaked his feet in the cold, running water of the *jube* as any old Persian peasant man on a hot summer's day would do. He sat there patiently waiting for Major Imbrie to show up. It was important to Malcolm, to physically be there and witness his operation. He wanted to make sure everything went according to his liking and his plan.

From his position, he could see the holy *sagha-khaneh* clearly. Visitors were crowding the site, offering prayers and burning candles. Street vendors were selling summer delights with their melodious calls. The sour, green plums, Persian ice cream with rosewater and pistachios, and *faloodeh,* which was chilled vermicelli and rosewater, were among the most popular summer treats. Young kids were running and playing around the vendors. All the women were covered with *chadors.* However, due to the heat of summer, the solid black *chadors* were outnumbered by lighter ones in various shades of gray as well as white with darker imprinted designs.

People were arriving at an increasing tempo on foot, in horse carriages, bicycles, and some were even riding donkeys. Malcolm noticed the number of men arriving on the scene was increasing in proportion to women. He observed a gathering of a group of rough-looking young adults and teenagers. He knew they were not at the shrine for religious purposes.

Around mid-morning, two men began to unload some equipment from a carriage. They were quite a distance off—perhaps fifty meters or so. Malcolm squinted his eyes to see them better. It was Imbrie. The show had begun. He didn't recognize the other tall blond man. It didn't matter. The two men moved toward *sagha-khaneh* with their equipment.

Malcolm searched for Ibrahim, who was supposed to be in place. He turned his head slowly and looked at each person in the square, one by one. After a few minutes, his sharp eyes spotted Ibrahim talking to a man on a bicycle, next to a butcher shop across the street.

Imbrie and the other man set up the equipment near *sagha-khaneh*. At first, a few curious kids gathered around them, then others began to notice the two foreigners and their equipment and gathered around Imbrie.

Imbrie appeared to ignore the crowd, but the sound of their voices grew loud and rather disquieting. It was apparent to Malcolm that the people were angry. The man on the bicycle, once he had finished talking to Ibrahim, steered near the crowd and screamed, "Don't let the Baha'i men get close to the *sagha-khaneh*. They will poison the water, kill us and our children."

Malcolm smiled. So far, the plan was working perfectly. He knew very well that, especially in his trade, there were always unknown factors that could pop-out and change the course of even the most well-constructed operation. Since this particular one was extremely delicate, he was prepared for contingencies.

He pulled an old Persian pipe out of his pocket and lit it. For now, he intended to smoke his pipe and enjoy the show.

13

THE MOB

Friday morning, July 18, 1924

FOR THREE DAYS, every morning, right after his breakfast shift at the teahouse, Ali went to Sheikh Hadi street and sat near the miraculous *sagha-khaneh*, hoping to find Major Imbrie there and to warn him of the danger. He didn't know when Imbrie would show up, and he had made up his mind to do this for several more days. Imbrie had not shown up yet. Was it possible that he had forgotten about it?

Along his route, he often saw a crippled old beggar man who sat on the street corner and recited prayers nonstop as people passed him. Today, the man was there. Ali stopped in front of the old beggar and searched his pocket. He only had a few coins left, but he decided to give it all to the beggar. "Here you go old man, please pray for me." He put the coins into the waiting hand of the beggar.

With a surprisingly swift action, the beggar grabbed Ali's wrist as he bent to put the coins in the hat on the ground. "Today is a different day, boy! Turn around and save yourself! It's a sabbath in the month of *Muharram*."

Ali's eyes locked with the old man's eyes for a split second. One of them was white and Ali understood it was blind. The beggar's face was filthy, and coarse black hairs covered his chin. Three dark teeth hung loosely in his mouth. Ali shivered in spite of the warm sun. "I know. Today is Friday and it's *Muharram*. I'll be fine old man. But pray for me!" He yanked his hand free of the old man's grip.

"Go back! Go home!" the old man yelled as Ali walked away from him, shaking off the impression of danger and disgust.

Ali found a shady spot in a corner near the *sagha-khaneh*, squatted down and waited for Major Imbrie. As usual, kids were every where, playing and running around. Mothers with one hand gripping their *chadors*, preventing them from falling or opening, and with the other, holding on to their unruly children, had gathered near the *sagha-khaneh*.

A street vendor selling watermelons stopped his dirty white donkey in front of Ali, blocking his view of the area. Ali repositioned himself and noticed a much larger crowd than usual was visiting the *sagha-khaneh* that day. The growing throng brought to mind the horrible images of the mob that had gathered outside Dr. Moody's house. These images haunted him, often in his dreams, and sometimes during the day as well. The clamor, the vigor of the shouting, the pungent odor of sweat mixed with fear, the pushing and tugging. The reason for the mob, bothered him even more. He never imagined demanding the death of a person, especially a woman. Ali couldn't understand why the mob did it. He considered Islam peaceful and compassionate, a religion that is good for everyone—a religion that helps people to get closer to God by being kind, truthful, and loving. Wasn't violence the way of the infidels such as Yazid, who killed Imam Hussein, the grandson of the Prophet Mohammed in a brutal battle some thirteen hundred years ago?

He remembered that in the month of *Muharram*, Yazid martyred Imam Hussein. This can't be good for Major Imbrie.

In the past, he considered the month of *Muharram* as an exciting month, albeit in a strange way. He knew Muslims mourn in the holy month of *Muharram*. Grief, and an atmosphere of melancholy, were predominant everywhere for adults. But for kids, it was a month of unique adventures. He vividly remembered that during the nights of *Muharram*, he and his father spent hours at the local mosques and gorged on the free and delicious food people brought for prayer warriors. He recalled his favorite rice dish given in mosques was *gheymehpolo,* a mix of rice, diced stew lamb, split peas, turmeric, and saffron. And when *Muharram* fell in winter months, his favorite dish was the hot *ashe-reshteh*, a thick noodle soup filled with lots of greens and beans. The camaraderie and solidarity he felt with people during *Muharram* seeped exuberance.

He took a mental note to take his brothers to the mosque. His preoccupation with Major Imbrie's problem and his many jobs had taken him away from his family. He asked God for forgiveness in neglecting his brothers.

Since his father's passing, Ali had been more than just the breadwinner for his family. His younger siblings looked up to him as their protector. For his brothers, he was a compass guiding them through the complex realm of a man's world and behavior. He wasn't ready for all these premature and imposed duties. But, he thought, God had plans for him, and as long as he stayed true to his faith and performed all the proper deeds, God would put forward the right path for him. He often asked his father's spirit to give him strength and guidance.

He closed his eyes to bring back his memories of his father. He remembered clerics reciting Quran and other chants with beautiful voices in religious gatherings. Most of all, he loved it when his father took him to teahouses that sponsored *taziehs,* the theatrical reenactments of the historical events in the month of *Muharram.*

Tazieh shows were extremely entertaining with props, actors in colorful costumes, and sometimes even live animals.

The most intense days of *Muharram*, the tenth and eleventh, carried climatically the sum of all actions. He loved it. He would go to the streets with his brothers and friends to join the parade of his local mosque. During the parade, he and his friends would chant at the top of their lungs and beat their chests in unison to the rhythm of the chant. He felt the most joy when his hands hit his chest in the exact synchronized manner with the rest of the men. *Boom, boom*, the sound of many hands hitting chests all at the same time was incredibly eerie. On the other hand, he had never joined the chain group in any of the parades. He never liked the idea of tearing his skin with a chain, or any other device for that matter. However, the unison sound of *swish*, when the chains hit the bare back of over forty men, created euphoria. The entertainment factor of the whole experience excited him when he was younger.

The colorful flags, banners, the rose water sprays, the free drinks and food provided by families, the kindness, and the complete feeling of camaraderie uniquely separated the holy month of *Muharram* from other months. He smiled as he remembered all that. He sensed the smells, the tastes, and the excitement.

But now, the reality of the moment settled in. He realized that the real reason adults paraded, chanted, beat their chests, hit their backs with chains, and cut themselves was to demonstrate their willingness to sacrifice their lives to preserve, protect, and guard Islam.

His smile dropped to a frown. *Muharram* was not a good month for nonbelievers! It was dangerous for them. People were charged with emotions of retribution and revenge. Non-Muslims were perceived as threats.

A chill ran through his body. He had to warn Imbrie, as he was probably not aware of the holy month of *Muharram*, and how he could easily aggravate people to violence.

Looking toward the *sagha-khaneh*, he noticed more people had gathered than the other days. And more men than usual.

A group of teenage boys gambled with a coin-toss game near him. They were loud and vulgar. Ali frowned. Muslims were forbidden to gamble in Islam. Why were they gambling near a holy site? They must be thugs. What were they doing there? Clearly, they were not there for religious reasons. Otherwise, they would not be gambling. But there were many of them and they were older than him, so he didn't say anything.

He mustered some courage, stopped a man nearby and asked, "Excuse me sir, what's the story here? Is there a miracle with this *sagha-khaneh?*"

The man looked surprised that Ali asked the question. "Well, yes. Sometime ago, a Baha'i man drank the water and walked away making no contribution to the saint's bucket. And as a bigger insult, he prayed to a Baha'i holy man. The miracle enacted and turned him blind. He received his sight back only after he repented, converted to Jafari Shiite, and paid a handsome contribution to the saint's bucket."

"Did you see that yourself?"

"No, but everyone knows about the miracle of this *sagha-khaneh* and the curse of Baha'is!" the man exclaimed.

Ali finally understood the extent of the danger. Given the back story, he realized how explosive the situation was. The last thing anyone needed was to insert a foreigner there with a camera. The locals would not tolerate it. He prayed Major Imbrie had forgotten all about the photo shoot.

Just then a Cossack soldier walked by where Ali was standing. "*Salahm sarkar*. Hello, officer!" Ali waved his hand and greeted the soldier. He felt his heart flutter at the sight of the elite Cossack.

The soldier nodded, acknowledging Ali's greeting, and continued his stroll as he shooed off some kids running around.

"Is there a military base nearby?" Ali asked the same man who had told him about the miracle.

"Yes, it's a Cossack brigade, our beloved Reza Khan's favorite."

Ali was filled with pride. "Oh, yes, my father was one. They are tough and extremely loyal to Reza Khan."

"This base is the home to the same unit where Reza Khan served his military life before he became a politician," the man answered and walked away.

The presence of a capable and strong military base nearby gave Ali a renewed sense of comfort and relief. If a disturbance began here, the Cossacks would intervene. He found another shady place and sat down.

On the corner opposite Ali, two men, one taller than the other, unloaded some equipment from a carriage that must have arrived when he was distracted by the conversation with the man about the miracle. The two men moved toward the *sagha-khaneh*. They didn't look like local people. In fact, they looked very much like foreigners, taller than most Iranians. One of them had blond hair. Heads turned toward the strangers, scanning them, and especially their odd equipment, with keen curiosity.

Ali heard a few locals on the street grumbling to each other. "What are these strangers doing here? What is that contraption?" A man in the crowd yelled, "Is that apparatus a photo camera? They are to take pictures! People, people, shoo them away. There are women present, for God's sake!"

Hearing that, Ali stood and searched for the two men, who were surely the source of complaints. He saw them moving their equipment near the *sagha-khaneh*.

Was that Major Imbrie? Who was the other man?

Ali hustled toward them and slowed when he got close enough to hear their conversation.

The tall man with brown hair spoke in English, "This is fantastic! *National Geographic* would love it. My new equipment is going to catch all that color. Handle it with care, Seymour! It'll be dandy if I can capture the faces of these people, especially during their prayers."

Allah-o-akbar, that was him. It's Major Imbrie himself! Ali debated what to do. He considered the pros and cons of warning the two men at that point. He was there to help them and to prevent any potential problems. In addition, the equipment looked very impressive to him. Perhaps Major Imbrie would show him the equipment. But what if he made fun of Ali and shooed him off? Major Imbrie's persona emitted such a confidence that Ali was intimidated. He decided to wait a bit longer. Perhaps Imbrie could manage it without incident.

He followed them for a few minutes.

"But boss, isn't it risky?" asked the blond man whom Imbrie had called Seymour. He stood a few centimeters taller than Imbrie, was heavier, and seemed rougher, not as sophisticated as the American major.

"Seymour, that's why you're here, man! Why else do you think I would slog along an oil field worker and a jailbird? You're my protection, man! It's a pretty day, have some fun. We're doing some decent work here. No guts, no glory, my boy."

"I'm not after glory, boss. I didn't ask for this. These folks look hostile," Seymour argued, his voice a bit shaky.

"Nah, just keep your head down and do as I say. I've been around situations like this many times before. These are simple folks and are just curious. You'll be all right. Would you rather stay in a brig?"

People began to gather around Major Imbrie and Seymour. Imbrie ignored the crowd's uneasiness and set up his equipment near the shrine. The crowd's grumble grew louder. A man on a bicycle approached the two men and their carriage and began to circle around them.

Ali was surprised. It was the same biker from Dr. Moody's mob incident.

The man steered his bicycle near the crowd, said something to the teenage thugs, and then screamed in Farsi, "Don't let the Baha'i men get close to the *sagha-khaneh.* They will poison the water, kill us and our children." The thugs yelled in support of the bicyclist.

Imbrie ignored them, obviously not understanding his Farsi screaming. The crowd's curious gaze turned to agitated stares. Another man shouted a few words of protest. Soon after came a second shout. Thick Persian eyebrows tightened, and the disturbed stares turned into angry shouts. Mothers called their kids away from Imbrie and Seymour, grabbed hold of the hands of the younger ones, and put a safe distance between themselves and the now-gathered angry men crowding around the two foreigners.

The man on the bicycle stopped. Ali rushed over to him and asked, "What's going on? These two men are not Baha'is."

The bicyclist stared at him. His eyes were dilated, as if he was amped up on some kind of drug. It seemed as if he hadn't heard Ali's question, nor his declaration that Imbrie and Seymour were not Baha'is. The bicyclist sucked in a big gulp of air and turned to face the crowd.

"Kill the infidel Baha'is before they kill us!" he screamed. Then he turned to Ali, "Go brother, run and help us to catch those bastards."

Ali was frustrated by the man's behavior. Why was he so determined to agitate the people? Why didn't he believe him that the two men were not Baha'is? He opened his mouth to try again to reason with the crazed man, but the biker peddled away. Ali decided the best thing for him to do was to warn Imbrie and Seymour. Putting his fears aside, he ran toward the two unsuspecting foreigners.

Seymour's large body became even more intimidating when Ali stood near him. His pink face was wet with sweat. His mouth was open and stretched sideways and his eyes were darting back and forth. "Major, what are they saying?" he said to Imbrie, who was busy with his camera, still ignoring the crowd.

Imbrie pulled his head out from under the black cloth that covered his equipment. He looked up and started to notice the people around them. "I don't know! Just ignore them." He stuck his head under the cloth once again.

Seymour checked the perimeter. "You know, I don't like the way they're looking at us, boss. Their tone sure doesn't sound friendly to me. Let's get out of here."

Ali finally mustered courage to speak, praying his English would be sufficient. "Hello, sirs. You not safe here. People angry. No like photo. You must go!"

Imbrie took his head out of the black cloth again and looked at Ali. With a cocky smirk on his face, he asked, "And who are you?"

"I am Ali. You must go now!"

Imbrie looked around and observed the crowd again. He shook his head. "Darn it all. Sure doesn't seem like a welcoming committee. What a damn shame. All right, Seymour. Let's pick up the gear and get outta here."

Seymour didn't need a second invitation. He grabbed the biggest pieces and practically ran toward the carriage. Imbrie followed close behind, but at a more dignified pace. Ali walked with them, hoping to somehow ensure their safety.

"Major, are they following us?" Seymour called out over his shoulder.

"I don't know, and I'm not going to look back to find out. We don't want to aggravate them. Don't look back," Imbrie commanded, and picked up his pace to catch up with Seymour.

But curious Seymour turned his head toward the crowd anyway. If he had known any Farsi, he could have understood the shouts of the man on the bicycle. "Don't let them get away, those dirty Baha'is are trying to kill us by poisoning our water. Catch them, defend your faith people!"

Ali heard that and stopped following Imbrie and Seymour. He turned toward the crowd, held up his hands and shouted, "No! They are not Baha'is, and they are leaving now. Don't harm them! Leave them alone!"

Seymour saw people following them with fists raised and

angry-sounding shouts. "They are chasing us, Major. Run!" he screamed. Then he ran faster.

"No, keep calm!" Imbrie warned, his voice stern and befitting his rank.

But Imbrie's warning came too late. Seymour was already at a full-out run toward the carriage. Imbrie picked up his pace to keep up, and slowly turned his head to see what had spooked Seymour. The angry crowd had ignored Ali's advice and were approaching rapidly.

Ali turned to Imbrie and shouted, "Run!"

Imbrie ran as Ali held out his arms, trying to stop the people from chasing the two Americans. In the midst of the commotion, Ali thought he recognized a familiar face. He stepped on a large rock and lifted himself up to get a better view.

It was Ibrahim. Ali wondered what he was doing there. Was it a coincidence?

But Ibrahim disappeared into the crowd quickly and Ali couldn't find him again. So, he turned to locate the foreigners. Seymour had reached the carriage and was throwing the equipment into the opened door. He jumped in after, and Imbrie raced up and followed him inside, barking some instructions to their driver. The horse was stomping and shaking its head, perhaps sensing the urgency and danger.

A few people reached the carriage just as the driver was flapping the reins. One man tried to stop the horse and others pounded on the back of the carriage with their fists.

Another angry man managed to open the door, allowing a few men to reach inside and drag Major Imbrie out of the cabin.

Imbrie struggled to release himself from the grip of the mob. "*Amrikaie! Konsul! Amrikaie,*" he shouted in Farsi to no avail. The mob's hysterical noise drowned Imbrie's voice.

His efforts to defend himself proved useless—there were too many men holding him down. Others were beating him with fists and sticks, striking Imbrie's head, face, and stomach mercilessly. "Stop!" he cried. "Amrikaie Konsul!"

Seymour stood on the edge of the cabin shouting something. His call was muffled by the shouting of the mob, the screaming horse, and the thuds of pounding punches.

Ali ran toward the carriage. Those teenage gamblers had joined the mob and were busy shouting and throwing rocks. He pushed his way next to the carriage where the men were beating Imbrie.

The crowd had totally overtaken the carriage. Seymour jumped out to help Imbrie, putting himself right into the fray. Rocks flew around his head as men threw punches into his muscular back. Somehow, he managed to reach Imbrie and do his job as the bodyguard.

Ali pushed people away and blocked some of the beatings. Seymour pulled a blackjack club from Imbrie's pocket and wielded it feverishly. He managed to get Imbrie up from the ground. Imbrie raised his hand to show his gratitude for the help as Ali and Seymour wrestled him back into the carriage. For a moment, Ali and Imbrie made an eye contact. Imbrie gave Ali a quick, but weak smile.

Ali felt proud helping the Americans. He didn't care that he would be judged or scolded by those radicals. They were not normal Muslims. In fact, he noticed most of the people who were hitting and throwing things were thugs. In honor of his father, he had to do what was right.

With all his might he shouted, "They are not Baha'is, stop beating them!" But it didn't help. Rocks continued to fly and angry shouts of "Kill the infidels!" permeated his head with fear. Frantically, he helped Seymour get into the carriage next to Imbrie, who could barely sit. Bloody-faced, Seymour reached over to slam the door and lock it.

"Go, go!" both Imbrie and Seymour shouted at the driver and pounded the cabin. But the driver wasn't immune from the mob's violent anger.

Several men yelled at the driver, "Stop the coach, you traitor! Do not move!" They climbed up the side of the carriage and tried to push the driver off his seat. The driver used his whip, fists, and legs to keep control and ordered the horse to take off.

The carriage began to move. Ali hopped onto the side rail, kicking and shoving the attackers who continued the chase.

"Good, the carriage is moving," Ali heard Seymour say.

"But there are too many of them. They are catching up," Imbrie replied, his voice weak.

"No, no, we are moving. Go faster, faster!" Seymour yelled and pounded the cabin's wall with his big fist. The coach traveled toward the direction of the Cossack barracks.

Frustrated from his inability to stop the crowd, Ali jumped off the side rail and rushed toward the bicyclist, who was still circling around and agitating the people. "You're spreading lies. You'll go to hell if you don't' stop! Tell the mob to stop."

The bicyclist glared at Ali, pushed down hard on his pedals, and rode off in the direction of the carriage. The carriage hadn't moved more than thirty or forty meters when the frightened horse reared as the bicyclist blocked its way and spooked it.

Ali ran to catch up with the carriage. The mob, now several hundred strong, reached the carriage as it approached the Cossack parade ground and pulled the driver down. People from every direction rushed to join the mob. Ali, heavily engaged in a tug of war with the mob, stood by the carriage and tried his best to stop them. But he knew he was no match.

14

THE POLICE

Friday, July 18, 1924

MALCOLM PUT his hand on his brow to block the sun and squinted to see if he could recognize the fellow who seemed to be talking to Imbrie. He knew well, that Imbrie couldn't speak Farsi.

"Blast me!" He cursed out loud when he saw who it was—the kid from the teahouse. Ali. What was he doing there?

Suddenly, Imbrie and his assistant grabbed up the photography equipment and started back toward the waiting carriage. Ali stayed with them. Then they started running when the crowed followed, throwing rocks at them as they ran. The man on a bicycle shouted again, "Don't let them get away, those dirty Baha'is are trying to kill us by poisoning our water. Catch them, defend your faith people!"

The angry crowd chased Imbrie, his assistant and the teahouse boy to the carriage. They succeeded in climbing in, but just as the driver was flapping the reins, one man stopped the horse and others pounded on the carriage with their fists. Seconds later, the entire crowd arrived and surrounded the carriage.

Malcolm sensed that the crowd was getting too aggressive and large. It was time to put his contingency plan into action. He took his feet out of water, sighed just like an old man would, put on his *givehes* and stood up. Nearby, a middle-aged fellow was pulling his donkey with a light load of salt rock. Malcolm waved at the man. "*Agha*, sir, come here!"

The man saw him and walked over to where he stood.

"Take me on your donkey to the nearby police station. I'll give you ten *shahies*. I'm old and can't walk fast. Hurry up and help this old man. Allah will give you back tenfold in heaven."

A big smile appeared on the man's face when he saw the money. He helped Malcolm to get on the back of the donkey and started running while pulling the donkey's harness.

Riding on the boney rear end of a donkey wasn't the most joyful riding experience Malcolm had ever had. The brisk, bumpy ride jostled every organ in his body. He made a mental note not to do that ever again. But for now, he needed to stay undercover and make sure his plan succeeded.

When he arrived at the police station, he dismounted the donkey, used his cane to climb up four short steps and entered the building, remembering to stay hunched over. He found a vacant chair in the waiting room and sat.

The police station was in an old building. The entrance hall had two wooden benches and three rickety chairs. On the wall was a picture of Imam Ali, the first Imam of Shiite Muslims, seated and holding a huge, curved Arabic sword. A few people were sitting and waiting in the lobby as well. One man was pressing a handkerchief on his bloody face and moaning. A loud argument between two people could be heard from one of the nearby rooms. It was sweltering inside the windowless lobby and smelled of sweat and body odor.

"Excuse me, *sarkar*, may I see the officer in charge?" Malcolm asked a policeman walking by.

"He is very busy. What do you want, old man?"

"Well, people are beating two men near the *sagha-khaneh!*"

The policeman chuckled. "Don't worry, they will get tired and eventually will stop. If we run to every quarrel out there, we would need to have forty more men. Go home and rest, old man."

Malcolm couldn't allow his plot to fail, the stakes were too high. If Imbrie died under the mob attack, the outcome could impact his future, as well as at least one nation's future, if not more. He used his cane and stood, staying hunched over, and raised his shaky voice. "No! I have to see the officer in charge. I'm talking about a mob *killing* two men. They could set shops on fire and, God forbid, worse acts of violence can come out it." He started to amble toward one of the rooms, using short steps and leaning on the cane.

The policeman blocked his way. "Okay, wait here. I will talk to him first."

Malcolm stopped and stood in the middle of the hall. A few moments later, the policeman pushed the two men who were arguing out of the office and invited Malcolm inside.

Inside the room sat an officer in his mid-thirties at a writing desk. Behind him, a picture of Ahmad Shah, the king of Persia, hung on the wall. The officer was scribbling away on a tablet.

"*Ghorban*, sir, this is the old man who reports about a mob attack near the *sagha-khaneh.*"

The officer looked up and studied Malcolm for a moment. Malcolm worried that the officer would suspect his disguise, but he didn't flinch.

"I'm Lieutenant Ali-mamad. How can I help you?"

"Good morning, sir. I was sitting by the *jube* near the *sagha-khaneh,* soaking my old feet in the *jube's* cold water, when I saw a group of angry villagers attacking two men!"

"Which *sagha-khaneh?* Why they were beating these two men. Who are the two men?"

Malcolm cleared his throat as an old man would. "Sheikh Hadi's *sagha-khaneh.* I don't know why they were beating them. I heard someone shouting about dirty Baha'is. But the trouble, Lieutenant, is that I saw more men were joining the mob as I left. I'm afraid they may kill those two Baha'is, or whatever they are, and then start burning shops."

"Damn it! This is the last thing I need to happen today," the lieutenant exclaimed and immediately shouted from top of his lungs, "Ahmad, send Akbar and Farhad to Sheikh Hadi's *sagha-khaneh!*" He looked at Malcolm and continued, "You can go home now. We'll take care of it." He returned to his writing.

Malcolm let himself out of the lieutenant's office, went back to the lobby, and sat on the same chair. The two policemen, assumedly Farhad and Akbar, ran past him and then outside and toward the *sagha-khaneh.* Malcolm decided that the police station lobby was the best place to receive reports on how the day progressed, so he stayed put, hoping no one would pay attention to him.

He wasn't sitting long when a messenger rushed into the police station with a note in his hand and went directly to the lieutenant's office. The office door was open, and Malcolm had a clear view of the inside. The lieutenant stood up when he opened the note, paused after reading it, played with it a bit, and then tore the note into pieces. He called another policeman. "Run after Farhad and Akbar and tell them not to get involved with the mob. Ask them to return to the station immediately. Hustle, hustle."

"But Captain, if we don't get involved, the mob may kill them!" the policeman protested.

When Malcolm heard the policeman second-guessing his superior officer, he knew for certain that the lieutenant would reprimand this rookie for his insubordination. But it didn't happen, not that day anyway. Instead, the lieutenant dropped his head and in a weary voice said, "Do as I say and don't ask any questions. Tell them not to get involved. We all have to follow our orders." He paused to rearrange a few items on his desk. When he looked up, the policeman was still standing in front of him. "Why are you standing here and staring at me, you imbecile? I said *now! Run!*" he barked.

The policeman ran.

This is not good, Malcolm thought. The game had changed. What was in that note? Who sent it? It must have been from an important person higher up in his command; otherwise, the lieutenant wouldn't have stood when he read it.

Malcolm remained seated on his chair, waiting for further developments. It was too late for him to effect any more changes to the course of events. He was curious if the higher-up authority who sent the note was on Ibrahim's payroll, or if there could be a new player in the game.

Sitting in the lobby, he contemplated possible ways to collect the pieces of the ripped note.

15

THE IGNOMINY OF DEATH

Friday, July 18, 1924, at the mob scene

DODGING ROCKS, Ali looked up from his struggle with the mob at the carriage containing Imbrie and Seymour just as two policemen with their batons drawn hustled toward them.

He yelled in English to Imbrie, "See, two police come to help!"

From the opposite direction a few Cossack soldiers were approaching the mob.

The carriage driver, who had been pulled to the ground by the mob, was receiving relentless beatings. Imbrie rose from his seat and reached for the door.

"What are you doing?" Seymour shouted.

Imbrie opened the cabin door. "We have to help the driver."

Seymour shouted, "Look! Cossack soldiers, let's wait, let them handle—"

The mob yanked away the door and pulled Seymour and Imbrie out onto the street.

Farther back, a young mullah wearing a white turban and a

green handkerchief wrapped around his neck shouted into the already excited mob. "Let the blood of these infidel dogs avenge the death of our beloved Imam Hussein. Don't let them get away! Our Imam Hussein was martyred by infidels. These Baha'is poisoned our *sagha-khaneh*'s holy water, attempting to kill our children. Don't let them get away!"

Ali recognized the voice. He twisted his neck to be sure, but yes. There he was—Seyyed Hussein! Ali couldn't mistake his dark brown robe and long white shirt, and the ever-present prayer beads on his left hand.

As the soldiers and police approached closer, Seyyed Hussein made his rhetoric louder and more potent. "They poison our youths' minds. They poison our Islam. They drain our resources. Don't let them get away. Avenge, people, avenge!" he screamed.

Seyyed Hussein's powerful shouts projected above the crowd's mayhem. His words evoked reaction from the mob. However, the outcome of his fiery speech had a more visible effect on the Cossack soldiers. They drew their swords and rushed toward the carriage, their faces flushed crimson.

Imbrie pushed hard toward the injured driver amid an unmerciful rain of punches and kicks. He appeared determined to reach him, despite his own bloody injuries visible under his torn shirt. He fought back and evaded as many blows as he could.

Ali rushed toward the driver also and made it through the crowd about the same moment as Imbrie. Both men stared at the driver's lifeless body, soaked in blood.

Imbrie put his fingers to the man's neck to check for a pulse. He looked up at Ali and shook his head.

This was the first violent death Ali had ever witnessed and the second dead person he had personally seen. His father had been the first. For a moment, he froze until a flying rock hit his leg, and the pain brought him back to the urgency of the moment.

Ali rubbed his shin and looked at Imbrie. "What now?"

He pointed to the two policemen approaching. "Surely they

will help." Imbrie climbed up onto the carriage, pulled his consul ID card from his pocket, stood up on the porch of the coach, and swung his arm wide. "*Amrikaie! Konsu!, Amrikaie*," he shouted, waving his ID at the officers.

"I tell them," Ali said, rushing to the approaching policemen, waving his arms to get their attention.

But the mob grabbed Imbrie, pulled him down off the carriage and started thrashing him, just as Ali reached the first policeman. Gesturing wildly, Ali yelled over the mob's riotous noise, "They are not Baha'i, they are foreigners, they are American. They need your help."

The policemen pushed their way forward and found Imbrie and Seymour brawling with the mob. Ali pointed to the policemen and shouted, "Major, Major! He knows." Imbrie looked up, and at that moment a fist landed on his bloody jaw. The stench of blood and sweat was overwhelming in the heat of the Tehran summer afternoon. Ali felt dizzy but shook it off.

The policeman pulled his baton and began striking the men in front of him in order to reach Imbrie, who was crouched on the ground, covered in blood. Seymour reached Imbrie a moment later. Together, the policeman and Seymour pulled him up and fought their way back into the carriage, which sat only a few steps away.

Thwack! A rock hit Seymour's head, and he dropped face first onto the ground. The mob pushed into the carriage, overwhelming the policeman.

"Akbar!" He shouted to his partner, who stood by the driver's dead body. "Get over here and drive the coach. Take these two foreigners to the hospital."

Akbar ran into the fray and began to wield his baton ferociously to gain access to his partner trapped in the carriage. "What are you doing in there?"

"We have to take them to the hospital," Farhad replied.

"These are Baha'is, let them be."

130

"No, I don't think so. This one showed me his ID card. They are Americans. I don't know who said they are Baha'is, but it's a mistake. One of them is a diplomat," Farhad explained. "I will throw them in the carriage and you drive them to the hospital," he continued.

"I will help you," Ali interjected. "Where is the nearest hospital?"

"The police hospital is only three kilometers away," Farhad replied.

"Don't be a fool, the mob will kill us," Akbar pleaded.

"Come on," Farhad argued, "It's the right thing to do. It's our religious duty to save innocent lives. God will not be happy with us if we let them die here."

Akbar shook his head in disagreement, but moved toward the porch of the carriage anyway, striking two people with his baton as he jumped onto the driver's seat. With great difficulty, Ali and Farhad wrestled both Imbrie and Seymour into the carriage. "Go, go Akbar, God be with you," Farhad shouted as loud as he could. Akbar whipped the horse hard and kicked a few men who tried to climb up to stop him.

The carriage gained speed and ran over the people who blocked it. Ali and Farhad stayed behind to push back the mob and keep them from following the carriage. A moment later, a tall Cossack soldier with a big bushy Hungarian moustache came face to face with Farhad. The Cossack's eyes were blood red with rage and his face wet from sweat. He spat on the policeman's face and roared, "Traitor!" Then he sliced Farhad's neck with the sword.

Shocked, Ali rose to the policeman's defense. "No, no, he was helping! Those men are not Baha'is, they—"

"Shut up, boy!" The soldier slapped Ali's face with the back of his hand and ran after the carriage.

Stunned, Ali fell to the ground next to the policeman Farhad, who lay crumpled and still. A large puddle of dark red blood forming underneath him. Ali shook the policeman's body and yelled "*Sarkar, sarkar,* officer, say something so I know you're alive!" The body stayed still and silent. Men running and chasing the carriage passed Ali and a few bumped into him. No one stopped to help.

This was the second violent death Ali witnessed that day. The proximity of the murdered man made Ali's flesh crawl with revulsion. Bile rose up in his throat and he vomited.

Moments later, a third policeman arrived at the scene only to find his colleague's lifeless body on the ground. He checked his pulse. "He is dead! What happened?"

Ali's mouth was bleeding. He wiped the blood from his mouth. "One of Cossacks hit him with his sword, and then the mob ran over him. He hit me too."

They both looked at the direction of the carriage. The mob, like a swarm of bees, was chasing after it.

"Where is Akbar?"

"He is driving the carriage," Ali answered. He stood up on wobbly legs, feeling weak and shaken. Although the coach had made a good distance from the mob, the mob seemed relentless in pursuing Imbrie.

In spite of the dead man on the ground near him, there were still lives to save. Ali was determined to help Imbrie. But he could not catch up with the coach, even if he could run. He looked around and saw a teenager with a bicycle standing and watching.

"Take me to the carriage, right now. Move!" He sat on the middle bar of the bicycle. The excited teenager beamed, jumped on his bicycle's seat, and pedaled as fast as he could to catch up with the coach, which was nearly out of sight.

They came within about four meters of the coach, having difficulty weaving in and out of the men in pursuit. Ali could see that Akbar was riding the carriage horse, holding the harness in one hand, and in the other hand he wielded his baton, striking and repelling those who were still trying to climb onto the carriage.

When the bicycle came alongside the coach, Ali jumped off, ran a few steps, and jumped onto the railing of the carriage.

"*Sarkar*, I'm here to help." Ali made the policeman aware of his presence.

The man on the bicycle, the one who had been inciting the riot, caught up with the coach and traveled parallel to it. Akbar saw him and used the horse whip to hit the man. But the bicyclist maneuvered away from the reach of the whip. He pedaled harder to gain speed, then turned sharply in front of the horse, spooking the already agitated steed. With some difficulty, the policeman gained control of it and moved forward.

A few people threw rocks and sticks at the wheels in attempt to stop it. The bicyclist tried harder. He caught up with the coach again and shouted, "Stop this carriage now!"

"Go away. You'll be in a lot of trouble when we catch you," the policeman shouted back at him.

"Stop and give us the dirty Baha'is!" the bicyclist ordered again.

The policeman again snapped the whip at the bicyclist. The man maneuvered away, sped up and rode alongside the horse. He opened a large switchblade knife and stabbed the horse several times in its chest.

The poor beast dropped with a loud whinny. The carriage crashed and turned over. Both the policeman and Ali jumped off before it hit the ground.

The bicyclist stopped. With his chest puffed out and a big arm gesture he pointed to the coach and shouted, "Infidels, infidels, don't let them get away. Protect your faith, people."

The crowd's fury escalated when they saw the carriage had turned over. A loud "*Allah-o-akbar*" arose as they rushed forward.

Ali saw a third policeman approaching on the back seat of a motorcycle. He jumped off the motorcycle when he reached the coach and the motorcyclist accelerated and disappeared from the scene. The policeman looked for his comrades. Seeing Akbar on the ground, he rushed to his aid.

"Praise God that you are here," cried Akbar. "Help me take these people to the hospital."

"No, stop..." the third policeman panted. "Captain's orders are not to get involved. Stand down. We are not to take any action."

"I don't understand," Akbar replied. "The mob is about to tear the bodies of these foreigners apart. Perhaps the captain is not aware of the severity of the situation." He stood up and climbed up the overturned carriage. Ali followed Akbar to help.

"Those are our orders. Do not disobey," shouted the third policeman.

"I'm sorry, but I'm a man of faith first and then a policeman. It's my duty as a Muslim to protect these men. Come and help me get them out. Then go to the army base and get their commander out here. These soldiers have joined the mob. They are chasing us with drawn sabers," said Akbar.

Ali added, "*Sarkar* Akbar, you are right. One of the soldiers killed the other policeman. I saw that happen. I was right next to him, and then he hit me in the face when I told him that these poor souls are not Baha'i."

"Shut up, kid. I don't care. The captain will punish me. I'm not disobeying his orders," argued the third policeman.

"What? Farhad is dead?" asked Akbar. Ali nodded his head.

Akbar turned his face to the other policeman and raised his voice, "You should be afraid of God, not a creature of God. At least stay a bit longer and guard us. We must get them out!"

"No, no! I'll report to the captain that you disobeyed him."

Ali understood he was alone in this rescue attempt. He jumped onto the coach and slid inside the cabin. Tucking himself underneath Seymour and using his legs, he pushed the big man up toward Akbar, hoping he would pull him out.

Akbar, still trying to convince the other policeman, barked, "Be brave! Get ahold of yourself. Be a man! Even if they have done vile, this is no way to deal with it. Our *sharia* is clear on this. Men need to be tried in front of a judge." He yanked Seymour's body out of the carriage. "Don't be intimidated by the mob. The mob mentality has always been played by evil people to bypass the system. Submitting to the mob mentality will make us weak."

The third policeman shook his head in disapproval, but he hit the first man from the mob with his baton who had reached the coach. Then he turned and ran back to the station.

Imbrie, half alive, moved his head and opened his eyes as Ali attempted to lift him, but the boy could not manage the American's large, heavy body. Covered with blood, Imbrie groaned, and then seemed to muster every ounce of strength he had left. He propelled himself out of the cabin and fell to the ground. Moaning something unintelligible, he lost consciousness.

Several people from nearby businesses rushed to the scene. "What is going on, sarkar? How can we help?"

"Here, you two, help us with these two injured men. The rest of you keep the crowd away from us," Akbar ordered.

The mob volume increased moment by moment. People rushed from every direction, some stood on the side of the street and watched, but a substantial majority joined the attackers.

"We still have about two more kilometers to go. It is impossible to take the two large injured men that far by foot and not be overtaken by the mob," Akbar said while looking around in search for a solution.

Just then, a car turned in to the street and drove toward him. Without hesitation, Akbar jumped in front of the car and stopped it. "Open the door, I need to take these two men to the police hospital around the corner."

The driver saw the two men laying on the ground and shook his head. "God is my witness, I want to help. But these men are all bloody. Are they dead? What happened?"

"No time to explain. We need to move before the mob gets here!"

"Mob? This is an expensive car. The mob will destroy it. And I have a family to feed, officer. I don't want to die!"

"I order you to take us to the hospital. It is not too far. If you hurry up, you will be gone before the mob reaches you. Don't force me to commandeer your car."

"*Allah-o-akbar*, God is great, officer, you don't leave me any choice. Let's do it fast." The driver jumped out of the car.

"Hey, boy, you come with me," Akbar ordered Ali.

Imbrie, now half-conscious, tried to stand. But his height made him an easy target for a flying rock. The projectile hit Imbrie's forehead and blood gushed out, splattering everywhere. He lost his balance and fell to the ground, unconscious once again.

"The mob is catching up with us!' Ali warned.

Akbar, Ali, and the driver of the car threw both men into the back of the 1922 Lincoln and sped away.

"Go faster, we have to put some distance between us and the mob," ordered Akbar.

Ali noticed the retail stores on both sides of the street were shut and locked, most likely to avoid damage and looting by the mob. Imbrie and Seymour lay unconscious in the back of the car, bleeding heavily. The driver turned his head around and looked at the passengers behind him. He shook his head and pressed the accelerator to the floor.

A few minutes later, the car stopped in front of the hospital, a small brick building with a modest sign. Akbar jumped out and pulled out the first unconscious man. He didn't wait for the hospital staff to come with a stretcher, but placed the body on his shoulders and ran for the hospital door. Akbar was much smaller than Major Imbrie, and his knees buckled under the lifeless weight. He stumbled, but he managed by shouting for help as he entered the building. A few people hurried to help.

A staff person rushed out the door just as Ali was dragging Seymour out of the car. The staff person hoisted Seymour's body over his shoulder and disappeared through the hospital door. The driver of the Lincoln took off in a whirl of dust.

When Ali entered the hospital, the on-duty doctor had just

come out of his office into the hallway. Wearing an unbuttoned white lab coat, with a stethoscope around his neck, he looked at Akbar carrying Imbrie on his shoulders and asked, "Who is this man?"

"I don't know! He and his friend were attacked by a mob. He is a foreigner," Akbar replied.

Ali stared at the physician. He had never seen one wearing a white coat and a stethoscope. The only doctor he knew was their local one who would come to their house wearing regular attire. He was about to answer the doctor's question, but the hospital staff person couldn't keep Seymour's body on his shoulder any more. He collapsed, and Seymour's motionless body fell to the floor with a heavy thud. Ali and the helpers hustled to pick him up again.

The doctor took a quick look at the unconscious Imbrie and ordered, "Take him to the surgery room at once."

"Who is this one?" he pointed to Seymour.

"He is a foreigner also, possibly an American. He is called Seymour," Ali replied.

The hospital staff member who was helping Ali carry the massive body joked, "Dr. Shafa, look at his hair. He looks like a blond gorilla."

Nobody laughed. Dr. Shafa tightened his brows and examined Seymour. "He can wait. Put him in this room and have the nurse attend to him." The doctor rushed toward the surgery room. As soon as Seymour was hoisted onto a bed, Ali followed the doctor.

The surgery room was just like the other rooms with a bed in the center and a few tables with tools and a special light. Nobody stopped Ali, so he went inside the room and observed. He had never been in a hospital before. Even when his father was sick with pneumonia, the doctor visited him at home where he rested. His mother had also delivered all her children with the help of midwives at home. He had no idea how to act in a hospital or what protocol to follow.

In the surgery room, they were searching Imbrie's pockets. A nurse found his ID card, "Sir, look at this."

"Aha! He *is* an American!" Dr. Shafa took a small notebook from his pocket, adjusted his big round glasses on his nose and wrote a note.

"Yes, sir, his name is Major Imbrie," Ali announced.

Dr. Shafa turned to see who spoke, nodded his head, and handed the note to the nurse. "Send someone to the American embassy at once and give this note to them." He quickly wrote another note. "Send someone else to the American Hospital and give this note to them to bring Dr. Packard here immediately."

An uproar in the hallway distracted them.

"No, no, you can't come in ... no!" A hospital aide shouted. It sounded as if the mob was pushing into the hospital. Ali and Dr. Shafa's assistant, Issak, ran out into the hallway. Despite his slender, boyish body, Issak charged toward the crowd, both his hands up in front of him signaling no entrance. "No, no, go back," he cried. "This is a hospital, you can't do this!"

"Get out of our way!" a Cossack soldier roared, "unless you want to end up like those Baha'i dogs. We're here to finish them. Where are those infidels?" He raised his sword above his head.

"But this is a hospital—"

Issak didn't get a chance to finish his sentence. The Cossack grabbed the young man's thick, curly hair with his huge hand and swung him aside.

"They are not Baha'is!" Ali screamed, hoping to stop the Cossacks. But the soldier threw Ali against the wall as if he were a kitten.

Ali groaned, then mustered all his strength and struggled to his feet.

One of the mob apparently discovered Seymour's motionless body unattended in the exam room. "Here is one of them!" he yelled. Crazed people rushed into the room to see.

"Let me through, get out of the way," the Cossack soldier

ordered. He stared at Seymour for a moment, and said, "Let's go, this one has already gone to hell."

Ali thanked God that they left Seymour alone. He followed after the mob and struggled to push through to reach the soldier, but it was too late. They were already bursting through the doors to the surgery room.

"What are you people doing here?" Dr. Shafa bellowed. "This is a surgery room, get out, get out!"

"Is this the Baha'i infidel?" the Cossack soldier barked as he pushed the nurse out of his way to get to Imbrie.

"No, we don't have any Baha'i here. Now, turn around and leave. I insist!" Doctor Shafa yelled.

"That infidel dog must be slain. Get out of my way if you don't want to be sent to the same hell where he is going!" Then with a powerful blow, the Cossack shoved the doctor out of his way. Dr. Shafa's back hit the wall and he collapsed onto the floor.

Ali couldn't believe his eyes. "He is not a Baha'i!" he screamed.

But Ali's voice was drowned out in the deafening shouts of crazed men thrusting through the hospital hallways and into the surgery room. The soldier, who stood next to Imbrie's body lying on the surgical table, raised his hand to strike him with the sword.

Ali pushed his way to the soldier and saw Imbrie, half conscious, turning away to attempt to avoid the blow. His movement caused him to fall from the table to the floor. The mob, which had crowded around, began another barrage of frantic beatings.

Ali felt a sharp thud on the back of his own head. The room spun in circles. He reached down to steady himself on the table where Imbrie had lain, but it wasn't there. Everything went dark.

16

INCERTITUDE

16:05, Friday, July 18, 1924

THE THIRD POLICEMAN rushed into the police station, passed Malcolm sitting on the bench in the lobby, and went straight into the Lieutenant Ali-mamad's office. Malcolm had a clear view of the lieutenant's office. The policeman's clothes were splattered with blood, and he was short of breath. "Farhad is dead! They killed him!"

"What? Who killed Farhad? Where is Akbar?" the lieutenant shouted, recoiling from the sight of the policeman.

"A Cossack. There were a few of them among the mob. They had their swords drawn and were chasing the two foreigners!"

"Foreigners? I thought they were Baha'is. Did you say Cossacks? What were they doing there? Where is Akbar?"

"He said that the two men were foreigners and he wanted to help them. He took them to the nearby police hospital."

"Good for him, *barikallah*. We need to go to the hospital," the lieutenant said.

"But sir, you ordered not to get involved and stand down."

"My orders were not to get involved with any *Baha'is* trouble. No one mentioned foreigners." The lieutenant looked for his hat and continued. "Go get the carriage ready. We need to go to the hospital at once!"

The lieutenant didn't follow his policemen; instead, he went to his trash basket and collected pieces of torn paper and set them on fire in a plate on his desk.

Malcolm had heard enough. He stepped out of the police station, hired a coach, and headed back to his apartment. This was not the kind of news he had hoped for. One dead already. Why did Cossacks have to get involved? Maybe Ibrahim wanted the theater to be more dramatic. How bad had Imbrie been injured? He wasn't concerned about the dead policeman, but the total number of mortalities for this operation would come into question during any sort of assessment or inquiry. Blast it all! These despicable Persian fools!

At home, Malcolm threw off his peasant disguise, no longer needing to move about undetected. He was needed elsewhere in a different capacity. He quickly changed into his usual grey business suit and trousers and hurried to the street to hail a coach to the hospital.

Malcolm's coach pulled up just as Dr. Packard from the American Hospital and two other Americans were arriving. Malcolm distanced himself a few meters behind them. Although the name on the building said Police Hospital, based on western standards it was more like a small clinic. He didn't want to be recognized—at least not yet.

Dr. Packard led his group inside the building and Malcolm followed. The scene was surreal. Pieces of broken glass littered the floor. Broken medical equipment and damaged doors told a story of extreme violence. The air in the lobby was thick with the pungent odor of chemicals mixed with blood and sweat. The sound of crunching glass echoed in the hallways as the American team progressed. A male nurse staggered into the corridor holding his injured head. Dr. Packard asked the nurse for Dr. Shafa. The nurse pointed to a door a few meters away.

As they walked closer to the door he had indicated, a scuffed and bruised Dr. Shafa appeared, bent over and supporting his lower back with his hand. "Oh, Dr. Packard, *je suis désolé.*"

"Good God, what a disaster." Dr. Packard observed. "What the hell happened here? Sorry, my French is rusty. Can you speak in English?"

"Yes, of course," said Dr. Shafa, "but my English is not good. Umm... basically, a mob overpowered us. We could not *protéger,* um ... protect him. He is in the surgery room. I am so sorry." Dr. Shafa extended his left arm, pointing the way to the surgery room.

Dr. Packard and the other two Americans followed his directions to the surgery room and Malcolm lagged just a few steps behind, still unnoticed amid the chaos in the hospital.

A heavy air of morbidity hung inside the room where Imbrie lay. Broken chairs and tables lay scattered all over the room; blood and scuffs on the walls and on the floor told the difficult tale. No words were needed to describe what had happened there. On the bed, the lifeless body of Imbrie was covered by a white sheet. Dr. Packard went straight to the still form and removed the white sheet. The man's clothes were torn to pieces and his exposed body was severely mutilated.

Examining the body, Dr. Packard said, "The deceased is so badly disfigured that it'll be hard for anyone to identify him. Do you know who he is?" Dr. Packard asked Dr. Shafa, who had followed them to the surgery room.

"*Oui*, he had an identification card. Uh...," he searched his coat pockets. "Yes, here it is." Dr. Shafa pulled out Imbrie's ID card from his pocket and handed it to Dr. Packard.

"Robert W. Imbrie, Vice Consul of the American Emb ...." Dr. Packard's voice faded.

Malcolm closed his eyes and pressed his lips together.

Dr. Shafa added, "He and his *collègue* were brought here by a policeman and a young boy. They had been attacked and beaten by the mob. He was barely alive when they arrived. A few minutes after arrival, the mob rushed into the hospital looking for him and his friend. We tried to stop them but …." He shook his head in remorse.

"Where is the other one?" Dr. Packard asked.

"He is in the recovery room. His condition is stable now. My guess is that the mob thought he was dead and left him alone," Dr. Shafa answered.

Dr. Packard examined Imbrie's body closer. "Lord! This is awful. There must be over fifty wounds on his body. His jaw is broken, and this particular head wound has cut his scalp clear to the bone. Dr. Shafa, did you record the time of death?"

"Fifteen hundred hours. He was a strong man."

Packard pulled the sheet over Imbrie's head. "Horrible violence. What caused this brutal aggression?"

"*Je ne sais pas vraiment*, oh *pardon*, I don't really know. I heard shouting about Baha'is. I am still in shock. I have never seen frenzy like this before." Dr. Shafa pressed his fingers against his temples.

"Let's see the other one."

"Follow me, *s'il vous plait*." Dr. Shafa led the way to the room where Seymour was recovering.

As the doctors were leaving, Malcolm approached Imbrie's body and lifted the sheet. He inspected Imbrie's face but did not react to the bloody mess he saw there. He called, "Dr. Shafa!"

Everybody stopped at the doorway and looked at Malcolm, apparently just noticing his presence for the first time.

"Yes?" Dr. Shafa replied, an expression bewilderment on his weary face.

"These wounds on his head are more like a saber cut. Were there any soldiers among the mob?"

"Yes, *monsieur*, the mob was led by two sword-waving Cossack *militaire*," Dr. Shafa answered.

"Who are you?" Dr. Packard asked.

Malcolm covered the body swiftly. "James Malcolm, from the British embassy and a friend of the family. I shall notify Katherine, Major Imbrie's wife right away."

"Yes, of course." Dr. Packard dropped his head and followed Dr. Shafa to the room where Seymour was kept. Malcolm tailed them.

In the recovery room, Dr. Packard examined Seymour. With a note of excitement in his voice exclaimed, "This one's alive! We'll take him into our facilities. I need to contact the embassy."

One of the men who escorted Dr. Packard approached Malcolm and whispered, "Mr. Malcolm, we'll contact the vice consul's family. No need for you to get involved at this point."

Malcolm nodded. "Yes, of course."

Shortly after that conversation, more investigators from the American embassy, police, department of justice, military and other officials began arriving. Malcolm took his leave so as not to be questioned.

Or suspected.

17

THE RUSSIANS

Sunday, July 20, 1924

A FEW DAYS LATER, in a dark corner of the same teahouse, Malcolm met with Colonel Fraser and Ibrahim. The gurgling of several *ghalyans,* mixed with the sounds of the water fountain splashing and birds tweeting, provided a good cover for their soft-spoken conversation.

"Good Lord, that's all we bloody well need! I want to know what went wrong." The colonel's agitated voice created tension among the three men. "He wasn't supposed to die!"

Malcolm kept silent and flipped a small rectangular matchbox with his hand over and over again, making it land on one of its narrow sides. Ibrahim glanced at Malcolm, shrugged his shoulders and said, "I don't know! I guess the Cossacks lost control and went overboard."

"This is changing the game," the colonel snapped. "We are getting a lot of heat."

"Heat from whom? Americans?" Ibrahim asked.

"No, not Americans, at least not yet." Fraser fiddled with his slim-waisted tea glass. "But we are getting heat from the public. Rumors are rampant about British involvement in this fiasco, and newspaper articles are appearing one by one, accusing the British government. As always in this country, when anything goes wrong, we're the first to be accused."

Ibrahim leaned back. "Relax, Colonel, this is Iran. No one cares about the public's view. Moreover, Reza Khan is closing down newspapers and arresting the loudmouth editors and writers anyway. Actually, if you ask me, I say it's going really well." Without wasting a breath, he shouted an order. "Hassan *agha*! Bring us some *ghalyans* here!"

Malcolm calmly sipped his tea, taking in the banter between his two co-conspirators and judging their moods. Finally, he spoke. "Cossacks went after Imbrie because they were ordered to do so. An order this precise can only come from two sources—either their commander, Reza Khan, or their old bosses, the Russians."

Ibrahim leaned toward Malcom. "But you Brits took over the Cossack brigade and dismissed the Russians. Didn't you chaps promote Reza Khan to General of the Cossack brigade and then have him march to the capital?"

Malcolm ignored Ibrahim and continued. "The Prime Minister, Reza Khan, wasted no time using Major Imbrie's tragedy to order martial law and arrest religious leaders."

"Well, I see your point. Like calculated and premeditated moves on a chess board, huh?" a calmer colonel added.

"Hey, you chaps and your Russian friends didn't waste any time coming up with some creative arrangements either. Pretty crafty!" said Ibrahim.

"You shouldn't complain, Ibrahim." Malcolm retorted. "you and your friends were very well compensated."

"Yes, but our work is not quite done yet," Ibrahim suggested. "The U.S. is pressing the Persian government very hard for justice and punishment of the guilty parties. Reza Khan is moving quickly, arresting a lot of people." He then shouted in Farsi, "Hassan *agha*, what happen to those *ghalyans*? Bring us some more tea!"

The proprietor rushed a tray of hot tea and three *ghalyans* to them. As he set the tea glasses down he looked at Ibrahim. "Sorry, Ibrahim *agha*, I'm shorthanded these days. Ali was a great help, but he's disappeared. Nobody knows what happened to him."

Ibrahim looked up at the proprietor. "You mean Ali the camel driver?"

"Yes, yes, do you know him?"

"No, I just know him from here. Maybe he is riding a camel somewhere, and he'll be back soon." Ibrahim let out a loud laugh.

Malcolm shot Ibrahim a look to shut up. He didn't want to attract others' attention to their corner. Ibrahim stopped his laughter instantly. "I'm sure he'll come back soon."

The shop keeper left their table. All three men exchanged a look, saying nothing.

Colonel Fraser broke the silence. "It's all about this political chess game that the PM is engaged in. Arrests of the opposition leaders, media censorship, armed forces reorganizations, and consolidating his power are all part of his calculated moves. But I want to know precisely, what went wrong with Major Imbrie's incident?"

Ibrahim jumped in. "It's not just Reza Khan, gentlemen. Don't even think for a second that I don't understand. The United States' persistence on justice for this incident has diverted their attention from Sinclair's proposal for the northern oil fields, which suits you, Standard Oil, and your Russian friends."

"Russia is not our friend," Colonel Fraser protested, just as a meaty hand gripped his left shoulder.

"Did I hear our name?" A heavy-set, balding man stood behind the colonel. His words were heavy with a Russian accent.

"Ah, Mr. Boris Mironov, good timing." Malcolm said gingerly. "Please be our guest and have a seat. We were about to order bread, greens, and feta cheese. Join us." Malcolm offered the man his most welcoming smile.

The Russian pulled out a chair and gave a hearty laugh. "What a gathering in a humble teahouse! Colonel Fraser, James Malcolm the translator, and Ibrahim a carpet merchant." He looked at everyone as he called their names. "All right, but only for a few minutes, comrades."

"You know Ibrahim *agha*?" Malcolm asked.

Boris answered, "Yes, of course, I have bought many carpets from Ibrahim. I know him well."

Boris lowered his heavy body next to Malcolm. "This evening, I'm having a small private celebration at my house and you are all invited."

Colonel Fraser rubbed his shoulder. "What is the occasion, if I may ask?"

Boris smiled. "Well, we are celebrating the good news with some quality Russian vodka!" Boris let out a thunderous laughter and gave Malcolm a heavy pat on his back.

"What good news?" Ibrahim asked.

"Haven't you heard? Americans are leaving with their tails between their legs . Sinclair is not getting the support he needs to deliver the contract for drilling the northern oil fields. That means, no American oil company will drain our oil reservoir on this side of the border," said Boris, grinning broadly.

Ibrahim took a sip of his hot tea and nodded. "I've heard that Sinclair is going to ask Russia for help. He has the permission of the Persian government for drilling. Do you think your government will work with him?"

"I doubt it. We don't like to work with Americans," Boris answered.

"Sinclair is caught in an intriguingly perplexing dilemma," Malcolm explained. "His government is extremely upset with the Persian government over Major Imbrie's unfortunate death. Therefore, not only will he have a tremendously challenging time raising the promised ten-million-dollar loan, which is the condition for the Persian government's permission; but also, politically and morally he cannot afford to show leniency toward the Persian government."

"So basically, Sinclair is out of the picture," Ibrahim surmised.

"Check," uttered the colonel, using the game of chess' lingo.

Everyone turned their heads toward him.

"I beg your pardon. Never mind," the colonel apologized.

Boris leaned forward in his chair. "Yes, Ibrahim. But a word of caution to my British comrades. Don't you people even for a second think that we will allow your beloved APOC to drill the northern fields."

"Boris, don't you find Major Imbrie's tragedy a bit peculiar?" Malcolm asked, changing the subject. He didn't care where Boris was going with his comments.

Boris rubbed his head. "It was unfortunate for Major Imbrie. But it is no secret that we Russians were not fans of him." He laughed loudly again, then changed to a more serious demeanor. "Actually, Americans are enjoying Reza Khan's swift actions on the Imbrie case. So far, he has arrested over twenty people. Soldiers, mullahs, and even a few teenagers."

Ibrahim and Malcolm exchanged a quick look.

"Good man!" said Fraser. "If he continues to play the game correctly, he may end up with what he covets the most."

"And what is that?" Ibrahim asked.

"Military upgrades, mate," Fraser replied.

Ibrahim looked at everyone's faces, one by one. For a few moments, no one spoke.

Malcolm circled the rim of his tea glass with his index finger and listened to the gurgling of the *ghalyans*. Finally, he broke the silence. "Gentlemen ... I believe we are witnessing the dawn of a new dynasty!"

Ibrahim leaned back, paused for a brief moment, and said, *"Allah-o-akbar!"*

A few more moments of silence passed. Then Ibrahim exclaimed, "Then let's go to Boris' house and celebrate the Russian's victory the Russian way!"

They all laughed and got up to leave the teahouse. Colonel Fraser pulled Malcolm aside and whispered, "I won't go to his house. But you go and find out what these bastards are up to."

18

THE BRITISH EMBASSY'S KITCHEN

Monday afternoon, July 21, 1924

MALCOLM RETURNED from lunch and saw a note pinned to his door. He was summoned to the colonel's office.

Colonel Fraser's secretary was unusually busy. His desk was crowded with many papers and incoming telegraphs. Two men were hovering over his desk. One was a messenger delivering a package marked "Confidential" and another one asked for the colonel's calendar. The secretary saw Malcolm and gestured for him to go in.

After a quick rap on the door, Malcolm entered. Colonel Fraser was sitting at his desk, furiously writing something. He glimpsed at Malcolm and went back to writing. "Well, Malcolm, what did you find out?"

"Forgive me, sir, but I don't have anything to report yet."

The colonel stopped writing and looked up at Malcolm. "You went to the Russian's party last night. Couldn't you extract any worthy information?"

"No, sir. They were careful. I left early, but Ibrahim stayed. My thought was that they'd ease up once they noticed the British were gone."

Ibrahim was late in his report. It was unusual for Ibrahim not to respond promptly when a task was assigned to him. Malcolm felt uneasy about it, but he didn't let on to Fraser.

"Keep your antenna up, Malcolm. I don't trust these new Bolshevik Russians. Something went wrong with Imbrie's situation, and I suspect the Russians. Remember what Adam said? We're walking a thin line here."

"Yes, sir." Malcolm turned to exit the office.

"Incidentally, were you aware Adam from the Foreign Office managed to have several meetings with APOC mangers and the Standard Oil representative when he was here?"

Malcolm stopped and looked back. "Intriguing! No, I wasn't aware of that."

"This asset of yours, Ibrahim, I don't trust him. He could have turned," the colonel said as he wrote something on a piece of paper.

"Will you consider sharing it with me?"

The colonel continued his scribbling. "Sharing what?"

"What triggered your suspicion of Ibrahim?"

Fraser stopped writing, looked up, played with his pen, and after a short pause, he replied. "He was your operator in the mob theater and the results were not what you expected. Actually, it turned out disastrous. Interestingly enough, he did a superb job at almost the same scene with Dr. Moody, controlled and well executed. One should question that. Who would benefit the most from Imbrie's death?"

Malcolm leaned forward and put his hand on the desk. "Are you implying that he is working for the Russians now?"

"Ibrahim, like most of the indigenous assets, is a creature of greed and self-interest."

Malcolm interpreted Fraser's suspicions as some cautionary

advice, but nothing more. "I never take the locals' loyalty with certainty, Colonel."

"Yes, I'm sure of that. Nevertheless, look into it."

"Yes sir, I shall."

Malcolm left Fraser's office with the strong suspicion that his operation had been compromised. Other players were involved, but who were they? What was their game? Whoever they were, they had advanced knowledge of the plot. The game had changed. He wasn't sure if it was for better or worse. He needed to collect more information.

Malcolm spent most of the day in his office reading various reports about the Imbrie incident, searching for any clues that would point him in the right direction. Time was of the essence. He needed to be efficient. No time for a wild goose chase. But as the hours went by, he became hungry and decided to visit the kitchen for a quick snack.

As he strolled the hallways of the British embassy's main building toward the kitchen, an unexpected rush of air brushed his face as a woman in a nurse's uniform whizzed past him. He slowed down and watched as she went into the dining hall and took a sharp left turn into the kitchen.

He followed her and approached the door silently. With the tip of his fingers he slowly pushed the door open, just enough to see the inside.

The nurse had approached a tall Persian man dressed as a cook. "Excuse me! *Agha*! Sir, excuse me!" she said.

The man appeared to be in his early thirties. He looked around and replied in English, "Me?"

She raised her voice slightly and in a deliberate slow tempo asked, "Yes, do you speak English?"

He put his thumb at the end of the first digit of his index finger, indicating a small amount. "Yes. A little." A gentle smile appeared on his face.

"Is Ali your cousin?"

"Ali?" He whispered and quickly checked his surrounding to see if anyone else heard.

"Yes, is Ali your cousin?" The nurse repeated the question much louder.

He immediately put his index finger on his nose and reacted with a whisper. "Ssss, who are you?" He quickly gestured with his two hands for the woman to speak softly.

"I'm Rose. I've been teaching him English. He hasn't showed up for many days. I'm quite worried about him. Is he your cousin?" the nurse asked in a softer voice.

He put his right hand on his chest. "Yes, I am his cousin. I am Majid."

"Is he sick?"

"No, no.! He is hiding!" he whispered.

Malcolm let the door go and turned his back to lean on the wall for a second. She knows about the boy. Who was this Rose, and how much did she know? He returned to his listening post.

"Oh, my Lord! Why is hiding? What happened?"

"American man dead. Major Imbrie dead!" He closed his eyes, stuck his tongue out, tilted his head, and acted dead.

"You mean that horrible incident—and that savage mob attack murdered Vice Consul Imbrie?"

"Yes. And Ali is hiding."

"Why? I don't understand! What tie does he have with that tragedy?"

"No, nothing. He is no bad boy. He is a good boy. But Cossacks looking for him! He is afraid."

"It's a mistake! I'm sure of it. Oh, God!" She covered her mouth and looked around for someplace to sit. Seeing none, she leaned on a table nearby. She fanned herself a bit and took a deep breath.

Majid shook his head, his face drooped in sorrow. "Ali very good boy!"

"Yes, yes, I agree wholeheartedly! Maybe they just want to ask questions. Was he there? If yes, why was he there in the first place?

What did he do? Do you know?" Rose dropped those questions on Majid at a rapid pace—too rapid for him to grasp.

Majid shrugged his shoulders.

After a few moments of silence Rose said, "He did ask me about Major Imbrie a few weeks ago. Ali was very curious about Major Imbrie during the banquet."

Malcolm let the door go again and leaned his back against the wall.

Banquet! That's right. She was the woman who called his name. Intriguing, Malcolm thought. He turned and softly cracked the door ajar again.

"Banquet!" Majid pointed his index finger and radically bobbed it up and down. "Yes, yes, banquet. Ali ran away when English man in kitchen asked questions about Ali."

"An English man? Who was he?" Rose asked.

He shrugged his shoulders and raised his thick black eyebrows upward.

"Can you at least tell me—what did the Englishman ask?"

Malcolm fidgeted at the doorway. He had forgotten about the head waiter at the banquet. It's becoming more complicated. This was not good.

"He ask, where Ali work and, and if Ali speak English," Majid answered.

"Yes, Ali said something about that," Rose acknowledged and moved toward the door.

Malcolm quickly let the door go, jumped behind a table in the dining hall and hid. The door opened.

"I need to see him! I'm positive he's innocent and has no reason to hide," Rose declared. Then she went close to Majid and whispered something in his ear.

Malcolm couldn't hear what she said, but Majid nodded in agreement as Rose left the kitchen, hurrying away as fast as she had arrived.

Malcolm stood and watched her disappear down the hallway.

What else did she know? He entered in the kitchen and faced Majid. "Pardon me, do you have a sandwich? I would like to have a snack."

"Yes, sir, right away. Chicken okay?"

Malcolm nodded. A large pot of soup was cooking over the stove. The aromas of cooked potato, parsley and cilantro, turmeric, and a few other spices filled the room.

"I just bumped into an attractive young nurse. It seemed that she came out of the kitchen. Does she work here in the embassy?"

"Yes, sir."

"Do you know her?" Malcolm asked.

"No, sir." Majid answered as he sliced a chicken breast with a large sharp knife.

"What was she doing here?"

"She ask kitchen time for dinner. Here, your sandwich, sir. Thank you." He handed Malcolm a plate with a sandwich on it, gave a half bow and left.

"Wait a moment!" Malcolm ordered the man.

He stopped and turned toward Malcolm. "Yes sir?"

"Was it you that I asked about a waiter named Ali at the banquet?"

Majid knotted his brows and looked at Malcolm. "I don't know, sir."

Malcolm walked closer to Majid. Sweat appeared on the Majid's forehead.

"Do you know Ali the waiter?"

"Yes, sir, my cousin. He is my cousin." Majid looked at the pot of soup and asked, "May I stir the soup?"

Malcolm ignored Majid's question and asked, "Where is Ali?"

Majid stood there, looked alarmed, turned his head quickly, scanned the area and with a softer voice replied, "I don't know, sir!"

"Is he hiding? Where is he hiding?"

"Oh, no, no sir, he good boy, very very good boy. I don't know where he is." Majid shrugged his shoulders.

Enraged, Malcolm grabbed the man's shirt and yanked it toward himself. Their faces were a few centimeters apart. He could smell the onion on Majid's breath. In perfect Farsi, Malcolm asked, "You wouldn't lie to me, would you?"

Majid, wide-eyed with sweat now dripping off his face, stuttered his reply in Farsi, "No, no sir, never!"

"Then, tell me who was that nurse."

"I really don't know, sir."

Malcolm grabbed a butcher's knife from a block on a nearby counter and put it against the trembling man's throat, then pressed it a bit. "I can cut your throat like a sheep and toss your miserable dead body in the trash without anybody noticing it. Tell me the truth if you want to live. Who is that nurse."

"I swear, sir, I swear on my mother's grave, sir, I don't know her. I know her name is Rose and, and she knows Ali."

Malcolm tightened his grip on Majid and yanked his face closer to him. He pressed the knife harder, drawing blood. "What was she really doing here? Do you know any of her friends?"

Majid closed his eyes and gasped. "I don't know, sir, I swear. All I know is her name and that she is teaching Ali some English. That's all. Please let me go, sir. I have a family. I have a wife and three children. They need me. Please let me go."

Disgusted, Malcolm threw the man on the floor, tossed the knife onto the table, grabbed his sandwich, and left.

19

HOMING PIGEONS

Wednesday, July 23, 1924

WHEN ALI TURNED the corner leading to his home on Friday evening after the attack, two Cossack soldiers stood guard at the door to his house. Terrified for his family, he knew better than to approach. Instead, he fled to his friend Ahmad's place. Ahmad had snuck him into the house and taken him to the roof. Nobody, not even Ahmad's parents and sibling were to know. Ali hid on Ahmad's flat clay mud roof and slept near his friend's homing pigeons, which were kept in a large cage.

Ali had asked Ahmad to try to find out why the Cossack soldiers were posted at his house. Ahmad confirmed that the Cossacks were looking for him and had ordered everyone to inform them as soon as they heard of Ali's whereabouts. In spite of the danger, Ahmad agreed to continue hiding Ali in his house in secrecy.

It was in the late afternoon on Wednesday, five days after the horrible mob attack, that Ali heard a loud clanking of the heavy metal knocker on the front door. He moved behind the cage, just in case it was the police. A few minutes later, his friend poked his head out of the opening on the floor of the roof, announcing that he had visitors—his cousin Majid, who worked at the British embassy's kitchen, and a woman.

Ali stepped on a wooden ladder that connected the roof to the hallway in the house and climbed down through the opening into the hallway.

His cousin rushed forward and gave him a tight hug along with the two customary kisses. Majid cradled Ali's face with the palms of his hands and looked closely into his eyes. "We waited till everyone was out of the house before knocking. Are you all right, Ali-jon?"

Ali nodded. "Thanks, Majid, but why are you here? It could be dangerous for you to be seen with me."

Majid put his long arm around Ali's shoulder. "Look who I brought here to see you?" With his other arm, he pointed to the woman in *chador*, who had been holding the cloth around her face so tightly that only her eyes were visible.

But the moment Ali saw those clear blue eyes he knew. "Rose?" Goose bumps rose across his entire body and a rush of blood to his head made him slightly dizzy.

"Yes, Ali, it is me!" Rose released her grip on the *chador* and let it drop on her shoulders.

"What are you doing here?" Ali asked.

"I want to know why you're hiding and if I can help."

Majid asked Ahmad if they could go into a room instead of standing in the hallway. Ahmad guided them to a room at the end of the hallway and then excused himself to make hot tea.

There were no chairs in the room, just a large, dark blue Persian rug that covered the entire floor, and a few cushions. They all took their shoes off, entered the room and sat on the floor. Rose set her *chador* on the ground next to her.

Majid said in his broken English, "I go help Ahmad. But I say, two days ago, a dangerous man asked about you."

"Dangerous man! Who was it?" Rose asked.

"Same man who ask about Ali in banquet. He little shorter than me. Has long face and black mustache."

Ali immediately recognized the description as Malcolm. "He is the same British man in *ghahve-khaneh*. He is the one who asked Major Imbrie to go to *sagha-khaneh*—"

Rose cut him off. "All right, just calm down, Ali. Let us reexamine the situation a bit. What happened Ali? Why are you hiding?"

Majid excused himself and left the room.

Ali's hands were trembling. Rose noticed and grabbed hold of them. He didn't pull back, even though he knew such contact was against the rules of proper conduct. Her soft hands felt good to him. Her touch calmed his nerves.

"It will be all right, Ali. Take a deep breath and tell me what exactly happened. Why are you hiding here?"

Ali pulled his hands away and crossed his arms. He didn't want Majid or Ahmad to see their hands were touching. "I not know. I go to *sagha-khaneh on Friday...*"

Rose corrected Ali's English. "You *went* to *sagha-khaneh* on Friday."

"Yes, sorry, I went to *sagha-khaneh* to help the American Major Imbrie. There were many people there. I went to warn him. Then, many men hit Major Imbrie at *sagha-khaneh*. He and his friend were hurt very very bad. Cossack soldiers hit him with *shamshir*—"

"What? With what? *Shamshir?*"

"Yes, a very big knife." Ali swung his arm in the air like a swordsman.

"Oh, sword, saber, all right go on."

"Yes, sword. I took him to hospital and then many men and soldiers went to hospital and kept beating him. I tried to help but somebody hit me, and I went sleep—"

Rose cut off Ali again. "Sleep? No, you were knocked out, unconscious. Oh my God. What a horrible tragedy!"

"Yes, I woke up in alley. Someone drag me there. I went back to hospital, but many police and *gendarme* guarding it. I didn't go in. How Major Imbrie? He okay?"

Rose's left hand had covered her opened mouth as she stared at Ali in disbelief. "Oh dear, you haven't heard. Have you?"

"What?"

"He died that day from the injuries. But his friend lived."

Ali dropped his head down in sorrow when he heard the news. "Poor man," he muttered. He looked up, tears rimmed his eyes, "Nobody should die like that." Although his interaction with Imbrie included only a few short sentences, he had felt close to him. Sadness overwhelmed him and his heart felt heavy as a stone. He was ashamed that people behaved so savagely and was sorry that Imbrie had to endure such agonizing pain.

Ali sniffed a few times, then in a hoarse voice, barely louder than a whisper, "I saw two men die that day. I am sorry for Major Imbrie."

"But Ali, if you were helping him, then why are you hiding here?" Rose asked, just as Ahmad and Majid returned with a tray of hot tea.

Ali shrugged. "Cossacks were by my house asking about me. They look for me. I am afraid."

In the room, Ahmad couldn't take his eyes off Rose. Majid noticed it and ordered in Farsi, "Don't stare at her."

Rose smiled. "Is this the friend you talked about? The pigeon fancier?"

"Yes," Ali replied, "His name is Ahmad. He has many pigeons. Do you want to see them?"

Rose glanced at Ahmad. "Perhaps some other time."

Ahmad poured hot tea in two small, slim-waisted tea glasses, placed them on china saucers, and put one in front of Rose and one for Ali. Then he left the room.

"Maybe the Cossacks just want to ask you some questions and

not necessarily arrest you. Have you considered that?" Rose asked, bringing the conversation back to the situation at hand.

Majid poured tea for himself and said in English, "Why Cossacks and not police?"

Ali touched back of his head. "I know Cossack soldier hit my head with saber."

The three of them drank their hot tea while pondering the dilemma.

Rose tilted her head as if wondering about something and asked, "Why did you go there anyway? Why did you get involved? It wasn't like you knew Major Imbrie!" Her eyebrows formed a knot and she pursed her lips, visibly upset with him.

"I wanted to warn him. Dangerous taking photos of Muslim women. I wanted to say him that men will beat him hard! I wanted to save him!" Ali exclaimed, waving his arms around.

"But he was quite an experienced adult." Rose replied, leaning forward and speaking intently. "He was called Major, and that means he had a high rank in some sort of military. In the news, they said he was a vice consul. That means he was also a diplomat. Obviously, he knew what he was getting into, dangerous or not."

The word dangerous bounced in Ali's head a few times. It reminded him of the first time he heard the word in the *ghahve-khaneh.* Ibrahim had said it about the very event where Imbrie was killed. The images of Ibrahim flashed back in his mind, He had been in the alley during the trouble with Dr. Moody and then in *sagha-khaneh* right before the mob attack on Imbrie, then the image of the same British man in the banquet enticing Imbrie to take photos.

"So everyone was aware of the danger," Rose continued. "Ibrahim, the English man, Major Imbrie. Then why did you go?"

Ali responded, "I go there to help the American because … I thought he didn't know. I must help, I tell myself."

"Well, you were wrong, and now you are in big trouble," Rose snapped.

Majid placed his empty tea glass in the tray and said in Farsi, "Ali, Rose is correct. It was not your duty to warn him. He was a grown man. You have a family to support. That's where your priority should have been."

"What about doing the right thing?" Ali retorted in Farsi. "How about saving a man's life?" He was frustrated. But quickly calmed himself and with a softer tone said, "Maybe it was a trick."

"What did you say?" Rose asked, "Say it again in English."

Ali shook his head. "Sorry, Rose. I say, maybe it was trick."

"Are you speaking of a set-up? Like someone was setting up Major Imbrie?" Rose clarified what Ali tried to say.

Ali raised his eyebrows. "Yes, I think maybe." He finished his tea and placed his empty glass on the tray.

After Rose finished her tea, Majid stood up, looked at Rose and said, "We should go back."

Ahmad returned, and in his hand was a wooden cage with four pigeons in it. He was wearing a big smile. He said in Farsi, "This is for lady Rose."

Ali laughed and translated for Rose. Bur she already understood Ahmad with her slight knowledge of Farsi. She smiled and said, "Thank you very much, but I have no place to keep them. Maybe some other time."

Ahmad was baffled, as he didn't understand English. Rose repeated her polite refusal in Farsi. "*Nah, merci, Ja nadaram*, No thanks, I don't have a space."

Ahmad insisted that she keep them.

Rose's eyes were sparkling, "What do I do with them?"

Majid replied, his eyes alight with joy. "Use them send English messages to Ali." They all laughed.

Rose nodded her head and took the cage.

She faced Ali, held his hand and said, "Ali *jon*, please do be careful. Stay in contact with me and let me know if I can help. Hopefully, this ghastly trouble shall pass soon, and I'll see you in the garden again."

Ali nodded. "Rose, you are like sprinkle of sunshine!"

All three of them laughed, expect Ahmad, who didn't understand the English words. His puzzled face turn to a big smile and then to laughter as he desperately looked at everyone's face, searching for a clue.

Ali held the cage while Rose put on her *chador*, covering herself well. Majid hugged and kissed Ali good-bye.

When they left, an emptiness settled inside Ali's heart. He thought about his family and how much he was missing them. He missed his freedom, even his jobs. He prayed that Rose was right, that the trouble would be over soon. But dark doubts began to cloud his hopes.

The wooden ladder stood in the hallway, beckoning him back to safety on the roof. He clutched both sides of it and climbed up.

20

PRISON

Saturday, July 26, 1924

THREE DAYS LATER, Ali sat on the dirt floor in one of the corners of the crowded ten-by-twelve-meter cell. There were no chairs, benches, or beds to rest on. Just a small pile of damp hay in the opposite corner. The only illumination was from a barred window on the brick wall behind him. Cockroaches, ants, and spiders were the permanent residents of the cell, and once in a while, a mouse would dare to challenge the twenty-plus inmates to a frenzied race of "catch me if you can." Ali didn't mind the smell of sweat and body odors, but the pungent smell of urine was nauseating to him.

He pulled his knees as close to his chest as he could and tried to distract himself with thoughts of his family. He wondered who was taking care of them. Did they have enough money to buy groceries? Were his younger siblings suffering from hunger? He wasn't even sure if his mother knew where he was. He prayed that his family didn't think that he might have run away.

A flood of self-blame took over him. He knew that Cossacks

were guarding his house. Why didn't he stay longer at Ahmad's? Why did he go home so soon?

"I am so stupid!" he muttered.

Blood rushed to his head and in frustration he punched the wall next to him. Immediately he cradled his fist and uttered a cry of pain. His bones ached from sleeping on the hard floor. His empty, wrenching stomach bothered him. Most of the food was devoured by the larger, more aggressive inmates the moment it appeared. Timid prisoners like Ali were left hungry most of the time. The tougher men also took all the hay to use as bedding. But for Ali, the worst pain of all was that he wasn't entirely sure why he was there. No one had said anything to him.

"Hey, what's the matter, kid? This your first time?" a prisoner mocked.

"*Akh*, leave him alone, he'll get used to it," another responded.

Ali inspected the faces around him, one by one. Their soulless eyes and leathery faces indicated a different breed of men. Not like him. He put his head between his knees and stifled a sob. He wanted to cry, but he couldn't. Not there.

Instead he prayed and asked God to help him understand why he was there. He hadn't done anything wrong. Was it part of a larger plan God had for him?

"Hey kid, you haven't said a word since you got here. What's your name?"

Ali didn't answer.

"Hey kid, *agha* Reza asked you a question. Answer him!" The order came from a large thug sitting on a stack of hay, enforcing *agha* Reza's demands. The question had come from *agha* Reza, a man who wasn't a big man, but he sat like a big man—erect, cross-legged, his arms extended on his knees. He was stocky and muscular around the neck and shoulders. Two inmates sat on either side of him like bodyguards.

Just then, the door opened, and two guards entered the cell. One of them shouted, "Ali, step forward!"

One of the prisoners stepped forward and said, "I'm Ali-Reza, but my friends call me Ali."

The guard struck him on the arm with his baton. "Well, I'm not your friend! Did I say Ali-Reza?"

"Ali, step forward. Now!" the guard barked again.

Ali looked around and saw that no one moved. He stood and said, "Yes sir, here." As he stepped toward the guards, one of them grabbed the back of his neck with his large hand and pushed him out of the cell into the hallway. Ali stumbled, smacked against the clammy wall of the narrow hallway, and fell to the ground.

Another guard pointed in the direction he wanted Ali to move. Ali staggered to his feet and shuffled through the dim corridor. "Where are you taking me? Why am I here? I haven't done anything!"

The guards looked at each other. One of them said, "Don't ask any questions, kid. You'll find out soon enough." They turned and walked down another corridor that was a bit brighter. At the end of it, one of the guards opened a door to a room, looked inside, and said, "Get in."

Ali stood in the doorway. The room had dirty off-white walls. The plaster had fallen off one wall in a few places, and brownish mud and straw were visible. The room was bare of furniture expect for three chairs in the middle. In one of the chairs sat a woman covered in a white *chador* with imprints of many little pink roses. She held the *chador* tightly; her face was hard to see. Next to her stood his cousin Majid, who smiled the moment he saw Ali. Two more guards stood by a door on the opposite side of the room.

His guards pushed him into the room. "Go, you have visitors."

"Mother?" Ali cried as he propelled himself toward the woman. He dropped on the ground to kiss her feet, only to realize that those feet didn't belong to his mother. He looked up into the woman's face.

"Oh Ali, dear, what have they done to you?" Rose whispered in English and extended her right hand to touch Ali's bruised face.

"Don't touch!" the guard barked in Farsi.

Ali pulled back and whispered, "Rose!"

His cousin bent over to pull Ali up. He greeted Ali with a big smile and said in Farsi, "Ali *jon*, dear, how are you?" As he pulled Ali up he whispered, "I brought Rose here for you, so she can help you. But guards think she is your sister, so play along."

Ali nodded in agreement, stood up, pulled a chair in front of Rose and sat, facing Rose and Majid.

"Ali, what happened? How did you end up here?" Rose whispered.

Ali spoke softly. "Rose, you shouldn't be here. This no good place for lady!"

"Tell me exactly what happened, please. I want to help you!"

"I not know. Day after you leave, I walk at night to see my family. I thought in dark night no guard would be there. But before I see my family, Cossack guards took me here."

"Did they tell you the reason for your arrest? What are the charges?"

Ali shrugged. "I not know. They tell me nothing. I say to them I help Major Imbrie and police. But they don't listen."

"Are you certain that you are placed in this prison for charges related to Major Imbrie's murder? Could there be anything else?"

"No, nothing else. I work, I go home every day. I do no bad thing. Ahmad said that Cossacks tell my mother I killed American."

"Oh dear, that's not good." Rose sighed.

Ali suddenly remembered something, "That very bad day, two police with me helped Major Imbrie. One went to hospital. He see me ... saw, he saw me. He saw me helping!" Ali exclaimed. "Rose, find the good police, he will say to you. He will say that I was help-ing!" He pointed his fingers and became animated.

"But if your incarceration is related to Major Imbrie's murder and you were helping him, then you shouldn't be here in this prison at all. I'll see if I can find the policeman. Do you have a solicitor?"

"A what?" Ali asked.

"A solicitor, barrister, lawyer!"

"What? I don't understand those words."

"Oh, good God! Someone who defends you in the court and gets you out of the jail!"

"No, Rose. Those only for rich people. I have only you and Majid." Ali dropped his head. Then he had a new thought. "How is my family? Do you know?" He toggled his eyes between Rose and Majid.

Majid replied in Farsi, "They are fine. I worked very hard to get the permission to bring them to you. But officials allowed only one visitor for now. I decided Rose should be the first one to visit you. Perhaps she can help you to get out of here."

Rose interrupted. "I'll send some money to them through your cousin."

Tears flooded Ali's eyes. "Thank you, Rose. May Allah reward your kindness a thousand times."

One of the door guards yelled, "Visiting over!" He strode over to Ali and yanked him out of the chair by the back of his shirt.

"Ali do take care. I shall help you!" Rose said.

"Know that I not bad. I am not bad, Rose!" Ali exclaimed.

The guard kneed Ali in his stomach. "What is this devilish tongue you're speaking? You traitor scum. Move on!"

2 1

THE INQUIRY

Sunday, August 10, 1924

"MALCOLM, do come in please and take a seat," Colonel Fraser instructed. "Shut the door. I want to speak with you about a delicate matter." He was sitting behind his desk reviewing some files, as usual.

"Yes, sir, good morning." Malcolm gently closed the door and took a seat in front of the colonel's desk.

Fraser looked at him and with concern in his voice said, "Apparently, there are some inquiries about the Imbrie incident within our own embassy. Will you please see to it? I do not want any unnecessary trouble in my own house."

"Of course, sir. May I ask who is inquiring?"

"A nurse from our clinic in the embassy. Pearce is her name. She has inquired of a few people about what happened to Imbrie." Fraser went back to his file and started to write something.

Malcolm sat back and crossed his legs. "Nurse Pearce. What does she stand to gain from these inquiries?"

"My hope is," the colonel responded as he continued writing, "that you will have the answer to the question soon. Do you know the lass?" He looked up, awaiting Malcolm's answer.

"I'm not certain, Colonel. I may have met her."

He put the pen down and stared at Malcolm. "I beg your pardon?"

"No, not in that way," Malcom answered, brushing off his leg. "A few weeks ago, I overheard a nurse talking to someone in the kitchen." He stopped and quickly said, "I'll look into it."

"Right you are! Then get on with it, and report back. Off you go." Fraser's attention went back to the file on his desk.

"Yes, sir," Malcolm replied, got up and left.

A few hours later, after making some preliminary inquiries and a detailed study of Nurse Pearce's personnel file, Malcolm stepped into the embassy's small clinic. He asked the reception clerk for Pearce's whereabouts. She pointed to the corner of a large area, where a nurse was busy attending to a man's wound. A few steps into the room, he recognized her face. She was the same nurse who had been in the kitchen asking about Ali a few weeks prior. He stopped and decided not to disrupt her work. On his way out, he asked the clerk if there were any other nurses on duty that day. He was pleased with the answer.

Malcolm went to a small patio near the rose garden. A few people were strolling about. He waited as a man passed by, and then when no one was in sight, he lifted his pants and rubbed his ankle against a rose bush. With his pocket knife he made two small superficial cuts on his ankle, just enough to draw blood. With blood dripping, he limped toward the clinic.

Rose sat at the front desk when he arrived. She rushed to his aid and guided him to a vacant examining table nearby. He felt her muscular strength as she assisted him up to sit on it.

"So, you say, a rose bush did this to your ankle?" Rose quipped.

"I'm afraid so." Sitting on the bed, he searched for a glimpse of her eyes while she moved her medicine tray near him. "James Malcolm, at your service."

She looked up, smiled, and answered, "Pearce, Rose Pearce." She paused. "Your face is familiar to me. Do you work here?" Her blue eyes were piercing and kind.

"Yes, I'm a dragoman here at the embassy."

She rolled up his pants up to his knee, exposing his scar from his childhood fight with his stepfather.

"From the Great War?"

Malcolm shook his head. "No, I was fourteen years old when I acquired this beauty. But, I do have other ones from the Great War."

"A childhood mishap?" Rose asked as she cleaned the wound.

"Is a fourteen-year-old a child?" Malcolm kept his eyes fixed on hers, expecting her to look up.

She did, and their eyes met for a moment. Rose quickly looked back to his ankle and pressed the cotton soaked in alcohol on his cut. However unexpected, the sting wasn't enough to make Malcolm jolt. He sat unmoved and watched her carefully.

"How long have you been stationed here?" He knew the answer, of course.

"It'll be two years next week," she answered without looking up.

He shifted his weight to his other hand. "How do you like it here?"

"Lovely, for the most part." She applied red mercurochrome to disinfect the cut.

"I detect a sort of hesitation, Miss Pearce. Is something bothering you? Are locals rude to you?"

"Oh, no. Quite the opposite. People and their customs are just lovely here. It's..." she paused. Malcolm remained silent and kept his eyes on her.

"It's the politics that bothers me," she confessed, "but then, politics by nature is a complicated beast, isn't it?"

"Yes, but perhaps we should leave it to the diplomats to worry about politics."

Rose nodded and tightened the dressing. "All done, Mr. Malcolm. Stay away from rose gardens for a few weeks." With a smile she rolled down his pant leg.

"Much obliged, Miss Pearce. Looking forward to seeing you again soon," he said as he carefully got down from the exam table and limped away.

Dr. Morison, the resident physician at the embassy, had an office nearby. Toward the end of her shift, Malcolm arranged to use the office. He shut the door, sat behind the desk of Dr. Morison, lit a pipe and put his feet on the desk. A moment later, he heard a quick knock on the door and before he could answer it, the door flung open. The nurse who opened the door, physically jolted when she found Malcolm behind Dr. Morison's desk.

"Oh, I'm so sorry. I was sent to meet Dr. Morison. It must have been a mix up," she apologized and was about to close the door.

"On the contrary, Miss Pearce, there is no mix up. Will you come in please?" Malcom rushed his reply, "I requested that you be sent here. Have a seat please."

Rose left the door open and stepped in the office. "Well, when you said soon, I wasn't expecting immediately! How may I assist you, Mr. Malcolm?"

Malcolm took his feet off the table, blew smoke into the air, and locked eyes with Pearce for a moment. "It is I who am here to assist you." He moved to the edge of his chair. "Please close the door, Miss Pearce."

Rose gently closed the door and stood next to it.

"I'm here to answer all your questions about the incident involving Major Imbrie."

Rose tilted her head slightly, pressed her lips together, and her brows formed a knot. "Major Imbrie? The American?"

"Yes, I've been told that you have been making some inquiries about him."

A cynical smile appeared on Rose's face. She rubbed her neck and moved her head to one side to accentuate the questions. "So, the rose bush incident was a ruse?" She shook her head, and without giving Malcom a chance to answer the question continued. "On our earlier encounter you mentioned that you are a dragoman here? Tasked with translations, isn't that correct?"

"Yes."

"Forgive my doubt, Mr. Malcolm, but how can a translator possibly be in possession of the facts about the murder of Major Imbrie, an American vice consul?" She shook her head, her voice was filled with concern. "Who asked you to see me? Was your visit to the clinic earlier part of your investigation?"

"Miss Pearce, let's presume that I wear more than one hat. I can assure you that I am well-versed in Major Imbrie's subject matter, and I can satisfy most, if not all, of your questions about him." Malcolm drew on his pipe. He was curious as to how deeply she was involved with anything related to the Imbrie incident.

Rose went toward the door and turned the handle. "Mr. Malcolm, I have no desire to be rude, but I do need to know who has asked you to meet with me." She opened the door and continued, "If you can not disclose that information, I—"

"Very well, Miss Pearce," Malcolm interrupted. "It is Colonel Fraser who asked me to meet with you. As you are aware, part of his responsibilities are the security and safety of the consulate staff."

Rose shut the door and walked back a few steps toward the middle of the room. She stopped next to a chair and grasped the top of the chair with her right hand.

"Oh, I see." She paused for a moment and continued. "Well, this is a bit unorthodox." She pulled down on her shirt. "Very well, my first question is regarding safety. Am I safe here? Is it safe for Westerners anymore?"

"The Persian government has taken precautionary measures to

assure the safety of Westerners." Malcolm sat back on the chair and drew on his pipe. "My recommendation is to limit your outings for the next few months and pay attention to the curfews."

"Oh, jolly good," she replied and fidgeted a bit. "I'll limit my activities to my flat and the embassy's compound till things settle down." Rose didn't move to sit on the chair. She remained where she stood in front of Malcolm and fiddled with her hands.

Malcolm remained seated and continued to smoke his pipe.

Rose looked at the door. "Well, I have work to do Mr. Malcolm; if you are satisfied with our conversation, I shall get back to my station."

Malcolm took his pipe out of his mouth and glanced up at Rose. "Let's stop pretending Miss Pearce, shall we? We both know that your questions are not limited to just safety issues. Everything I told you was written in a communiqué by the consulate and distributed many days ago. Tell me what is really on your mind."

Rose glared at Malcolm for a second, then she moved forward and sat on the edge of the chair in front of the desk, her knees touching each other. "Well, Mr. Malcolm. That's what you said your name was, right?"

"Yes."

"You know, last year, at a banquet," Rose pressed her hand together and continued, "I overheard Colonel Fraser gloating to a few gentlemen about the fact that we made Reza Khan first a general of the Cossack army and then the Prime Minster." She looked down at her hands for a moment and then looked up at Malcolm. "Now, I'm not ordinarily interested in politics, but in lieu of the recent events, politics have piqued my interest."

Malcolm leaned forward. "That is a peck of hearsay and not the facts. The British government has no such claim. Colonel Fraser, as the British military attaché, knows better to refrain from such announcements."

"Well, people act a bit differently after a few drinks at parties.

Nevertheless, my point is, with such influence at the highest level of Persian government, can't we bring some civility to their barbaric justice system?"

"I'm having difficulty following you, Miss Pearce. Can you elaborate?"

"Yes, of course." Rose crossed her legs and leaned back on her chair. "I've read in the English newspapers that during the brief investigation into Major Imbrie's incident, Persians have charged and sentenced two minors." She stopped and collected her thoughts. "I'm speaking of the sentencing of two underage teenagers to life in prison for the murder of a well-trained, strong, and capable American military man. One of these teenagers is only fourteen years old. We are British!" she exclaimed, her voice rising both in pitch and volume. "We take pride in our high morals and advanced civilization. Can't we in any way assist these boys?"

Malcolm drew on his pipe and pretended to ponder Rose's question. She knew more than she should. Where did she get her information? It couldn't be just from the newspapers. He had to diffuse her meddling somehow.

Malcolm chuckled, hoping to lighten the mood. "They have also apprehended and charged two Cossack soldiers and sixteen other individuals!" He took the pipe out of his mouth, held it with his right hand and locked eyes with Rose. "Miss Pearce, it appears that you are not in possession of all the facts. However, you have shown a keen interest in this subject matter. What exactly is the nature of your intrigue?"

Rose fidgeted on her chair. "I read it in the newspapers, I heard it over the wireless, and most importantly, I am concerned about the safety of myself and my colleagues."

"Forgive me, Miss Pearce, but the welfare of two Persian teenagers accused of murdering an American diplomat is hardly considered a safety issue."

Rose glared at Malcolm. "Nevertheless, can the embassy assist?"

"You are proposing that the British government assist in exactly what ways?"

Rose moved closer to the edge of her chair. "Reports indicated that Major Imbrie suffered over one-hundred and thirty wounds and a deep saber cut to his head. It is hard to believe that two minors caused all those wounds. The newspapers reported that over two thousand people participated in the riot and —

"Hardly reliable," Malcolm interrupted. "The local rags are full of exaggeration and propaganda."

"But don't you agree that investigators should at least look into who were the real perpetrators?"

Malcolm glared into Rose's blue eyes. He didn't like where the conversation was going. Why was this nurse so interested in Imbrie's case? She is the one who inquired about the boy, Ali, in the embassy's kitchen. How close is she to that boy?

Malcolm stood up. "I'm afraid I don't see it that way, Miss Pearce. It is not our concern at this point to delve into Persia's internal affairs, or their justice system. This incident is exceptionally sensitive. The Americans are very agitated and are extremely persuasive for speedy resolutions to this affair. They are the ones who are actually asking for the death penalties." Malcolm walked toward the door. He needed to investigate this nurse further. Pearce could potentially become a risk.

"What?" Rose raised her voice. "This is absurd! How can we allow this to happen?" Rose was relentless.

He stopped and looked at Rose. "You are giving us too much credit regarding our influence with the Persian government, Miss Pearce." He paused for a moment, tilted his head and asked, "Do you have any personal connection to this matter, Miss Pearce?"

Rose shook her head.

Malcolm opened the door.

Rose remained seated on her chair, her back toward the door. Then she turned toward Malcolm and, as if suddenly remembering something said, "He's beating you at your own game!"

Her comment stopped Malcolm's retreat. Game? What is she talking about? How much does this woman know?

"Yes, an uneducated Persian soldier is beating you at your sophisticated political game, and you're afraid."

Malcolm decided to ignore her comment and simply walk away. He knew she was referring to Reza Khan. But, it wasn't prudent to engage further with Pearce till he learned more about her.

"I know about Ironside!" Rose exclaimed.

Malcolm stopped halfway out the door, turned his head back toward Rose and, without a word, responded with a directed gaze that could only mean one thing. Pearce had gone too far.

Malcolm left the room and went straightaway to Colonel Fraser's office. With a quick knock, he opened the office door and stepped in. The colonel sat behind his desk, busy with paperwork as usual.

"We need to talk."

Fraser stopped his work and looked up. Malcolm strode across the room and sat on the chair near the colonel's desk. "She knows about General Ironside's role in Reza Khan's coup d'état."

Fraser took off his readers and set them on his desktop. "Are you referring to Miss Pearce?"

"Yes."

"Hmm, that's not good. You need to investigate her. Where does she get her information? How deep is her knowledge? And what does she stand to gain from it?" He paused and looked at his paperwork. Suddenly he gasped, as if he remembered something horrible. "How about Lieutenant Smyth? Does she know about his involvement in the coup d'état?"

Malcolm lifted his brows and shrugged his shoulders.

Fraser pointed his index finger at Malcolm. "That's classified information and a secret. If she does, she will need to be dealt with swiftly. We simply cannot run the risk of exposing this sensitive matter. You know that, of course. Good day, Malcolm." The colonel went back to his writing.

Malcolm understood the reason for Fraser's tone and brusque dismissal. Ironside's and Smyth's activities in bringing Reza Khan to power were covert, and still highly classified.

He let himself out.

22

THE DINNER PARTY

Early evening, Thursday, August 21, 1924

MALCOLM CHECKED the address again to be sure he had the right place. The handwritten invitation from Jane Berkley had been passed to him by a waiter at the tennis club a few days prior. He hadn't noticed her there, but apparently, she had seen him. He was intrigued by the invite's mysterious aura. Malcom had no idea who else would be present at the dinner party.

He adjusted his necktie, lifted the large brass ring that was gripped in the mouth of a brass lion head door knocker and rapped it smartly against its backplate. He admired the door knocker, a British lion.

The door opened. In front of him stood a teenaged girl, "May I help you?"

He smiled. "Yes, yes, I am James Malcolm. Mrs. Berkley expects me."

The teenager measured him with an appraising eye, smiled and said, "Just a moment, please." She closed the door and screamed, "Mum, there is a Mr. Malcolm at the door!"

A faint voice from deep inside the house answered, "Yes, take him to the drawing room."

She reopened the door. "Please come in, Mr. Malcolm. I'm Agnes Berkley."

"A pleasure," he replied.

Malcolm entered the house and took off his hat. The house felt unusually British to him. It was hard to find a house with a British floor plan in Tehran. But this one had a beautiful wooden floor and a foyer. To his left was a staircase going up to the second floor. Immediately to his right was a place to hang jackets, hats, and a place for wet or muddy items such as boots, umbrellas, etc. A painting of a handsome horse wearing a British saddle hung on the wall in the foyer. The house even smelled British, with the aroma of Sunday roast beef, tobacco, and the fragrances of summer flowers.

Jane Berkley glided to the door. Her dress's lace overlay flew behind on the air. "James, welcome." She offered her right hand while with her left hand patted her head to tame any stray hairs.

Malcolm took her hand and kissed it lightly. "Mrs. Berkley, what a splendid house."

"Jane, please. Come on in." She turned her head toward the hallway and yelled, "Charles, Charles, come and greet our guest!" Then she turned back to Malcolm. "Let's go to the drawing room, shall we?" She put her right arm through his left arm. Malcolm liked the gesture. He hung his hat on the hallstand and let Jane guide him to the drawing room.

In the drawing room, flowers in vases were scattered through-out. Bunches of lilacs, delphiniums, sweet peas, irises, some carna-tions and roses, masses of roses everywhere. An upright piano was standing against the wall near the entry to the room, and two carved chairs and a table between them were at the far corners. In the center of the room, sat a sofa, a loveseat and two chairs of the same design with dark red velvet cushions.

Charles Berkley entered the room drawing on his pipe. He locked eyes with Malcolm when he saw him on Jane's arm. Pointing his index finger at Malcolm, he took his pipe out of his mouth with his left hand. "James Malcom, the dragoman, right?"

Malcolm nodded with a smile. "Yes, sir."

Mr. Berkley let out a loud laugh and extended his right hand to Malcolm. The two men shook each other's hand vigorously.

"Charles, you know James?"

"Oh, yes dear, he is the embassy's dragoman, a translator. He has helped me on several occasions in the finance department with translations. He's a very talented man." Mr. Berkley laughed some more and patted Malcolm's back.

"Well, he is a talented tennis player as well." Jane pulled Malcolm closer to herself, their elbows still linked.

The doorbell rang.

"Agnes, darling, could you get the door, please." Mrs. Berkley called out to her daughter, who was still in the hallway. Mrs. Berkley turned her head toward her husband and continued, "Charles, I met Mr. Malcolm at the tennis club a few days ago. We played tennis against a cute American couple. I've forgotten their names. Who were they, James?"

Everyone became distracted by Agnes' delighted cry. "Oh, Miss Anderson! I didn't know you were invited."

Mrs. Berkley released her grip on Malcolm's arm, pressed her skirt with her hands and rushed to greet the new guest without hearing the answer to her question.

"Let me pour you a drink, James." Mr. Berkley guided Malcolm to the drawing room.

"Patricia, I do adore your new hairdo," Jane exclaimed, her voice echoing in the acoustics of the entry. "It is so chic and short."

"Miss Anderson, I love your headband and your dress is so lovely," Agnes added.

"Thank you, both of you. What a lovely house."

Jane entered the drawing room, locking elbows with Miss Anderson. Agnes had Miss Anderson's right arm, mother and daughter both guiding her to the room where Mr. Berkley and Malcolm were standing silently next to each other observing ladies entering the room.

"Gentlemen, may I present Miss Patricia Anderson. She is the librarian at Agnes' school." Jane introduced the two men. "My husband, Charles, and this fine gentleman is James Malcolm, single. I presume." The women chuckled.

Malcolm gently kissed Miss Anderson's right hand. "How do you do."

"Mr. Malcolm." She gave Malcolm a charming smile.

Malcolm looked Miss Anderson in the eye and said, "Emer-aude, comforting yet almost haunting."

"Oh, Mr. Malcolm, you know your perfumes! And yet I used such a small amount! You must have a sharp sense of smell," Miss Anderson exclaimed with a wide smile and admiration.

Malcolm did have an excellent sense of smell, and it wasn't all about body odors, blood, gun powders and other scents of his rough world. Since childhood he could easily tell ingredients of foods that he was familiar with or the type of fragrances his mother and other women in his life would wear. In his adult life, he enhanced that ability by practicing every chance he got. It had served him well in many occasions, personal or professional. Ladies loved it.

"Oh, how magnificent! Let's see if you can tell what I'm wear-ing!" Mrs. Berkley came close to Malcolm and before he had a chance to say anything, she extended her neck close to his face. Malcolm already knew exactly what she was wearing, but he enjoyed observing her slender, elegant neck from close up and was not going to stop her by answering too soon. Her neck almost touched the tip of his nose. He took his time, slowly inhaling the scent. No one spoke a word. Perhaps they were in shock at the intimate display. Malcolm closed his eyes and held the breath in his lungs for nearly half a minute, and softly exhaled as he stepped away from Mrs. Berkley and opened his eyes.

Agnes' eyes were pinned on Malcolm and a small smirk showed her amusement with the clever parlor trick. Both Mrs. Berkley and Miss Anderson's eyes twinkled in anticipation of the results.

"Chanel No. 5," announced Malcolm.

The loud laughter and clapping of the ladies confirmed his correct answer.

Agnes strolled closer to Malcolm and in a silvery voice asked, "Well, Mr. Malcolm, since you're such an expert in perfumes, what is your opinion about Tabac Blond?"

"Oh, Agnes, dear!" Mrs. Berkley scoffed, "Why do you bring up such a contentious subject when we have company?"

Miss Anderson said, "Actually, I'd like to hear Mr. Malcolm's response."

Malcolm smiled. "Tabac Blond with its sweet, aromatic odor of Virginia tobacco and leather, is considered seductive and a daring flair for its wearers. Therefore, it's not suitable for gatherings like tonight and most definitely not suitable for discussion by young ladies like you, who have such a decent upbringing."

Jane jumped in, "Thank you, Mr. Malcolm. Agnes, please go to the kitchen and bring us some more ice."

Malcolm noticed Miss Anderson beaming with admiration. He enjoyed this cheerful, charming brunette's persona, and found her flawless, white complexion and slender limbs most compelling.

Miss Anderson sat on a floral armchair and crossed her legs. Malcolm followed her with his eyes, admiring her good taste in fashion and appraising the possibilities of establishing intimacy with her, and the advantages that might accrue.

The doorbell rang again.

Since Agnes was by the door, she opened it and shortly after she announced, "Mum! Dr. and Mrs. Morison and Miss Rose Pearce have arrived."

Malcolm was engaged in small talk with Miss Anderson when he heard the announcement. He stopped talking and watched the entrance to the drawing room.

Mr. and Mrs. Berkley greeted the new guests. Rose stopped for a moment when she saw Malcolm in the room. Their eyes locked. He gave her a polite, brief smile which she didn't reciprocate.

He couldn't be distracted. This was a good opportunity for him to get to know Rose better. He had to solve the mystery of Rose's in-depth knowledge of the UK's meddling with the Persian government. How did she know so much about Imbrie's case? He knew she had taught English to Ali. But how close were they? How much had Ali told her? Where and how did she learn about their operation with Reza Khan?

According to Rose's personnel file, she was a twenty-six year old nurse from Bristol who had never married. She studied nursing at the University College in Bristol. Prior to her post in Tehran, she was stationed in India.

Malcolm slowly approached Rose after Mrs. Berkley poured her a drink.

"Miss Pearce, we meet again!"

"Mr. Malcolm." Rose gave him an obligatory short smile. "It has been over ten days since our last meeting."

"Oh, has it been that long?"

Rose moved closer to Malcolm and with a voice nearly whisper asked, "Have you made any progress?"

Malcolm was saved by Mrs. Berkley's loud soprano voice announcing, "Everyone please proceed to your seats at the dining table. Dinner will be served shortly!"

At the dinner table, Mrs. Berkley had assigned Malcolm's seat next to Miss Anderson. Rose sat across from Malcolm. Dr. Morison and his wife sat next to Rose.

Malcolm noticed a peculiar restlessness about Rose during the dinner. Although she talked to Dr. Morison's wife, Rose took frequent glimpses at him, but moved her attention quickly back to the Morisons when he tried to make eye contact.

Malcolm decided to change the subject from the boring monologue that Miss Anderson had carried about her school's activities since dinner was served.

"Mrs. Berkley, I mean Jane, I must congratulate you on your delightful taste in British décor and flowers. Your roses are especially magnificent. It is so very comforting to see a totally British house in this country. You have my gratitude!"

A wide smile appeared on Mrs. Berkley's face. "Oh, thank you, James." She gave him an appreciative look, took a sip of her wine and continued. "I have seen too many people who have totally immersed themselves in this Persian culture! Every item of decor in their homes is from some part of Persia. In some of the houses, you can hardly find a chair to sit on. During a recent visit at a friend's house, who will remain nameless, it was agonizing for me to sit on those awful large cushions. The host had to borrow a chair from her dining room for me."

"Well, we live in Persia, dear." Charles finished chewing his food quickly and continued, "I don't see anything wrong with having a little bit of local culture infused in the décor."

Miss Anderson chewed her bite quickly and added, "There are many aspects of the Persian culture I find fascinating. For example, their miniature paintings—"

Mrs. Berkley cut her off. "Charles! We are British, and I am proud of that. Do you see any non-British object in our house?" She didn't let him respond. "I love my utterly British house. Doesn't it remind you of our lovely place in Bristol?"

Mr. Berkley nodded his head in agreement. Agnes rolled her eyes. No one spoke.

Rose broke the silence. "Mr. Malcolm, your job as a translator for the embassy must be quite demanding."

Malcolm didn't look at Rose, pretending to be busy cutting his food. He nodded his head in reply.

Mr. Berkley jumped in with enthusiasm, "And he is a very good one, I may add. His fluent mastery of German, French, and Russian are commendable ..."

"Well, most of us are in possession of such fluency in those languages," Rose interrupted.

Charles nodded and replied quickly, "But what fascinates me, is his fluency with Farsi and many dialects of it."

Malcolm bobbed his head in appreciation and with a smile put a bite of food in his mouth.

Rose glanced at Malcolm and asked, "With such an abundance of talent, Mr. Malcolm, it is possible, is it not, that one could assume you have been involved with many diplomatic conversations?"

Malcolm hesitated, chewed his bite, bobbed his head slightly and replied vaguely, "Your point?"

"Can you assist us in understanding this tragedy with Major Imbrie and the Persian government's behavior?"

Malcolm worked hard not to show any indication of his shock over Rose's question. He didn't expect such a direct hit. She'd put him on the spot.

"Imbrie?" Mrs. Berkley gasped. "Is that the same..."

Malcolm acknowledged her with a solemn nod.

"Oh dear! This is most disconcerting." Mrs. Berkley instinctively put her right hand to her chest, but her demeanor and words were calm. "Such a tragedy; a few days prior to that horrible calamity, I played tennis with Major Imbrie and his wife. Remember that, James?"

Rose's eyebrows went up with the last comment. "You knew Major Imbrie personally?"

Malcolm finished chewing his bite, set his fork down and replied, "Major Imbrie was a fine gentleman and frankly, the entire episode of what happened to him is truly horrible."

Everyone was looking at him. This conversation had potential traps, and he wasn't sure what Rose might ask next. He moved to end the topic. "The Persian government is moving rapidly to ease tension. The Americans are agitated and are extremely persuasive for speedy resolutions to this matter, and the Persians are complying."

"But regarding safety," Mr. Berkley asked, "With our family here with us, is it safe for Westerners anymore?"

"The Persian Government has taken precautionary measures to assure the safety of Westerners. My recommendation is to limit your family's outings for the next few months and pay attention to the curfews." An uncomfortable silence settled over the table. Malcolm noticed a piercing stare from Rose.

"Now, I am on the edge of my seat, Mr. Malcolm," Rose said without taking her eyes off him, "What kind of a person was Major Imbrie? Was he ambitious? Was he unpretentious? Was he secretive? Tell us about him, Mr. Malcolm."

Mrs. Berkley jumped in, "Oh, he was handsome, tall, polite, humorous, and overall a real gentleman, I would say. Wasn't he, James?"

Rose kept her eyes fixed on Malcolm, obviously not willing to let up on him until he responded.

"Yes, that's right, Jane. He was all that and more. He had keen interests in photography. As a matter of fact, his photos had been published in the *National Geographic* a few times."

Rose broke her stare and looked down on the table when she heard mention of the *National Geographic* magazine. It appeared that she was reminded of something. Malcolm made a mental note.

After dinner was over, Mrs. Berkley invited everyone back to the drawing room. There, Rose slowly walked toward Malcolm. "Well, Mr. Malcolm, do you have any answers for me?"

Malcolm pretended he didn't know what she was talking about, "I beg your pardon?"

"Have you made any progress?" Rose asked again, looked slightly agitated.

"About?"

"Oh, come now, Mr. Malcolm," Rose's angry voice went up in volume. "Surely you know what I'm asking about! Will the British embassy help the two incarcerated Persian boys in the Cossacks' prison?"

"Miss Pearce, please control yourself and the volume of your voice," Malcolm answered with a firm whisper. "These matters are highly sensitive and require delicate treatment."

He turned around facing away from Rose and whispered again, "I never said that I'd help."

Mrs. Berkley walked toward Malcolm and asked, "James, do you sing?"

She locked her elbow with Malcolm and walked him away from Rose.

"Oh, no. I'm afraid my voice is utterly undesirable."

"How about piano-forte? Do you play it?"

"Yes, I can find my way around it."

"Great! That settles it then. You play piano-forte and Patricia and I shall sing. Patricia dear, you sound like your voice is an alto, is that right?"

"Yes, that's correct."

"Then let's start with the beautiful *Standchen* by Shubert. Are you familiar with it, James?"

"Yes, of course." Malcolm replied. "I beg your pardon, but before we start, I should use the W.C."

"Oh of course, go to the end of the hallway and turn left."

Malcolm walked down the hallway. He heard the piano. He was about to open the door to the W.C when he heard the creak of a door closing near him.

His instinct pressed him to investigate. When he found the door, he stood by it and eavesdropped.

"Don't be silly, Rose," It was a man talking, assumedly Berkley.

"You must forget the boy. There is nothing else we can do about it!" After a moment of silence, Berkley continued. "Rose, dear, I thought I clearly explained this to you before. I'm in the financial section and have no influence whatsoever on the matters of operations, politics, and military. Your demand is unreasonable."

He heard Rose's voice, soft but insistent. "Charles, I need your help in understanding this situation. You're my only hope."

Malcolm raised his eyebrows.

A moment later, Charles said, "All right, let's go over it again. What's on your mind?"

Rose continued in a quite calm, almost matter-of-fact manner. "Ali, the fourteen-year-old boy, worked at a teahouse when he wasn't tending the garden at the embassy. One day, he overheard two British men and a Persian man talking about some local shrine, a miracle connected to the shrine, Major Imbrie, and the danger involved with it. Then, in the embassy's banquet, where Ali worked as a server, he heard the same British man entice Major Imbrie to photograph the very same shrine! Ali told me that during the banquet, the same British man, our mystery man, chased Ali once he found out that Ali could understand English, suspecting that he was the same boy who worked at the teahouse. And—"

Charles interrupted her. "Rose, stop! Are you insinuating that this is a British conspiracy? Killing a high-ranking American diplomat?"

Malcolm put his ear closer to the door.

"Not exactly, Charles. I'm simply lining up the facts the way Ali witnessed them."

"But, these are not the facts dear, far from it! They are simply a convoluted interpretation of events from a dreadful mind! I fear you have been deceived by this Ali character!"

"Well, do you remember Dr. Moody's incident with the mob last month?" Rose asked.

"Yes,"

"Ali was there—"

The screech of a jerking chair obscured her words, and Charles interrupted her again. "Ah ha! Why did he go there? He participated, didn't he? He joined the mob, didn't he?"

"No! *He wasn't* ... sorry, I didn't mean to raise my voice. Please be patient and listen to me."

"All right. Go on."

"The boy was there to observe, not to participate. He told me that the same Persian man from the tea house showed up before the trouble began. The man paid a bundle of cash to two mob agitators. And he saw the very same man right before the mob attack on Major Imbrie at the shrine!"

A moment of silence, then Rose spoke again. "Charles, all these sightings are telling me that this was not an accident, or even a coincidence of some sort. It shows me that someone or some group of people worked together to make this horrible thing happen. If the British were not involved with the plot, they certainly knew people who had influence over the outcome! We need to find the mystery man. He can tell us exactly what happened and, hopefully, help us release poor Ali from prison."

Moments later Charles said, "Hmm, Intriguing. In some bizarre way, your story may have some merit. Did the boy mention any names?"

"Only Major Imbrie and a Persian named Ibrahim *agha*."

Malcolm stepped back. This was not good, not good at all.

"Well, I shall poke around the embassy tomorrow. But let me tell you about—"

"James! James!" Malcolm heard Mrs. Berkley calling. Her calls became louder every second. She was getting closer. Malcolm swiftly moved toward the W.C. and met Mrs. Berkley in the middle of the hallway.

"Oh, here you are, we started to worry about you!"

"Here I am! Sorry, I got turned around. Now, let's go make some music, shall we?" Malcolm put his hand around Jane's narrow waist, turning her toward the drawing room. Jane smiled, moved closer to Malcolm, and sashayed along with him toward the piano.

Rose and Mr. Berkley walked in the room a few minutes after Patricia and Jane took turns singing while Malcolm accompanied them on the piano.

Rose looked preoccupied for the rest of the evening.

Colonel Fraser would be enraged to hear about Berkley's involvement, Malcolm thought, and decided to keep it to himself for the time being.

23

THE RUMOR

MALCOLM HAD JUST SETTLED into his chair next to Rose in Colonel Fraser's office when a brief rap on the door alerted him to Charles Berkley's arrival. He braced himself for Berkley's reaction to her presence there.

"May I enter?" Berkley said.

When the colonel invited him in and gestured for him to sit, Berkley instead rushed to the chair near the desk where Rose sat, wringing her hands.

"Rose!" Berkley exclaimed. "Are you all right?"

Rose nodded.

Berkley's wary eyes looked up at Colonel Fraser and at Malcolm, who stood next to the colonel. "What is the purpose of this meeting?" he asked, standing and facing them.

"Relax, Mr. Berkley, have a seat. We need to talk." Colonel Fraser extended his hand toward a chair next to Rose.

The colonel leaned in toward his desk and picked up his pipe.

He took his time lighting the packed tobacco and taking a few quick puffs. Finally, he spoke. "Mr. Berkley, we called you and Miss Pearce here as a protective measure."

"Protective? I'm afraid I'm not following you, sir," Berkley said,

After a strong draw at his pipe, Colonel Fraser, in a slow and deliberate manner explained. "There are reports of rumors circling in regard to British agents' hands in the murder of Major Imbrie. Eyewitness reports are indicating that Miss Pearce was, indeed, the source of these unfounded rumors—"

"This is absurd!" Rose interjected.

The colonel ignored her. "We all know that the political situation in this country is highly sensitive these days. Naturally, we brought Miss Pearce here to protect her against any potential harm. And ... to ask her a few questions."

"That is unfortunate, but why am *I* here?" Berkley asked.

"We are also intrigued by these rumors and are curious about the origin of some of the information," continued Colonel Fraser calmly.

Rose changed her position on her seat, "This looks to me more like a charade! To what extent have British agents been involved?"

"We'll ask the questions here, Miss Pearce," Malcolm interjected.

"Is that so? I wasn't aware that this was an official interrogation!" Rose protested.

Berkley glared at Malcolm. "Mr. Malcolm, just what is your role here? Are we in need of translations?"

Fraser jumped in. "He is assisting me with the inquiry."

"My apologies for being redundant," Berkley moved to the edge of his chair, "and I have no desire to be rude, but still, I'm not clear as to the purpose of my being here in this meeting. I have a busy office to run."

"We have reasons to believe that you have assisted Miss Pearce with some privileged and sensitive information," the colonel replied.

Berkley sank back in his chair and rubbed his chin. "Well, I'm certain that we can resolve this issue in an amicable way." His tone was oddly conciliatory.

"Gentlemen," Rose said, "may I make a suggestion to get on with the matter at hand without any further delay. Shall we?" She sounded irritated.

The colonel swept his right hand forward, gesturing for Rose to go on.

"Persian authorities have arrested an innocent fourteen-year-old boy among those who are accused of murdering Major Imbrie. This boy was forced to drop out of school to support his mother and siblings after his father's unexpected and early death. He has no wealth, no connections, and no representation. The boy was at the wrong place at the wrong time, but with good intentions. He was there to help." She paused. The room was quiet. Her eyes toggled between the colonel and Malcolm. "I'm soliciting your help to free this boy!"

Mr. Berkley looked at the two men and sighed. "She is right. We ought to be able to do something for the poor boy rotting away in the prison."

Fraser cleared his throat. "It is unfortunate to see that a young lad's life is wasted like this. But it's their internal affair—the Persians, that is, which is fueled by America's demand. Our hands are tied in the matter."

Rose crossed her arms and twisted in her chair. "Well, Ali doesn't deserve this!"

Fraser leaned forward and rested his arm on his desk. Malcolm, alerted, moved closer to Rose. "Ali?" he repeated, "So you know this lad?"

"Yes, Ali! An innocent fourteen-year-old boy who worked here at our embassy as a gardener. I got acquainted with him this past year and taught him some English." She looked down on her hands clutched together in her lap. "For what it's worth, he is a sweet, dutiful child who has been thrown into this senseless adult world by misfortune. This entangled world of conspiracies and the expediency of temporary alliances between strange players is consuming his life."

Malcolm asked, "How well do you know this Ali?"

"I don't understand that question!" Rose looked up at Malcolm. "He doesn't deserve to be thrown in prison among hard-core criminals for a crime he hasn't committed. He went to the location to help. What is the matter with you people? Aren't you human? Do you have any dignity left in you?" Rose raised her voice with each question.

Malcolm glanced at Colonel Fraser and noticed Berkley's glare at Rose--appearing shocked at her outburst.

Fraser cleared his throat again. "As I said, it is unfortunate. But, Americans are demanding severe punishments. Our hands are tied."

"Perhaps we can talk to the Americans," Berkley pleaded. "Who is in charge of the investigation?"

"Mr. Murray, Wallace Murray," Fraser replied. "However, I do advise you against it. He is adamant to see some Persian blood shed in reprisal."

Rose jumped in. "Perhaps we should talk to Mrs. Imbrie. I shall be more than happy to plead and beg Mrs. Imbrie to forgive Ali."

"We don't know if Mrs. Imbrie is still residing in Persia," Berkley replied.

"Actually, she is," Malcolm replied. "But Katherine is not in any shape to entertain such a plea. She is devastated. Her husband's body was destroyed with well over a hundred wounds. I am afraid she is eager to take comfort in justice."

"Justice? Ha," Berkley added sarcastically.

"So, you know her!" Rose perked up. "That's right. You were there at the banquet with them, and according to Jane, you also played tennis with them. I remember now. If you are on a first name basis with her, then I'm certain you can get me an audience."

"I should hope so!" Berkley said, glaring at Malcolm.

"No, no, it won't work. She is overwhelmed and distressed. I shall not do such a thing," Malcolm protested, shocked at how easily Rose could ambush him.

"Don't treat me as a naïve person, Mr. Malcolm. You would do well to remember that, sir!" Rose warned.

Malcolm, intrigued by the way Rose conducted herself, and especially with the way she had challenged him, pulled a chair over and sat near her. He looked her in the eyes. "What exactly do you know?" His dark eyes rested on her.

Rose sat back on her chair, appearing a bit frightened by the menace in his voice. She adjusted her skirt and crossed her legs. With a controlled and calm voice, as if she owned the place, replied, "Gentlemen, I know a lot more than you think."

Berkley turned his head and looked at Rose with raised eyebrows. Malcolm leaned back on the chair and crossed his arms, continuing to glare at Rose with a hint of a sneer. Colonel Fraser leaned back on his chair also, took another draw on his pipe, and looked straight at Rose.

She locked her eyes on the colonel. "Shall we proceed?"

24

AN OLD FRIEND

Thursday, September 4, 1924

ALI PACED BACK and forth in his cell, the same one-hundred-twenty-square-meter box he had endured for several weeks. The rancid smells were part of his daily existence now as his own body had succumbed to the absence of normal hygiene. He had surrendered to sleeping on the hay on the hard floor, and the prison food was tasteless—not enough to sustain even a child. But the pain of hunger had taught him to be more aggressive when food was thrown in the cell. It was about survival.

Ali didn't like the way the guards treated them, like they were animals, pushing, shoving, hitting them every chance they got. Despite all that, he stayed diligent with his daily prayers, even though some of his cell mates ridiculed him. He had a commitment to God, which mattered more than what these criminals thought of him. For the most part, he stayed quiet and remained in a dark corner to avoid contact with anyone.

But that day, he was agitated. He paced back and forth. He

missed his family terribly. He had heard no news about them or from them. Since his last visit with Rose and Majid, he'd had no other visitors. Every morning, he scratched a small line in the corner of the wall where he slept. The lines on the wall showed him that it had been thirty-eight days since her last visit. Had she given up on him?

"What you here for, kid?" asked a new inmate squatting in the corner of the room.

"Nothing, a mistake," Ali answered and continued his pacing, hoping the inmate didn't continue pestering him.

The inmate chuckled. "Sure, aren't we all!"

"I swear to God," Ali protested, "I haven't done anything wrong. They accused me of killing an American." He said all that without looking at the inmate or breaking his pacing. Suddenly he turned and grabbed the bars on the cell door. "Guard, guard, please, I have to go to the bathroom!" he yelled.

A guard responded from down the hall, "Shut up, camel boy. It's not time for toilet run yet."

The new inmate stood up, alert. "Wait a minute. The camel boy!" Another inmate walked toward Ali and said, "Oh, the camel boy! I have heard of you! You are Ali Rashti! *You* killed that filthy infidel Baha'i!" A third inmate approached Ali, patted his back and said, "Hey, brother, you're our hero!" With a big smile plastered on his face, he turned to the others and shouted, "Brothers, he's the one who killed that foreign Baha'i man!"

Ali turned toward the group, his eyes wide open, and waved his hand. "No, no, I didn't kill anyone. I didn't, I swear!"

A tall, well-built inmate stood up and sauntered toward Ali. His shoulders were wide and his neck was thick. His body stood over Ali like a great tower. He looked straight at Ali's eyes. His large face came less than three centimeters away from Ali's face, spooking him with its serious gaze. Ali took one step backward while staring at the man's eyes to determine his intention. The man stared back and stepped forward silently, then grabbed Ali's shoulders, lifted him up, and quickly kissed each of his cheeks. "You are our champion!"

The men in the crowded cell cheered and lined up to embrace Ali. Each inmate planted a kiss on each of his cheeks and said, "*Marhaba*, congrats. You're a hero."

Ali stood motionless and amazed. He wasn't expecting this reaction from the inmates.

Once they all paid their respects to their newly found hero, one inmate put his head in between the bars and shouted out a call to a guard he knew. "Ahmad *agha*, Ahmad *agha*, please take Ali *agha* to the bathroom!"

For a moment, Ali enjoyed being called *agha*, mister, for the first time. Nobody had ever called him *agha* before. He walked to the cell door looking into the dark hallway with a smile on his face. But he quickly reminded himself that the flatteries were not deserved, and he shouldn't allow it.

Soon a guard named Ahmad opened the door and asked who needed to go. Ali raised his right hand with his index finger erect like he was in a classroom.

The guard pulled him out of the cell and led him to the bathroom area. Two other inmates jumped up and asked to be allowed to go also.

"We'll be your bodyguards," one of them whispered, beaming with delight.

Ali shook his head, but secretly enjoyed the attention.

On the way, they passed through dim corridors reeking with the strong stench of mildew and urine. He heard voices of inmates arguing, chatting, and even singing. But the most eerie of all were the sounds of captive men weeping.

The stink of sewage grew stronger as they came near to the stalls. There was a small courtyard and a line of men waiting for the toilets in the corner of the yard.

"Move faster." The guard pushed him into the line.

Ali stumbled forward. The line moved slowly. After a few steps, he turned back and looked behind him into the hallway. He couldn't believe who he saw. Or who he thought he saw. He stood on his toes to see better. The light was rather diffused, perhaps it was an illusion. He rubbed his eyes and looked again. Is it really him?

He yelled at the man standing a only few meters behind him. "Seyyed, Seyyed, is that you?"

"Ali? Is that Ali Rashti?"

"Yes, Seyyed its me."

"What are you doing here?" Seyyed Hussein shouted back. A guard hit Ali with the butt of his rifle and demanded silence. The sharp pain on his skull stopped Ali's answer.

He saw Seyyed still standing in line as Ali returned to his cell. Seyyed looked much different without his turban and robe.

Ali had mixed feelings about the encounter with his friend. On one hand, he was happy to finally see a familiar face after such a long time being kept away from his friends and family. On the other hand, he was sad about seeing a friend in such an awful place. He wouldn't wish the torture of captivity in such a grotesque place on his enemies, let alone his friends.

In the cell, the other inmates circled him and demanded to hear how a fourteen-year-old boy had killed an infidel American military man.

"You are our *Rostam!*" one of them exclaimed and extended his arms toward Ali, a sign of admiration.

"No, he's Hercules. Hercules is stronger than Rostam," said another inmate.

"Shut up, Rostam is our own hero. Hercules is a foreign hero. To hell with foreigners," another one shouted and they all cheered loudly.

***

Early the next morning, two guards opened the cell door and asked Ali to step out.

"*Sarkar*, officer, where are you taking me?"

The two guards looked at each other and shook their heads.

"What? Please tell me! What is going on?" Ali begged.

The guards stayed quiet and pushed him forward. After about a hundred meters, they stopped by another cell, opened the door and pushed Ali inside.

The new cell seemed empty and, like the other one, had a window to the outside, high on the east wall. Beams of sunshine descended to the floor, illuminating dust particles in perfect shapes of geometric cones. But it was smaller than any other cell he had been in. He decided to stay by the door till his eyes got used to the darkness of the room. He put his hands behind his back and felt the door, and then took a few small steps till he felt a wall. He slid down with his back touching the wall and squatted.

He didn't notice it first, but as his eyes adjusted to the diffused lighting, he saw that he was not alone! A man was sleeping on the floor in a cradle position, facing the wall. He got up and carefully approached the man, turning him over to see his face.

"What? ...Seyyed Hussein, is that you?" He shook the sleeping man. "Mullah! Mullah!" he shook him again.

Seyyed Husain, with eyes half opened and in a groggy voice replied, "What ...what? Who is this?"

"This is Ali, Mullah. Are you all right?"

"Ali?"

"Yes, Mullah. Ali. This is Ali," He helped Seyyed Hussein to sit up.

Seyyed squeezed his eyes and glared at Ali's face for a moment. "Ali, what are you doing here?"

"They brought me to this prison a week after that miserable day! They've made a mistake. They think I killed the American. How about you? What are you doing here?"

"Oh, nothing, just a cover up, I'm sure. I'll be out soon. I'll get you out too."

"So, you've been here since that day?"

Seyyed Hussein nodded his head. He pulled his body back and leaned against the wall behind him. Ali sat on the floor next to him. The two sat quietly on the floor for a few moments without speaking. Ali contemplated what just transpired.

Not too long after, the cell door opened again and the guards threw another person into the cell. He fell on the ground head first.

"Who are you?" Seyyed Hussein asked.

The man stood up and shook the dust off his body. "Morteza!"

"*Agha* Morteza ... hmm." Seyyed Hussein nodded his head and asked, "*Agha* Morteza, who did you kill to earn the privilege of being in a cell with two killers of an American infidel?" He enunciated the end of his sentence clearly and deliberately, similar to a theatrical presentation.

The newcomer stared at Seyyed Hussein. He squinted, perhaps to see better, and then his eyes widened as he recognized him. Ali saw fury in his eyes. With a loud exhale, he jumped on Seyyed Hussein and wrapped his large hands around his neck. "Little rats like you are making life miserable for all of us!" He squeezed Seyyed Hussein's neck.

Ali didn't expect the attack on his friend. He reacted immediately and jumped on Morteza and struggled to release his grip on Seyyed Hussein's neck. "Please, *agha* Morteza, forgive him. He's a Seyyed, a direct descendant from Prophet Mohammad. We're not to harm Seyyeds. Let him go, please!"

"He said he's a killer. I'm here to end his miserable life and his sinister attitude!"

"No, no, he was joking. He's wrongly accused, just like me. We are not killers. We didn't kill any American. Let him go!"

Morteza looked at Ali, his facial features eased up, and he loosened his grip on Seyyed Hussein's neck. "What are you? Fifteen, sixteen-years-old kid?"

Ali helped Seyyed Hussein, who gasped for air, to get up. "No. Actually, I'm fourteen."

Morteza stood. His tall, strong body loomed over them. "Fourteen? How about you?" He pointed to Seyyed Hussein. "Now that I'm looking at your ugly face in the light, you look like a kid too!"

Seyyed Hussein picked up his prayer beads and pulled himself into a darker corner. With his knees in his arms he answered, "I'm not a kid. I'm a member of the *rohanion*, respected spiritual leaders."

"Shut up and answer my question, you miserable weasel!" Morteza raised his left arm to slap Seyyed Hussein's face.

He ducked and mumbled, "Seventeen."

Morteza snickered and rubbed his huge, square jaw. "They put me in a cell with a fourteen- and seventeen-year-old." He looked at both of them with a serious face and shouted, "Boys, I'm the boss here. I'm older, stronger, and as a soldier I can kill you both in under a minute with my bare hands."

"Soldier?" Ali asked.

"That's right! A Cossack soldier, not one of those ordinary, wimpy soldiers you see around."

Seyyed Hussein struggled to his feet. "Cossack soldier? You don't look that much older than us. You must be a deserter—a coward deserter who's afraid of action!"

Morteza jumped on Seyyed Hussein again and grabbed his neck. "I'm not your age, kid. I'm a nineteen-year-old Cossack soldier who will proudly break your pitiful neck."

Ali intervened again, pulled Morteza off of Seyyed, and assured him that they both would respect him and his seniority. Morteza let go of Seyyed. All three sat on the floor, exhausted.

"*Agha* Morteza, just out of curiosity, why are you here?" Ali asked, "Isn't your regiment in charge of protecting the king and fighting with the enemies of our country?"

Silence took over the cell. Morteza looked uncomfortable.

Ali continued, "I hope I wasn't out of line asking you that question. You don't need to answer it." Morteza remained silent. Ali continued, "It was rude of me. Of course, it's none of my business. My father, peace be upon him, was a Cossack too."

Morteza smiled for the first time, shook his head and looked at Ali. "Do you ever shut up, kid?"

"Sorry, sir."

"What happened to him?" Morteza asked.

"To whom? My father?"

"Yes, did he die in action?"

"No, pneumonia, a little more than a year ago."

A few moments of silence passed. Finally, Morteza spoke again.

"I disobeyed an order. When the call for the riot came, my commander ordered me and a few other Cossacks to go out and make sure the foreigners were killed. We were told that they were spies. But when I saw how the merciless crowd beat the hell out of the two bastards, I hesitated." He pointed to Seyyed. "When I saw how a weasel, like this one here, fanned the mob's fury with his words, I decided not to be part of it. I walked away. I'm no murderer."

"So, you're here for disobeying your commander?" Seyyed mumbled.

"What will happen to you?" Ali asked.

"I don't know. I may be stuck here for a few years."

"I've heard deserters get the firing squad," said Seyyed Hussein.

Morteza turned his head swiftly toward Seyyed and with his eyes wide open replied, "I didn't run away. I'm not a coward! I simply returned to my base."

Ali jumped in to divert Morteza's attention away from Seyyed. "What I don't understand is, why did your commander want the Americans dead?"

"Ali *jon*, you're so naïve," Seyyed Hussein cut in. "The two Americans were dirty Baha'i infidels who were converting our youth and poisoning their minds." His cynicism didn't help his stand with the other two. They both gave him a look that suggested they thought he was the naïve one.

Ali shook his head swiftly. "No, no, he wasn't a Baha'i. I saw Major Imbrie at the British embassy where I worked. I'm not sure if he even knew what Baha'i was. He was there to take some photographs. An English man told him about *sagha-khaneh*."

"Oh, Ali, you simple boy, I know for fact that he was a Baha'i—"

Morteza's booming voice froze Seyyed Hussein into silence. "Quiet, you filthy mullah! I've had it with you. We all hate mullahs, all the way to our general. Even Reza Khan hates them with a passion. Mullahs like you take our hard-earned money and brainwash our people, so they can stay in power." He turned his back to him and faced the door. "Reza Khan soon will end their miserable existence."

Ali remembered something. Something important.

"Wait a minute, Seyyed Hussein. You know Ibrahim *agha*, you talked to him before the riot. What did he tell you?"

"Who's Ibrahim *agha*? I don't know him." Seyyed Hussein turned his face away and looked up at the window.

"Yes, of course you know him," Ali insisted. "He paid you right before the Baha'i doctor's riot and then he paid a man on a bicycle. On the day that the American was killed, I saw Ibrahim again, right before the same man on the bicycle started shouting. I saw that with my own eyes."

Morteza squinted at Seyyed Hussein and moved toward him, grunting.

Seyyed Hussein inched away from Morteza. "Oh, *that* Ibrahim *agha*. Yes, he's the one who said the Americans were dirty Baha'i infidels and were planning to poison our beloved *sagha-khaneh's* holy water."

Morteza didn't waste another moment. He jumped on Seyyed Hussein again and this time he punched his face. "You lying scum!"

Ali didn't stop Morteza this time. Seyyed deserved it.

"All right! Stop! I will tell you what he said. Please, stop beating me!" Seyyed Hussein begged.

Morteza backed off.

"Ibrahim *agha* said that the American was a Baha'i sympathizer and that some of his friends wanted to scare him a little. He paid me a little bit of money to rally people."

Morteza jerked his tight fist near Seyyed Hussein's face.

Seyyed Hussein stooped, raised his hands to cover his face, and said, "I swear to God, that was the truth! Please don't punch me again! Please!" He started to weep.

Ali tapped Morteza's back and gestured for him to go to the corner with him. "You know, I remember Ibrahim talked to an Englishman in the *ghahve-khaneh.* The same Englishman was at the embassy's banquet. I heard them talking about the *sagha-khaneh.* This was the same Englishman who told the American about *sagha-khaneh.*"

Morteza laughed out loud and pointed his index finger to Seyyed Hussein who lay on the floor across the cell. "You were fooled, man."

"What do you mean? I'm nobody's fool!" cried Seyyed Hussein.

Morteza stood up and leaned against a wall. "We Cossacks hate mullahs, and if it was up to our commander, he would kill them all like cockroaches. But Reza Khan is a politician now, so he has to play games. You are a sacrificing pawn in this chess game."

"I'm nobody's pawn. I got paid well!" Seyyed Hussein admitted.

"Shut up, you miserable cockroach," Morteza persisted, "you're just a kid, what do you know? They played you well. Reza Khan tried to work with the clerics, but those fools didn't play with him. He needed a reason to shut you hoodwinkers down. What better reason than killing a high-ranking diplomat, and not just any ordinary diplomat, but an American diplomat." He couldn't stop himself anymore. "As soon as the news broke, Reza Khan declared martial law, arrested a whole bunch of mullahs, and shut down all newspapers sympathetic to mullahs. Why do you think you're in this jail? What is your sentence? Do you even know? Let me guess, life?" A fleck of foam appeared on Morteza's thick lower lip.

Seyyed Hussein silently nodded. His face turned white and he breathed heavily, fear written all over his face.

Ali looked at Seyyed Hussein, feeling horrible about their fate but still wanting to do the right thing--to give hope to his old friend. "But Ibrahim *agha* is very influential. I'm sure that he'll get Seyyed Hussein out!"

A thick layer of silence permeated the atmosphere of the cell. He felt Seyyed Hussein shiver when he put his arms around him.

25

THE HOPE

Sunday, September 7, 1924

MALCOLM FOUND himself staring at Rose's front door, located not far from the embassy compound. He wondered about the wisdom of what he was about to do. He took a quick breath, lifted the black iron ring of the door knocker, and let it drop against its back plate. The loud clanking of the heavy metal knocker echoed somewhere beyond.

A brunette woman about Rose's age opened the door. Grinning, she said, "You must be Mr. Malcolm."

"Yes, indeed. James Malcolm, at your service," he replied and lifted his hat.

"Good afternoon. I'm Belinda, Rose's flat mate. Come in, please." She opened the door for him to enter. "Would you care for a cup of tea?"

Rose rushed down the stairs. "No need, we are leaving. But before we leave, which one of these do you think I should wear?" Rose held out two *chadors* in her hands. One was pitch black and shiny, and the other was a white one, with many little pink rose imprints.

"What are those?" Belinda exclaimed.

Rose gazed at herself in the mirror on the wall of the entry room. She opened the black *chador* and placed it gently over the top of her head. With a motion of her wrists, she folded the top part over her forehead, slid her hands around her face, and pulled the mate-rial tight under her chin. "There, now if I can only hold it this tight for a few minutes." The rest of the *chador* material draped over her shoulders and covered her entire slender body.

"Oh, my lord!" Belinda exclaimed, "These are the covers women here wear! What do they call it?"

"*Chador,*" Rose answered.

"You just look like a typical Persian peasant woman." Belinda quipped. "Why do you do this to yourself? Covering your lovely hair with this hideous piece of cloth!"

Intrigued by Rose's question, Malcolm smiled and said, "I like the white one with the little rose imprints."

"Good, that's my favorite one too. That settles it. I'm ready!" Rose responded. She placed the black one on the hall table, picked up a bag that was resting there, and carried the white *chador* with her outside where an embassy car waited at the curb.

Once they arrived at the prison, but before getting out of the car, Rose put on the white chador so it covered all her hair and her forehead. No one could tell she was British if she didn't look up or utter a word.

Malcolm accompanied Rose to the warden's office. He spoke in Farsi with the warden and handed him a piece of paper. The warden stood at attention at the sight of the document. He gave an order to his assistant and asked Malcolm and Rose to follow him.

They traveled through hallways and several check points. Once they arrived at the visiting room, a guard opened the door. The room was poorly lit. It had only one small window. The assistant ordered the guards to set up two chairs in the center of the room facing each other and another chair on the side by the door for Malcolm. Guards also brought a few kerosene lamps and placed one near each sitting area and two by the other door. Rose gracefully approached one of the chairs in the center of the room and sat. The entire time Rose had a firm grip on her *chador* under her chin to assure the material didn't slip. Under no circumstance was her blond hair to be revealed. Malcolm sat on his chair and a guard stood inside the room by the door.

A few minutes later, the other door slowly opened with a loud squeak. From the dark of the hallway, Ali appeared, tired and filthy. His faced brightened when he saw his visitor, and he lurched forward toward Rose. His guard, noticing Ali's sudden burst of energy, stuck out his booted foot and tripped him. Ali went down hard, slid on the floor, and hit the second chair. His face stopped just short of Rose's feet.

Rose stood, obviously shocked by the rough treatment, and sighed loudly. But she never let loose of her grip on her *chador*. The guards in the room sported loud laughter at Ali's expense.

Ali got up quickly, straightened the chair, and sat on it with a big smile on his face. "Rose!" he whispered.

"Shh. I'm Miriam, your sister!" Rose whispered back.

His guards shouted, "No whispering! Speak normally or I'll take you back to your cell!"

"*Salahm*, Miriam *jon*," Ali said out loud in Farsi, turned back and glanced at the guards in the room.

Malcolm whispered a few words in Farsi into the ear of the warden's assistant. The assistant then spoke loud and clear so all the guards could hear. "Guards, leave the room. Guard the door from the other side." The guards obeyed and left the room. He also left the room. Malcolm had positioned himself in the shadow. He didn't want Ali to recognize him, at least not yet.

"Very well, my dear!" Rose used her quiet voice and continued, "How are you holding up?"

Malcolm's sharp ears could hear their conversation clearly from his seat in the corner.

"*Alham-dolelah*, praise God, I am good."

"I'm diligently working to get you out Ali, talking to many people and I am very hopeful."

"Rose! Rose! Be very careful!" Ali whispered. He looked over his shoulder and said, "They put a Cossack soldier in my jail. He say government doing this. I not know why. But you must be very careful. Many bad people, many!"

Rose extended her hands and held Ali's hands. For an instant like a reflex, Ali tried to pull his hand away, but Rose held them tight. "I know. It's very complicated. Rest assured, I've asked a few friends in the embassy to help."

Ali stopped resisting and let his hands be held by Rose.

"How is my mother? Good? How are my brothers and sisters? You heard?"

Rose gently let his hand free. "I have asked your cousin to regularly check on them and gave him some money for their expenses. Last week, I asked about them, and he said they are fine. Your brother is now working for the local baker."

Ali dropped his head down and looked at the ground. Rose extended her hand, pulled up Ali's chin and looked at his tearful eyes. "You miss them terribly, don't you?"

Ali nodded, looked down on the floor again and wiped his tears.

Malcolm adjusted his body on the chair, it creaked. Ali looked up toward the sound. Malcolm's position had changed, and his face was not in the shadow any more.

Ali's eyes stopped at Malcolm. He turned away quickly and dropped his head.

"Ali, what is happening? You suddenly turned white. Are you all right?" Rose asked.

Ali whispered something very quietly in Roses' ear. Rose cut him off and said, "Are you certain?"

Ali vigorously shook his head up and down in agreement. "Yes, yes, he dangerous. Rose, be careful—"

"I know, Ali." Rose interrupted him again. "His name is James Malcolm, and he is helping me to get you out of here! Relax." She moved her head closer to Ali and in a soft voice continued, "I suspected him of being involved with all this. Now you confirmed it. So, he is actually the one in the tea house." She paused for a moment and continued, "Rest easy. It's all under control. I've already made a deal with him."

Ali didn't take his eyes off Malcolm. "What deal? Do not trust him! He no good. He *Sheitan!*"

Malcolm smirked. He figured that Ali had recognized him.

"Satan, we call it Satan or devil. Yes, I understand, he is a mysterious man, but he seems very influential and we need his help to get you out of here."

"Rose, do not trust him!"

"I hear you, Ali. But you mustn't worry. Trust me, I know what I'm doing." Rose gathered the *chador* around her chin and smiled. "Let's change the subject. Did you enjoy the cookies I sent you last week?"

"Cookies? No, nobody gave me cookies."

"What? That is strange! I sent them to you through your cousin Majid. He said he brought the bag here. They didn't let him visit you but assured him that you'd receive the cookies!"

Ali shook his head. "Maybe guards took for themselves."

"Oh well, here." She reached under her *chador* and pulled out a small package from her bag. "Take this. It's a cake I made for you."

Ali grabbed it, removed the wrapping and took a big bite right there. It had been a long time since Ali had a decent meal.

Rose chuckled. "You don't have to devour it right now. Gosh! Leave some for later."

"I am very very hungry. If I don't eat now, guards take it."

"All right, enjoy it then." Rose replied, watching Ali's every move with concern etched across her face.

A guard opened the door and yelled, "Time is up. Get up, Ali."

Rose leaned forward. "Ali, I'm working to get you out. Soon, I shall free you. Keep the faith, keep the hope, stay strong!"

Ali nodded in agreement. *"Khodahfez*, good-bye, Rose."

Rose stood and watched as Ali disappeared into the dark hallways. Malcolm heard her snivel but was grateful she kept her composure. The visit was a risk—a significant risk. But in his judgment, it was necessary to keep Rose amicable and nearby. As for Ali, he was just a street rat to him. Not worth a thought.

The ride home from the prison was quiet. Rose remained silent. Every so often, Malcolm could hear her sniffling.

After dropping Rose off at her home, Malcolm decided a walk would be an effective way to shake off the filth of the prison. He dismissed the driver and took a longer path to the British embassy that would take him past the Russian embassy. Although he wasn't in disguise, he enjoyed checking in on the Russians every chance he could get. The large compound of the Russian embassy was on a busy street, and he could easily hide in the hustle and bustle if needed.

The sidewalk was crowded with people, bicycles, and many street vendors peddling their goods. As he passed by the giant, wrought-iron main gate, he noticed a short, plump man with a bald head sneaking out onto the street from one of the smaller side gates. He only saw that man for a fraction of a moment, but he felt that he recognized him.

Malcolm decided to follow. He picked up his pace to get closer to the man. It was important to identify him. Shortly after, a passerby bumped into the man hard enough to turn him sideways so Malcolm could see his face.

Malcolm stopped in his tracks. It was Ibrahim.

He stood still in the busy street, a few people jostling him as they passed by. One of them was a Cheka agent that Malcolm knew. He had a hunch that the Cheka agent was actually following Ibrahim too. So Ibrahim had left the Russian embassy and a

Russian agent followed him. This was becoming even more intriguing for Malcolm.

He followed both men at a safe distance. After two blocks, Ibrahim went inside a local grocery store. The man tailing Ibrahim went inside as well. Malcolm slowly approached the window of the store. He peeked in and saw Ibrahim putting some cherries into a bag. A worker was calling out about the high quality of the grapes they had that day and was encouraging the customers to buy them before they ran out. There were heaps of grapes, cherries, and sour cherries on display. The store was busy, and the owner stood behind the scales weighing customer purchases and collecting money.

Malcolm saw Ibrahim take an envelope from his side pocket and put it in his bag of cherries. A well-dressed Persian man approached the cherry pile. Ibrahim placed the bag on top of the pile, made a sharp turn to his left, and slowly moved toward a pile of apples. The man picked up the bag and added more cherries into the bag as if it was his bag. Turning away, the man pulled the envelope from the bag and put it in his side pocket, and went in the opposite direction of Ibrahim, straight to the front of the store to pay for the cherries.

Ibrahim selected some lettuce and greens, paid for them, and was coming out of the store. Malcolm didn't want to be seen by Ibrahim, so he jumped into the butcher shop next door. The smell of fresh cut meat was strong and there were more flies in there than outside. Malcolm watched the grocery store's only entrance from inside of the butcher shop.

"*Agha*, what kind of meat do you want today?" The thunderous voice of the butcher brought Malcolm's attention to inside the shop, where a large man with a thick, bushy mustache, and a cleaver in hand, stared at him, expecting an answer.

Malcolm had to think quickly. He didn't need any meat. "One kilo stew lamb, please."

The butcher acknowledged the order and started preparing it

for him. That gave Malcolm a moment to look outside the window again. To his surprise, across the street stood another man he knew well. Boris!

Boris waited till the agent who followed Ibrahim came out of the shop, gave an inconspicuous and quick nod to Boris, and disappeared. Ibrahim, unaware of all that, stepped out of the shop with his bag of greens in his arms. Boris put some fingers from his right hand in his mouth and gave a short but rather loud whistle. Ibrahim looked up. Boris jerked his head sideways and walked. Ibrahim followed Boris.

Malcolm tossed some coins onto the counter—more than enough to pay for the meat, and dashed out the door to follow them. After taking only a few steps, he saw Boris turn into a narrow alley. Ibrahim followed.

A street vendor was selling fresh walnuts by the entrance of the alley. On a large round metal tray sitting on top of a wooden box he had meticulously arranged the whole, shelled walnuts in multiple small pyramids. Malcolm stopped by the vender and ordered a hundred grams of the nuts as he watched the two men. From where he was, Malcolm had a perfect view of the alley. Boris and Ibrahim were talking near the other end of it. Boris nodded and put his right arm around Ibrahim's shoulder, slipping him an envelope with his left hand. Ibrahim nodded his head, took the envelope, and put it in his pocket. The two men departed out the back of the alley, never realizing they were being watched.

26

THE RUSSIAN SPY

Monday, September 8, 1924

QUESTIONS WERE PILING up in Malcolm's head. What exactly was Ibrahim doing in the Russian embassy? Was he gathering intelligence, or had he truly turned? Who actually ordered the killing of Major Imbrie? He had to find out. Everything depended on knowing the truth. His career, his standing in his profession, even his life perhaps. This was his project.

He was running out of time. He needed answers soon. Rumors of England's involvement in this fiasco were getting strong. It was time to invoke the deep sleeper protocol.

From his closet, he took out a tin box with pastel colors and faded images of flowers. The box contained several keys of assorted sizes with different labels. He fondled a key labeled 126 S for a moment, hesitating, contemplating if it was prudent. He had to be certain. Then, with a burst of decisiveness, he yanked the key from its resting place and put it in his pocket.

After dressing in his disguise as an ordinary Persian man, he headed for Shahriar Street, not too far from the Russian embassy. Once out on the street, he walked briskly. The air was cool on that late afternoon, fall was approaching Tehran fast. Shop keepers and street venders were aggressively pitching their last sales calls to the pedestrians rushing home before dark. About thirty minutes later, Malcolm stopped in front of building number 126. He removed the key from his pocket, gave the door a good shove after turning the key in the lock, and opened the door.

The building 126 on Shahriar Street, a yellow, two-story brick building, was one of several safe houses in Tehran for British intelligence operators. The house was minimally furnished and vacant. Once the darkness of the night spread through the city, he turned on two gas lamps, went to the second floor, and placed one lamp in front of the third window facing the street. He picked a book and sat on an armchair away from the window, placed the second lamp on a table next to the chair, and read the book for two hours. Then, he turned off the lamps and left. He repeated the process three nights in a row at the exact same time.

On the fourth night, again disguised, Malcolm went to a mosque in Sadi Street. In the mosque, he proceeded as a typical Muslim worshipper. The man on top of the east minaret was loudly reciting *azan*, the call for prayers. Several men were washing at the large round pond in the center of the mosque's courtyard. Malcolm approached the pond, crouched by the edge facing the pond and started the typical process of washing before prayers, *vuzoo*. He washed his hands, cupped his right hand and threw water on his face three times, cupped his right hand again and poured water on his left elbow and washed from the elbow down. He repeated the same for his right hand, and then put three fingers on top of his head and slid them down to his forehead.

He took note of his surroundings, scanning the washing area for any possible tail, or other spooks. In his world of shadows, operators, spies and informers could be found in any setting, including mosques. However, any foreign spook had to be well trained in local customs and vernaculars in order to fit in and act naturally. That day, the local informers were more of a threat to him, and what he was about to do, than any foreign ones.

More men arrived and started their washing for prayers, so he couldn't skip the last part of the ritual. He took off his shoes and socks, placed his soaked fingers on his right foot, slid them from toes up to his ankle, and repeated it for his left foot.

Next was prayers. He put his socks in his pants pocket and proceeded to the mosque's main hall where he took his shoes off, paired them neatly, and placed them in the corner next to many other pairs of shoes before he entered.

The large hall had a tall ceiling decorated with blue and green tiles. Many colorful Persian rugs covered the floor. It was divided in two by a wall of thick, mahogany-brown cloth separating the men's section from the women's. An abundance of rosewater scent effectively minimized the pungency of body odors.

Malcolm knew exactly where to go, the third pillar on the left. Fortunately, nobody was sitting there. He sat on the floor and leaned his back on the pillar. Mass prayers hadn't started yet, so he took a set of prayer beads made of wood from his coat pocket and started counting them, just as a Muslim would do.

He wasn't there for too long when a Persian peasant sat next to him. The peasant greeted him and started praying with his own beads.

"Does this mosque have mice?" the peasant asked Malcolm.

That was it, the secret phrase.

Malcolm scanned the area. It was a perfect time. There were not too many people in the mosque. He turned and looked at the man. "I don't know. I've only seen cockroaches," he replied with the correct answer.

He recognized the man. Beyond the well-applied disguise, he was agent Henry Shaw. They served together in the Great War for a brief time, until Malcolm was captured by the Germans. A few years later, their paths crossed again in early 1918, in Petrograd in

Russia, and then in Moscow, where they both worked undercover, carrying on clandestine operations. Malcolm reported to Commander Cromie and assisted him in destroying the Royal Navy submarine flotilla at Helsingfors before it fell under German control. Shaw joined Cheka and worked undercover with another agent, Sidney Reilly. Reilly was an ace of an agent, well connected and effective in every mission to which he was assigned. Shaw stayed with Cheka all these years, and he was in deep undercover as a member of the Russian diplomatic and security team in the Russian embassy in Tehran.

"What is the occasion?" Shaw asked in Farsi to avoid any suspicions.

"Did Imbrie's kill order come from the Russians?" Malcolm asked in Farsi in a quiet tone.

"I don't know," Shaw whispered

"If it did, I need to know the names. Or at least, the name of the lowest ranking person in the know."

"I'll find out. But Aliev is back on the scene. He is in Mashhad under an alias, Asef-e-Bakoie."

Malcom continued with his prayers in Arabic, "*Astagh-firullah*," he repeated three times.

"Monitor him closely. Watch for my signal and meet in the second place," Shaw said in Arabic, pretending that he was quoting verses from the Quran. Malcolm guessed he was hedging his bets on the fact that most Persians in that mosque did not know Arabic and had only memorized the Quran's verses in Arabic. Therefore, to them any Arabic sentences spoken in the mosque must be verses of the holy book Quran or some prayers.

"*Allah-o-akbar*," Malcolm said, loud enough for people around him to hear, and rubbed his face with his hands, as a typical Muslim would do when finishing a prayer. After that, he stood up and left the hall as the men gathered to stand shoulder to shoulder next to each other for the mass prayers.

For the next two days, Malcolm walked by the same mosque.

On the third day, the words "Ya Ali" were written with green chalk on the east wall of the mosque. That was the cue.

The next afternoon at six p.m., Malcolm walked into a fresh produce store in Monirieh street, several kilometers away from the British and Russian embassies. Again, disguised as a Persian man, he picked up a bag and went to the grape pile. Within moments, another Persian man appeared next to him and said, "These ruby grapes are fantastic this year. Have you tried them?" Malcolm looked at the man. It was Shaw.

"No, are they any good?"

"The answer is yes. But there were others," said Shaw and moved toward a pile of apples. Malcolm followed him and whispered, "What do you mean by *others*? Who else?"

Shaw examined an apple but didn't take it. He moved back to the grape section. Malcolm went the opposite direction and picked a bunch of green onions and walked back to the grape section where Shaw was adding more grapes to his bag.

Shaw said, "We don't know yet." and with his eyes indicated his bag. He left his bag on the pile of grapes. Malcolm put his bag next to Shaw's, picked up two more grape clusters, and added them to Shaw's bag. He took the bag to the shopkeeper for payment.

Outside the store, he found a shaded place next to a *jube* and sat down to eat the grapes. He searched the bag discreetly. At the bottom of the bag he found a piece of paper with one name written Kerensky.

He knew Kerensky. Malcolm tore the paper to pieces and threw them in the *jube's* running water. Kerensky was a capable Cheka agent and second in command, reporting to Boris.

If he was the lowest rank in the know, someone else must have carried out the plan. Someone outside of the Russian embassy. Someone hard to trace. But who?

The next day, early morning, Malcolm took an unmarked car with a large trunk from the embassy lot and parked it a few blocks from the Russian embassy. Disguised as an old beggar, he camped out across from the Russian embassy on the corner of the side-walk. Dressed in torn pants, a wig of long, dirty grey hair, a money pan and a cane, people passing by took pity on him and dropped a coin or two in his pan. Donkeys carrying loads, people on bicycles, street venders pushing produce carts, and many pedestrians made up the traffic on the sidewalk where he sat watching the move-ments in and out of the embassy. In mid-morning, Kerensky walked out of the embassy's main gate. Malcolm sat up and followed him with his eyes. Kerensky wasn't alone. Two other people were with him. They returned an hour and a half later.

Malcolm was doing well as a beggar—making a decent day's wage. He had to empty his money dish a few times. Three times he had to shoo off a few obnoxious kids with his cane who wanted to steal his earnings.

It was late afternoon when Kerensky finally walked out of the embassy alone. Immediately, Malcolm got up and followed him. He anticipated Kerensky's path, used a short cut, and got ahead of him. He signaled a kid nearby, enticed the kid with a handsome reward, handed him a couple of raw eggs and tomatoes and sent him to intercept Kerensky.

The kid, about twelve years of age, excited about his mission, ran toward Kerensky.

"Dirty Russian. Death to Bolsheviks. Death to Bolsheviks," the kid shouted and threw the raw eggs and tomatoes at him.

The eggs and tomatoes found their targets easily, and within moments Kerensky's head and body were covered with eggs and tomato stains. The provocation worked, and he chased the kid. Malcolm was waiting for him on the corner of the predesignated alley. The moment Kerensky arrived, Malcolm, who was hiding in a corner shadow, hit him in the head with a club. Kerensky went down fast and lay unconscious on the ground.

Malcolm quickly covered Kerensky's head and shoulders with a gunny sack and used another one for the rest of his body. Fortu-nately, Kerensky was a small man. Malcolm threw the unconscious body over his shoulder and briskly carried him to the embassy car, which he had parked a block away.

He opened the trunk, which he had lined with a few layers of sheeting, and dumped Kerensky inside it. He removed the gunny sacks and tied up his hands and legs and gagged his mouth with a piece of cloth. Malcolm then drove the car to a secluded area in the outskirts of south Teheran.

He sat in the car and waited. When he heard kicks and motion in the trunk, he drove the car in circles for about fifteen minutes. He purposely drove over bumps and made many sharp turns to make Kerensky more uncomfortable.

He stopped the car, put a mask on his face, got out of the car and opened the trunk. The pungent odor of vomit escaped the moment it opened. Malcolm took the gag off of Kerensky's mouth. He coughed out the rest of his vomit.

"Who carried out the kill order for Imbrie?" Malcolm asked in Farsi. He reckoned it would be impossible for Kerensky to detect his national origin.

"I'm a Russian diplomat. You can't do this to me!" Kerensky exclaimed in Russian.

Malcolm yelled back, "Say it in Farsi!" even though he understood what Kerensky said.

"No Farsi," Kerensky replied in broken Farsi.

Malcolm yelled back, "*Almani? Sprichst du Deutsch?*"

Kerensky nodded. Malcolm repeated his question in German. Kerensky repeated his original response in German.

Malcolm shut the trunk lid without any more words and calmly returned to his seat behind the wheel. He drove in circles for another twenty minutes.

Again, he stopped the car, kept the engine running, opened the trunk and repeated his question.

"Who carried out the kill order for Imbrie?" Malcolm asked in German.

Kerensky moved his head rapidly back and forth and with his

eyes fluttering fast, then shouted in perfect German, "Go to hell!"

Malcolm shut the trunk again without speaking. He got back in the car and drove it to a garage he had secured earlier, located not far from his flat. He locked the dark garage and left Kerensky there, crumpled and bound inside the trunk.

The next day after his breakfast, Malcolm retrieved the car from the garage and drove to the slums in south Tehran. On his way, he stopped by a street vendor and bought a skewer of *kabab*, barbecued meet, and flat bread. When he arrived at a secluded location he stopped the car, put on his mask, and opened the trunk. The stench of vomit, urine and other foul odors assaulted Malcolm's nose like a rogue wave. Kerensky appeared weak and half-conscious. His body fidgeted a bit, and he tried to open his eyes despite the brightness of the daylight.

Malcolm removed the damp, sticky gag from Kerensky's mouth. "Who carried out the kill order for Imbrie?" Malcolm asked.

Kerensky squeezed his eyes and tried to look at Malcolm. "I don't know. Get me out of here."

"What's the matter? Hunger eat away your memory?" He waved the sandwich he made with the *kabab* and the bread around Kerensky's nose. Malcolm knew that the aroma of kabab for someone who hadn't eaten for eighteen hours would be unbearable. Kerensky's nose went active, smelling the sandwich in short bursts of inhales, just like a hungry cat. His neck was extended and as Malcolm moved the sandwich in small circles near his face, his nose followed it. Then Malcolm took it away.

"Give me the name and you can have the food."

Kerensky released his neck muscles and dropped his head to the floor of the trunk. Hopeless of getting any bite of that delicious smelling sandwich he mumbled, "I don't know."

Malcolm brought a water canister and swung it over his face. "How about water? Hmm? Are you thirsty?" He spilled one drop on Kerensky's cheek.

The moment Kerensky felt the drop on his cheek, he moved his face rapidly toward the direction of the drop, hoping to catch the next few drops. But Malcolm stopped pouring from the canister and asked again, "The name?"

Kerensky stretched his tongue vigorously on his cheek trying to catch that one drop of water. His efforts were in vain.

"Give me the name and you shall receive the food and the water. And I'll let you go."

Kerensky shook his head. "I don't know it." This came out in Russian. Kerensky was apparently too delirious to speak in German any longer.

Malcolm shut the trunk, sat in the car behind the wheel and drove in circles again for about twenty minutes. He stopped the car and opened the trunk. Kerensky was unconscious. It was a sweltering day. It was even hotter inside the trunk. Malcolm opened the lid on the water canister and poured water on Kerensky's eyes and his nose. He reacted to the water and moved.

"Just imagine how it would feel if you had that water in your mouth. What is the name of the person who carried out the kill order for Imbrie?" Malcolm spoke deliberately and clearly.

He was about to shut the trunk again when he heard a weak mumbling from Kerensky. He couldn't fully understand it. Despite the horrific odor of body fluids, he bent over and moved his head closer to Kerensky's mouth and said, "I can't hear you."

A weak and shaky voice out of Kerensky uttered, "Reilly"

"Who?"

"Sidney Reilly." He coughed.

Malcolm shut the trunk, took off his mask and leaned on the car.

Was he toying with him? If Reilly, the British master spy, was in the country, Malcolm would expect to be notified.

He put his mask on and opened the trunk again. "Are you playing with me, you piece of dirt? You want more pain? You want to suffocate in your own vomit? Be my guest." He shut the trunk, got in the car and drove in circles for another fifteen minutes. Then he stopped the car, replaced his mask and opened the trunk.

"Who did it for you?"

Kerensky was coughing hard, blood was dripping from his mouth. "Ibrahim." He mumbled with a weak and shaky voice.

"Ibrahim? Did you say Ibrahim?"

Kerensky nodded. "A Persian named Ibrahim. He got paid well," he said in Russian.

Malcolm stood up and shut the trunk. Kerensky made some attempt at shouting in protest, but it was very weak.

"So, it's true. That lousy bastard Ibrahim played us all," he mumbled.

Malcolm took a few minutes to collect his thoughts. He grabbed a knife and his black jack, then opened the trunk and hit Kerensky in the head with the blackjack. He lifted his motionless body out of the trunk and dumped him on the ground. After cutting the ties on his hands and legs, he threw the food and the water canister at him and drove away.

He glanced at Kerensky one more time in his rearview mirror. The man lay motionless in the fetal position, blood pooling under his face.

27

THE BATHHOUSE

Tuesday, September 16, 1924

MALCOLM CHANGED into his peasant disguise later that afternoon. The baggy brown pants, long white shirt, and dark green cloth that served as a belt had become like a second skin to him. He liked the feeling of invisibility and anonymity. Finally, he put on an old, worn-out coat and black felt hat, and left his apartment. Taking the back alleys that had no names, he began his walk to the Fatahie Bathhouse, where he had arranged a meeting with Ibrahim.

Even the dusty back alleys were trafficked frequently by street venders pushing their cart or pulling their donkeys and calling out or singing to announce their trades. During the summer, more than any other seasons, children played on the streets near their houses, adding more noise and busyness to the backstreets. Although in general Malcolm was irritated by the sights, sounds, and smells of the Persian culture, he knew he would learn more about them, and also look less conspicuous, if he traveled through residential streets. And the more he learned about them, the better he could manipulate the people.

Every few minutes he stopped to tie his shoelaces or adjust his coat, or some other excuse to look behind him to see if he was being followed. Two days prior he had discovered two Russian tails on him, and that was a bit disconcerting. Was he a suspect in the Kerensky incident?

He knew Cheka's protocols fairly well. As a matter of fact, he was there when Cheka was born in December 1917. Its full name was All Russian Extraordinary Commission for Combating Counter-revolution and Sabotage. The name was so long that the Bolsheviks had to abbreviate it twice, once to *chrezvychaynaya kommissiya,* extraordinary commission, and then to Cheka.

His espionage assignment in Russia had been one of his favorites. Despite the extreme winter cold, excessive danger, and intensely explosive political situation, he felt a special fondness for the time he spent there. His talent in linguistics had helped him to master the Russian language, taught to him by Russian inmates when he was in German prison during the Great War. His fluency in Russian and German primed him for the assignment in Russia. The British government was skeptical of the new Bolshevik government in Russia. Trotsky was all about exporting the proletarian revolution, and the West didn't like it.

Malcolm's goal had been to infiltrate Cheka, along with his friend Henry and the legendary master spy, Sidney Reilly. Malcolm was assigned to Commander Cromie, the chief of British intelligence operations in northern Russia for the British Naval Intelligence Division in Petrograd.

Malcolm revered his memories with Commander Cromie and had enjoyed his missions under him as they were diverse, dangerous, and exciting. He felt a great remorse that he hadn't been at the side of his commander, defending the British embassy the night of Cheka's attack. Commander Cromie lost his life that night.

Malcolm was deep in his thoughts when something struck his

leg. Looking down, he saw a wood dowel the size of his hand and as thick as his thumb, nicely filed. He picked it up and scanned the area. Thirty meters away a few boys stood in a group, pointing to him and laughing.

A moment later a young boy ran up to him. *"Agha,* that's our wood. Give it back to me."

"What are you kids doing?" he asked in Farsi.

"We are playing *alak-do-lak.*"

"Alak-do-lak? How do you play it?"

The boy stepped back from him. "You don't know how to play *alak-do-lak?*"

"Are you going to answer me, or do I take the stick away with me?"

"No, no I will tell you." The boy jumped up and down, his face twisted in horror at the prospect of losing his stick. "In *alak-do-lak,* first we place the *dolak,* which is what you have in your hand, on two bricks lying on the ground parallel to each other." He went to the ground and set two rocks next to each other to demonstrate. "Then we take a wooden bat, called an *alak,* and hold it in between the *dolak* and the ground. The *alak* is then thrust upward so that the *dolak,* the dowel, goes flying and the player then tries to hit it before it reaches the ground. When he hits it, then the people of the rival team will try to catch it. If they do—"

"That's enough," Malcolm interrupted, suddenly irritated. It was just another silly bat-and-ball game like baseball or cricket, except instead of a ball they used a wooden peg.

"Why were you and your friends laughing at me?"

"No, *agha,* we weren't laughing at you. I swear. We were just happy to see our stick flew so far! Can I have my stick back now?"

Malcolm scanned the area again and noticed a dog sitting in a small shaded area, hiding from the children and the hot afternoon sun. An image of George, his step-father, hugging and kissing his dog flashed in his mind. Feelings of disgust came over him. He always thought George cared for that mutt more than he did his mother. The dog was about fifteen meters away. Without hesitation, he threw the stick with all his strength at the dog, hitting it on the head. The dog yelped and ran away. He hated dogs.

A burst of laughter exploded among the kids. A few of them chased the dog farther and threw some rocks at the mangy cur. Malcolm laughed, pleased and impressed by his accuracy in throwing a piece of wood, and his understanding of the local mentality.

Malcolm continued his walk. The bathhouse entry was located on a main street. When he arrived at the bathhouse, but before he entered, he checked again to see if he was followed. The street was not as busy as usual, but the old woman with a black *chador* shuffling away from the corner couldn't possibly be a tail.

He paid his entrance fee and proceeded to the undressing area, a few steps below the entrance corridor. It was a large vaulted room lined with wooden benches and covered with blue and yellow tiles painted with flowers and birds. Some of the benches were covered with Persian carpets. In the center, there was a small decorative pond inlaid with blue tiles. The air was humid, warm, and the smell of tobacco with a hint of rose water was noticeable.

Malcolm had been to this bathhouse before. He undressed and put on a maroon colored *lowng*, a loincloth, covering him from the waist to the knees. He saw Ibrahim busy drinking hot tea and smoking *ghalyan* in the far corner of the room near the entrance to the second hall. He walked slowly toward Ibrahim. The air in that part of the room was even more humid and heavy with the fragrance of tobacco and the pungent odor of the soap they used in the second hall, the wash hall.

"I see you don't waste any time getting started on your beloved *ghalyan*," Malcolm said with a smile as he sat next to Ibrahim.

"Oh yes, and let me order a hot tea for you." Ibrahim immediately shouted the order to a bath house worker nearby.

Malcolm jumped right to the business at hand. "The Russians are becoming a nuisance."

"How so?"

"They are becoming bolder, fueling the underground communist parties, sabotaging and getting dirty with politics. What do you have for me on them?" Malcolm asked.

The hot tea arrived. Malcolm, like Persians, put a sugar cube in his mouth before drinking his bitter, hot tea.

Ibrahim waited for the worker to leave. Wiping sweat off his forehead, he replied, "Nothing. I haven't heard anything in particular."

Malcolm kept his cool. He had dealt with operatives like Ibrahim before. It was time to be more direct. "Who gave the kill order to the Cossack soldiers?"

Ibrahim shrugged. "The Cossack base is near that place. It's natural for them to show up. Perhaps the soldiers were sucked into the drama like a whirlpool, and rage took over." He paused and smoked his *ghalyan,* exhaled and continued. "Especially with the fiery rhetoric of the young mullah who was there that day. I think he is in jail now."

"Well, what you just said is the cover. I'm asking what did *you* do?"

Ibrahim chuckled, his big belly moving up and down rapidly. "You paid me and asked me to make it real. I paid the Cossack commander and asked him to send a few of them there for show."

Malcolm wasn't amused. "But they were not there for show. They actually participated. I saw the saber cuts on Imbrie. They were deliberate. How did it happen? The kill wasn't on the menu." Malcolm scanned the area, looking for signs of other operatives or any overly curious onlookers or eavesdroppers to their conversation.

Ibrahim leaned closer to Malcolm and whispered, "Cossacks' loyalty is to Reza Khan first, and money second. I thought the plan was for you to inform the PM about the riot in advance. I assumed you used your usual contacts." Ibrahim took a deep draw on his *ghalyan,* which was followed by a loud gurgle sound. "Maybe he changed the order for a reason, or perhaps, bypassed the chain of command and gave the soldiers a direct order," Ibrahim continued.

"You are not a fool, Ibrahim. You know Cossacks are still influenced by Russians. Besides, it wouldn't serve Reza Khan well to have an American killed on the streets. Especially now, more than ever, he needed the loan that was promised to him by the Americans."

"Yes, I know Cossacks were established by Russians, but General Ironside, your countryman, took over a few years ago. I know for a fact that he handpicked Colonel Reza Khan to organize a *coup d'état* and take over Tehran—just two-and-one-half years ago. Don't worry. The Cossacks follow British orders now."

Malcolm looked deeply into Ibrahim's black eyes. They seemed dilated—but with what? Fear, drugs, or?

Ibrahim turned his face away. "It's our turn. Let's go get washed." Ibrahim stood.

Malcolm remained in his seat, looked up at Ibrahim and asked, "You never told me about what you found out at the party at Boris's house. Did you identify any new intelligence officers? Any new info?"

"No. You were there yourself. You know those Bolsheviks, they are pretty tight lipped," Ibrahim replied. "There were only a bunch of drunk, wild Russians."

Malcolm stood up. "You knew the Russians had a big reward for Imbrie's head, didn't you?"

Ibrahim sniggered. "Yeah, who didn't?" He walked toward the second hall.

Malcolm followed him down the stairs. On his way, Malcolm took two additional loincloths.

Ibrahim noticed that. "You don't need all those *lowngs*, you know."

Malcolm put one across his shoulders and one on his head, which disguised his face. "I like my head to feel the heat when I'm bathing." He wasn't the only one. There were other men who placed loincloths on their heads.

The large, octagonal second hall featured walls and ceiling decorated with mosaics. The floor was white marble. Two large, water-filled basins decorated with intricately painted blue tiles sat in the middle of the floor.

When they entered the second hall, they greeted those present. Malcolm observed a few men being scrubbed by the bathhouse workers with a *keesa,* a rough glove to remove dead skin. Others were being washed with soap and were totally covered in foam. Their eyes were closed to avoid the soap. A few men were rinsing in the basins and heavily engaged in a political discussion.

The hall had several recessed nooks for those desiring a more private setting. Each area was the size of a small room with tile seating about two-and-a-half meters wide and a meter-and-a-half deep.

Malcolm pointed to one of the private areas in a less crowded section of the hall. Ibrahim nodded and made his way into it. Two other men had entered the second hall a few steps behind them. Malcolm took a mental picture, one skinny and short, and the other chubby.

Right at that moment, Malcolm felt a hand tapping on his back. He turned around, away from Ibrahim, to find a bathhouse worker. "Sir, you left your tea back there, would you like me to bring it to you with your *ghalyan?*"

"No, it's all right; I don't need it, thank you."

"Are you sure, sir. It's no problem for me. Tea is recommended while bathing."

The man was beginning to annoy Malcolm, but he wanted to stay in character, which required politeness in the bath house. "Your concern is appreciated. But I prefer no tea, today."

When he turned his head back, Ibrahim was slumped on the tile platform in the corner of the private nook. He seemed to be dozing.

Malcolm entered the nook and sat on the tile platform near Ibrahim. He took the loincloth off of his head and set it on his lap. He surveyed the outer area again. It appeared that everyone in the hall was busy and no one noticed them. A few people were leaving the second hall and a few people were walking into it.

"Are you having a nap?" Malcolm asked.

There was no answer. He touched Ibrahim's shoulder.

Ibrahim's head tilted toward Malcolm, and he saw blood. A lot of it. A chill traveled down his spine. Somehow, when his back was turned, someone had slashed Ibrahim's throat with a sharp knife or razor. The loincloth wound around his neck had absorbed the bulk of the seeping blood.

Malcolm had to think quickly. There was no time to wonder about who did it or why. He put one more loincloth on Ibrahim's face and gently laid his body flat on his back on the tiled platform they were sitting on, to make it look as if he was taking a nap. A typical activity in the public bath houses.

Malcolm quickly stood up and put a loincloth on his head to cover his face for his return to the first hall. He already had committed to memory the whereabouts of each person present there. Now he realized one was missing—the skinny, short man. He had been sitting across from them in the waiting room and moved along with them to the second hall. Was he the assassin? How had he slipped in and out so quickly and silently?

Watchful of a possible ambush, he crossed the room. Before leaving, he glanced back at Ibrahim for the last time. His body lay motionless as if he was in a deep slumber. A few scarlet drops stained the tiles of the platform. Malcolm knew he had only seconds before someone noticed the blood.

Back in the dressing room, he quickly changed into his disguise clothing. As he left the building, he heard shouts coming from the washing hall.

Stepping out into the busy street, Malcolm vanished into the crowd.

28

THE MESSENGER

Sunday, September 21, 1924

"HIS HIGHNESS IS NOT HAPPY!" The translator, an overweight man in his fifties, wiped perspiration from his forehead with a white handkerchief.

Malcolm, standing in the corner to the right of Colonel Fraser's desk, faced the two Persians who had been sent to the colonel's office to deliver the message from the Persian high command. The messenger, Major Rahimi, stood erect with his clean and well pressed military uniform, holding his hat in his right hand at his side. His head was rather large in proportion to his body and his oiled, Hungarian moustache made his face seem even larger. His intense focus and discipline made his persona much bigger than his small body warranted.

"He is a prime minister, not a king," Colonel Fraser protested.

"Not yet, anyway," Malcolm muttered. The colonel gave a look to Malcolm to warn him to keep quiet.

The translator did his job, but the messenger ignored the

comments and said, "Russians are asking for too much. Americans are demanding heads, and you are not delivering the weapons that were promised to us. How do you suppose we proceed?" The messenger spoke rapidly and his left arm moved energetically as he spoke. The translator had a hard time catching everything.

"We'll handle the Russians. Do not concern yourselves with them," Colonel Fraser replied.

"Russians had a large reward in gold for Imbrie's head, so they are actually quite happy. It is their nature to play deceptive games. They'll never stop pushing," Malcolm said.

The colonel leaned over his desk, put his elbows on top of it, and with his left hand covered his chin. "What did you say the Americans are demanding?"

"Americans are not satisfied with the arrests. We have arrested hundreds of people, issued over twenty guilty verdicts, and sentenced three with life in prison for the murder of Major Imbrie. But they want blood. They are demanding executions. We, on the other hand, need weapons to bring peace and stability to the region. As you well know, we are having operations against the Kurds, Lurs, Bakhtiyar, and most importantly against Sheikh Khazal in the south," the messenger answered, followed by the translator.

The colonel pushed back on his chair. "Oh, trust me, we understand why you need military assistance and new weaponry. We too, are interested in a strong central power in Persia. We don't believe for a moment that these tribes and regional ethnicities who are demanding independence can provide stability to the region. But, please tell your leader, Reza Khan, that we ask for his patience."

"I'm curious, what are the Americans' specific demands?" Malcolm asked.

The messenger listened to the translation and replied, "They want us to execute the people responsible for Major Imbrie's murder. They are not satisfied with the life sentences that we have given them."

Malcolm lit a cigarette. "Those you have charged with murder are minors, aren't they?"

"Except the soldier. He is nineteen. We have offered his head first. But Mr. Murray, the American chargé, is very impatient and is pushing for more than just one head. So, we have to execute the seventeen- and fourteen-year-old boys who are charged with the murder," the messenger answered.

Malcolm drew on his cigarette. "Isn't death a somewhat harsh sentence for a fourteen-year-old boy? After all, he is a minor. Isn't a life sentence more adequate?" The words were not out of his mouth when he asked himself about the wisdom of his question. Why did he care?

Images of his lifeless stepfather, the pool of blood on the floor, and his hysterical mother hovering over the dead man, paraded across his mind. He was fourteen at the time. No one had demanded his life as a punishment.

"Not satisfactory for the Americans, Mr. Malcolm," the translator said. Hearing his name brought Malcolm's attention back in the room. The translator continued, "We don't care how old they are. The Americans don't care, and the Russians don't care. Why do you care? We need to move forward fast. They are what you or the Americans call...." The translator took a moment and searched for the correct word and then said, "Collaterals."

Malcolm, back in the cold and calculated mindset of a spy, couldn't agree more with that logic. It made sense.

Colonel Fraser leaned back on his chair. "You have already arrested quite a lot of people. You have declared martial law. You're moving in the right direction. Executing minors is not a terribly civilized behavior. It is not a habit of mine to tell you people what to do; however, do ask Reza Khan for leniency on the boys."

Malcolm jumped in, worried that Major Rahimi would misinterpret the colonel's request. "Change their sentences back to life in prison. Replace them with two adults. The world may look at Persia with a kinder eye." Ali knew too much, Malcolm did not want him to be released.

Colonel Fraser glowered at Malcolm while the translator conveyed the message.

Major Rahimi's eyes traveled back and forth between the colonel and Malcolm and a crooked smile on his face indicated his amusement with what just transpired, "What about the Americans?"

Fraser answered, "Just give the Americans time, they'll come around. Any news on the loan Mr. Sinclair promised the Persian government? Have you received the funds yet?"

The translator wasn't totally finished translating when the messenger burst into laughter, then spoke a long tirade which the translator attempted to repeat.

"American money? What money? Mr. Sinclair's representative has already left the country for Russia. He said that the deal for northern oil fields is off due to the misfortunate incident. We have actually paid the United States $110,000 for the transport of Major Imbrie's body, $60,000 to Mrs. Imbrie, and $3,000 to Mr. Seymour." The messenger stopped until the translator caught up and then continued, "Colonel, the collapse of this country will only help the Russian takeover of the northern oil fields and spread communism in the region. We have plenty of people. What we don't have is time. We need arms and we need them soon!"

Fraser nodded. "Very well, we shall consider the urgency of this matter more diligently and shall attempt to expedite the arms delivery. However, I still recommend a more lenient punishment for the two minors."

Malcolm was surprised to hear that from the colonel. He thought he didn't care about the boys either.

"I shall inform my leader of your advice, Colonel, but please understand that my leader is a serious and direct man. Political games displease him. If you don't fully deliver on time, we shall find other avenues!"

The Persian messenger snapped his heels, gestured a half bow, and removed himself from Colonel Fraser's office. The translator followed.

Malcolm exhaled his last puff and extinguished his cigarette in the colonel's ashtray. "I didn't realize that you cared about those two teenagers."

Fraser walked to the liquor table and fixed two drinks, giving one to Malcolm and looking straight into his eyes as he handed it to him. He walked to his desk and sat down. "I like this Reza Khan; he's a man of action. He doesn't waste time, doesn't mince words. He's a straight shooter. Is the Ibrahim problem solved?"

Malcolm took a sip of the drink, wondering why Fraser was avoiding his question. "Yes, he's silenced. I have a hunch that it was courtesy of our Bolshevik friends."

The colonel took a sip of his drink and then pressed his lips together, as if savoring the liquor. "It doesn't feel right. It's too topsy-turvy. Situations can change rapidly. There are too many players in the game. In addition, we have this new nuisance of Berkley and Pearce—a situation we must resolve. I don't want to get demoted to some African hell, and I'm certain that you don't want to end up like Imbrie. The nurse must be contained. What are your plans for those two?"

"They can be silenced," Malcolm replied.

"No, not like Ibrahim. They are British, for Pete's sake. Don't you see?" Fraser snapped. With one upward toss of his glass, he finished his drink.

Malcolm looked into his glass, rotated it and asked, "Do you know of Reilly? Sidney Reilly?"

"No, who is he? Do I need to know him?"

"He is a well-connected SIS agent. Apparently, about fifteen years ago, through a clandestine operation, he smoothed the path for Mr. D'Arcy to sell his newly acquired Persian oil concession to the British government rather than to a French company. I heard he was in Tehran in early July of this year."

"That was about the time Adam from the Foreign Office showed up,"

Malcolm nodded. "Yes. Not too long ago, you mentioned that Adam had a few meetings off compound. Do you know whom he met? Or where?"

"Not really. Come to think of it, he was quite secretive about those meetings. He even refused the typical security escort. He asked only for a car and a driver. But there are rumors that his meetings were with APOC people."

Malcolm emptied the rest of his drink into his mouth.

The colonel looked up at Malcolm, boring into him with his eyes. "About the duo, Berkley and Pearce. Find a better way. Don't harm them."

Malcolm set his glass down and made his way toward the door. The last words he heard as he exited were in Fraser's firm, commanding voice.

"Malcolm, fix it!"

29

THE PLAN

Tuesday, September 30, 1924

THE ONE WINDOW, high on the east wall of the prison cell, had become a source of extraordinary joy for Ali. Every dawn, he woke up to the chirps of happy birds announcing the arrival of pleasing narrow rays of sunshine, bearing with them the impression of hope. He had a favorite game. Every morning, he watched the dust particles illuminated by the first rays of sun to see whose image would appear. Then he would name the day after that person and devote the entire day to the memories of that person. This game kept his mind busy and his heart full.

But not this day. Ali woke in the darkness to the clang of a key turning in the cell door and then by the loud screech of the door opening. Two guards entered, carrying a lantern to cut through the gloom. One guard brought the lantern near Ali's face.

"Not this one," he growled.

The other guard barked, "Morteza, get up!"

Groggily, Morteza rolled over. "Wha … what is it?"

The guards followed the sound and brought the lantern near his face.

"Yes, that's him."

The guards yanked Morteza's body up off the ground where he slept. One slapped him hard across the face. "Wake up, time to go!"

"Go where?" Morteza murmured.

"You'll find out soon enough. Hurry up, move!"

After they left, Ali shook Seyyed Hussein, who had managed to stay sound asleep throughout all the ruckus. "Seyyed, Seyyed, wake up. They just took Morteza!"

Seyyed rolled over and yawned. "Good, I hope he doesn't come back."

"But the sun is not up yet. Isn't it odd?"

"Shut up and go back to sleep." Seyyed rolled over and pulled his thin blanket over his head.

Ali couldn't possibly go back to sleep. He stood up, but he couldn't see anything in the pitch-dark cell. He searched near the ceiling and found the window high on the east wall. Extending his hands, he moved forward until he hit the hard bricks. Pressing his left ear to the wall below the window, he listened for any sound—any clue as to what might be happening with their cellmate. The wall was very thick, but the prison courtyard was on the other side of it.

He thought he heard the heavy marching footsteps of a few men wearing boots and some sort of military command was barked after the marching stopped. A thunderous sound of multiple rapid rifle shots jolted his body. The sound shook Seyyed out of his slumber.

"What was—"

Seyyed stopped his words. The cell was still dark, but the silence, the silence that took over the cell, was darker. A heavy air of sadness and fright permeated the small space.

A few minutes later, Seyyed began mumbling, the reality of

what they had heard apparently dawning on him. Ali guessed he was saying some sort of prayers, perhaps.

An hour or so later, when the birds started their chirps and the first morning light cut into the darkness of the cell, Ali saw Seyyed's frightened face, his form bundled in the corner of the cell with his arms around his knees, rocking himself forward and backward. Neither one spoke. They both preferred silence.

Eventually, a guard shoved the breakfast into the cell. Only two trays. They both stared at them. Despite their hunger, they didn't touch the food.

"Toilet run!" A guard shouted. They both jumped up and stood by the door.

While in the line for the toilet, Ali decided to question the other prisoners. Maybe they had also heard the sound, and perhaps someone knew for sure what exactly that horrible noise had been about.

"What was that loud sound early in the morning?" he asked the man in front of him.

"It was the firing squad. Some poor soul was executed," he answered woodenly.

Another one added, "I heard that he was a soldier, perhaps a deserter."

Another prisoner said, "We have a window in our cell that looks into the yard. We heard lots of noises. I climbed up on my mate's shoulders and peeked out. It was dark, but they had lights in the yard. I saw many people witnessing the execution, and some of them looked like foreigners."

Ali couldn't take it anymore. He had to know for sure. "Does anyone know Morteza? And where he is now?"

"The kid soldier?"

"He was nineteen. He wasn't a kid," Ali replied.

"Nineteen is a kid. How old are you? Sixteen or something?" A few inmates laughed.

"Everybody shut up!" one of the guards shouted. "It's not good to laugh at the expense of a dead person. You all will go to hell!"

Ali had to gasp for air. He felt dizzy. His knees quivered, and he felt like he was about to throw up. Ali looked for Seyyed. He had squatted onto his heels and held his head with his hands facing the ground. Ali squatted next to him.

"Are you kids sick?" someone asked. "Don't throw up here, for God's sake. They'll make us clean it up." He shouted at the inmate in the front of the line, "Hey, Akbar! Let these kids go to the toilet in your place, they are about to barf!"

All heads turned, and many eyes stared at the two squatting teenagers. The sound of discontent rose from a low murmur of a few people to loud shouts. The guards intervened, yanked the two from the ground, and pushed them to the front of the line.

Later, back in their cell, Seyyed and Ali went over every bit of information they had. Seyyed openly talked about his contact with Ibrahim.

"The first time I saw Ibrahim *agha*," Seyyed said, "was in a carpet store in the bazaar. I was having tea with Reza *pahlevoon* and Mohmmad *agha,* the owner of the carpet shop. Ibrahim *agha* knew the owner. He was very worried about the spread of Baha'is."

Ali shifted his legs and moved a bit closer to Seyyed. "Yes, my first time was in *ghahve-khaneh* and he was explaining the miracle of *sagha-khaneh* to an English man. He spoke English very well."

Seyyed nodded his head. "Right! He was worried about the influence of the foreigners in the spread of the Bahaism. He took me aside that day and said that he was looking for a passionate religious authority to lead a demonstration against an American Bahai woman—"

"You mean Dr. Moody?"

"Yes. So, I organized the protest—"

"But he paid you! I saw that. He also paid another man who was riding a bicycle."

"Yes, but it was more about stopping the spread of Baha'is."

Seyyed stopped talking for a few moments. He seemed to be trying to recall the event. He scratched his beard and continued, "I was actually surprised by the type of crowd Ibrahim *agha* brought that day. They were the ones who went wild and turned the protest into a violent one."

They both went quiet.

Ali broke the silence. "I don't think Ibrahim is a good man. I remember that he was in cahoots with another English man, Malcolm. They had something to do with the story of *sagha-khaneh*'s miracle."

"I don't know. I still think Ibrahim *agha* will get me out of here." He paused for a moment, "How about you? Is your family helping to get you out?"

"Yes, my cousin is helping." Ali didn't want to tell Seyyed that Rose was his benefactor. He worried about being labeled as someone who worked with infidels or Seyyed accused of being a British spy. He quickly changed the topic, "What if he and Malcolm plotted all this to get to the American?"

Seyyed shook his head. "*Astagh-firullah*, God forgive us."

Ali nodded as an eerie fog of silence penetrated the cell. A few minutes later, Ali shared what he heard at the banquet. But he didn't say anything about Rose. The more they talked, the grimmer their situation appeared.

Ali worried about Seyyed. Given how the Cossacks felt about clerics, Seyyed could be the next to go in front of the firing squad.

Ali sat in a dark corner of the cell and closed his eyes. He remembered how in Ahmad's house he was so stressed that his hands shook uncontrollably. And then Rose sitting across from him, held his hands. Her touch calmed him. He searched for Rose's image in his mind. He wanted to feel her touch again. Since Islam forbade contact between unsanctioned men and women, he had never actually initiated a touch but ... he had felt it. When she grabbed his hands, secretly, every fiber of his body, every cell in his skin quivered with the sensation of her touch. It felt good.

His mind played games with him and didn't let him have the comfort of a dream. Would Islamic laws apply to his dreams too? What if he imagined touching Rose's hand? Would God punish him? Was God reprimanding him? "God, what have I done wrong that you're punishing me like this?" he prayed.

He knew he could ask Seyyed Hussein if dreams were forbidden too. But at that moment, the dark quiet corner of the cell turned out to be a good sanctuary for him. He didn't want to disturb the moment by speaking to Seyyed. He searched for a feather, hoping that one of his chirping birds might have dropped one, but none was to be found. He brushed his fingers across his pile of filthy hay and thought about his old mattress, which was filled with feathers. But immediately his fingers felt the sting of the straw under his nails, a painful reminder that his bedding on the floor was made with straw.

He cleared his mind of the clutter and allowed only the image of Rose to appear.

I'll deal with the consequences later, he thought.

Committing a sin by imagining Rose felt like a spice that makes the taste of good food memorable.

***

The next day, near noon, the guard called Ali to the door. He reluctantly complied.

"Where're you taking me?"

"You'll find out soon," he said, and then laughed.

Ali recognized the same long, dark corridors. They weren't headed toward the prison's courtyard. That was good. No firing squad. At least, not today.

The guard opened the door to the visitation room. Ali saw two women seated in the center of the room, one in a black *chador* and the other one in a white *chador* with small pink roses. He glanced across the room and saw two men standing by the door. He took one step back. One of the men was the Englishman, Malcolm.

Ali furrowed his brows and clenched his fists. What was he doing there again? This guy was nothing but trouble. Ali hesitated at the doorway.

A guard pushed him forward. "What's the matter, kid? Don't you want to see your mother?"

Quickly his eyes returned to the two women. Goose bumps rose across his arms. He rushed to the feet of the woman in black and dropped to the floor.

"My dear mother, it's been so long!" He broke down and wept. Guards rushed toward Ali, but a halting gesture from one of the men by the door stopped them. The woman lifted Ali up. He kissed her hands and wept uncontrollably. His mother took him in her arms and kissed each cheek several times.

Rose, again wearing her white *chador,* sat next to Ali's mother. Teardrops streamed down her cheeks as she witnessed the mother and son reunion.

"My dear son, you disappeared on me! No one knew what happened to you! No one knew. Finally, your cousin Majid found out that you were held in prison for murder! I haven't seen you for more than two months, son!" She wept.

"Mother, I'm innocent. Don't believe what you hear!"

"Some say that you killed an infidel spy. I tell those people that my son is not a murderer, but if he has killed an infidel spy, then I tell those people that my son is a hero!"

Ali shook his head. "No, Mother, I haven't hurt anyone. I'm no hero. I'm just tired and want to come home." He wiped his tears with back of his hand and mumbled, "I'm frightened. Mother."

"My dear," his mother reached for his hands, her eyes soaked with tears. "You have always been smart. Keep your wits, keep your faith, and stay strong. Submit yourself to God's will. You have always been a good son and a faithful Muslim. God will protect you, my dear son. You know, cousin Majid is working with some people to get you out."

He had rarely seen tears in his mother's eyes. It was a gut-wrenching sight for him. He decided to lighten up the conversation and put a smile on his mother's face, "You know, here they call me Ali Rashdi, the camel driver!"

"The camel driver? Where did they get *that* from?"

"I suppose from those few times I helped Uncle Jaffar with his caravan."

They both chuckled and wiped their tears.

Rose didn't understand their chat, but their laughter put a smile on her face as well. She wiped her tears.

They talked, laughed, and cried for a while. A few minutes later, Ali's mother, with her left hand, gently raised her *chador*, blocking her face from Rose's view, signaled Ali with her eyes and whispered, "Who's this woman? Why is she here?"

"She's helping me, Mother. Her name is Rose," Ali whispered.

"Rose? Just like the flower?"

Rose noticed her name was mentioned a few times. She looked at Ali and smiled. Ali returned her smile. He turned to his mother and said, "Yes, mother, she is a British nurse. She has taught me English and she is helping me. She is a good person. One day, Mother, when I'm out of this place and have a job, after all my brothers and sisters are graduated from school, I want to marry someone like her!"

Ali's mother shook her head. "*Astagh-firullah,* God forgive. Son, you are too young to think about these things. Plus, I have your cousin Nargess in mind for you."

Ali blushed. "Nargess?" he smiled. "Maybe brother can marry Nargess."

A guard tapped Ali's shoulder, time was up. Ali stood and embraced his mother, then kissed her hand. Rose also stood and walked over to Malcolm, who was standing by the door, and whispered to him. Malcolm turned to the assistant warden who stood next to him and said something. The assistant ordered the guards to give Ali and Rose some time alone, and with a softer voice asked Ali's mother to leave the room with him.

"Ali *jon*, God protect you, my son! You are a hero. We all are proud of you, son," his mother said as she departed.

The guards pushed Ali back on the chair. Tears ran down Ali's cheeks. Rose sat on a chair in front of him. She stared at Ali's tearful eyes. "I'm sorry you are going through this. Hopefully, it'll end soon and you will be released."

"Thank you for bringing her." Ali looked down on the ground, wiped his eyes, sniffed, and said, "Look Rose, they killed Morteza!"

"Morteza? Who's he? And who killed him?"

"He was Cossack soldier. They ask him kill Major Imbrie. He say no. He was here in *zendan*, jail, with me. Yesterday, very early morning, they take him to yard and bang bang. Killed him!"

"Oh God, it's started!" Rose mumbled.

"What?"

"Never mind, please continue. Who asked him to kill Major Imbrie?"

"Cossack commander. Someone say he saw *farangee*, foreigner people, watched the bang bang. Many!"

"Probably they were the foreign observers like Americans and Russians."

"No, *Engilisi, Engilisi*," Ali insisted.

"Yes, probably some British officials too. I'll find out. But he was a soldier. The rules are different for the soldiers. They won't do that to you." Rose reached for Ali's hand, which was resting on his knee. But he dropped his hands to his sides, to prevent the guards' fury.

"I am scare, Rose!"

"I know. I am too. But I shall get you out. Colonel Fraser has already asked for leniency for you."

Ali shook his head, "I not know him."

Rose replied, "It's all right, he is an important British military man. Believe me, I shall release you. I'm putting more pressure on the British officials to ask for your freedom. God will not let an innocent young man, a loving boy like you to die. Pray and pray, and God will hear you. I will get you out." Rose extended her hands to hold Ali's hands again but retracted them quickly when she saw guards walking toward them.

"Rose, if they do kill me, my dead body may drop the ground, but my life with no body, will continue. I protect you from heaven." Ali pointed his index finger up toward the sky.

Rose's eyes were soaked with tears. She pressed her lips together and sniffed.

Ali then turned back and saw two guards were coming for him. He looked into Rose's eyes. "All I have is you. And hope."

The guards tapped Ali's shoulder. Time to go. Ali rose from his seat, thanked Rose in Farsi, and turned his back to exit.

Rose stood up, grabbed Ali's arm, turned him toward her and whispered. "Soon I shall come here with your release paper in my hand! I shall free you! I promise!"

Ali looked at Rose, smiled, and gave her a quick nod.

The guards forcefully separated her hands from Ali and pushed her back angrily. "What devilish tongue is that?" he roared.

The push forced Rose backward a step, but she kept her balance and didn't fall.

Ali jerked his shoulders hard to release himself from the guards' grip so he could assist Rose. But their holds were firm and his reaction earned him a painful strike of the baton on the back of his knees. He fell, but never took his eyes off Rose.

As the guards dragged Ali out of the room, Rose looked on, her face drenched with tears.

30

THE THREAT

Malcolm smiled, amused by how the guards dragged Ali out of the visiting room. However, his pleasure was more driven from the guards' harsh treatment toward Rose. He hoped, perhaps, the well-deserved rough treatment would convince Rose to change her path. He waited a few short moments before approaching her.

"Are you all right?"

She didn't answer. Instead, she turned around, and with a determined walk, exited the room. Malcolm followed her, and the assistant warden followed him.

"Ali said that they executed a soldier who was in the cell with him!" Rose exclaimed, not slowing down or looking at Malcolm.

"Yes, the soldier was involved with Major Imbrie's death. I witnessed the execution."

"Ali is frightened. He thinks he'll be the next. You told me that you have talked to Persian authorities and that he'll be released, not executed!"

"I said no such a thing!" Malcolm retorted irritably. "I agreed to trying to lower his sentence. And I have asked them—"

Rose cut him off. "Have you heard back from them?"

"No, not about Ali's sentencing. This is a dangerous world, Miss Pearce! Politics is complicated. It changes direction like the wind, swift and hard to predict. And sometimes the punishment is severe. People lose their lives or their fortunes."

Rose increased her pace. "Spare me the lecture, Mr. Malcolm. You ought to make certain that he is released. Otherwise, I predict the consequences will not be pleasant for you or your friends."

Malcolm grabbed her arm, stopping her just outside the prison entrance. He felt her stiffen against the force of his hand. "What do you mean, exactly?"

Rose pulled her arm away from Malcolm's grip and gave him an angry look. If only she wasn't British, he thought. He could resolve the problem swiftly. For now, he had to use diplomacy and patience.

"Americans are insisting on executions," Malcolm explained walking behind her. "I'm afraid they want it fast and in multiples. Persians put a soldier in front of the firing squad to calm the Yankees yesterday. Yes, he was only nineteen years old. Believe me, we're working every angle to prevent execution of the minors. But there are no guarantees."

Rose rolled her eyes. "Then I suppose there won't be any guaranties for the consequences of promises not delivered!" She stopped and looked into Malcolm's eyes. "Mr. Malcolm, I can and shall hurt you if you don't save Ali."

Malcolm slowed down. How much tolerance does this matter require? He let her go on.

"May I remind you that in this matter, you must be a man of great sense and clarity. I advise you to use every possible resource at your disposal to mend this situation."

The embassy car was waiting for them. The driver started the engine as they approached.

Rose was a few steps ahead of Malcolm. When she reached the back door of the car, Malcolm spoke up. "What is it with you and this kid? What do you see in him that is worth all the trouble?"

Rose hesitated a moment, and then without answering, she opened the car door and got in the car. Malcolm sat in the front seat next to the driver.

A few minutes into the drive, Rose spoke in a soft voice. "He reminds me of my younger brother Paul. He had a keen sense of pride and dignity and a mind full of desire to help others. Ali is like that, despite life's senseless pounding. When he smiles, his whole face opens up and two dimples appear on his cheeks. Just like Paul."

Malcolm turned his head around and looked at Rose. She was smiling. "What happened to Paul?"

"We lost him to consumption when he was fourteen." Rose turned her head and gazed through the side window at the buildings and people rushing past her.

Malcolm faced forward again and remained silent the rest of the trip.

Once they arrived at the embassy, Rose turned to Malcolm. "Mr. Malcolm if you want me to stick to my end of the deal, you need to deliver." Without waiting for a response, she opened the car door, got out and walked away.

Malcolm chose to maintain his silence. The woman was stubborn, and a problem. But his instructions from Colonel Fraser were clear. Malcolm got out of the car but stayed back, lit a cigarette and observed as Rose disappeared. She presented a threat and needed to be dealt with in an appropriate way.

He took the long way to his office through the garden. Fall was at its peak. The sycamore, birch, walnut and other trees in the embassy's compound were in full display of every imaginable shade of yellow, red and orange. He stopped by the rose garden and picked a healthy red bloom on his way inside the building. Approaching the reception desk where Sandra worked, he hid the rose behind him and sidled up behind her. Sandra didn't see him as she was reading a document. He slowly brought the rose near her nostrils.

The appearance of a rose from behind her startled Sandra, but a wide smile quickly replaced her surprised appearance. She closed her eyes and inhaled deeply, enjoying the fragrance.

"Hello, Sandra," Malcolm whispered into her left ear, in a low, sexy voice.

Sandra closed her eyes and rubbed her cheek on Malcolm's cheek near her. "James, what has brought you to this part of the building?"

Malcolm had a perfect view of the appointment book Sandra had opened in front of her. He quickly skimmed it. A general was visiting the colonel.

"Dinner tonight?" Malcolm asked with the same low sexy voice.

"My place or your's?" Sandra answered, the smile on her face in full bloom.

"Your's. At 1900?" Malcolm answered.

"All right. What else? I know better. You just didn't walk here to ask me for dinner in my own home!"

"Well, all right. Since you insist, I have a small question." Malcolm walked to the front of her desk and sat on a corner of it.

Sandra followed him with her eyes, "All right, ask away."

"Who drove Mr. Adam from the Foreign Office to his off-compound meetings in early July?"

"Oh, that was a few months ago. Let me check the July book." She opened her drawer and took a notebook out. "It was O'Connell."

"Thank you, dear. See you tonight at 1900." Malcolm placed a quick peck on her cheek and left.

On his way to the embassy's garage, where all the cars were kept and repaired, he came across Colonel Fraser who was walking in the hallway toward him, preoccupied in thought.

"Good morning, Colonel."

"Good morning," Fraser answered as he walked by him, unaware who had greeted him. Then, "Oh, blast, Malcolm! Wait up."

"Yes, sir?"

The colonel scanned the area and looked for a safe place to talk. "Here, follow me." He walked about five steps to open a door to a small, empty courtyard.

Malcolm followed. Fraser seemed nervous and somewhat agitated.

The colonel looked around again to make sure no one was listening and approached Malcolm's face, whispering, "Yesterday, the body of a Russian citizen was found in the slums of south Tehran. He was mutilated. Did you have anything to do with it?"

"Colonel, you need to give me more information. Who was he?"

"His name was Kerensky, Viktor Kerensky. He was a Cheka agent. It looks like he was at the wrong place at the wrong time. Again, did you have anything to do with him?"

"I interrogated him. I was in disguise and nobody saw us. He is the one who told me about Ibrahim. When I left him, he was alive with no signs of any physical harm."

"I warned you to be extra careful, Malcolm. Now the Russians are agitated too. If the Russians suspect us, they may retaliate with military action. They are looking for an excuse."

"Colonel, I didn't kill him. But I'll look into it."

"Tread carefully, we have enough trouble on our hands already. Get back to me soon."

"Yes sir," Malcolm said and left the courtyard. He had miscalculated the Russian agent's strength. At the time, he was certain that Kerensky could handle a few thugs in the slums of Tehran, where he had left him. If it wasn't the thugs, then who finished the job? On the other hand, the world was no doubt safer with one less detestable Cheka agent.

The garage was a loud and busy place. Three mechanics were working on two cars. Two mechanics were singing an Irish ballad. Smells of grease and exhaust permeated the air. Malcolm recognized one of the mechanics.

"Good day, Finch."

"Oh, hello, Mr. Malcolm. What has brought you here today, sir?" Finch stood up and cleaned his hands with a rag that was on his shoulder. He was a tall, skinny man with a long, happy face.

"Looking for O'Connell, have you seen him?"

Finch pointed to a door at the end of the garage with his long arm. "He's back there drinking beer."

Malcolm approached the door. Seeing it was ajar, he gently pushed it open with his fingertips. O'Connell, a stocky Irish man with auburn hair covered by a flat cap, was sitting alone, drinking and reading a paper.

"Good day, O'Connell." Malcolm entered the room.

"Oh, good day to you too, sir. Would you care for a pint?"

"Yes, please." Malcolm sat on the bench next to O'Connell. The room was small and dirty. It functioned as a storage room for parts, oil, and also as a breakroom for the staff. The two men made small talk and drank beer for a while. Finally, Malcolm saw an opening to probe for the information he had come for.

"Do you, by any chance, remember the gentleman from the Foreign Office who visited us in July?"

"Do you mean Mr. Adam, sir?" O'Connell answered in his thick Irish accent.

"Yes, that's right, Mr. Adam. He wrote to me to ask you the name of the place you took him. He grew quite fond of the place, but he cannot remember its name."

"Oh, yes sir. If I remember rightly," he took off his cap and scratched his russet hair. "The first place was Tehran's Grand Hotel in Lalehzar Street. The second one..." O'Connell tightened his jaws and rubbed his jaw with the flat of his thick, stained hand.

"What is it, O'Connell?" Malcolm asked.

"I can't remember the name of the place, sir. It was east of Tehran. I'd never been there, and frankly don't wish to go there again. I was sure glad he didn't ask me to wait for him."

"What do you mean? How did he get back?" Malcolm asked sharply.

"Some bloke was waiting for him. They went to a teahouse. I'm glad he wasn't dressed up. Otherwise, the locals would have mugged him."

"Was he wearing sort of a disguise-type clothing?"

"Right you are, sir. He looked more like one of the locals.""Who was waiting for him? Was he a British chap or a local guy?"

"Honestly, I couldn't tell. He was dressed like a local guy. He was average height and not fat, not skinny, dark hair, black eyes, and his skin was more like yours."

"How about the Grand Hotel, was the same bloke there waiting for him?"

"No, there were two men waiting for him. I've seen those fellows here at the embassy before. They're the oil people."

"Do you mean the APOC people?"

"Sorry sir, I don't know those fancy names." O'Connell shook his head and continued, "From what I reckoned, they were in some sort of protection or security for the oil people."

Malcolm raised his mug, cheered O'Connell, and gulped the rest of it.

"Bless you, O'Connell, I'm certain Mr. Adam will appreciate your help." Malcolm put down his mug and headed back to his office.

"Now I know why I didn't like him. That sly Adam," he muttered.

31

ABDUCTION

Sunday, October 5, 1924, 7:30 pm

MALCOLM WORKED LATE THAT DAY. The Bolsheviks were expanding their operations in large cities near the Soviet Union such as Tabriz and Mashhad, which bothered him to his core. Stopping the Bolshevik expansion, and better yet, dismantling the communist regime of the Soviet Union, was his passion. As a prag-matist, Malcolm knew that in order to get a long-term post as an operative in the Soviet Union, he needed to prove himself in Persia. He was convinced other British agents were involved with the Imbrie incident, but he needed more time and resources to ferret out the details. Why wasn't he in the loop? Under whose command were they serving? How could he find their identities?

Since the evening was clear and pleasant, he decided to walk home and let the chill of the air calm his restless mind.

Malcolm hadn't gone more than three blocks from the embassy when two meaty hands grabbed him by the throat. He tried to release himself, but the grip was strong. Seconds later, he felt a blow to his head, which seemed to crush his skull. The world turned dark.

HOURS LATER, his consciousness returned accompanied by a burst of a sharp pain in his head. He tried to open his eyes, but a blindfold had been strapped tightly around his skull. He kept his eyes open, hoping he could see something through the material, but instead, he watched sharp, colored fragments racing across his vision. He was terribly thirsty. The room seemed to be dark. He was tied to a chair, sitting upright, his arms and hands bound behind his back. He closed his eyes and let his other senses become sharper by the darkness and absence of sight. He felt the cold of caked blood on his neck. The air smelled damp and old, but he also detected the stench of grease, indicating he was in a mechanic shop of some sort. He also detected whispering somewhere in the room.

The whispering stopped. Whoever was there must have noticed that he was awake. The crescendo of approaching footsteps made him brace himself.

A low, rough voice spoke in heavily accented English. "What is your name?"

Malcolm figured that they must have searched his pockets and seen his British embassy ID.

"James Malcom," he croaked. "What is the meaning of this? I'm a British diplomat. You need to release me immediat—"

A firm slap to the side of his head, stopped him from finishing his sentence.

"Shut up. Only answer the questions we ask," the voice ordered. "What happened to Kerensky?"

His face burned from the slap. Direct and to the point, he thought. No style, no theatrical twist to their interrogation technique.

"You are playing with fire," Malcolm snapped. "You cannot

treat a British official like this."

He was barely finished with that sentence when a heavy blow landed on his face with a thud. He tasted the metallic tang of his own blood. His jaw went numb.

"What happened to Kerensky?"

"Who?"

Another punishing blow hit his face, this time on the left side. "Viktor Kerensky?"

The pain was substantial, but well within his tolerance level. Their interest in Kerensky gave the impression that they were Russians. He remembered his training: during torture, always remember to dislike them, his instructor had said, they will treasure what they get out of you. He stayed with his initial disposition. "Why would I know him? Who are you people? I protest this brutality."

This time the punch landed right above his stomach on his diaphragm, cutting off his breath. He knew he had to wait, but his body's reflexes pushed to inhale, which was impossible. A sensation of suffocation came over him.

He figured that at least two men were present. They could be Russian or Persian counter intelligence. The accent was closer to a Persian one, but it was hard to distinguish completely, especially through the pounding in his head.

"You filthy cowards will pay for this dearly—"

Another blow to his face stopped his words. Blood gushed out of his mouth.

"All right! Stop! Isn't he the Russian chap who was found dead in the slums?"

A brutal blow by something made of metal landed on his rib cage. The excruciating pain that followed indicated a possible rib fracture.

"Did you kill him?"

"No!" Malcolm grunted. "I am … just a low-level employee. You … you picked up the wrong person."

Another blow to his face rocked his head back, nearly snapping his neck.

"Do you know Sidney Reilly?"

"No." Malcolm spat blood. That was it. Persians wouldn't know much about Reilly, but Cheka was obsessed with him.

"What he was doing in Tehran?"

"I don't know this man. I haven't met or even seen him in the embassy, or anywhere!"

Suddenly his hair was yanked back and the icy cold steel of a knife blade rested right below his Adam's apple.

"I will cut your throat from ear to ear if you don't cooperate. And then throw your dead body into the desert for the wild dogs to chew."

Malcolm figured if they were working for Persian authorities, but were following a Cheka directive, they wouldn't kill a British diplomat. But if they were on Russia's payroll, with no connection to the Persian government, then this could very well be his last day on earth. Either way, he decided the best bet for him was to continue to play his cover as a British embassy clerk.

"I don't know, I swear. Please don't kill me. I haven't done anything. I don't know these people. I'm just a clerk."

Malcolm felt a sting on the skin of his throat.

"*Beboram?*" His captor asked permission to cut his throat in Farsi.

Malcolm was less than a second away from death. The fight and cutting of his stepfather flashed in his mind, then his mother's image appeared. Not the terrified face, but her kind face with a warm smile. That frightened him. He thought his mind was preparing him for death.

"Stop!" he screamed. "Please stop. I might be able to help you!"

The pressure of the knife on his throat subsided.

Malcolm cleared his throat. Warm blood trickled down his neck and under his shirt collar, its odor disturbing. "I can get access to certain files. I can get them for you. Just tell me what you want. My office is near Colonel Fraser's office." Blood mixed with saliva gathered in his mouth and he spat it out. "Maybe I can get you transcripts of certain meetings. Would that help?"

A pause, and then he heard a soft whisper farther away from where he was sitting. As if someone was telling them what to do.

"What?" One of the abductors whispered in English.

There must be a third person in the room who doesn't speak Farsi. He heard footsteps coming toward him.

"Sidney Reilly. We want to know what he was doing here. We will give you three days. Put the information in a bag and hand it to the same butcher that you visited on September seventh and say the bag is for Heidar Khan. We know who you are and where you work. If you fail, we will come and get you. And this time you won't leave alive. Do you understand?"

Malcolm nodded. He detected a definite Russian accent. His anger overcame his good sense. "I understand, you don't have the guts to do your own dirty work. You rotten pigs..."

"In three days," said the man and immediately another hard blow crashed against his jaw, and his world went dark again.

BEFORE HE OPENED HIS EYES, he felt a soft hand caressing his arm. Gradually, wincing from the sharp pain shooting through his temples, he tried to open his eyes. Only the right one responded. Through blurred vision, Sandra from the embassy emerged.

"Where am I?" he mumbled and reached up to touch his face.

"Oh, thank you, Lord," Sandra prayed. "James, you are in a hospital. How do you feel?'

"Bloody awful, what is this place?"

"You're in a hospital, as I said. Local people found you beaten up and unconscious on the street. They took you to the hospital and the doctor here found your ID and called the embassy."

Malcolm felt pain all over his body. He tried to raise up, but Sandra gently pressed his chest back toward the bed. "No, you cannot leave yet. You have three fractured ribs, a broken nose, and your left eye is covered with bandages. What happened to you? Who did this?"

He ignored Sandra's questions. "How long have I been out?"

She took her hand away. "They found your body last evening, I came here this morning and it's about noon now." She put the back of her hand on his forehead, checking his temperature, and slowly slid it down the right side of his face, where there were no bandages. "You're running a fever. Why don't you rest now? Colonel Fraser asked me to inform him when you are awake. I'll go and get him."

Malcolm nodded his head in agreement, but the movement sent shock waves of pain through his face. He was in a private room with minimal furniture. The bed was small and not comfortable. He rested his head on the pillow and dozed off.

He woke up sometime later when a nurse came in to check his vital signs. Behind the nurse stood Colonel Fraser, looking down on him. "My dear chap, perhaps it is time for you to realize that the fight clubs no longer suit you."

The nurse finished her job and left. The colonel moved closer to Malcolm's bed and continued, "Your bruises are a perfect reminder that you are no Kid Lewis." Colonel Fraser laughed loud at his joke. "Anyway, do you feel better?"

"I suppose so," Malcolm hesitated. "Those sods beat me up quite good."

The colonel closed the door and returned to Malcolm's bedside. His face now lined with concern. "Who did this to you? Russians?"

Malcolm sighed and tried to sit up. "Yes, quite possibly. They asked about Viktor Kerensky and Sidney Reilly."

"Sidney Reilly? The master spy you were talking about a few weeks ago?"

Malcolm offered a small nod.

Fraser folded his arms across his chest. "How on earth did they know about him? I made some inquiries about Reilly, after our conversation a few weeks ago. He is like a ghost. Not too many people know when and where he is."

"Well, Reilly worked undercover in Cheka for several years. He was an exceptionally effective operator. Naturally, the Russians are searching for him."

"So, then your assailants were Russian?"

"That is how it looked. But, I have to be open to other possibilities. The truth remains unseen. Reilly's mission, if any, could be unrelated to the Russians." Malcolm pulled himself higher in the bed. "Colonel, I need to get out of here. I have work to do."

"Not so soon, lad. Your injuries need healing. Like it or lump it." Fraser chortled at his own humor. "Rest today, and I shall get your release order from the doctor tomorrow."

"Yes, sir," Malcolm lowered himself down in the bed and laid his head against the pillow. Unamused, he closed his eyes.

32

MAGNA CARTA

Thursday, October 23, 1924

MALCOLM'S INJURIES took longer to heal than he had anticipated. The incident had isolated him from tracking the recent burgeoning movements of certain shadowy figures. That morning, he had become aware of a meeting in Colonel Fraser's office with an important visitor. He decided to invite himself into that meeting, regardless of his bruises.

When Malcolm reached the office, the secretary stopped him. "Pardon me, sir, but Colonel Fraser has company."

"Good, then I'll join in." Malcolm proceeded to open the door, but the secretary jumped up from his chair and stood in front of the door, extending his arms out to block him.

"Sir, the colonel asked me to hold all visitors."

Malcolm backed off. "Who is in his office?"

"The general and Major Thompson."

"In that case, I must be there. Soldier," he ordered in the

manner of a military commander, "announce my intention to the general and the colonel immediately!"

The secretary took a moment to assess Malcolm and his demand. Then he turned around, opened the door and entered the office, closing the door behind him. Seconds later, he opened the door for Malcolm to enter.

"Yes, come in, Malcolm," Colonel Fraser said. "We are going over the recent turbulences in the self-proclaimed autonomous regions of this troubled land."

All three men were dressed in civilian attire, which puzzled Malcolm, as it appeared to be a military briefing. However, the meeting and the visit had not been formally announced. Major Thompson reported on his northwest region and then the men discussed some troubles that required urgent attention for the entire country, region by region. Forty minutes into the meeting, the general left.

Twenty minutes later, Colonel Fraser turned his head toward the door where he heard shouts and commotion. "What is all the noise about?"

The office door opened with force and Rose propelled herself into the room, followed by the colonel's ruffled secretary brandishing a pistol.

"Miss Pearce, this sort of behavior is beneath you!" the colonel exclaimed. Malcolm grabbed her arms.

Rose twisted around to face Thompson. "General Ironside, I beg an audience with you, sir!"

Thompson chuckled. "Ma'am, General Ironside is in England. I'm Major Thompson, British Military Attaché, Mashhad at your service. How can we help you?"

Malcolm looked at the colonel and chuckled. He released Rose after a slight nod from Fraser. The secretary put his pistol back in its holster and left the room.

"But I heard General Ironside was visiting," Rose said, her eyes widened in surprise.

"Not General Ironside. We had a visit from General Salmond. He left twenty minutes ago. What is it you want, Miss Pearce?" Fraser asked.

Rose's shaky but determined voice filled the room, "Forgive me, gentlemen, but you all know Reza Khan, and he knows you. I am here to ask you once more, and if need be, to beg you, to encourage him not to execute the youth being held in prison." She took a few steps closer toward colonel's desk. "Furthermore, any subsequent punishment or sentencing should be done in due course and by due process of law." Rose paused a bit and waited for a reaction.

Getting none, Rose continued. "Come now, gentlemen. We are duty-bound by our great civilization and the wisdom of our fore-fathers to educate and improve upon the status of this desolate country."

Malcolm had been waiting with growing irritation since she barged into the meeting. He could not stop himself any longer, "Does it ever get cold on the moral high ground?'

Thompson looked like he was about to explode with laughter. But he controlled himself.

Rose gave a disappointed look to Malcolm and without acknowledging his comment, continued. "We are Britons! From the land of our great King John. We wrote the Magna Carta, which declares that no man shall be put to death before he has a fair trial and—"

Impatient, Colonel Fraser interjected, "You are nudging imper-tinence, Miss Pearce. We all know about the Magna Carta. You have inappropriately interrupted our meeting to what purpose? To teach *us* a history lesson?"

The men chuckled.

Unfazed, Rose kept on. "Just a few years ago, General Ironside made Reza Khan a general. Reza Khan became the Prime Minister with the assistance of Lieutenant Colonel Smyth. Didn't he? Reza Khan will listen to you!"

Silence filled the room. The men looked at each other and burst into loud laughter.

Major Thompson said, "Miss ..."

"Pearce."

"Yes, Miss Pearce, you cannot possibly be serious!"

"Yes, Major Thompson, I assure you, that I'm indeed quite serious. You gentlemen have the influence needed to stop this atrocity. In the name of humanity, why don't you *do* something?"

"Miss Pearce, mind yourself," Colonel Fraser warned. He turned his head, glaring at Malcolm and visibly displeased. "Malcolm, I thought this subject was handled!"

"These two kids are street rats, Miss Pearce. Why do you concern yourself with the subject?" Major Thompson inquired.

The colonel picked up his pen. "This is an internal issue we have with Miss Pearce here. Major Thompson, you have a long trip back to Mashhad. You are excused."

"Yes, sir." Major Thompson snapped his heels, gestured a half bow to the colonel and left the room.

Fraser wrote something on the open book in front of him. Malcolm and Rose remained silent and avoided eye contact while he wrote. Finally, he spoke. "Miss Pearce, my patience is running quite thin. And I warn you being tested does not bring out the best in me." He leaned back in his chair and continued, "We have asked Persian authorities for leniency for the boys. However, there are other important elements at play. Recently we have formed a partnership with Standard Oil, an American enterprise. With rising competition and other political changes, we have lost a good percentage of our control over the oil fields of Iraq and the Arabian Peninsula. We cannot lose any more. Our security and future depend on it." He took a linen handkerchief from his inside coat pocket and wiped his forehead. "Now, America's government, in support of other American oil companies, has entered the scene of the Persian oil fields. We don't like it."

Malcolm jumped in. "Russians equally don't like it."

The colonel without pause continued, "Americans are new in the politics of this region, and the Middle East is a dangerous region full of death traps." A hint of a grin appeared on Fraser's face as he looked at Malcolm. "The pun was not intended, of course."

Malcolm walked to the corner of Fraser's office where fancy bottles of hard liquor sat neatly on display. He set out three glasses, dropped two ice cubes in each glass, and poured a bit of whisky in each one. He placed one glass on the colonel's desk in front of him and turned to Rose. "On the other hand, the new communist Soviet Union is becoming aggressive at an alarming rate." He extended a glass of whiskey to Rose as he continued. "Their thirst and desire for Persian oil and access to the free waters of the Persian Gulf in the south is rapidly increasing. We need a strong and stable government in Persia to act as a buffer for Russia's potential aggression and expansion to the south."

Rose looked puzzled. She refused the drink and shook her head. "Gentlemen, not to change the subject, but if we, as you proclaim, Colonel, are after stability in the region, then why was Mr. Berkley asked to approve funding for a rather large supply of arms and ammunition for Sheikh Khazal of Khuzestan's province in the south of Persia just a few years ago? He is clearly opposing Reza Khan by demanding independence. This actually will push the region into further chaos!"

"For Christ's sake," the colonel snapped, "How would you, a nurse, know about this?" His voice had the peculiar sound of a very angry man.

Rose gave a passive look at Fraser and nonchalantly answered, "A month ago, Mr. Berkley felt nauseous after a rather contemptuous meeting with a fellow from London. He asked me to check his blood pressure. I saw a document about the aid on his desk. If my memory is correct, the number was 3,000 guns."

Malcolm couldn't wait anymore. Ever since the dinner party at Mr. Berkley's house he had a burning desire to ask the question. "Now that we are freely alluding to concealed scandals Miss Pearce, I'm curious as to the nature of your relationship with Mr. Berkley!"

Rose looked at Malcolm in disgust. "Scandal? I have no concealed scandals, Mr. Malcolm! Charles Berkley is my cousin."

Colonel Fraser gave a look from the corner of his eyes to Malcolm and exhaled. "Miss Pearce, the arms deal you referred to was about four or five years ago! At that time, we thought that Sheikh Khazal of Khuzestan was the answer. Now we believe Reza Khan is the answer." Colonel took a sip of his drink.

Rose shook her head. "Politics gives me nothing but headaches. I didn't mean to deviate. Let's return to the subject at hand—how to prevent a pair of teenagers from being executed without due process. Your keen acquaintance with Reza Khan is admirable; support him all you want. But if you doubt his willingness to reconsider sacrificing the life of two children for his political gain, then for God's sake, ask your colleagues at the American camp to wake up and demand the Persian authorities find the real instigators. Prosecute the real criminals, not children!"

Malcolm gazed at his glass. "Miss Pearce, we understand and appreciate your cry for justice." He paused to take another sip of whisky. "Believe me, we do. I also appreciate your tireless efforts on behalf of these two boys and especially Ali. But what puzzles me is why you are going through so much trouble to save two street rats. You demonstrate such a passion for their fate."

Fraser leaned forward on his desk. "Yes, particularly for the one named Ali. Is this really about justice? Or is it something deeper?"

Both men pinned their eyes on Rose. She shifted her weight on the chair and crossed her legs. After blinking several times, she softly replied. "Ali reminds me of my young brother, who died at fourteen from consumption. I've already mentioned that to Mr. Malcolm."

"Miss Pearce, I—"

Rose cut the colonel off and raised her voice. "And I shall do everything in my power to help save this poor boy's life."

Colonel Fraser sat back in his chair, speechless.

Malcolm emptied his glass. "Miss Pearce, you must forgive me. Your strength in the nursing field is commendable, however, when it comes to the science of politics, I'm afraid you are a bit, hmm … inexperienced. The only concern the Americans have at this point, in this part of the world, is the integrity of their prestige. In fact, Mr. Murray, the American chargé d'affaires, told me that they made sure both boys have passed puberty. Do you know why?"

Rose shook her head. "No, actually I'm bewildered as to the purpose of this."

Malcolm smiled. "Islamic law in this country forbids the execution of children who have not reached the age of puberty. Understand that Murray doesn't actually care about Islamic law. He just doesn't want any obstacles to a quick resolution."

Fraser jumped in. "Moreover, the United States demanded and has received a handsome sum of blood money. They have dug their heals in and are serious about their prestige. All parties are eagerly awaiting a quick resolution."

"And no one cares for justice or truth?" Rose asked, rising from the chair.

A long, awkward pause took over the room. Rose shifted her weight on her feet.

The colonel shook his head. "Miss Pearce, surely you can see the predicament here. I strongly advise you to waste no more of our precious time. Good day, miss." He pointed to the door.

Rose's face turned red. She hesitated for a second, looked at both men, and without a word left the room in haste.

"She and Berkley are becoming major irritations. We simply must find a way to remedy the situation," Fraser said, once Rose was gone.

"You don't seem to like my methods. Do you have any suggestions?" Malcolm asked.

The colonel looked out of his window for a moment. "I might have found a way to get rid of them." He turned toward Malcolm. "And I now have to get to it. You are dismissed."

33

MAJOR THOMSON

Malcolm found Major Thompson waiting for him in the hallway outside of Colonel Fraser's office. "Thompson, you are still here! I thought you were on your way to Mashhad by now."

"No, I'm not leaving without having a few drinks with my old chum."

"All right then, let's go to my office and drink gin."

"Proposal accepted."

Both men laughed. Malcolm put his right arm around Thompson's shoulder and then slid his hand to his neck and squeezed it on their walk to Malcolm's office. Once inside his office, Malcolm went straight to the liquor table and fixed two drinks.

"You have been quite busy lately," said Thompson as he accepted a drink from Malcolm.

"Yes, a lot has happened."

"What an awful end Major Imbrie suffered," Thompson mused. "Poor bloke, all that torment for what, a few lousy photographs?" He shook his head and took a sip of his gin.

"Don't fret. Sometimes lives are lost for a greater good. He knew very well what he had signed up for," Malcolm quipped.

"Are these curtains actually covering up a window?" Thompson pointed to a set of heavy, dark velvet curtains draped to the ground.

Malcolm nodded.

"Then, do you mind terribly if I open them. It's awfully dark and musty here." He didn't wait for Malcolm's response. Thompson pulled the curtains aside and opened the window, allowing sunshine to brighten the room. "There, now we have light and fresh air."

Malcolm didn't object. He sat on the edge of his desk, stared out the window, and sipped his gin.

"Who is this attractive young nurse, Rose Pearce?" Thompson asked. "Why is she so concerned about the camel driver?"

"She's just a temporary nuisance. Her concern about executing a fourteen-year-old boy shall soon pass."

"A fourteen-year-old *murderer*," Thompson corrected.

What Thompson said triggered a flashback in Malcolm's mind. Again, he saw himself covered in his stepfather's blood. His heart pounded faster and a chill went up his spine. His mother's bloody face hovered over his sister, Emma. George, his drunk stepfather, raised his fist to strike them both when he charged him. He was fourteen when he killed that bastard. He was also a fourteen-year-old murderer.

"Are you worried about the Americans' reaction?" Thompson asked, jolting Malcolm back to the present.

"What's that?" he sneered. "No, not at all. The Sinclair Oil representative has already left the country. Americans are scaling down their operations here. The Russians are the ones we need to watch carefully."

"Right you are," Thompson agreed. "They have become quite active in Mashhad lately. They're rigorously promoting, supporting, and expanding communism."

"Since we are on the subject, I'd like to ask you for a favor, Thompson."

"What's that?"

"Perhaps you know of a man called Asef."

"Asef, hmm, are you referring to Asef-e-Bakoie?"

"Spot-on." Malcolm reacted.

"He's a notoriously brutal man." Thompson said, "We have tracked him to many communist activities in Mashhad. We believe that he is one of the major instigators of the Turkman's rebellion, for which we are currently aiding Persian military. And let me tell you, good sir, that it is not pretty. What about him?"

Malcolm took a drink. "He is actually a Soviet intelligence officer. His real name is Nicolai Aliev. He's fluent in several languages, including Farsi. He is a man of many secrets. He often disguises himself as a Persian. One of his aliases is Asef-e-Bakoie. I want you to arrest him and send him here to Tehran."

"He is a difficult man to pin. We are aware of many of his crimes, but can't pin him. What do you stand to gain from having a troublemaker like him in your backyard?"

Malcom contemplated for a moment, "He is a very clever man with deep contacts. You can't get him officially. It has to be a covert operation."

"But you didn't answer my question, Malcolm. Why here in Tehran?"

"I want him to lead me to the hornets' nest. Let's say, just recently, an opening of sorts has happened that I want him to fill."

"Are you referring to Kerensky?"

"What do you know about him?" Malcolm probed.

"I read it in my intelligence report that he was a *Cheka* agent and his dead body was found in the slums of south Tehran. But this Asef fellow is an extremely dangerous man. I don't want to lose any of my men over this operation."

Malcolm looked Thompson in the eyes. "This is important. Do I need to remind you that on more than one occasion, I've saved your neck?"

Thompson chuckled. "Saved *my* neck? I don't recall any major incident. Please do elaborate."

"Don't be daft!" Malcolm retorted. "All right, how about the incident in Damascus with Minna? My friend, not only I saved your honor, your career, but most importantly, your life."

"My honor? My career? What a lot of absolute nonsense, old chap. I'm still not over your intrusion with Minna."

Malcolm looked him in the eyes. "Intrusion?"

"Yes, intrusion. There I was, on my holidays enjoying a conversation with a charming young lady with a slight hope of a wonderful holiday romance." Thompson recounted, "Then you barged in with a ridiculous, fabricated story, punched me in the face, and spooked her forever from my life. What part of *that* saved my honor or career, or even my life?"

Malcolm laughed loudly. "Poor chap! You didn't even know what a dangerous affair you were getting into. Her complete name was Minna Weizmann. She was the mistress of a German intelligence officer, Curt Prüfer. We knew for a while that she was spying for the Germans in Egypt against Great Britain."

"Weizmann? Isn't that a Jewish surname? It is awfully familiar."

"Yes, she was a Jewish immigrant from White Russia."

"If I recall correctly, she said that she was a doctor. If that was correct, I'm puzzled by why a charming young Jewish doctor would spy for Germany?"

"Well, we knew that Curt Prüfer had developed a successful Jewish spy network in Egypt. And my friend, you were not charming her, it was quite the opposite. Her objective was to seduce you. As a young British officer stationed in Cairo, on a short recreation trip to Damascus, you had valuable intelligence for her ringmaster."

And suddenly, with the clarity of a man too long deceived, Thompson understood the shocking truth "Oh, my lord! I was a mark! That is riveting. And why did you never reveal this to me before?"

"I'm afraid that is classified intelligence—above your clearance level."

"Why are you telling me now?"

"It was sensitive intelligence during the Great War. The Germans lost. Prüfer is no longer a threat."

"Weizmann, why is that name so familiar to me?" Thompson pondered.

"Chaim Weizmann is a high-profile Zionist activist," Malcolm replied. "Minna is his younger sister. Sort of the black sheep of the family, I suppose."

"Yes, yes, they believe Palestine belongs to the Jews." Thompson crossed his legs and smoothed his trousers. "But why did she spy against us for Germany? We had been very accommodating to the Jews."

"She detested Russia and what they have done to Jewish people," Malcolm answered. "I suppose she subscribed to the notion of 'the enemy of my enemy is my friend.' During the Great War, Germans were archenemies of the Russians. Plus, she was Prüfer's lover."

"What was your role in all this?"

"My objectives were to get close to her and find out all about the Jewish spy network and neutralize them. So, my friend, be grateful to me. She was a smart and effective operator. You could have been accused of treason and court-martialed."

"What a ghastly ordeal! I must concede, you have done some good to me. Perhaps, it will do me good to remember it. I'm indebted to you, my friend." Thompson moved closer to Malcolm, put his arm around Malcolm's neck and embraced him, causing him to wince. "So, what happened after you got me out of that mess. Did you get to know her?" Thompson quipped, grinning.

Malcolm smiled. "No, according to my command, I jeopardized the mission by saving your neck. I was transferred to Russia for about a year and a half and then here, to Persia, land of chaos and poverty."

"Oh, no, what I meant was, did you get to *know* her?"

Malcolm shook his head.

"Is there any special one in your life?"

Malcolm continued to silently shake his head in response.

"Nothing to tie you down, huh? Then what is in the future for you? Another mission? Another espionage?"

Malcolm took another sip of his drink. "I live in the present, mate. The only..." He stopped, catching himself.

"Go on mate, say it. It's all right. It's just me."

"I must concede that it would be nice to get out of this rotten place," Malcolm admitted.

"Come now!" Thompson raised his voice. "This place is the land of opportunities. With all these recent discoveries of oil fields in Persia, our country will profit significantly. Militarily, this is the place we stop the mama bear's ever-expanding territory. This place is becoming a hotbed of spies from all over. So, you have oil, politics, espionage, and military actions all in one place. We've got it all, mate. Persia is like a candy store for people like you and me."

"I suppose," Malcolm muttered.

"No, seriously, where would you prefer to be if not here?"

Malcolm stared at his gin, swirled it in the glass, and took a small sip. "Europe, or better yet, back in Russia."

"Why Europe? Nothing noteworthy is happening in Europe now. All the action is here!"

"Quite the opposite, my friend," Malcolm persisted. "I believe the Paris Peace Conference didn't finish the job correctly. The ruling apparatus is still largely intact. That, old chap, in my view, will leave Germany to easily rebuild its alliances and eventually come back at us with a vengeance. I want to be there to stop it. And if I can't, I want to be in Russia to stop the Bolsheviks from spreading their communism germs all over the world." Hunching forward, he stared at Thomson and continued. "But instead, I'm stuck in this God-forsaken chaotic land, witnessing the execution of a few barbarian children and—" Malcolm noticed he was ranting and stopped, worried he had already revealed too much. Too much gin, perhaps.

"My friend, you are being pessimistic," Thompson reacted. "This dark, windy tunnel does have a light at the end. Reza Khan is our boy. Once he becomes the king, we will completely dominate this region." Thompson paused, and then he smiled a roguish smile. "As you're well aware, all major navies of the world are converting their ships' fuel from coal to oil. It's a substantial race, old chap, and this country can help us to lead it."

Malcolm shook his head. "I know all that! You are repeating facts—"

Thompson cut him off. "Sorry mate, but it's an old habit of mine. I have to go through the motions. The U.S. is exiting the scene, thanks to Major Imbrie, may God bless his soul, and we are expanding our control and influences here in Persia. You may get the chance to establish a new intelligentsia. We'll train Reza Khan's new military, and that means more money and security for us."

Malcolm wanted to change the subject. He didn't share Thompson's enthusiasm. "Going back to the favor I asked of you. Will you deliver?"

"I hope you know what you're getting into. Are you in possession of all the facts? This one is not a pretty Jewish doctor."

"This is my chess board. I know what I'm doing." Malcolm played with a match box flipping it on its sides over and over again, waiting for Thompson's agreement with growing irritation.

"Would it be possible, in your twisted mind, to find a way to explain to me why I should endanger my men for this strange request of yours?" Thompson looked straight into Malcolm's eyes.

"All right." Malcolm smiled. This was a great chance to educate his friend in what he believed was the art of Machiavellianism in espionage with a British touch. "Beliefs such as religions, political doctrines, etcetera, traditionally are amongst the best tools to control the public of any society. Bolsheviks are eager to export their brand of communism. Aliev is very effective with what he does. He is focused, pragmatic, and cold hearted. I have prepared a stage for him to play on, so to speak."

"Oh, how is that?"

"Let's say, there is an eager group of young minds, thirsty for learning about the great fruits of socialism, ready to accept a strong leader, here in the capital. Aliev will not return to Mashhad if he can have a stronger group under his talons here. Boris, the head of Cheka here, will not allow him to leave." He paused a moment as a new thought struck him, then he continued. "Keeping him close to me allows me to influence his network and activities. Who knows, his head can become a valuable gift for a certain new king who may need to prove himself to the powers that be."

"You sly fox, Malcolm, always planning several steps ahead of the game. So, in other words, Aliev will become a sort of job security for you. Isn't that right?"

Malcolm pushed his lower lips upwards and shrugged his shoulders.

Thompson leaned toward Malcolm, and with a lower and softer tone said, "I think it's also personal with you. What have these Russian chaps done to you that you hate them so much?"

"It's not the Russians, per se," Malcolm tossed the match box on his desk. "It's the communism that I hate. I think of it as a form of cancer. The sooner it's eliminated, the better it is for the rest of us. So, what is it, Thompson, will you do it?"

Thompson raised his glass. "Consider it done." He swiftly chugged his drink and placed his glass on the table with a loud thump.

The two men shook hands and Thompson departed.

Malcolm remained in his office. He topped off his glass with more gin and thought about his rant to Thompson. His mind persistently circled around one topic, witnessing the execution of a few barbarian children. "Children, rats, they all are nuisances," he thought.

The image of Ali appeared in his mind over and over again. A fourteen-year-old pawn who showed up at the wrong place at the wrong time? A hard-working kid he secretly dressed as a murderer. Does his life matter?

He again pushed his lower lip upward against his upper lip, the facial equivalent of a shrug. He reminded himself to do a better job at compartmentalizing what was happening to Ali. He concluded that there were far larger plans at play, and the life of a camel driver boy would not matter.

A moment later he muttered, "Or would it?"

34

THE END GAME

Saturday, November 1, 1924

Malcolm couldn't sleep, so he decided to start his day early. It was 6:30 a.m. when he arrived at the embassy's dining room. He was drinking his tea and reading the paper when Colonel Fraser dropped his hat onto the table and sat in front of him. He had his full uniform on.

"You are going to be very busy today, Malcolm."

Malcolm folded his newspaper neatly and put it away. The colonel didn't wait for Malcolm's response.

"I requested an urgent transfer for Pearce and Berkley last week. I've received it. Today, you are going to supervise their departure. It is of the utmost importance that they leave today. We simply cannot have them here when they execute the teenagers."

"And that is tomorrow at dawn." Malcolm added.

"Yes."

"It would be hard for Berkley's family."

"I am not without compassion, but it must be done!" Fraser

282

rubbed his stubbled jaw. "I have asked Sergeant Simpson and his squadron to report to you. Take him and his men to facilitate their speedy removal today. Use force if you must. They simply cannot be here tomorrow. Are you clear?"

"Yes." Malcolm's eyes drifted to his newspaper on the table and his fingers continued tapping. A waiter came by the table and asked the colonel for his order. He asked for a glass of water.

"What is it, Malcolm, you seem preoccupied."

"Apparently, Adam had separate meetings outside of the embassy with APOC and Reilly during his July visit."

"What of it?" Fraser shrugged. "I fail to see the significance."

"These meetings took place near the time of Imbrie's mob attack. Reilly doesn't get involved with small matters. Besides, I don't trust the Standard men. There is a reason for Standard Oil's infamous reputation. Their greed overrides everything else."

"What are you insinuating, Malcolm? That the Americans killed their own man?"

"They have done worse. Profit is their only god."

"Well, if Reilly was involved and he operated without our protection, then that must have been an important covert mission. You said it yourself, Reilly is well-connected. Therefore, the order must have come from the high command. Let it go."

"What if APOC and Reilly were the ones that—"

Fraser cut him off, "What's done is done. Let it go. We have a lot to do." The waiter brought a glass of water. Both men remained silent until the waiter disappeared. The colonel leaned on the table and continued in a low voice. "The plan worked. Americans are licking their wounds and exiting the scene. APOC is dominating the Persian oil affair. It is between us and the Russians now." He took a sip of his water. "Reza Khan is on the right track and we are pleased with him. I have just authorized the delivery of weapons, and soon he will be on his way to stabilizing the region. If he passes his test and calms the country, then we'll be in the saddle. That is a victory. Now, off you go, you have a full day ahead of you." The colonel emptied his glass of water and left the table.

***

Later that morning, Malcolm stayed a few feet away from Berkley's office door and gave a nod to Sergeant Simpson, who was closer to the door, to proceed. Sergeant Simpson was a short, slender man who stood purposefully. The sergeant gave three strong knocks.

A male voice ordered, "Enter."

"Good day, Mr. Berkley. I'm Sergeant Simpson. I have been tasked with facilitating your transportation, sir."

"Oh great! Now they have sent a military man to spy over me," Berkley grumbled.

"No sir, my objectives are to use my team and any resources possible to ensure safe, comfortable, and speedy transportation for you and your family to your destination."

"Oh, I see."

Malcolm slowly walked into Berkley's office. The moment he saw Malcolm, he burst into an outrage, "Oh, remarkable! Now there are two spies watching over me!"

Malcolm's head was down. He patiently waited for Berkley's rage to subside.

Sergeant Simpson said, "I have men and trucks standing by, sir."

"Nonsense! I haven't even told my family yet. What's the rush?"

Malcolm looked at Berkley. "We need to talk, Berkley. The plan has changed." He turned to the sergeant, "Give us a minute please."

The sergeant nodded and left the room. Malcolm shut the office door.

"What in heaven's name has happened now?" Berkley asked.

"They are going to execute Ali at dawn tomorrow."

"What? This soon? I'm certain Rose will insist to file an appeal!"

"This is a military court. No appeal processes. Besides, the order came straight from above. Reza Khan will not get what he wants unless this matter is resolved. He is running out of time. The country is on the verge of collapse. This must be done. We want you and your family out of here before the execution. You are leaving tonight."

"This is totally preposterous! We can't possibly be ready in such a short time! I just received my transfer order telegram this morning! There is no indication of such an urgency. How about Rose?"

"Miss Pearce is reassigned as well. I'll go to her as soon as I'm satisfied that your family has all the resources needed for the move. I have arranged for a number of men to assist you and Mrs. Berkley in every feasible way. A driver with additional security personnel will be at your door before dark tonight. This is for your family's safety."

Berkley dropped his pen and slammed shut the book in front of him. "I must go home now." He grabbed his coat and left the office in a hurry. Malcolm followed him. The moment the sergeant saw them, he rushed and led them to his vehicle. The three men drove to Berkley's house.

Malcolm shadowed Berkley as soon as they arrived. He couldn't afford to let Berkley out of his sight, or to have anything go awry with the plan to get the Berkley family out of the county as soon as possible. Colonel Fraser would make certain that Malcolm receive a substantial reprimand if Rose or Berkley interfered with the execution.

Malcolm followed Berkley into the house. It looked as if no one was home. Berkley called his wife a few times before the men heard a faint response, "Here on the terrace!"

Mrs. Berkley was outside, hosting an afternoon tea with two of her friends. The table was neatly set with a tea pot and cakes. As the autumn weather had already settled in, the women were enjoying Tehran's pale fall sunshine. Trees in the yard were in full display of their colorful leaves.

Berkley and Malcolm quietly approached the ladies. It seemed like Berkley wanted his wife to enjoy every tranquil second before hearing the bad news. A woman in a pleated red skirt sitting to the left of Mrs. Berkley set her tea cup on the table, and with a dramatic gesture said, "I just adore the Duchess of York's fashion style—"

Mrs. Berkley interrupted, "Absolutely, have you seen her—"

Mr. Berkley put on a fake-looking smile, approaching his wife from behind and interjected, "Good afternoon, lovely to see you all. Aren't you ladies chilly sitting outside?"

She turned her head and exclaimed, "Oh, Charles!" then she saw Malcolm, "James?" her brows raised in surprise.

A woman replied, "Mr. Berkley, we are simply soaking up every minute of this magnificent tapestry of color and the warmth of Tehran's last autumn sunshine. Would you and your friend care to join us?"

"Thank you for your kindness, Mrs. Johnson, I'm sure it is lovely. However, I'm here for an urgent matter. May I borrow Mrs. Berkley for a moment?"

Jane, for once, was speechless at the interruption to her gathering. She kept toggling her glare back and forth between Malcolm and her husband. Berkley went to his study and his wife followed him, a worried look darkening her face. He closed the door. Malcolm gave them some privacy and waited outside. He couldn't help but overhear Jane's loud outrage over the news.

"Charles, how could you do this to me? How could this be possible? Who can even imagine a family to evacuate in such swiftness? I refuse to believe it! Go back and explain to your superior that a move of such magnitude takes days, no, weeks, to prepare! Do you hear me?"

A few moments passed and then another outburst by Mrs. Berkley. "This is absurd, Charles. You must have done some horrible act and your superior is punishing us for it. You simply must go back and fix it." Malcolm couldn't make out what Mr.

Berkley said, as he kept his voice low. But soon after, he heard Mrs. Berkley concede, this time in a more controlled volume.

When they emerged from the room, Mrs. Berkley looked at Malcolm in utter disbelief. "James, can you assist us in delaying this treacherous ordeal?"

Before Malcolm could respond, Agnes' voice came from behind him. "Papa, what is happening? What are those men doing outside?"

"Agnes! You are home much earlier than usual, what is the matter, dear?" her mother asked.

"The principal dismissed me early. She said that I'm needed at home. What is happening?"

Mr. Berkley answered, "Darling, go on into the study and talk to your mother. She will explain everything. I must speak with Mr. Malcolm concerning a private matter and shall finish soon."

Agnes gave a strange look to Malcolm and followed her mother who was already on her way to apologize to her friends for the unexpected interruption, and to see them out.

Berkley guided Malcolm outside. "What are all these men doing here? Must we have such a display?" He pointed to the five British soldiers standing by a truck.

"They are here to help. You are faced with an enormous task in a short period of time. I doubt you can afford to refuse any help, Mr. Berkley."

Before Berkley could argue, his wife's guests came out the front door, said their good-byes, and left amidst a gaggle of whispers.

Agnes appeared at the front door shouting, "Papa, I must talk to you now! Will you please come inside right away?"

Malcolm looked at Berkley and raised his brows.

"Don't have them touch anything until I come back," Berkley looked at both Malcolm and Sergeant Simpson who was standing next to him.

"Actually, I'm on my way to talk to Rose." Malcolm took out a pack of cigarettes and offered one to Sergeant Simpson, who declined it. Then he returned to the embassy vehicle.

Back in the embassy compound he found Rose in the clinic, sitting behind a wooden desk writing a report.

"May I have a moment please?"

Rose looked up, paused, and replied, "If it's about the telegram, I received it this morning."

"Yes, but it's even more urgent, I'm afraid."

Rose informed a colleague nearby that she was taking a break and asked Malcolm to follow her to a small patio facing the embassy's garden. The patio's floor was carpeted with colorful fallen leaves of the surrounding trees. She took a cigarette out. Malcolm immediately lit it for her with his lighter.

Rose exhaled a puff of smoke. "What dark shadows are you going to cast now?"

Malcolm looked around to make sure no one else could hear their conversation. "My orders are to get you and Berkley's family out of Tehran tonight."

Rose looked into Malcolm's eyes. "You are testing me, Mr. Malcolm. I warn you, being tested does not bring out the best in me."

"My orders are clear."

"I shall not remove myself from this city until Ali is free or his prison terms are clear."

Rose's stern tone didn't settle well with Malcolm. He decided to be more direct with Rose. "Ali is to be executed at dawn tomorrow."

Rose's eyes didn't move from Malcolm. She stayed quiet and continued glaring at him as tears welled up. She shivered, and a moment later, tear drops rolled silently down her cheeks.

Malcolm took his eyes away from her, sat on the edge of a half-wall separating the patio from the rest of the compound, and remained silent, giving her privacy in her obvious grief.

She pointed her trembling index finger at him. "I won't let you get away with this." Her voice was shaking. "You ...you think you've calculated every move? You think you're in control? No. Not this time! This one is different, Mr. James Malcolm. You have underestimated me. I shall *not* let you get away with it!"

A cool wind blew from the south and swept through the area. Leaves scuttered across the patio, augmenting Rose's temperament, as if they too were protesting the unjust fate of Ali.

Malcolm kept his face impassive. Detachment, or at least the display of it, was easy for him. He wasn't bothered by her threats. What he didn't like was that she accused him of not being in control. He was always in control. He had to be. Rose was a nuisance, but she was still manageable in his assessment. He quickly surveyed the patio to see who else might have witnessed her outrage. No worries there, no one was around. Malcolm decided to ignore Rose's outburst, but to stay vigilant of her actions and focus on the task at hand.

"Nevertheless, I'll pick you and Berkeleys up around 10 p.m. You'll be driven to a port in the south to board your ship."

Rose dashed out of the patio. Malcolm decided not to follow her, but to enjoy a smoke in the quiet and think. When he finished with his cigarette, he extinguished it and went back to the clinic. No sign of Rose there. He inquired from the front clerk about her. Apparently, she had left the building after their meeting.

Malcolm acquired an embassy car and motored slowly toward Rose's neighborhood. Considering her state of mind, she couldn't have gone too far on foot. But he didn't see her on the streets. After arriving at her flat, he decided to confront her at home. He knocked on the door. Her roommate answered.

"I'm here for Miss Pearce."

The roommate sneezed, and through a stuffy nose replied, "Pardon me, uh, she isn't here. She's at work."

Malcolm nodded, got back to the car and drove around for another ten minutes in search of her. Giving up, he returned to the embassy. Inside the main building, he checked the kitchen and the library, but found no trace of Rose. Time was being wasted in all this searching--but perhaps she needed to let off some steam, collect her thoughts, and control her emotions. He envisioned that soon she would return to her flat to pack. Orders were orders.

He decided to take a short break, check his messages, and have a sip of whisky. Malcolm unlocked his office door and entered.

"Change of plans, Mr. Malcolm?"

Pieces of broken glass lay scattered on the floor underneath the French casement window, and a breeze blowing the drapes indicated Rose's clever entrance to his supposedly secure, private office.

"You broke my window!"

"That doesn't matter. The important thing is for you to sit behind your desk quietly and listen to my new plan. That is, of course, if you don't want to be exposed."

Malcolm kept his eyes focused on her every infinitesimal eye movement as he slowly approached his chair behind his desk.

"Exposed?" Malcolm asked. "What exactly are you going to expose, Miss Pearce? And to whom?"

Her eyes were red-rimmed and still wet with tears. She corrected her posture and looked directly at him. "Your despicable plot, your ruthless plan, and your lack of compassion for the innocent lives that your schemes have destroyed." She sniffed a bit and finished. "To the press, of course."

Engaging a young woman in a fruitless argument wasn't intriguing or productive for Malcolm. He decided to take a different approach. "All right, tell me about your new plan." Malcolm sank into his chair and put his arms on his desk, making a steeple with his fingers.

Rose sniffed and wiped her tears with a handkerchief. "I don't know much about politics, but I'm certain that the brutal death of an American diplomat and blaming and executing a fourteen-year-old child ..." She stopped to wipe a stray tear trickling down her check. Taking a deep breath, she fought to compose herself. "And

... and executing an innocent fourteen-year-old will not be forgotten. It will become history. It appears that the course of the events cannot be changed." Pausing, as if for some dramatic effect, she looked directly at Malcolm. "Therefore, I want to be there to witness it. I want Ali to see me there. In the prison yard." Her look was determined, even as her lips quivered.

Malcolm remained silent for a few moments, pondering her proposal. He moved up to the edge of his seat. "Execution is an utterly gruesome ordeal. A young woman of your age shouldn't be exposed to such violence."

"I'm firm in my position, Mr. Malcolm."

"Miss Pearce, your proposal poses a substantial risk for me. The alternative for me is to enforce my orders and remove you from Tehran, willingly or otherwise, tonight. Your threat of exposing my so-called plot to the press, which is, of course, totally absurd and a product of pure fantasy, isn't substantiated with any facts."

Rose moved slightly in her chair and kept her eyes fixed on Malcolm. "I had a feeling this dreadful day would come. As a precaution, I've arranged multiple packages to be distributed among a number of journalists in case of my disappearance or harm. Each package reveals the details of a clandestine operation, sponsored by British agents, that resulted in Major Imbrie's murder."

Malcolm sat back on his chair, his gaze at Rose intense and penetrating. A few moments of silence passed. Then Malcolm broke the silence. "I am certain you are aware that my colleagues and I here at the embassy are the officers of His Majesty. Any accusation of wrongdoing is a serious matter and may suffer severe consequences."

Rose didn't flinch. "Distribution of these documents can be stopped only by me. And I shall stop it when I'm satisfied that my request has been honored."

Malcolm moved forward and put his arms back on his desk.

"Miss Pearce, wouldn't it be easier if you just proceeded with the travel and forget this God-forsaken place?"

Rose crossed her arms and sat up stiffly at the edge of her chair, glaring back at Malcolm.

Malcolm put on his most calm and controlled demeanor, even though he could feel his blood pressure rising. "What documents? Make believe ones fabricated by a deranged nurse?"

His bullying didn't deter Rose. "I have written a detailed report of your clandestine meetings with Colonel Fraser and a Persian man named Ibrahim, in places like *ghahve-khaneh*, where Ali worked. I know about your discussion with Major Imbrie and how you lured him to the shrine for the purpose of taking photos when you very well knew that the public at that location were quite agitated by provocations that you master-minded. I even included clippings of newspaper reports about the incident. Furthermore, I have highlighted, and cross-referenced them as evidence of my claim that you, Mr. Malcolm, are the responsible operator for such a calamity."

Malcolm shook his head. "No one will pay attention to such ramblings."

Rose smirked. "Quite the contrary, sir. Tabloids love drama. Are you willing to risk a wager on it?"

Malcolm leaned back in his chair, pushed it back a little and crossed his legs. "All right, what is my guarantee?"

"Once all my requirements are met, you will not see or read any references to this story in any press, nor would anyone gain the knowledge of it. Your secret, sadly, will be safe." Rose sat still as her eyes stayed focused on Malcolm's eyes. Only her right eyebrow slightly rose.

After a few moments of weighty silence, Malcolm lifted his eyebrows, and with his hands offered the impression that he was all out of options. "Well, I'm positive that you will not be the only woman present there. I shall arrive with a driver to pick you up from your residence at half past three in the morning. We'll drive to the prison yard. There, I will personally escort you to the prison's courtyard, where the firing squad will execute the two men. The driver will return with the Berkeley family. Immediately after the execution, you will join them and your trip to the port city of Bushehr in the south of Persia will begin. A ship will take you all to India, where your new prospective posts are assigned. Is this acceptable?"

Rose looked down and nodded her head quietly in agreement. Hot tears ran down her cheeks. Her sad eyes and her weary face exposed the dreadful impediment she surely felt. She stood up and quietly left Malcolm's office.

Malcolm didn't like Rose's plan. It was extremely risky, exposed, and entirely based on a moody promise of actions. A prudent course for him would be to find out the names of her cohorts, and how they were planning to distribute this potentially damaging information among the press. But it was too late for that sort of reconnaissance; he didn't have that much time left—only about twelve hours. He felt angry, as he had completely underestimated Rose. He should have investigated her more thoroughly. But who could have guessed an ordinary nurse could be so resourceful, or be so empowered with such determination? He had a lot to learn about this new generation of Brits.

He pounded his desk and cursed his bad luck.

He needed to devise a plan B. And fast.

35

FAREWELL

Sunday, November 2, 1924

AT PRECISELY 3:30 a.m. the next morning, Malcolm's driver stopped in front of Rose's residence. The window curtains on the second floor were pulled aside and the flicker of a lantern was detectable. Malcolm got out of the car and walked toward the door. Mr. Berkley also got out of the car. He had decided to accompany Rose to the dreadful execution. Malcolm gave the door a quiet tap.

Belinda, Rose's flat mate, opened the door but offered no greeting. She left the front door open for Malcolm and Mr. Berkley to enter and went to fetch her roommate. But Rose was already on her way down the stairs. She wore a long black coat with a black draped hat. A black lace veil completely covered her face. She carried a small wicker cage containing four white birds. When she approached the bottom of the stairs, she noticed Berkley.

"Charles!"

Mr. Berkley took his hat off and said, "I thought you could use a friend."

Rose nodded.

Malcolm stopped Rose and put his hand on the cage. "May I?"

Rose let Malcolm lift up the cage to his face and examined the birds.

"Homing pigeons! Why are you taking them?"

Rose snatched the cage back from Malcolm. "You will see." Without any further delay, she proceeded to the waiting car. Malcolm swiftly grabbed her elbow and stopped her.

"I'm sorry, I have to know before I let you move on."

"Mr. Malcolm, I suggest you focus on your task and deliver what I have asked of you. Once I'm satisfied, two of these pigeons will carry my code to stop delivering the sealed envelopes to the journalists." She yanked her elbow away from Malcolm's grip.

Clever girl. Very clever indeed, Malcolm thought. His plan B wouldn't work. Her cohorts would spill the story to the press and a huge fiasco would come upon the British diplomats. He would have to ride this one out.

The driver took a few pieces of luggage that were stacked by the door and placed them in the car. Mr. Berkley escorted Rose by her elbow, helping her through the door. No words were spoken between the two as they walked somberly to the car.

Malcolm sat in the front. Mr. Berkley and Rose sat in the back with the cage resting on her lap.

The city was covered in darkness. Not a gleam of a solitary star penetrated the blanket of clouds hanging heavily in the November sky. The chill in the air warned of the early arrival of a long and cold winter. Only a few stray dogs in search of food were visible on the empty streets.

Once they arrived at the prison, the driver opened the car door for Rose and helped her get out. Rose left the bird cage in the car and asked the driver not to touch it.

A cold breeze swept through a pile of dead maple tree leaves at

Rose's feet. The air smelled of death. The sky had turned from black to grey, and silhouettes of naked trees became visible, adding to the eerie atmosphere at the prison. Malcolm usually enjoyed being a part of these ghostly, secretive events that only a few selected people could bear to witness. It helped him to justify his actions and provided him with a certain degree of self-importance. But that dawn, he felt different. He wasn't sure why.

Malcolm processed them through the guards at the main gate and walked with them into the prison yard. Rows of chairs awaited observers. He offered Rose and Mr. Berkley seats in the middle of the second row. Rose refused his offer, choosing to sit at the edge of the last row. Mr. Berkley sat next to her.

Malcolm preferred to sit in the front row at such events, but he needed to keep an eye on Rose, so he sat next to Mr. Berkley. No one spoke.

A few minutes later more observers arrived, some British officials, Persian authorities, American diplomats, and a woman dressed in a long, heavy coat and hat draped in black walked by them and sat gracefully in the front row.

A few dim lampposts and a grey sky were the only sources of light in the yard. The air was chilly, the silence and suspense were disturbing, even to Malcolm. This was a risky arrangement for him. There were British, American, and other officials present, and Rose was a wild card. The chance of exposure of the British role in this affair were very high.

Finally, the gate to the west of the prison yard opened and the firing squad marched in. Eight Cossack soldiers with their Russian-style uniforms, black lamb's wool hats and rifles on their shoulders started a slow procession to the loud marching count of their commander. Their knee-high boots pounded the ground in unison, creating an even rhythm as they stepped together. Their somber faces were indicative of the gravity of what they were tasked to do.

The squad stopped in front of a wall.

"Squad left!" The commander ordered.

The Cossacks used the toes of their right foot and the heels of their left to pivot to their left. Stamping into squad attention, they faced the wall. If there had been more light, observers could have easily seen dozens of bullet holes and old blood stains. Malcolm knew they were there.

A small wooden door on the east side of the yard creaked opened, and two prisoners, their hands tied and feet chained, shuffled toward the wall, sandwiched in between two guards. Seyyed Hussein in front and Ali behind. Seyyed Hussein walked in short steps with his shoulders drooped and his back hunched forward. He whimpered as he proceeded. Malcolm thought he heard Seyyed mumbling over and over that he was innocent and shouldn't be there.

Ali however, exhibited a good amount of self-control. The chains on his feet forced him to take short steps, but he managed to walk tall and look straight ahead. His face appeared malnourished and tired, but the way he carried himself radiated bravery. He walked as if he understood the sick joke destiny had played on him, but he wasn't willing to succumb to it. A small hint of bravado in the way he carried himself sent a chill up Malcolm's spine.

Malcolm, concerned that Rose could react with an emotional outburst, watched her intensely. She sat unmoved.

When Seyyed Hussein reached the front row chairs, he turned to the observers, dropped on his knees and cried loudly in Farsi, "I'm innocent! I haven't committed any murder! Please have mercy on me! Don't let them do this! Please have mercy on me!"

Malcolm leaned over to Berkley and whispered, "In the Persian justice system, the victim's family can forgive the accuser and stop the execution at the last minute. He is begging for mercy."

"So presumably, Mrs. Imbrie can stop this execution. Am I correct that she is the stately woman sitting in the front row?" Berkley whispered back to Malcolm.

"Yes, but don't get any ideas. Mrs. Imbrie completely understands that this is much bigger than one person's vendetta. She is fully committed to the process," Malcolm explained.

Berkley nodded. They both glanced at Rose. She looked as if she were glued to her chair, sitting tall, and looking straight ahead.

A translator for the American delegation explained and translated Seyyed's plea word by word for Mrs. Imbrie and the other Americans and Brits attending. They sat unmoved.

Guards pulled Hussein up from the ground and shoved him toward the wall. Ali, on the other hand, didn't beg for his life. He stood tall. Hussein's howling made the situation impossible to bear. Malcolm had experienced executions in almost every shape and form, including cries and begging, but nothing like the show Seyyed Hussein put on.

Perhaps it was due to his youth. He was a seventeen-year-old teenager, after all.

Malcolm observed Ali who stood tall and appeared calm. The kid couldn't be proud of his actions, as he didn't do anything wrong. How he is keeping it together? He wondered if he himself could remain so collected, so at peace, in the face of a firing squad. How would he have reacted at age fourteen if he had been sentenced to execution for murdering his stepfather? He found himself admiring Ali's brave behavior.

Malcolm turned his head to check on Rose. He could detect her trembling through the edge of the lace veil and hat, illuminated by the light behind her. Her friendship with Ali and her fondness for him was obvious. He could no longer deny their bond. She could have easily chosen not to get involved and forget about the boy. Instead, she was sitting in a dark, cold prison yard that reeked with death and suffering to witness the execution of her young friend.

From somewhere he couldn't explain, the words of poet George Elliot bounced into Malcolm's head, "Only in the agony of parting do we look in the depths of love." He'd never known that kind of love. And right then, he envied the depth of their devotion to one another.

A guard shouted at Seyyed Hussein, "Stop wailing and start your last prayers!"

Hussein stood up and with a shaky voice joined Ali in reciting their last prayers out loud, *"Ashahdo-an La-ellaha ell-allah,* I testify that there is no God other than the God. *Ashahdo-an Mohammadan rasool lell-allah,* I declare that Muhammad is the messenger of God ..."

Rose stood up.

Malcolm saw her move, and his heart pounded faster. He sat alert, on the edge of his chair, ready to detain her if she did anything crazy. What was she up to?

Rose quietly walked behind the last row of chairs. Malcolm watched her disappear into a dark corner. Then he looked at Ali, who was still praying and hadn't noticed Rose. Or perhaps he didn't recognize her in the dim light of dawn with the black veil over her face.

The guards lined the two men against the wall and offered them each a blindfold. Seyyed Hussein accepted it, but Ali refused the blindfold with a shake of his head and continued his prayers. Finally, Ali raised his head up and stared at the spectators. His face showed no emotion—neither anger nor fear.

The commander ordered the firing squad to prepare their rifles. The unison sound of multiple rifles cocking echoed in the small, enclosed yard. The commander raised his right hand, which held a sword.

Rose had not returned to her seat.

Where had the woman disappeared to? What was she doing? Perhaps she changed her mind about watching the execution. Malcolm thought he should have followed her.

"Aim!" The commander's order boomed in the yard.

Just then, Rose ran into the yard. She wore a solid, bright white dress, her long blond hair exposed and floating in the air as she ran. In her right hand, she waved a piece of paper.

Ali saw her, and his face opened up into a huge smile.

Rose ran closer to Ali, screaming as loud as she could, "Ali, Ali, you are free! You are free, my dear! I've got your release paper in my hand! You are free—"

"FIRE!" The commander shouted, unfazed by Rose's spectacle, which he couldn't understand.

Bam! The thunderous sound of eight rifles shooting in unison echoed in the prison's courtyard.

Two lifeless bodies, riddled with bullets, dropped onto the ground.

Malcolm rose and rushed to the front of the chairs where Rose was kneeling, just a few meters from the bodies, crying. Her crumpled form looked like a bundle of white carnations against the dark grey surroundings. In her hand, she clenched a piece of white paper.

Malcolm slipped it out of her hand to examine it. The paper was blank. There was no release paper for Ali. It was just a ruse, designed to give her beloved young friend a moment of joy, of hope, before he left this world. In his last moments of life, Ali welcomed the cold, hard bullets with a smile bigger than life itself. Rose had been there to make certain of it.

A single, unexpected tear rolled down Malcolm's cold cheek. He quickly wiped it away, not used to feeling such emotion, or especially, displaying it.

He was the only one there who understood what Rose had done.

Berkley arrived, carrying Rose's dark coat and hat. He covered her with the coat, turning the white bundle to black. He spoke softly to his cousin, and then helped her to stand. Together, they departed the execution yard and headed back to the car. Malcolm followed respectfully behind them.

Jane Berkley and Agnes, who had been fetched by the driver,

waited inside the vehicle next to the cage of pigeons. Jane took Rose into her arms and let her weep. Mr. Berkley sat on the front seat. There seemed to be nothing to say.

A few minutes later, Rose took the birds out of the cage one by one and attached a note to each bird's foot. She rolled down the car's window and released them.

Malcolm signaled the driver with two short taps on the hood of the car. The travelers' journey to India began as the four white pigeons soared together above the prison yard, then flew into the dawn of Tehran's morning sky.

EPILOGUE

Malcolm sat at his desk in the embassy, his curtains fully opened and his repaired window cracked, letting the frigid air of Tehran's late autumn rush into his office. The chill kept him sharp. His ashtray held several cigarette butts, and his burning cigarette was sending swirling smoke into the air. He started to pick up his pen to begin writing his report, but instead picked up his cigarette and gave it a good draw, slowly exhaling the tobacco smoke.

He stopped for a moment and gazed into the dancing smoke. The events of the previous weeks had stirred an unfamiliar emotion in him. An intriguing sense of longing for a feeling he had wished for as a young man, before the Great War and the life he had chosen since.

The recollections of the young nurse Rose, whom he had considered an irritant, could not be shaken from his mind. Her efforts, despite powerful obstacles of pursuing what she believed, were impressive. But what captured Malcolm's attention the most was her ability to understand, shift, and adapt to the ever-changing circumstances without losing focus on delivering the most important gift of all to the young boy: hope.

He had never known such a headstrong woman. Nor such a clever one. This must be what most would call compassion and benevolent selflessness. Her plot was not for herself—not even to ensure justice. She had simply allowed Ali to die with the knowledge of her love and true friendship—feelings Malcolm had never experienced.

Yet for a brief moment, just before the rifles sent the two boys to their deaths, his hardened heart *had* felt something. For an instant, he had wished that he, too, could exist in that space, where indifference and apathy is replaced by warmth and love.

But now there was work to do. He looked at the telegram for his next assignment, folded the paper and put it in his pocket. Leaning on his desk, he stared at the painting of the single white rose on the wall in front of him. He walked toward it, took it off the wall, and as he prepared to wrap it, he muttered, "You are going with me to Russia."

***

Reza Khan became Reza Shah, the king of Iran (Persia), in 1925.

***

AUTHOR'S NOTE

Why is the world the way it is? This is a profound question that active minds regularly ponder. In the view of some, this query is among the basic building blocks that form the human quest for progress.

Traditional history is often tainted with the colors of the select few who wrote about it. Today, however, the enormous resources at our disposal and convenience allow us to paint history with our own brushes. In an era where raw news reaches the public in the blink of an eye, history now forms itself differently than it has in the past. No longer are we bound to a set, prescribed view; individuals can interpret history through their own lenses, including the lens of storytelling.

Although *In the Shadow of the Kingmakers* is a work of fiction, some of the key people and events in the book reflect actual ones, most significantly the murder of American Vice-Consul, Major Robert Imbrie, by a mob in Tehran. This incident drastically shifted America's role and policies in Iran post World War I. The swift and premature departure of the U.S. from Iran's politics left this highly strategical region open to the ambitious European powers.

The oil business and diplomacy had deep influences in the region's politics at the turn of the twentieth century. Petroleum companies such as Standard Oil, APOC (Anglo-Persian Oil Company) and others often manipulated and inserted their hold over candidates for positions of power. The American businessman Harry Sinclair's involvement and proposal for Iranian northern oil had rattled the prevailing establishment and formed an imposing impact on the politics of those years. Oil companies, powerful and unchecked at the time, were suspected to be among the cooperates of Major Imbrie's death by popular belief.

These fascinating entanglements of power, politics, wealth and intrigue can be further researched with resources readily available online or in print. While the complete list into these subjects is very long, the following may be a place to being:

Specific to Major Imbrie's murder:

- "Imbrie Murder Laid to Religious Hate," published in *New York Times* 1924-07-24.

- Smith, Murray W., "Report on Baha'is of Iran, 1925", U.S. Embassy, Tehran

Legation of the United States of America, Teheran, Persia, January 8, 1925, Department of State Department of Near Eastern Affairs.

- Zirinsky, M. (1986), "Blood, Power, and Hypocrisy: The Murder of Robert Imbrie and American Relations with Pehlavi Iran, 1924." *International Journal of Middle East Studies,* 18(3), 275-292. doi:10.1017/S0020743800030488.

About the region:

- Anderson, Scott, *Lawrence in Arabia, (Doubleday, 2013 or Anchor, 2014).*

- Oren, Michael B., *Power, Faith, and Fantasy: America in the Middle East: 1776 to the Present,* (Norton, 2006).

- Phillips, Tomas B., *Queer Sinister Things: The Hidden History of Iran*, (Lulu.com 2011)

- "The Making of the Modern Middle East" A video of an interview and discussion with Scott Anderson at Intelligence Squared, a forum for debate and intelligent discussion. www.intelli-gencesquared.com (2014)

ACKNOWLEDGMENTS

A project like this would not be possible without the help of others. The initial spark for this project was given to me many years ago by my late uncle, Dr. Djafari, when he told me the story of Major Imbrie's fate, which deeply affected me. I am forever grateful and often fondly remember our candid conversations as we walked along the shores of the Pacific Ocean in California.

My first attempt was a short story. Later, it was Jeanette Morris, my insightful editor's, strong encouragement that persuaded me to develop the story into a full novel. I'm very thankful for her perceptive counsel. The journey took eight years of research, edits, and revisions. My gratitude and appreciation goes to the many people who were instrumental in encouraging me to push through the ups and downs of this complex project: Carole Eckhardt for her constant support and encouragement, Todd Summer for his critique and edits in Chicago, the team at Artful Editor in Los Angeles, Susan Leon for her astute critique and edits in New York, and Jeanette Morris on California's Central Coast, my team of readers CM Powers, Tracy Losson, Walden Bohnet, Jessica Hylek, and Heidi Honeyman who helped me navigate this road with their enthusiasm and cheers, and my son David, who took many hours from his busy PR schedule in NYC to advise and provide me with resources for the countless issues involved in this project. My special thanks to Norma Hinkens who was instrumental in formatting and designing the inside of the book and to Germancreative for the cover art.

However, none of this would be possible without my wife, Kathryn's, grace and patience during the entire length of this project; I'm eternally grateful for her support.

Naji and the mystery of the dig

An award-winning children's book for middle graders

This award-winning cultural book is inspired by a true story. One summer morning, 8 year old Persian girl, Naji woke up to an unusual sound. Three strangers were digging in her courtyard. Naji's sixth sense warned her: something suspicious was lurking down there. As events unfold and suspense rises, readers will enjoy the many colors of Persian culture, cuisine, folklore, history, geography, religion, language, and intrigue through Naji's eyes and heart. No one was prepared for the ending. Not even Naji. For middle graders to adults. Includes glossary, study projects and discussion questions sections. Lexile® Measures 690L.

For more information visit:

www.najistories.com

www.facebook.com/NajiStories

www.twitter.com/najistories

www.pinterest.com/najistories

http://alturl.com/37d9g

Naji and the mystery of the dig is
available for purchase at:
Barnes & Noble
Amazon

ABOUT THE AUTHOR

Vahid Imani was born in Tehran, Iran, and made the United States his home in 1979. He earned his master's degree in 1980 from Gonzaga University's School of Business in Spokane, Washington. At the turn of the century, he transitioned to the world of fine arts after a career in high-tech as a business executive. His opinions and insights about the arts, history, and international politics have been shared in articles, public lectures, and mass media. In 2014, he debuted as an author with his award-winning middle-grade novel *Naji and the Mystery of the Dig*. Imani is the father of three children, grandfather of three, and lives with his wife in California.